SMILE NUMBER SEVEN

MELISSA PRICE

BELLA
BOOKS

2019

Bella Books, Inc.
P.O. Box 10543
Tallahassee, FL 32302

Printed in the United States of America on acid-free paper.

First Bella Books Edition 2019

Editor: Medora MacDougall
Cover Designer: Judith Fellows

ISBN: 978-1-64247-038-3

Other Bella Books by Melissa Price

Skin in the Game
Steel Eyes

Acknowledgment

Thanks to Bella Books, the keeper of our stories. Thank you, Editor Medora MacDougall for guiding *Smile Number Seven* into the world.

To my fiercest and most trusted critics who inspired me throughout this work: Oana Niculae, John Daleiden, Jacob Shaver.

And to my readers, I am grateful for daydreamers everywhere.

About the Author

Melissa Price is a novelist who credits her former profession as a chiropractic sports physician for creating characters who make skillful leaps and bounds. While *Smile Number Seven* is pure romance, she describes her first two novels, *Steel Eyes,* and *Skin in the Game,* as "Lesbianage"—the word that characterizes her lesbian romantic intrigue. Melissa's current work-in-progress is a sociopolitical farce titled *The Right Closet.* She also co-wrote the screenplay *Toma-The Man, The Mission, The Message.* She is passionate about animal rescue.

A lifelong guitarist and avid swimmer, Melissa hopes to be reincarnated as a mermaid. Her motto is: Write. Swim. Read. Repeat. While Melissa's happy place is Jamaica, you can always find her at www.melissa-price.com.

Dedication

Dedicated to the memories of Nancy and Chick Price, who taught me to strive for excellence and originality. And for Andrea Price Goldsmith, to whose effervescent artistry I remain beholden.

CHAPTER ONE

For that singular moment, Katarina Verralta held her breath—ignored her racing heartbeat that rippled across the space-time continuum. *I'd trade two of my Oscars for this one!* she thought.

From the list of names the presenter read, all she heard was, "Katarina Verralta for *Allies of Night*." On the edge of her seat, she watched the actor pull the card from the envelope in slow motion. The name he repeated belonged to someone else.

The next instant would turn out to be her least appreciated performance of the year—the one for which no gold statue was at stake. Katarina convincingly cheered for her rival's Best Actress win.

If I'd been this good on-screen, I'd be walking up there right now! she thought.

Katarina smiled and applauded vigorously. She wondered how many cocktails it would take to erase the words from her brain: "And the Oscar goes to Britney Cavell." Like the incessant ding of an unanswered phone, the name echoed in her head. *Cavell.*

From her front-row seat, Katarina watched Cavell cradle the Oscar, then produce an on-demand tear that segued brilliantly into her rehearsed visage: feigned humility.

Katarina grunted. *Jesus, I taught her that expression! Just keep smiling.*

Cavell ended her acceptance speech with a nod to her competitors, singling out Katarina, "who I grew up watching and emulating. I share this with you, *old* friend."

The camera that broadcasted that moment around the world captured a cutaway star-shot of Katarina's ebullience—as Oscar-winning as Cavell's.

The bitch just had *to throw the age shots at me.* "Old *friend!" Grew up watching me? You're 39, for god's sake, not 19!*

Katarina responded with Award Ceremony Smile Number Four: plasticine encased in polyurethane, it beamed delight with a dash of nostalgia.

From the seat to her right, her assistant Gigi patted her leg and applauded her graciousness. The actress waved to her worldwide audience through the camera lens, but on the inside this amounted to making a disappointing cameo in someone else's blockbuster film, briefer even than the screen time of a supporting role.

Katarina scanned her costars from *Allies of Night* who had won Oscars for their work and smiled her seal of approval—the dethroned queen lauding her subjects with a nod. Suddenly, her Spanx felt very tight, the Versace gown strangled her ample breasts, and the theater temperature baked her two layers of makeup. She tossed back her long chestnut-brown waves and used Award Ceremony Smile Number Two to hide her broken heart.

Katarina toughed-out the Best Picture category, counting down the moments until she could leave. Upon her exit from the Dolby Theater, she signed some autographs and posed for the paparazzi.

"Katarina, Star Cable News. How about an interview?"

Katarina pivoted and smiled for the camera. "Sure, call my publicist," she said in a throaty alto Italian accent.

"Katarina, look this way!" another photographer called out.

Then, "Miss Verralta, over here."

One after the next, a hundred stuttering clicks delivered the message that the world still loved her. She knew how to dazzle in the lights—she'd grown up studying photos of every movie icon, and their class and style in Hollywood's golden age.

"Look! It's Britney Cavell!" a fan blurted out.

In a swarm, the colony of worshipers followed the clique of photographers; admirers surrounded Cavell, leaving Katarina Verralta a red carpet orphan.

Gigi had her limo timed perfectly; the door was open and waiting. Katarina paused before getting in. She filled her lungs with Hollywood night air and observed the parade of camera-ready faces vying for their moment in the press. The crowd swelled outward toward Cavell, with fans reaching, calling out to the Oscar winner from behind the barricades.

Britney posed, signed a few autographs, and searched into the near distance until her eyes met Katarina's.

"Get me out of this quicksand," said Katarina, turning away quickly for the refuge of her limo.

"Here." Gigi offered the actress a glass of champagne.

Katarina waved it away. "Pour me the hard stuff," she said as the limo pulled onto Hollywood Boulevard.

Gigi had the vodka waiting. "You were the one who deserved that award, Rina. Britney Cavell is nowhere near your caliber."

"Thank you, Gigi, but I pay you to say that."

Gigi took a swig of the champagne Katarina had declined. "Fine. But this time I mean it. As far as I'm concerned, they've snubbed you two years in a row. Everyone knows you're the biggest draw at the box office, and the world loves you."

Katarina downed the vodka. "A lot of good that did me tonight."

"Shake it off. We're going to have some fun at the studio after-party."

"I think I'd like to skip that. I don't want to see Britney Cavell again. Ever."

"Honey, you're the star of your movie. You can't bail."

"Okay, one hour. That's it. Then I'm out of there."

They rode in silence most of the way until Katarina's cell phone rang. Gigi pulled it from her purse. "Right on cue. It's Cavell."

Katarina took the phone, turned it off, and handed it back to Gigi. "There. One problem solved."

CHAPTER TWO

The following morning, Clay Hart drifted into Katarina's kitchen bright and early at noon. As usual, he entered through the sliding doors from the lush garden that led to the pool house he occupied. "Morning, Gigi." He smiled and reached for the coffee pot.

"You're a ray of sunshine this morning," Gigi answered from her seat at the table.

"You jealous that I met Harry Orlon last night?"

Gigi chuckled. "*Met* the man named by *People* magazine as the sexiest man alive? I'd say you two did more than meet."

Clay winked at her. "He just left the pool house." Clay poured coffee into his mug, added a tablespoon of heavy cream, a heaping teaspoon of brown sugar, and two shakes of organic cocoa powder.

"Really?" Gigi said, amused.

"Really," he replied matter-of-factly.

"So…was this but an Oscar-night dalliance, or are we seeing Harry again?"

Clay laughed. "I don't know about you, but I am." He planted his slight five-foot-nine frame opposite her and took a long sip of coffee. "Nectar of the Gods."

"That's wine."

"Not the South American gods. Where is she and how is she doing this morning?" he asked.

"How would I know?"

"You're her personal assistant."

"Well, you're her personal manager. Since it's noon and we haven't seen her yet, maybe she needs to be managed. Again—*your* domain."

"Managed and perhaps 'assisted,'" Clay smiled. "This is going to take a combined effort. She was so bummed last night. Poor baby. Rina poured her heart into that role. And I believe it was her best performance since *Spinning the Light.*"

"I agree. I've never seen her that despondent. What if something's really wrong? She's upstairs in her suite and we would never even know."

"Maybe I'd better go check on her," said Clay.

"I'll go. You look like you could use a little more time to rejoin the living."

"You're a kind soul."

"We're just a good team, Clay."

"I'll get up in a minute and make the queen a remedy."

The assistant climbed the two levels above the kitchen in the five-story Malibu mansion. The entire top floor was a home within a house—the sprawling private suite fit for a movie star of Verralta's stature.

Gigi entered the suite and crossed the marble foyer. She stopped and surveyed a sitting room so tidy that it was lifeless, sterile—even if adorned with expensive trinkets from her boss's travels. The tiled terrace bowed outward around the hillside, and on a clear day, a seat on the Roche Bobois ultra-modern couches afforded a view that reached across the expanse of sapphire Pacific to Catalina Island.

She tapped lightly on the bedroom door but heard no response. After rapping harder a second time, Gigi drew open the door one inch at a time.

"Rina?" she whispered into the blacked-out room. "Rina." She stepped across the threshold, pressed the button on the wall, raising the electric shades enough to be able to take in the disarray of debauchery.

Unforgiving daylight highlighted the woman, who, sprawled across her bed, lay surrounded by evidence of the excesses of the night before. Strands of her luxurious chestnut waves were plastered across her face, stuck to her cheeks with makeup she hadn't removed.

"Rina, wake up."

The actress didn't stir.

"And...action!"

Rina shot straight up to a sitting position. "Huh? What?" She lifted her sleep mask and peered at Gigi with startling green eyes that nested above her prominent cheekbones. "Go away."

"Not an option. What the hell happened up here last night?"

"My head. My stomach." Rina groaned, falling back onto her pillow, leaving the mask resting on her forehead.

"You're hungover." Gigi picked up the trash can and surveyed the debris on the floor. She flourished the first of several candy wrappers. "So then, this was the appetizer? Dark chocolate, 55 percent cacao. Really? Domestic?" She shook her head in disapproval.

"I was slumming," Rina moaned.

Gigi dropped it into the can and reached for the next one two steps away. "Imported Belgian dark, 75 percent cacao. Now we're getting somewhere." Another toss into the trash. "Here's a nice change of pace." She read from the empty box. "Chocolate swirl ice cream dipped in a hard chocolate shell." She sighed. "Rough night."

"I know, I know. Don't remind me." Rina hugged her pillow, holding it tightly against her abdomen. "Alcohol would have been more forgiving."

Gigi hovered, advancing her position until she stopped at the night table. "Chocolate chip cookies. Nice, there are two left out of the entire bag."

"Move away from the cookies!"

Gigi dropped the remains into the can.

"That's not what I meant."

"Okay, give it up, Rina."

"Give what up?"

The assistant held out her hand. "What's under your pillow?"

"Nothing."

Gigi stared down at the actress until the silence forced Rina to look at her.

"Now, please."

"Fine!" Rina groped underneath the pillow and tossed over the box of chocolate-covered cherries.

"And that pillow?"

Rina sneered at her before tossing her the package of unopened mini-chocolate cakes.

Gigi swept it all off the bed into the can and sat. "Jesus! Are you finished wallowing?"

"Don't make it worse. I already feel like shit."

"Honey, you know that chocolate is a cruel mistress. We've been down this road before and it never turns out well. What happened to throw you off this cliff?"

"I had to leave the after-party. The more Cavell drank, the meaner she became—even threatened to out me in the press. I wanted to smack her. But then I imagined all of the online photos, headlines, and TMZ profiles. So I left and came home."

"You mean you punished yourself instead of the person who deserved it. Do you think you might come back to the land of the living anytime soon?"

"Why, what did you have in mind?" Rina dusted the cookie crumbs from her blue silk pajamas.

The assistant softened and smiled. "How about we start out slow? Come down to the kitchen."

"I don't know what I'd do without you, Gigi."

"Of course you don't. Clay's downstairs whipping up one of his magic potions. Now, up with you. Go wash your face—and peel off those false eyelashes already. See you downstairs."

"But you were supposed to find me in bed with my Oscar this morning."

"I know." Gigi sighed. "Cavell's a bitch. Yada yada. Now get up."

* * *

Katarina entered the kitchen to see Clay standing at the counter blending a detox cocktail for her.

"There's my girl," he said. "Here's a little something to help you flush out all that sugar."

"Gigi ratted me out, huh?" She cinched her silk robe around her trim waist and took her seat at the kitchen table.

He waited a moment, then placed a glass of the concoction in front of Rina and sat quietly opposite her.

"I'm so disappointed, Clay."

"I know, honey. Me too."

"I poured my heart into this role."

"I know you feel it way worse, but I thought that we'd own the world today."

"I know you understand," she added. "Don't think for a moment I don't appreciate all the things you do to keep me desirable."

He patted her hand and smiled. "Let's be clear—you're desirable enough without me. We'll get it next time," he said softly.

Rina took a sip of her drink and crinkled her nose on the swallow.

Clay chuckled. "I know, but trust me, you'll feel much better after you drink it."

Her full lips curled upward on the right. "Well, I certainly can't feel much worse."

"There's no second-guessing this," Clay began. "Who knows why she was chosen over you."

"The Academy isn't to blame—my performance in *Allies of Night* was."

"That's crazy talk," he said. "Your performance was flawless."

"Then it was me. Whatever it was about me that just didn't break through to that level of runaway excellence."

"Don't you think you're being a little hard on yourself?"

"Perhaps it's time someone was."

"Britney Cavell can't compare to you, so you shouldn't ever measure yourself against her."

"I don't care anymore."

"Since when?"

"Since right now. Or maybe since about the fifteenth cookie."

"Rina, what is going on with you?" he asked. "You've been off lately."

"I don't know. Maybe I'm getting stale—irrelevant. Old. Even though the camera filmed my good side last night, on the large screen I just looked...old! An actress in her fifties in Hollywood might as well be a hundred."

"You can't be serious about being irrelevant. And you look like you're forty."

"I am serious."

"Irrelevant actresses don't get nominated for Best Actress awards. You're in good company. You have one more Oscar than Streep, and she's lost more times than you. Including last night. This is just the sugar dive talking."

Rina stared off into the distance wistfully. "I love Meryl. And I am younger than she is...Gigi, make a note for me to call her." She snapped back to the moment and looked at Clay. "I need a change. As much as I hate how I feel, maybe there's a valuable lesson in this."

"We don't have to talk about it right now, and I know it's a little soon to be asking, but have you given any thought to what you'd like to do next?"

"I'll wait to see what I get offered—considering I didn't win." She shut her eyes, gulped the concoction, scrunched her face after finishing it, and then opened her eyes. "Rehab!" she blurted out.

Clay laughed. "For what? You don't do drugs. You drink only socially…"

"For chocolate."

He laughed harder. "You want me to find you a *chocolate* rehab?"

"I don't care what kind of rehab. I need to get away from all of this for a while." Her gaze drifted over the room and then to Clay's eyes when he spoke.

"Would you like to go home to Italy? Maybe visit your mother? How about a cruise? I'll charter a boat in the Caribbean and you can float around."

She stared at him with Blank Expression Number Two—pursed lips and no blinking. "No, I don't want to go to Italy. The last thing I need right now is my hypercritical mother telling me why I lost and then everyone clamoring to get something from me. And I can't just float around, Clay. I need to get rid of this feeling."

"Don't think I don't know that you just shot me Blank Expression Number Two. What feeling?"

"The feeling of being…me. Of living a cloistered life—always under a microscope. The feeling of getting old—the fear of becoming irrelevant. You want more?"

"Wait a sec. Somehow you think rehab for a nonexistent addiction will fix that?" Clay stood and kissed Rina on the top of her head. "Why don't you go shower and dress, and we'll go shopping on Rodeo Drive. You can buy me something expensive. That always makes you feel better."

"Nice try." She smiled up at him. "I'm afraid not even Rodeo Drive could fix what's wrong with me today."

"I'm not going to let you sit here and wallow." He pulled out his cell phone and placed the call. "She needs you in one hour," was all he said before he disconnected. "Maribelle will be here soon."

"I can't believe you called my trainer."

"You always feel better after Maribelle." He thought for a moment. "All you do with her is work out, right?"

"Clay! I'm not interested in Maribelle."

"Okay, just checking in case I need to protect you." He turned to leave.

"Find me that rehab, Clay."

"You were serious about that?"

"Dead serious."

He scratched his head. "One chocolate rehab coming up, I guess."

CHAPTER THREE

A creature of habit, Julia Dearling always counted her tips and cleaned up at the end of the night. Tonight, however, her manager, Cass, took over the evening ritual of closing up the Starlight Diner.

Cass gave Julia the once-over. "You're not going out on your date dressed like that, are you?"

"No, I brought a change of clothes."

"Those sexy new jeans that show off your ass?"

Julia grinned. "Maybe."

"Go change for your date. Nicki's going to be here soon, and you know how she hates waiting."

Julia checked the time. "Damn, she'll be here in five minutes."

Cass looked up when the Mustang's headlights reflected off the diner's window. "She's early."

Julia grabbed her knapsack. "Keep her busy," she said as she raced for the ladies' room. Julia washed her face and changed into her new sweater and jeans. She freshened the eye shadow that Cass had said made her eyes appear even bluer, and while looking in the mirror, she wished that the bridge of her nose wasn't quite so high. Julia hastily brushed her long brown hair, put on some lipstick and blush, and stepped back from the mirror to see how it all came together. "This will have to do."

Barely one breath after, she reentered the dining room. "Hi, sweetie, I'm ready," she said with a hard exhale.

Dressed in black jeans, cowgirl boots, and a suede jacket over her custom-made shirt, Nicki strode over and met Julia midway. "I missed you," Nicki said. "You ready to go?"

"Can't wait."

"What movie are you going to see?" asked Cass.

"*Allies of Night*," Julia replied excitedly.

"The Katarina Verralta movie?"

"Uh-huh. I wish we didn't have to wait so long for movies to make it all the way out here to the desert. Especially her movies."

Nicki rolled her eyes. "I must really like you to agree to see a sappy chick flick."

Julia laughed. "You do like me! It's not a sappy chick flick. G'night, Cass."

"Have fun, you two," she replied as they left.

Nicki started the car, leaned in, and pulled Julia close. They spent the next minute kissing before Julia fell back into her seat.

"Whoa, that's some hello kiss."

Nicki grinned. "I'll say." She exited the lot onto the desert two-lane, heading for the only nearby town with a theater.

"How was your day?" asked Julia.

"Stellar. I sold two newer cars and made a bundle on them. That's the seventh sale in three days."

"You've built a good reputation, Nicki."

"Customers are coming from as far away as the Arizona line. The word is out!"

"Is it enough?"

"What?"

"Does owning a used car dealership make you happy?"

"I'm pretty happy right now, Julia. I made a lot of money this week."

"That's great. But that wasn't what I meant."

"Are you going to get all deep on me now?"

Julia smiled. "N-no. Let's just go enjoy the movie."

"I want popcorn—I'm hungry."

Julia reached into her knapsack and came up with a freshly wrapped turkey sandwich on rye.

Nicki glanced away from the road. "Is that for me?"

"Yes, I'm starting to get the hang of dating you. You change your mind every ten seconds. When you called today, you said you didn't want me to bring food to the movie for you—so I brought something anyway."

Nicki's hand crept across the console and caressed Julia's thigh, stroking it gently. "You're the best."

For the twenty-minute ride along the dark back roads between the two sleepy California desert towns, Julia found it hard to take her eyes off of Nicki, so confident and sexy in her tomboyish style, with her short black hair with the long bangs that fell across her eyes. And that lanky swagger she had—as much sensual as it was anything else. Finally, she looked away. "Oh! We're almost there. How fast were you going?"

"This new Mustang is sweet, isn't she? You ought to let me put you in something newer than that junker you drive."

"Maybe," said Julia. *A car's a car*, she thought.

"I mean if we're going to be dating, I can't have my friends thinking that I'd let you drive something like that."

"You care what your friends think about my car?"

"It just doesn't look right, you know?" Nicki pulled into the parking lot of the Indian Rock Theater.

"I'll let you know when I can afford a car payment."

"If business keeps up the way it's been going, I'll just give you one." Nicki pulled into a parking space. "Even the worst car on my lot would be a step up."

"I don't really want a different car."

"Sure you do. Everyone loves a new ride."

They walked to the theater entrance; Nicki, as usual, was five or more steps ahead of Julia. *If I stopped walking, I wonder how long it would take her to figure out I'm not beside her.*

"Two for *Allies of Night*," Nicki said, tossing a fifty through the cashier's window. She took the change and handed it to Julia. "Why don't you go get some popcorn or whatever and I'll find some seats."

"You mind sitting midway up and on the aisle?" Julia answered.

Nicki smiled. "See you inside."

A few minutes later, Julia juggled her popcorn and drink as she entered the sparsely populated theater. Her eyes had to adjust to the light before she found Nicki—who was all the way up in the second to last row and in the center seats. She sat next to her and whispered. "I don't like sitting in the middle of a row."

"There's no one else in the row," Nicki whispered back.

"How about farther down?"

Nicki issued an exasperated sigh. "Whatever."

Julia extended her hand to keep Nicki in her seat. "It's fine. Really."

"You sure?"

"Yeah."

Julia handed Nicki her sandwich as the movie theme began. Then, forsaking her surroundings, Nicki, and even herself, she sank down into her seat and allowed herself to be pulled into a montage of opening scenes set to a rich and melodic score. It transported her over the aerial expanse of Paris, soaring above the Seine and red clay rooftops. The ominously gray city, saturated beyond wet, was foreign to Julia in every way.

The camera zoomed in gradually to and through an old window of an ornate building as gray as the sky, as old as winter. The woman in the bed within opened eyes so mesmerizing that Julia thought they alone were worth the price of admission, mutable green eyes that the press had rightly said rivaled Sophia Loren's. To Julia, Katarina Verralta's beauty was unmatched—even by the likes of Charlize Theron, although Theron was younger.

Julia watched, immersed, as Katarina Verralta fell in love on the big screen again, like she had in so many movies before. This time around, the woman in the story put her life in jeopardy in a World War II movie about spies, saving her lover—and becoming all the wiser for having loved.

Once, about midway through the film Julia glanced over at Nicki, only to discover that she had nodded out. By the time the house lights came on, though, she was wide-awake and eager to leave. Julia, on the other hand, wished she had another minute, or an hour, to savor all the emotions the film had evoked in her. It had made her both happy and sad—happy that she'd spent the evening devouring Verralta's classic beauty and extraordinary talent, and sad that the film had ended.

Julia turned to Nicki as they approached the car. "How did she not win the Oscar for this picture? It's one of her best performances."

Nicki shrugged, then yawned when they got back into the Mustang. "Sorry, that film put me right out." She chuckled. "Guess you can call that movie a snore."

Julia remained quiet, replaying in her mind the scenes between the lovers—how they had craved each other's touch, had vowed their undying devotion. She wondered what it felt like to have that— someone who'd look at her that way. To love someone so much that all she ever thought about was her kiss or maybe the way she spoke her name.

"Right?" Nicki said.

Julia snapped back to reality. "Huh? I'm sorry. I was thinking about the movie."

Lingering still in the world of the film, Julia thought about the most beautiful woman God had ever created and how she had portrayed falling in love. She glanced over at Nicki, who while cute and tomboyish, lacked the soft sensuality that oozed from a seasoned and elegant woman like Katarina Verralta. Knowing it would be fruitless to try to persuade Nicki to appreciate what she did about the movie, she simply said, "I'm too tired to discuss the film. Mind if we do that some other time? It's been a long day."

"No, babe, not at all."

They rode in silence for twenty minutes until Nicki turned onto the road that led to Julia's ranch—the Y2, which her father had named for her and her sister. Julia hopped out, unlocked the gate, and waited for Nicki to drive through it before getting back into the car.

"Don't you want to close the gate behind me?" asked Nicki.

"Not tonight, sweetie. I'm tired. I think I just want to go to bed."

"And you don't want me in that bed next to you?"

Nicki rolled up to the house and Julia didn't give her the chance to put the car in park. She leaned over and kissed Nicki's lips. "Speak with you tomorrow," she said with her fingers on the door handle. "Will you…?"

"I'll close the gate on my way out."

"Good night, and thanks for the movie."

"Sure, but next time I get to choose. Prepare for a *Terminator* marathon."

Nicki waited until Julia was inside, and then her tires kicked up the driveway dust as they spun out.

Julia entered the house, poured a glass of pinot grigio to keep her company as she lay down by the small fire she built in the fireplace. There, she replayed the luscious textured scenes of a stormy Paris night and the way they had made her feel. Followed by a replay of the close-ups of Katarina Verralta in bed with a sheet barely covering her breasts. She fell asleep by the fire holding onto that vision.

CHAPTER FOUR

Julia met this sunrise astride Lightning, unencumbered and on her own terms. She rode toward a daylight that cast its first shadows on her. Lightning's hooves clopped against the taupe earth, straining to reach the far end of the trail. Midway up the hump of mountain on the distant side of the ranch, Julia scanned the disc-shaped lenticular clouds that hovered above the peak like a UFO.

She contemplated the expanse of desert below her and took comfort in the creaking of saddle leather when she shifted her weight. The early morning chill, made brisk by the breeze of a trot, carried the scent of morning mesquite and damp desert. *Is there anything better than this?* She took a deep breath and savored it before patting the side of the horse's neck. "Come on, boy, time to go back."

Lightning lazily swayed from side to side as he descended the elevation, while Julia reflected on her movie date with Nicki. She was glad she had spent the night alone. Had she invited Nicki to stay, she would have missed the intimacy of this ride and the sunrise, which surely never would be duplicated.

She breathed in the moist woody aroma suspended in the air around her and thought again of the rainy Paris scenes in the film she had just seen, daydreaming about visiting Paris, feeling the rain, falling in love. *I doubt Paris in the rain smells anything like morning mesquite,* she thought. She clicked her tongue. "Come on, Lightning. That diner doesn't run itself."

When the lunch rush at the diner ended, Julia poured a cup of coffee and sat at the counter. She yawned and rubbed her eyes. "I don't know how I'm going to make it to closing."

Cass passed her with an armful of bussed dishes. "Wild night on the ranch with your girlfriend?" she teased.

"I sent her home."

Cass deposited the dishes in the rubberized container. "Really?"

"Uh-huh."

Cass leaned against the counter. "You two have some kinda spat?"

"No. I was tired and I didn't want to miss my sunrise ride."

"I'll bet Nicki wasn't happy about being dismissed like that."

"I didn't dismiss her."

"I know you—yes, ya' did. I don't think she's heard the word 'no' very often. A lot of girls would like to go out with her."

"Thanks for the reminder."

Cass poured a cup of coffee and took the seat next to Julia. "What's the problem?"

"I'm thinking about last night. Shouldn't I know by now if I'm head over heels for Nicki?"

"You've only been dating for a few months. People don't just fall in love at first sight."

"Sure they do."

Cass smirked. "You've seen too many Katarina Verralta movies."

"You can never see too many Katarina Verralta movies. Isn't the beginning of a relationship usually when your excitement about it is off the charts?"

"I guess," said Cass.

"You don't think Nicki's a little stuck on herself?"

Cass nodded. "A bit overconfident, I'd say. But it's not like she doesn't have reason to be. She's good lookin', is a lot of fun, makes a great living…" She paused.

"But there's something missing," Julia interrupted.

"Like what?"

"If this is love, it doesn't feel the way I thought it would. I thought I'd feel more…I don't know—special."

"You're pretty special to me, girl," Cass offered.

"Obviously. We've been best friends since eighth grade!"

"What do you mean you don't feel special?"

"I don't know. I can't quite put my finger on it. It's me, not her. She was so sweet last night, she even offered me a new car."

"The woman offered you a car and you don't feel special?" Cass raised her eyebrows and stared at her. "Do you think maybe your standards are a tad high?"

Julia rolled her eyes. "She seemed most concerned about what her friends would think of me driving a forty-year-old car. When you put it that way, though, I sound like a bitch."

"Never. No one could ever call you that—not even you. Maybe you're overthinking this and need some time. She's pretty crazy about you."

"You're right. I'm reading too much into the little things. Like at the movies and at other times, when she asks what I want and then does whatever she wants to anyway."

"Not everyone's as sensitive to the needs of others as you are, Julia."

"Not everyone's been where I've been."

Cass gave her a light pat on the back. "You're always waiting for that other shoe to drop—not that you don't have your reasons, girl. For now, why don't you just try to enjoy the moment? If you want to go rest up for the dinner rush, I can handle things here until you get back. Besides, Jimmy is working with you tonight, so he can close up and you can get out early."

"You don't mind?"

"Nope. I still need to rotate the perishables in the cooler before we open for dinner."

"Okay." Julia stood, took off her apron, and fetched her purse. "See you later."

* * *

Even though she wanted to nap, Julia couldn't resist the tug from her sculpting studio when she got home. The natural midday light in the casita was a welcome change from the harsh bright bulbs she sculpted by at night. She'd spent many a late night holed up in that casita molding and shaping her visions, losing track of time until dawn pierced the skylight. Stocked with all her basic needs, the casita was her adult version of a tree house for her private club of one, a place where the world outside could be held at bay. She changed into the sweatshirt she wore when working and uncovered her latest work-in-progress.

Julia selected her knife and sliced through the next layer of malleable clay—studied it—ran her fingers across its smooth surface until her hands knew how they would continue to build the head and face. Holding the double-edged sculpting tool with the medium blade, she carefully finished carving the outline of the first human bust she'd ever sculpted.

Each painstaking stroke of her cutting tool shaped another long strand of wavy hair, as organically as if the knife was a comb. Building the chiseled cheekbones and nose, she added bits of clay shaping the slope from beneath the nose to the full lips.

The angle of light coming through the skylight had drifted far from when she had started. She glanced up at the wall clock.

"Dammit, I'm late!" Julia hastily covered the bust. She scrubbed her hands, changed into her work clothes, and headed back to the Starlight.

"Sorry I'm late, Cass," she said when she came through the door.

"Did you catch a good nap?" Cass leaned on the counter and tallied two checks.

"I wound up in the studio the whole time."

Cass chuckled. "I swear, you should just move into that casita. You're always in there sculpting."

Julia stowed her purse beneath the counter and smiled. "I had the urge to continue working on my new piece, and honestly I couldn't wait."

"You carving another Arabian horse? I like those the best."

"Not a horse."

Cass removed her apron and patted Julia on the back. "I'm heading home to plant myself on the couch in front of the TV. Jimmy, you're closing tonight."

"Why?" said the young man. "Julia's here."

Julia stared at Jimmy and then at Cass. "You know, I'd prefer closing tonight," she said. "Which means, you get to do all the clean up, Jimmy."

"Me and my big mouth," he said as he went to wait on the table of four he had just seated.

After the dinner rush came and went, Julia counted the cash and managed the receipts while Jimmy mopped the floor. She only glanced up when headlights reflected off the large window of the closed diner.

"Jimmy, please unlock the door and let Nicki in."

"Sure," he said leaning his mop handle against the wall.

Julia gathered the cash that she was in the middle of counting and walked back toward the private office. "Tell her I'll be out in a couple of minutes."

As Julia counted the last pile and entered the amounts into her ledger, her office door opened.

"Hi, beautiful," said Nicki.

"Oh, didn't Jimmy tell you I'd be right out?"

Nicki crossed the room and kissed Julia on the lips. "Yes, he did. But I couldn't wait to see you," she smiled.

"Give me one minute or I'm afraid I'll mess up." She checked her totals and placed the cash in the bank deposit bag. Julia walked to Nicki, sat on her lap, and put her arms around the woman. "Sorry about last night but…"

"It's okay, Julia. I know what it's like to work a long day and then go out afterward. Truth is, I didn't have much energy myself last night. Sorry I fell asleep at the movies."

"No worries. I'm off tomorrow. Would you like to come out to the ranch tonight? We can go riding in the morning."

"I would, but I have new inventory coming in very early tomorrow. Why don't we just plan on getting together this weekend?"

"Great." Julia smiled at the thought of spending more time in the studio until then.

"I'm putting you on notice to make sure you take off the two days after my birthday party."

"The diner is closed on Sunday and your party is Saturday night, so we'll have the day afterward."

"No, take Monday off too in case we want to…"

"I can't just take off, Nicki. But let's not worry about it, we have a few weeks to work it out."

"You're getting someone to feed the horses so you can stay over, right?"

"Already handled," Julia said politely.

"We can sleep in, make love. You could serve me breakfast in bed." Julia laughed. "Sounds like you've given this some thought."

Nicki pulled her close and gave her a lingering kiss. "I always give us a lot of thought."

"Breakfast in bed, huh?" Julia teased. "Maybe you should serve *me* breakfast in bed for a change."

"I'd love to bring you breakfast in bed. You like your toast light, medium, or dark?"

They both laughed.

"I'm going to take off," said Nicki. "I just wanted to stop by and kiss you good night."

Julia stood. "Thanks, that's so sweet of you to come all the way out here for that."

"Thanks for noticing. Night," she said and left.

Julia gathered her things and put the deposit envelope in her knapsack. She turned off the light when she left the back office. *Cass is right. She does care about me.*

CHAPTER FIVE

Rina disguised herself behind oversize Balmain sunglasses and a cap before her limo pulled up to the entrance of Namaste Rehabilitation Center West. She exhaled a hard sigh and savored what she hoped would be her last bite of Belgian dark chocolate. The gypsy in her soul would have to find a new, healthy addiction to replace this one.

The driver lifted her suitcase from the trunk and handed it to the male coordinator who came outside to greet Namaste's latest high-profile rehab-ee.

"Welcome to Namaste. I'm Mike." He pointed toward the sliding door. "After you. *Namaste.*"

She entered and surveyed the place. It was strategically painted in a boring hue of sage green, a sedate color, she decided, that was designed to elicit no emotional response. Rina had the opposite reaction. On the walls hung bland still-life paintings best described as paint-by-number. She hoped this wasn't going to be rehab-by-number.

"Welcome," said the crisp blonde approaching in a white polo shirt with the Namaste logo on it. "I'm Dr. Malinworthy. *Namaste.*"

Rina shook her hand. "Nice to meet you. I'm Rina…"

"No introduction necessary. I've been expecting you." The doctor turned to Mike. "After Intake completes the contraband search, please bring Miss Verralta's things to her room." She smiled at Rina. "Your purse, too."

Rina placed the Balmain sunglasses and case inside the purse. "Please be gentle with that purse, Mike—it's Hermes." She turned back around to Malinworthy. "Okay, now what?"

"Follow me, we're going to chat and then get you settled in."

"Don't I need to fill anything out?"

"No, your people have taken care of that for you. I have all your basic information, although we do need to go over the ground rules." The doctor led Rina down another bland hallway whose walls also were lined with homemade art.

"Who drew these pictures?" Rina asked.

"Our clients did them during art therapy. You'll be doing one too." She opened the door to her office and entered.

"You must be pretty smart," Rina said.

"What makes you say that?"

"The letters following your name look like alphabet soup." Rina had stopped to read them off the door. The alphabet code ended in PhD.

The doctor waited for Rina to enter and then closed the door behind them. "Make yourself comfortable," she said extending her hand toward the sofa. She placed a bottle of water on the coffee table, picked up a file and pen from the desk, then took the chair opposite Rina.

"Before we get started," Malinworthy began, "I want to assure you we're very exclusive. Many of our clients, like you, are either well known or famous. Everyone here goes to great lengths to protect your privacy. That means if someone offers personal information—whether privately or in a group situation, that knowledge never leaves these walls. So, as a matter of record," she laid a pen and paper in front of Rina, "would you please personally sign the confidentiality agreement?"

"Of course." Rina scribbled her name and leaned back into the sofa. "I hope everything here is that easy. What's next?"

"Why don't you start by telling me about your drug habit?"

"My drug habit?"

"Yes, why you're here."

"I don't have a drug problem."

"Ah, denial." Malinworthy began writing. "First, you have to be able to admit you have a problem, so what's your drug?"

"Dr. Malinworthy, I think there's been a mistake…"

"It's okay," the doctor interrupted, "a lot of people get here and want to bolt, thinking they've made a mistake."

"It *is* a mistake."

"I can assure you that we…"

"No, I'm saying there's an actual mistake in your information."

"Oh, forgive me." Malinworthy drew a line through her notes. "So then, you're an alcoholic."

"N-no. No drugs or alcohol—unless you consider enkephalin an actual drug."

The doctor put down the pen and paper. "I'm confused. Why are you here?"

"Enkephalin," Rina mumbled inaudibly.

"I didn't get that."

"Chocolate. Okay? Chocolate! Enkephalin in chocolate acts like an opioid. I'm here because I'm addicted to chocolate."

"Chocolate," Malinworthy repeated tentatively. She looked into Rina's eyes. "Really?"

"Am I in the wrong place?"

"No. You've just taken your first step toward recovery: admitting you have a problem. Now, did you come here of your own free will?"

"That depends if you consider emotional blackmail of oneself willing."

The doctor stared at her. "Do *you*?"

"I suppose so, since everyone around me tried to talk me out of this. I told them they were enablers."

Malinworthy fought back a smile. "I'll be honest with you, Rina. We've never treated a chocolate addict here before. I can't even confirm that's actually a thing. We're pretty old school. Drugs, alcohol."

"Is it a problem that I'm not a drug addict or alcoholic?"

"No. But I am curious."

"I self-medicate with chocolate. We're not talking a candy bar here. The night I lost the Oscar, I binged all night!"

"Did you purge it afterward?"

"No!" Rina rolled her eyes. "I got fat afterward. Which depressed me and only made me want more chocolate."

Malinworthy jotted down some notes and then signed the pages in the file. "You'll have your private therapy with me." She glanced up at Rina. "I'll admit I'm very intrigued."

"That I have a chocolate addiction?"

"There is that. But I'm more interested to know why you feel you need an intervention?"

"I can tell you."

"Okay."

"How can the most wonderful thing you know betray you every time and still you go back for more?"

Malinworthy studied her. "Are we still talking about the chocolate?"

"Yes, we're talking about the chocolate!"

"Are you sure?"

"That's why I'm here, aren't I?"

"Are you? Maybe there's more to this than chocolate."

"No. It's about the chocolate."

"What if the chocolate is a metaphor? Have you ever explored what chocolate represents to you?"

Rina scoffed as though Malinworthy was an obnoxious fan. "I don't know what you mean."

"Well, that's what you're here to uncover. I'll do everything I can to help that happen." The doctor stood. "This has been a good ice breaker. We'll have plenty of time to discuss this further, but right now would be a good time to find your room and unpack. You have a group session in half an hour, in the Community Room on the second floor. You're in a private accommodation on the third floor. Room 314. Any questions?"

"What time is dinner and where are the menus?"

"Any dietary restrictions were already submitted by your staff. Your individualized menu was based on a nutritional approach geared toward rehabilitating your body along with your mind."

"What if I don't like what's being served at a particular meal?"

"Then you're free to wait until the next meal or you can help yourself to the snacks in the kitchen. Don't worry, I'll see to it you have no access to chocolate." Malinworthy escorted her to the door. "We'll pick this up again tomorrow."

"What time?"

"Your schedule is waiting for you in your room."

"Good, I'll enter the appointments in my phone calendar."

"Um, your phone has been confiscated."

"What? Why? It's not chocolate."

"No outside contact while you're here. That's a rule. No one here has their phone."

"What if there's an emergency and someone needs to reach me?"

"Your emergency contacts have been instructed to call our main number and we'll get a message to you."

"Well…as long as I'm in good company, I can manage for the next few weeks."

"Be sure to get a good night's rest. Your first full day will be very busy."

Rina nodded and left. She found her room and marveled at its simplicity. Except for the picture window, it was more college dormitory than the Ritz. Still, the manicured grounds offered a peaceful view.

Rina glanced through the brochure on her desk. "So this was an orchard on one of the original ranches in Southern California. Hmm." Carefully, she scanned the property, which stretched through verdant hillside almost as far as the Pacific Ocean. A large man-made lake sat in the center of Rina's view, reflecting the peacock blue sky.

In the distance, a thin woman with medium-length straight brown hair meandered toward the lake and took a seat on the bench, her back to Rina. A brace of ducks waddled toward her even before she tossed them breadcrumbs.

What the hell am I doing here? Gigi was right. This was a mistake. She changed into a pair of worn designer jeans, her favorite classic crew T-shirt from Fred Segal, and sneakers. *Here goes*, she thought as she left for the first group therapy session of her life.

"Hi," said the therapist when Rina entered. "You must be Katarina. I'm Britt."

"Britt?" Rina improvised her first therapy expression, which she reluctantly named Therapy Are-You-Kidding-Me Number One. "As in Britney?"

"No. Brittany," she replied, adding the "a."

"Great." Rina thought of Cavell with an internal sneer. "Call me Rina."

"Have a seat anywhere, Rina," said Therapy Brittany while the other participants filtered in. She waited until the group got settled. "Everyone, let's get started today by saying hello to our new member, Rina."

A flurry of "hey," "hi," and "welcome" came her way from the small gathering of people, along with a muddle of names.

"Hello," she replied.

For the entire hour, Rina listened to people whose lives had been turned inside out from drug use. Since she was bad at recalling their names, she found it easier to identify them in her mind by assigning nicknames.

First to speak was "Jack Smack," whose heroin addiction had caused him to separate from his wife and kids. Then came "Bump," the woman who kept referring to her cocaine use as measured in "bumps."

A bump in the morning, a bump before, during, and after one event or another.

After Bump came "Notes," a famous musician, and then a woman in her forties whom she vaguely recognized and therefore named "Hollywood."

Lastly, the prescription drug addict—the girl from the bench by the lake. Young. Sweet. Liked feeding ducks but was pretty enough to be called "Swan." *If I had met this girl under different circumstances, I would never have guessed that she had a drug problem.*

The more everyone in the group shared their individual stories, the more Rina wished she had a piece of chocolate. Not a big one. Just a tiny taste to get her through the last of the session.

"Rina?" said Therapy Brittany.

Rina was jolted back to reality. "Yes."

"Do you have anything you'd like to say?"

"No."

"This process works a lot better if you share. Would you like to share with us what brought you here?"

"Not really."

"May I ask why?" said the therapist.

"I'm afraid of what everyone here will think of me."

"We're all familiar with that feeling and we're not going to judge you. We know what judgment feels like, and it's not useful to healing. So have at it."

Jack Smack snickered, folded his arms and sank down in his chair. "We're going to figure it out anyway. You might as well come clean. Besides, have you been listening? We've all done really bad shit."

"Yeah," said Bump. "What's your poison, Rina? Meth, blow, heroin?"

"Chocolate," Rina answered.

The circle suddenly became intensely still, as though the oxygen had been sucked out of the room. All eyes focused on her.

"You've gotta be kidding me," said Jack.

"Oh man!" said Bump. "You're not serious."

Rina turned toward the therapist and raised an eyebrow. "Now, what was that speech you gave about judgment?"

Swan sat up straight. "Settle down, people. Rina shared and that's what's important." She turned to Rina and tilted her head. "What kind of chocolate?"

CHAPTER SIX

The following afternoon, Rina ambled toward the lake and watched Swan toss the last of her bread scraps to the ducks. She stopped several feet before the bench. "Mind if join you?"

Swan turned her head and welcomed Rina with only a smile, then turned back toward the lake. Rina shared the bench and stared at the water.

"How was your first night?" asked Swan.

"Okay."

Swan glanced over at her. "I meant how was your first night without Belgian dark?"

"Boring. You'll have to excuse me," Rina began. "I'm really bad with names, especially when I meet more than one person at a time."

"Amanda."

Rina chuckled.

"What's so funny?"

"I had to give you a name in my head until I could ask you."

"What was it?"

"Swan."

"Swan?"

"I saw you feeding the ducks and geese yesterday, and neither of those names fit you."

"Hmm. Swan," said Amanda. "I like it. You can call me Swan."

"May I ask you a personal question?"

"Sure," Swan replied.

"Why did you choose this particular rehab?"

"I had heard that this is where all the movie industry people go."

"Ah, so you're in the business." Rina handed Swan a piece of bread wrapped in a napkin. "I took this for you at lunch time."

"Thanks." Swan tore the bread into pieces and tossed them to the ducks. "I like your movies. I hope you don't mind me saying so."

"No, it's what I'm best known for."

"Your eyes are overwhelming in person, you know."

"So I hear."

Rina glanced down at the legal pad on the bench. She wouldn't attempt to read what was on it without her reading glasses, and she wasn't about to wear her reading glasses in public while fighting back an urge for chocolate. "You like to write, Swan?"

"It's what I'm best known for. Although I have worked as a script editor for TV."

"What do you write?"

"Novels and teleplays, except now I'm working on a screenplay."

"Have you written something I might have read or seen?"

Swan shrugged and stared across the lake.

"How much longer are you here for?" asked Rina.

"A few weeks. Can I ask why you think you need to come to rehab for chocolate?"

"Dr. Malinworthy asked me the same question. It seemed like the right thing to do and the time to do it."

"You know, it's never about the drug. It's about answering the question of why we self-medicate. What could be so painful that we kill ourselves slowly, so that we don't have to feel what's causing the pain?"

Rina nodded. "I guess I'm about to find out. Have you figured out why you took drugs? I'm sorry. Is that out of line?"

Swan turned to her and smiled. "No, it's not out of line at all. I'm starting to get an idea of why I went off the rails. I'm glad to make a friend here. It's a good program, but I haven't connected with anyone in group."

Rina drew in a slow breath and then exhaled. "I'm glad to know you too. It's relaxing watching you feed the ducks."

Swan tore a piece of bread and handed it to Rina. "Give it a try. I think we could learn a few things from the fowl around here."

"Such as?" Rina asked in surprise.

Swan pointed to the geese. "Take Gary and Greta there."

"You've named them?"

"Only the ones I've become fond of. Anyway, Gary always positions himself to protect Greta when she eats. Did you know that geese pair for life?"

"I didn't."

"And if one of them gets sick or injured, their partner won't leave them, even if winter looms or all their friends are flying south. Now that's what I call loyalty."

"I agree. I can barely conjure anyone I know who's that loyal." Rina paused. "Maybe I can learn something from the geese."

Swan nodded. "That makes two of us."

The bell rang.

"Time for group, Rina."

The women walked back to the building and up to the second floor in silence.

"Hello, Therapy Brittany," said Rina as she took a seat.

Swan took a seat on the opposite side of the circle from Rina.

Therapy Brittany waited until the group was assembled. "Today we're going to switch things up a little and hopefully have fun." She had Bump and Jack Smack and Hollywood and Notes exchange addictions and role-play. When they finished, she looked to Swan and Rina.

"Rina, you now have Amanda's addiction to prescription drugs. Amanda, you're now addicted to chocolate. Amanda, you go first."

Amanda stood and strutted across the room, tossed back her imaginary long hair and mimicked Rina. Before she uttered a word, everyone except Therapy Brittany laughed.

"I don't just *love* chocolate. No, I'm *addicted* to it! Belgian Dark— 75 percent cacao." She turned to the therapist. "Do you have any chocolate? I wonder if there's any chocolate in this place. There has to be a piece of chocolate *somewhere*. I'd eat a Hershey bar at this point. Life is so boring without chocolate."

The addicts laughed again, none harder than Rina as she applauded Swan's performance. Swan curtsied and sat.

"Okay, Rina, here's your turn to get even," said Therapy Brittany.

Rina ripped a sheet of paper from her notebook, tore it into scraps, and made little paper balls. She pulled her chair into the middle of the circle, sat, and took a moment to get into character. She tossed the first paper ball at Jack Smack's head. "I love feeding the ducks and geese," she said wistfully. "Geese mate for life." She tossed paper balls at each person's head. "Did you know geese mate for life? They're *loyal*." And then with her worst melodramatic portrayal said, "I could go for some Oxy. Oxy! Got any Oxy? Wait, I'm asking the geese if they have Oxy. Come here, Gary and Greta. You're my fave goose couple." Rina continued tossing the balled-up paper at each person in the group, playfully aiming the largest one at Swan.

Slumped in her seat, Swan belly-laughed and batted the paper ball back at Rina.

Therapy Brittany applauded. "Great job, group. I'm going to let you go a few minutes early today because I want you to take some time to share what you saw and how you felt when your partner was making fun of your addiction. Then I want you to explain to each other why you chose to highlight the things you acted out. For example, Rina, why did you pick feeding geese? Take notes if you have to, because tomorrow we're going to share about it. Have a good night, everybody."

"Hey, Rina," said Swan, "you want to have dinner with me?"

Rina turned to her and mocked Swan's performance. "Do you have any chocolate?"

Swan laughed. "No. Got any Oxy?"

"No! And I wouldn't give it to you if I did."

"Then good luck finding my chocolate."

Rina smirked and then smiled. "You really know how to hurt a girl, Swan. After you," she said, following Swan out the door.

CHAPTER SEVEN

Julia finished feeding the horses. "Time for my breakfast now. No more rides for you guys until I finish that sculpture or it'll never be ready in time for Nicki's birthday." She patted the side of each horse before leaving.

When she heard the phone ringing in the kitchen, she sprinted for the back door. "Hello."

"Why are you breathing so hard?"

"Vitty! Is that you?"

"Hi, Sis."

"I called you a couple of nights ago but didn't leave a message."

"I saw that," said Vitty. "I haven't left the office before ten at night in over a week. Would you believe this is the first chance I've had to get back to you?"

"I would. We Dearling women are hard workers."

"Listen, JuJu, I have a meeting in a minute, but I wanted to give you a quick call to see when I can come home for a visit. My boss owes me a long weekend off and I want to see you."

"Sure!" Julia beamed. "Yeah, that'd be great. I have Nicki's birthday party coming up, but any other weekend is fine. I'll see if Cass can cover me when you're here."

"Great, tell her I said hi. I'll call you later with the details. Gotta go. *Muah*," Vitty said before the line went dead.

Julia dialed Cass while she juggled vegetable containers from the fridge to the counter for an omelette. "Hey," she said when her friend picked up. "I just heard from Vitty. She wants to come for a visit—I'm guessing within a few weeks. Any chance you can swap a Saturday with me?"

"You want to work for me today and we'll call it even?" asked Cass.

"Sure, I'll grab a quick shower and open."

"It's too dang early to sound that chipper."

"Vitty's coming home! Thanks, Cass."

Julia placed the food containers back in the fridge and raced upstairs.

"Yay! Vitty and Nicki can finally meet."

* * *

Julia bounded into the diner, flipped the OPEN sign in the window and entered the kitchen. "Morning, Isabella."

The cook raised her eyebrows. "What are you doing here?"

Julia stowed her purse and tied her apron. "I switched days with Cass. Vitty's coming for a visit."

"Why?" said the matronly fifty-five-year-old.

"She misses me."

Isabella snapped down the lid of a container with more force than necessary. "Julia, I promised your grandmother I'd watch over you. I know you love and miss Vitty, but if she's coming home it's because she wants something."

Julia pursed her lips. "No, we miss each other!"

Isabella shook her head. "I hope you're right, but I don't want you to be disappointed if she lets you down."

"Don't be ridiculous. We're sisters who live three thousand miles apart."

"When was she here last?"

"About a year ago."

"Uh-huh. And what happened on the third day?"

Julia thought about it. "Oh, she wasn't serious about selling the ranch."

"You sure about that, *mija*?"

"What is it with you and Cass? You always suspect Vitty of the worst. I'm proud of how successful she is."

"I watched you and Vitty grow up. You couldn't be more different. She flew the coop for New York, leaving you to handle all of Grandmother Lucia's affairs."

"Well, yeah. I was the executor."

"With good reason."

Julia thought about it. Isabella had been in her life forever, and she was the one who had comforted Julia when Grandmother Lucia had died—when Vitty left. "Vitty's strong suit was math, not cooking."

Isabella chuckled. "Boy, that's the truth! Luckily, one of you got Lucia's talent. Cass and I could package this stuff for sale. We could make a lot of money with these fabulous recipes."

Julia peeked through the window in the door. "Breakfast crowd is here." She flung back the door, grabbed a stack of menus, and set them down on the table of four women. The one she knew was a friend of Nicki's.

"Hi, Caroline. Nice to see you. You girls know what you'd like or do you need a minute?"

"So you're Nicki's current girlfriend," said the blonde on Caroline's right. "I used to date her."

Julia plastered a noncommittal smile on her lips.

"So did I," one of the remaining two women chimed in. "Guess it's your turn. Good luck."

"I'll give you all a minute to figure out what you want," said Julia. She turned away and rolled her eyes.

Is it a full moon?

CHAPTER EIGHT

The first week without her phone had been harder for Rina than the last two. She enjoyed eating the healthy meals and having time to explore who and what she was without her entourage talking in her ear. While she admitted to being homesick, there was no denying that the simplicity of her routine had left room to meditate on what was important. A smorgasbord of thoughts and feelings made their rounds on a daily basis. She thought about how she liked filming on location because it meant there would be people around her. But then she wondered how many more opportunities would come to a woman her age. And if that thought wasn't depressing enough, it was compounded by the fact that she lived a reclusive existence in her Malibu mansion.

But here in this Namaste place, she was finally able to admit to herself that she missed being the sexual and passionate woman that she was. It had been a long time since she'd been able to trust someone enough to allow them to get that close. Then she wondered if, like her career, the best of it was over and done.

Clay had left a message while Rina was in therapy, asking her to call back. He said he had good news—no, "great news"!

Her urge to scratch and claw her way to the next big role, like her urge to reach for Belgian dark, was no longer immediate. *I'll call him later.*

The chocolate addict then thought of how Swan had proved to be a good friend, helping Rina rediscover the value of laughter in the face of adversity. Sometimes, after dinner, they worked on Swan's screenplay, and during afternoon reflection time, Rina had taken to Swan's daily ritual of communing with waterfowl. She was beginning to feel like a regular person—the most challenging role she'd been offered in a long time.

"Okay," Rina said to no one as she leaned back on her bed pillows. "I have a choice—at least according to Dr. Malinworthy. I've made the choice to not have chocolate every day so far. So I choose not to have chocolate today. Huh. Could that have sounded any less convincing?"

She stood, walked to the mirror, and cleared her throat. "Who is this character? What is her motivation?" She thought for a moment, then tossed her chestnut waves and stared into the character playing opposite her in the mirror. Rina tried on three different facial expressions and settled on Determined Glare Number Four— distinguishable from Number Three by the raised eyebrow.

"You think you can control me! But you're dead wrong. I have a choice, and you're not it. I don't choose you, chocolate. *Get it?* Not interested. Now get out." She laughed. "And, end scene. Cheesy, but fun."

She turned toward the light tap on the door. "Who is it?"

"It's Swan."

"Hi," Rina said when she answered.

"Sorry to bother you. Is this a bad time?"

"Not at all. I was just practicing choosing in the mirror."

Swan chuckled. "In the mirror?"

"I *am* an actor, Swan. Come in."

"How does one practice choosing in a mirror, Rina?"

"Watch and learn. I've titled this scene, 'Breaking Up With Chocolate.'"

Rina performed a second take of the breakup.

Swan laughed and applauded. "Brava!"

"I'm sure it will get better with practice," Rina said sarcastically.

"You've acted it out, while I've actually written the scene in the screenplay."

"The whole scene?" said Rina.

"Yep. Except in my version, it's Oxy, not chocolate. Maybe I should change it to chocolate."

"Do you have the script?"

"For Oxy?"

"Nooo."

"I know what you mean. Yes."

"Let's see how far you've gotten. I never realized how much time I spent on my phone until I came here. I could use something creative to distract me. I'll act, you direct."

"Direct? I don't know anything about directing."

"You're in luck because I do."

"You're not kidding."

Rina opened the door. "Go."

"Be right back."

Rina held the door while Swan dashed to her room two doors down. Swan handed her a few pages when she returned.

"Do you think the story is silly, Rina?"

"No, it's different. A woman enters a rehab for prescription drugs, not realizing that it was predestined for her to meet someone there who will change her life in a mysterious way. It's a fantasy rom-com."

Swan moved across the room and sat in the chair by the window. "So the one thing she never counts on is that it's not just a rehab, right?"

"Yes. It's a mystical place—with a…what's that called?"

"A positive nexus. But she doesn't know that yet because she can't unlock her journey through the nexus until she uncovers the reason for her addiction. Once she 'sheds the old and embraces the new,' she gets a cosmic do-over. Then she can choose a different path in life knowing what she knows now, and that's when she finds the love of her life."

"It's a spin on the road not traveled," said Rina. "So because she takes the road that doesn't lead to addiction, the effects filter through her life and relationships from then to the present?"

"Right. But she's the only one who is aware of both worlds. In her new life, her relationships with family and friends are a result of the do-over."

"So, the Catch-22 is that only she remembers all of the bad stuff that happened between her and all those people." Rina paced across the room and turned. "I think it's very creative and different, Swan. It would make a good indie film."

"Really? You think so?"

"Why not? The major studios mostly put out the same crap over and over."

"Not so," said Swan.

"You don't think so?"

Swan smiled. "No. Every once in a while they redeem themselves and come out with a Katarina Verralta movie." She stood and held a copy of the pages she had given to Rina. "You're reading for Dolly."

Rina put on her reading glasses and paced while silently reading the scene. Across the room, she stopped with her back to Swan, and when she pivoted, she transformed into someone else.

"What the hell are you talking about, Simon? What the fuck is a 'positive nexus'?"

Swan read the part of Simon. "It's a direct connection with the universe—a portal of some sort."

"Aren't we connected to the universe already?"

"This is very different."

"How?"

"You're getting the opportunity to go back. You're one of the few who have made it this far."

"Back to where?"

"Back to where you made the wrong choice in your life. It's real—I've done it. But your time there is limited, so you need to know what you want to change and get it done quickly. If not, then you wind up right back here—an addict in rehab. If I could do it, so can you."

"What happens to all the things I know now?"

"You'll still know about now, but you'll also know a new now. One that's based on the changes you made through the nexus."

"What happens if I run out of time and don't get to change everything that needs to be changed by the time I come back?"

"Then you have to live with those choices. Those are the rules."

Rina swung her arms outward. "That's crazy talk. Then what, Simon? We all get medicated for our delusions?"

"It's not a delusion. It's how I finally became drug-free and started to live my dreams."

Dolly gazed at Simon through Rina's eyes. "Which moment did you go back and change?"

"We don't have time for the whole story now. But I went back to the night the opportunity first presented itself to take that shit. And I said 'no.'"

"Wow, I get to be twenty-five again!"

"Yeah. Think about it, Dolly. You'll still be you, but as if you'd never had the addiction—never had the bad relationships resulting from the drug use. Imagine what your life might have been like by now. It's all possible."

Dolly sighed. "Simon, have you talked to your shrink about this?"

"Sorry, Rina, that's all I have so far," Swan said with a frozen stare.

Rina removed her reading glasses and looked at the screenwriter. "Are you okay?"

Swan gawked at her. "I can't believe that Katarina Verralta just read one of my scenes with me."

"It's Rina. And I like it. The dialogue could use a little beefing up but…where's the rest of the script?"

"I'm writing it."

"Does it have a happy ending?"

Swan stared at her. "I don't know."

"For it to work, Swan, it has to have a happy ending. It's a fantasy rom-com. Older woman, younger guy rom-com."

"Huh. You're right."

Rina glanced at the clock on the nightstand. "It's getting late. Do you want to go to the lake before group?" She handed Swan a paper bag. "I gathered up everyone's leftover bread."

"Sure. A little fresh air with the ducks is always a good idea."

The two of them strolled almost the entire circumference of the lake before Rina spoke.

"What I wouldn't give right now for just a bite of dark Belgian 75 percent cacao."

"I hear you," said Swan. "Half a vicodin would be great. I wouldn't have been able to even feel a half a few weeks ago."

"Question."

"Uh-huh."

"Why did you want to check out?"

Swan shrugged. "I guess I liked feeling one step removed from life. Less painful that way."

"But why? You're smart, beautiful—talented. Have you ever been in love, Swan?"

"Unfortunately."

Rina looked her in the eye. "Why unfortunate?"

"Because I self-medicate to get rid of the feeling after the breakup. And the breakup is usually caused by obsessing over the relationship when I'm in it."

"Yet here you are taking back your life. Taking back your power."

"Working on the screenplay has had a lot to do with that. Thank you, Rina. It's healing me. Writing heals me."

"I get it. Acting does the same for me."

Swan's eyes flared. "Yeah? So, I'll ask you the same question about chocolate."

"That's different."

Swan stopped walking and looked into Rina's eyes. "Is it really? Because last I checked, you have a room here at rehab."

"Point taken," Rina acquiesced. "Maybe it's more the same thing than not. But, chocolate rehab is still experimental, at best."

They sat on the bench.

"What does chocolate cover up for you?"

"I've been trying to answer that for weeks. I don't think I've gotten very far."

"I may be able to help you with this one," said Swan. "When do you want chocolate the most?"

"When I'm awake."

"How often do you think about it?"

"When I'm not acting. Although, I do think about rewarding my work between takes when I'm filming."

"When was the last time you were in love?"

"No. This is about more than passion."

"Interesting."

"What?"

"I asked you about being in love, and you translated that to sex."

"And you think that has something to do with chocolate?"

"I think that you do. Sounds to me like chocolate has been a merciless lover for you. Really, really good and very, very bad."

"Maybe you are onto something, Swan. As delicious as she is, she sabotages me every time. Just like every woman I've ever been with. Oh! I think I just found an answer to what I cover up with chocolate."

Swan raised her eyebrows. "You're gay?"

"I thought you'd figured that out by now. I'm not out in the press, so I hope you'll keep that to yourself."

"Your secret is safe with me. Since we're on the subject, why aren't you out?"

Rina thought for a moment. "Maybe I would consider it if I had the right woman. I don't know—I don't want to go through that circus. Being my age makes it hard enough in the biz. But being gay too?" She shook her head.

"Have you ever thought it might help to shift people's views or acceptance if you came out?"

"No. What I think is that they'd stop casting me as an older romantic lead. Who am I kidding? They'd stop casting me altogether."

"No. Not you—you're too big a star for that."

Rina groaned. "No one is too big a star for anything in Hollywood."

They sat in silence watching the ducks paddle around the lake. Rina did some deep breathing. Swan stared at the ducks.

"I sure could use a piece of chocolate right now."

"It will pass." Swan's voice was soft—calm.

"Ready for group with Therapy Brittany?" asked Rina.

"Why do you always call her Therapy Brittany?"

"Because she's nice and I don't want my brain to confuse her with Regular Britney, whom I despise at the moment."

They got up and started back to the building.

"So Regular Britney is a villain, huh?"

"What makes you say that?"

"You hate her like a bad ex-lover."

"Very perceptive, Swan." Rina laughed in one short burst. "Can't I just hate her because she's an asshole?"

"Sure, that works."

"It will seem weird around here without you after tomorrow," said Rina.

"You'll be leaving yourself soon enough."

"I'd like to keep in touch once we're back in LA," said Rina.

Swan smiled. "I'd like that too."

* * *

Before dinner, Rina returned Clay's call. While waiting for her personal manager to answer, she noticed how slow was her breath—how still was her mind. The sensation of the phone receiver against her ear felt foreign—imposing.

"I've been waiting all day to hear from you," Clay said when he answered. "I was beginning to think they hadn't given you my message."

"Hi, Clay, how are you?" Rina said in an even tone.

"Fine. Are you all right?"

"I'm really good." It had been weeks since Rina had had any outside contact. Her focus had been about balance in her life—except for intermittent chocolate cravings. The cravings were no longer her fallback position, however, as they once had been. In this moment, she savored calm gratitude.

"You sound different, Rina."

She chuckled. "I am different. You're not used to hearing me calm."

"Honey, if they could do that for you in a few weeks, book me a stay."

"Is everything okay at home, Clay?"

"Yes. I know you're getting out soon, but I called because I need an answer right away. I've been putting out feelers for your next project. Brace yourself. Your favorite director, Reese Collingworth, wants a meeting—soon. Rina, this is the role of a lifetime in a blockbuster film, and he wants *you*."

"What's the part?"

"Lead actress in a drama. Reese wants to know if you can meet with him next Wednesday at his place in Palm Springs."

"What day is today?"

"Are you joking?"

"No."

"It's Wednesday. You're getting out on Saturday. There's time to come home and switch gears."

Rina paused in the silence to think.

"Are you still there, Rina?"

"Okay, I'll meet with him, but I need Gigi to have my car brought here. And have her book me into the Sierra Bella Spa in Scottsdale from Saturday night until Tuesday. I'll drive to Palm Springs after that and spend the night. I want to meet with Reese looking and feeling my best."

"Scottsdale, Arizona?" said Clay.

"Yes. I'd like full spa services and then hair and makeup. Gigi knows who to ask for."

"Why do you want your car delivered?"

"Because I'd like to drive."

"Alone?"

"Yes, Clay."

"Why? It's like a four-hour drive from Scottsdale to Palm Springs. And the drive to Scottsdale is longer from where you are."

"I have nothing but time."

"Who *are* you?" said Clay. "How about if I send a car and driver?"

"No."

"Fine," he exhaled. "Which car do you want?"

"The Jag. Thanks, Clay."

"You don't sound excited," he said.

"I think it's great," she offered.

"You're a great actress, and you're not even acting excited."

She laughed. "I'm just being present in this moment. Next week is a lifetime away."

"Are you sure you're okay?"

"Never better. Thanks for working so hard on my behalf."

"You're welcome. I'll let you go do…whatever it is you do there."

"It's pretty wild, Clay."

"Yeah?"

She smiled. "I'm about to end my daily reflection and have dinner. I'll call you from the spa next week." Rina hung up the phone and joined Swan, who was already eating.

"I saw you on the phone but didn't know how long you'd be," said Swan. "Everything okay at home?"

"Opportunity is knocking."

Swan swallowed her bite. "So, you ready to answer that door—without chocolate?"

"We'll see. I don't have any details yet about the part. I don't even know what the film's about."

"When the time is right, you'll know if the project is right."

"I agree. If the part is right, it's right. My personal manager, Clay, says it's the role of a lifetime."

Swan stopped eating and looked directly at her. "Whose lifetime was he referring to?"

CHAPTER NINE

Julia pivoted one last time in front of the full-length mirror, peering over her shoulder to see if she looked good from behind. She glanced out her bedroom window when she heard Cass's car rolling down the driveway and raced down the stairs.

"Wow!" said Cass when she came through the door. "You look beautiful. Nicki's eyes are going to pop out of her head when she sees you all glam."

"So you get what I'm going for here."

"Who wouldn't?"

"It's been a long time since I've worn high heels." Julia chuckled. "Make sure I don't tip over."

Julia knew the short skirt she was wearing with the heels would give her the chance to show off legs she usually hid under jeans and boots. The sleeveless scoop neck top allowed her sculpted arms to feel the soft sensation of her hair falling onto them. It was such a welcome change from the ponytail she wore all too often.

Before they headed out, Julia entered her casita and returned with the small padded crate she had constructed to transport Nicki's birthday present.

Cass opened the car door for her. "I can't believe I'll finally get to see this sculpture that you've been working on forever."

"I hope she likes it." Julia leaned into the back seat and secured the crate with a seatbelt. "There, that should do it."

Cass drove out slowly, then tackled the two-lane with a lead foot. "I'm looking forward to this party. It's time to blow off the stink."

Julia laughed. "I haven't heard you use that expression since high school."

"Well, it's true. No secret that we could both use more fun in our lives."

"I'm with you."

"You're staying at Nicki's tonight, so I'm sure you'll have some fun."

"You bet. She made a point of trying to get me to stay until Monday night."

"I told you I'd get someone to work for you if you want to do that."

"No. I'll be home tomorrow night."

They drove along the country road, singing to the radio until they arrived at Nicki's house. "Nice digs," said Cass when she pulled up in front of the Territorial style ranch home. "How many garages does the woman need?"

"You know Nicki and her toys. There are cars, jet skis, a motorcycle... I'm leaving the sculpture in the car until she starts opening gifts if that's okay."

"Great idea. Just give me the sign and I'll bring it in."

Nicki rushed out the door when Julia and Cass approached the walkway. She greeted Julia with a kiss. "Hiya, Cass, thanks for coming."

"It's the big 'three-oh' and I'm here to celebrate the passing of your youth."

"Attagirl." Nicki patted her shoulder.

"I'm going to put my gift inside with the others," Cass said, walking away.

Julia kissed Nicki again. "Happy birthday, honey. You'll get my gift later," she teased.

"I like the sound of that. You look gorgeous, by the way. But now I'm really curious."

"Hmm. Good."

"Come on in. My friends from LA have been waiting to meet you!" Nicki cradled Julia's hand in hers and led her inside to the party room.

Julia stiffened, tugged her skirt down, and tossed back her hair. She smiled at each woman as Nicki introduced them.

"And this is Marielle, my old college roommate," said Nicki.

Julia and Marielle hugged. "Finally," said Julia. "I've heard so much about you."

"Same here, Julia."

"Let's get you a drink, baby," said Nicki, escorting Julia to the bar. "What are you having tonight?"

"You."

Nicki looked away from the bottles and at Julia. "Before that," she smiled.

"White wine sounds good."

"I have your favorite right here." Nicki poured Julia a glass of pinot grigio and handed it to her.

Julia raised her glass. "To you, beautiful. Happy birthday." She took a sip and kissed Nicki.

"Thank you. Are you ready to get this party started? I think you'll like talking with Marielle. She's like you—loves horses." Nicki led Julia into the middle of the crowd.

"You mean she's like us," said Julia.

"Horses? I can take 'em or leave 'em. I only went riding with you because you wanted me to."

"I didn't know…"

Nicki kissed her. "Let's dance to this slow song so you can show off those legs."

"You know I need more alcohol if you're going to make me dance."

"I'll hold you close," Nicki smiled. "You look so hot in that skirt with those heels."

"I'm glad you like it—I wore this for you."

Nicki pulled Julia against her and whispered. "Good move."

Midway through their second dance, Marielle tapped Nicki on the shoulder. "Stop hogging your girlfriend. How am I ever going to get to know her?"

Julia smiled and touched Nicki's lips with her fingertip. "She has a point."

"You're right. Time to swap partners," said Nicki as she joined Marielle's girlfriend on the dance floor.

Marielle waited until the next song started before asking. "So how's my friend treating you, Julia?"

Julia glanced away and then back at the woman. "Fine, I reckon."

"And you've been dating how long?"

"A few months."

"Then she must really like you."

Julia smiled. "She does. But why do you say it like that?"

Marielle leaned toward her and spoke in hushed tones. "I love the girl to death, but where women are concerned, she has a short attention span. From what Nicki has told me, I think she's lucky to have you. I wouldn't give you two cents for any of her exes."

Julia turned in time with the beat, did a few spins, and smiled. "I could use some wine, Marielle."

Marielle smiled kindly. "That's easy to fix. Follow me."

They freshened their drinks and carried them to the back patio where Julia drank a second glass of wine and Marielle sipped her margarita.

"Do you ever make it up to LA?" Marielle asked.

"I want to, but between my diner, the ranch, and my addiction to sculpting, I never seem to get there. What do you do in LA?"

"I'm a studio hair and makeup artist."

"That sounds exciting. Do you ever work on famous people?"

"Sure, all the time."

Julia raised her glass and clinked the one holding Marielle's margarita. "Artists of the world, unite."

Marielle laughed. "I like you, Julia."

"Don't take my shyness for being aloof. I like you too."

Marielle pulled out her phone. "What's your number?"

Marielle typed it as Julia told her. Julia's phone rang a moment later.

"That's me calling," said Marielle. "Now we have each other's numbers. You know, just in case."

Julia looked at her quizzically. "In case of what?"

Marielle hesitated. "In case you get to LA and want to say hi."

Over drinks, they shared about art and horses.

"It's nice to have someone to talk to who can relate, Marielle."

Before Marielle could respond, Nicki came bounding onto the patio.

"There you are!" said Nicki. "I've been looking for you two. It's time to open presents and I need you both there."

Julia stood and walked toward the house. "Cass?" she called out. "Time to bring in my gift."

Julia waited until all the other presents had been opened to offer hers. She gulped the last of her third glass of wine and set the crate on the table in front of Nicki.

"What? No bow?" Nicki teased.

Julia playfully slapped her arm. "I made the crate. Lift the lid gently."

The room became quiet as Nicki peeled back the wooden top. She stared at the contents and carefully lifted out the sculpture. "Oh, cool." Nicki hesitated, then held it up for her guests to see. "A horse. Thanks, honey." She gave Julia a peck on the lips and placed the sculpture beside her other presents.

"Wow!" said Marielle. "Julia, where did you find that? I love Arabians!"

"I made it," Julia replied.

"No way! Are you serious?" said Marielle. "It's gorgeous."

"Thank you."

"Yep," Nicki added. "My girl sculpts. Although I'm partial to her sexy legs!"

"Kill the lights," said one of Nicki's friends as she entered with a lit birthday cake.

As everyone sang the birthday song, Julia watched Nicki's friends shower her with affection. A woman whose name Julia couldn't recall fawned over her, giving her a long close-mouthed kiss on the lips.

Hellooo. I'm standing right here! thought Julia.

Cass glanced at Julia and flicked her head in the direction of the kitchen. Julia slipped through the crowd and followed her silently out the back door and into the yard.

"You really outdid yourself, Julia. That horse is magnificent."

"Not to Nicki it isn't."

"Fuck her. You worked on that for over a month, and she just tossed it aside."

Julia shrugged.

"For all the trouble you went to, maybe you should've just gotten her a gift card."

"I'm sure she'll thank me later, Cass."

"She should be thanking you now. Here. In front of her friends. More than that…"

"She's had a lot to drink."

"You don't need to make excuses for her."

Their heads turned when they heard the collective roar from inside the house.

"Sounds like we're missing something," said Julia.

They made their way back to the party. Julia halted in her tracks when she got to the archway of the room. In the middle of the floor, Nicki sat on a small chair—with a stripper straddling her.

"Now *this* is what I call a birthday present!" Nicki said. "Thanks for chipping in, ladies!"

Cass whispered in Julia's ear. "You're a better woman than I am, Jules. The green-eyed monster would have bitten me in the ass by now."

"I guess she prefers the stripper." Julia stood on the outskirts of the room, pushing back at the jealousy that threatened to overwhelm her as she watched Nicki's hands slide all over the nearly naked woman's body. A boulder landed in her stomach with a dull thud, and although she'd been drinking, she suddenly felt stone-cold sober. "Can you give me a ride home, Cass? Now?"

"I thought you were staying over tonight."

Julia replied with a tightness in her throat. "So did I." She watched as the stripper nestled Nicki's face in her cleavage. Then Nicki kissed her hard. Julia knew what that kind of kiss usually led to.

"I have to get out of here right now," she whispered.

"Do you want to tell Nicki you're leaving?"

Julia shook her head. "Why? Does she look like she cares? I can't watch anymore."

* * *

Cass glanced over at her passenger after fifteen minutes of dead silence. "You okay? You haven't said a word since we left the party."

"Not really. I doubt she even knows I left." Julia remembered how Nicki had walked ahead of her at the movies, never once turning to see if Julia was at her side. Then, how she ignored Julia's desires, often coaxing her and succeeding in getting Julia to do whatever she wanted.

"I'm sorry, Jules. I do not believe how that woman disrespected you—you deserve better. Hey, why don't you stay at my place tonight and we'll watch funny movies, make popcorn?"

"No thanks," Julia answered listlessly.

"Aw, come on, we can trash Nicki. She deserves it."

Julia slumped. "You know that's not my style." She turned off her cell phone.

"Why did you turn off your phone?" Cass made a right onto the road that led to the ranch.

"Because I don't want to glare at it all night hoping she calls." Julia got out of the car to unlock the gate when she and Cass arrived at the Y2. She walked to the driver's-side window. "Thanks for the lift. I'm going to walk from here."

"But those heels will get all dirty on that long driveway."

Julia gave an ironic grin. "Ask me if I care."

"I don't want to leave you feeling this way, Jules. Especially when your phone is off and I can't check on you."

Julia mustered a sad smile. "I'll call you later to check in."

"Promise?" Cass stuck out her pinky.

"What are we, thirteen again?"

"Pinky swear. Promise me!"

Julia hooked her pinky around Cass's. "Promise," she said before wending her way down the dark and dusty driveway.

CHAPTER TEN

Rina adjusted her rearview mirror as she pulled away from the Arizona spa and wound down the mountain. She'd achieved the perfect blend of Rina-ness through a stew of balanced Ayurvedic Dosha, yoga, spinal adjustments, and facials. Now the archetype of calm and centeredness, she glanced in the visor mirror to see how all that body and mind rehab looked on her.

Even with the fillers I can still see the lines.

She took a deep breath and reminded herself that self-acceptance had been key to avoiding her urge for chocolate. Glad she had taken time at the spa to transition between rehab and "re-life," she decided she was as ready as she was going to get to meet with the A-list director. She passed an hour alone with her playlist-orchestrated thoughts. When the phone rang, she glanced at her dashboard display, then pressed the button on the steering wheel.

"Hi, Clay."

"How is it going? Where are you?" he asked.

"The Arizona desert, just past Tonopah."

"That's a desolate ride, especially after dark."

"I left the spa later than expected. I had a Reiki appointment and then hair and makeup."

"Everything okay?"

"I'm not sure if I'm tired or simply more relaxed than I've ever been. I should be in Palm Springs in under a few hours, although it's been raining on and off, so I'm taking it easy."

"I don't want to worry. Call me when you check into the Ritz?"

"I want to eat and sleep when I get there. I'll call you tomorrow after the meeting."

"I wish you'd have let me join you, Rina. You need your attack dog next to you in a negotiation."

Rina chuckled. "I'm not negotiating anything—especially without running it by you. I'm just going to listen to what Reese has to say."

"Listen to you."

"What about me?"

Clay laughed. "I feel like a proud papa who sent you away to summer camp—and you came home all grown up and knowing how to make your own bed! Is this the new you? Grounded? Secure?"

"Rehab was time well spent. I got a good view of my life there."

"What'd you see?"

"An up-close encounter with my fear of aging, of losing my desirability—both on-screen and off…"

"In rehab? What the hell does that have to do with chocolate?"

"You'd be surprised."

"Rina, this film is going to be huge. I'm so glad I could get this for you."

"Thank you, Clay—it's helping to quell my feelings of irrelevance."

"You'll never become irrelevant. Ya gotta believe, babe. Believe."

Rina laughed. "Good night, Clay." She switched to the satellite radio's Chill-Electronica channel, cranked it up, and set her plan of attack for the meeting.

Another hour and a half elapsed before Rina stopped for gas in Blythe, on the California-Arizona state line. Caught on a desolate stretch of Interstate 10 when a steady downpour began drenching the desert floor, she pushed ahead, driving through deep puddles that she couldn't see and gripping the wheel with a vengeance when she saw a Flash Flood sign. Her stomach growled, and the vigilance with which she was being forced to drive tired her. As the visibility deteriorated, she drove slower and slower. She should have taken the last exit, but she was past it before she could decide to do so. She coasted now while looking for the one the map on the GPS indicated was next.

The country road was barely visible when she pulled off the highway. Darkness pervaded the scene, as best she could tell through the sheeting of water across the windshield.

"Proceed to the route," said the disembodied voice on her GPS.

Her stomach growled again. "Restaurants near me," Rina told the GPS.

"I see one restaurant cafe four miles ahead. The Starlight Diner is moderately priced and has a four-star rating. I can call or get directions."

"Get directions," said Rina. "The Starlight Diner. It sounds quaint, like a throwback to the Fifties—in the middle of God knows where. I hope they're open."

* * *

"Jules," said Cass. "I have almost everything cleaned up and put away in the kitchen. If we'd had a minute today I would've asked why you spent Sunday alone. And why between yesterday and today at work you've probably said only six words."

"I sculpted all day Sunday. The only break I took was to feed the horses."

"Have you…"

"Spoken with Nicki? No. I've managed to avoid her calls since that disastrous party."

Somehow it was now three days later and the fog in her head had yet to lift. Still, she knew they were going to have to talk at some point. What would she say to the woman who had hurt her feelings more than once and humiliated her in front of a room full of people?

"I almost forgot my dinner." As soon as Cass disappeared through the swinging kitchen door, the diner phone rang. Julia reached behind the counter and picked it up. "Starlight," she answered.

"Don't hang up. It's Nicki."

The call didn't last long, but its effect did. Dazed by Nicki's words, Julia grabbed a rag and started moving the counter appliances, cleaning behind them. The harder she scrubbed, the more muted Nicki's voice became in her mind. She had opened with a profuse apology. The words that lingered, however, were: "I guess I'm not ready for a full time relationship with just one woman."

"What are you doing? It's quitting time," said Cass when she returned.

Julia moved the toasters back into position but said nothing.

Cass slung her purse over her shoulder. "Mind if I take off?"

"No. Night, Cass. Be careful out there. It's a flooding kind of rain."

"Jules."

Julia stopped and looked at her.

"That was her on the phone, wasn't it? Nicki."

Julia nodded and Cass hugged her. "You want to tell me what she said?"

"Maybe tomorrow." Julia shook her head. "Go home, Cass. I'm finished."

"I don't mind keeping you company."

Julia looked away. "I'd really like to be alone right now."

"You sure?"

"Yeah, I'm heading home." Julia put the blender back.

"Okay. Call me if you want to talk."

Julia nodded. "Good night."

The conversation with Nicki played on a continuous loop in her mind. "You're breaking up with me for that stripper from your party? A girl you just met?"

"We're over, Julia," Nicki had said. Then she'd had the nerve to repeat it. Twice. "I'm sorry."

As if that would change anything. Julia thought about it. *Admit it, you weren't in love with her. Think of all the times she discounted you and you ignored it. Ugh! Maybe I wasn't enough for her.*

With every tour her rag made of the counter, Julia wiped harder, determined to erase every crumb, every speck of a crumb—every crumbled illusion. Finally, exasperated, she tossed the rags and her apron into the laundry bin, grabbed her knapsack, locked up, and left.

Her ranch-worn boots scraped the crushed stone as she moved toward the lone car in the parking lot alongside the lonely desert two-lane. The rain had lessened somewhat and she breathed in the cool freshness of the wet earth. She tossed the knapsack onto the passenger seat of her 1974 Fiat Spider convertible and tilted her head back to feel the droplets tap her face before she got in. The usual sparkling celestial parade was shrouded in clouds so low that the night appeared more gray than black. She let out a deep sigh.

"I just want a glass of wine and a hot bath. Is that too much to ask?" Julia got behind the wheel and turned the key in the ignition.

Chug.

Click.

She tried again. *Chug, click.*

Click. The third time, the battery was so dead the car didn't even chug.

Tears burned her tired eyes, and while she rested her forehead on the steering wheel, she wondered whom she could call for a jump start—someone who wouldn't ask her any questions. *I'll figure it out in the diner and wait there.*

She sighed and grabbed her keys to head back inside. "Who did I piss off in my last life?" As she got out of the car, a set of brilliant headlights lit up the parking lot and blinded her. Julia shielded her eyes as a sleek Jaguar rolled up beside her, but to Julia's bedazzled eyes the driver's head looked like one big light bulb.

"Excuse me, Miss," said the woman. "Can you tell me if there's someplace open to get a bite to eat?"

Although the driver's face was enveloped in a halogen-esque globe, Julia recognized the driver's unique Italian accent, the unmistakable throaty timbre of the voice. The whole world knew that voice.

"Holy sh...ohmigosh! I grew up watching you; I've seen every movie twenty times—y-you're Katarina Verralta!" The light bulb effect had begun to fade, although the driver was still but a sketch of an outline.

Right there in her parking lot, on Old Saguaro Road, late on a Tuesday, was that some-kind-of-sexy that eradicated all doubt.

The actress confirmed it with a tired smile. "Actually, I'm a very tired and hungry Katarina Verralta. I'm sorry. I'm babbling and you're getting soaked."

"We're closed...but I was just heading back inside to call for a jump start. I'd be happy to get you some food. I'm rambling, aren't I? Did I say that out loud? Please. Come in."

"I really don't want to bother you," Katarina said.

"Honestly, it would be a highlight on an otherwise miserable day." Julia stood in the light rain, staring as her vision came back fully into focus.

Katarina Verralta's mutable green eyes were often compared to Sophia Loren's when they lit up the silver screen. Regardless, to Julia the woman was more beautiful than Michelle Pfeiffer, Charlize Theron, and Cate Blanchett all rolled into one, only with dark hair like Julia Roberts. At the moment, though, reflecting the indirect light through the prism of rain, her eyes merely shimmered and glowed. "I'll see you inside." Julia dashed toward the diner.

Julia left the door ajar and flipped on the lights. She entered her back office, changed into a dry sweater from her locker, brushed her hair, and put on some lipstick. It wasn't in every lifetime a girl got to meet her screen idol up close and personal. She heard her brain scream as she came out to greet the woman. *Katarina Verralta, Julia! Breathe for god's sake!*

Katarina made her entrance in the middle of a sentence while closing her umbrella. "...and then the rain became so heavy that I couldn't see the exit sign, but I took the ramp and that road led me here. I'm happy to take whatever you have prepared and eat in my car. Oh, and if you wouldn't mind, I really need your restroom."

Momentarily starstruck, first by the whirlwind of the moment, then by those luminescent eyes, all Julia could do was point to the ladies' room. She darted into the kitchen, fired up the mini oven on her way to the cooler, then tripped over a tray, nearly dropping the pan of her famous lasagna, which she'd served every Wednesday since she had taken over the place four years earlier.

She composed herself, reentered the dining room, and set a table. "Miss Verralta," she said when the actress returned, "I have a table ready for you right here."

The chestnut-haired beauty smiled. "I'm at a disadvantage. You know my name, but I don't know yours."

Julia managed a shallow breath. "I'm Julia Dearling, owner of the Starlight Diner." Her hand swept across the panorama of tables and booths before her right hand met Katarina's handshake.

Soft. Strong, Julia thought. She savored the velvety warmth of the manicured hand that was so unlike her own thanks to her work in a kitchen, in a sculpting studio, and in the barn. *I can't believe I shook her hand! Breathe, Julia!*

"Julia Dearling, you are a lifesaver. But I feel terrible for inconveniencing you."

Julia thought the woman's accent made her name sound exotic. Something like *Zhooliaah*. She smiled and it felt good. Until that moment, Julia didn't realize how long it had been since she'd smiled and meant it. "You have no idea what an honor it is to have you as my guest. Do you like homemade vegetable lasagna?" *Please say yes.* "It's my Grandmother Lucia's recipe."

"I'm starving and I love lasagna. Especially Grandmother Lucia's."

Julia fidgeted awkwardly. "I took a chance—it should be hot in a minute." The movie star's smile glued Julia's feet to the floor.

"Are all the people around here as nice as you?" Katarina asked, her long chestnut-brown hair framing the face that made Julia lightheaded.

"No, I'm the only one."

Verralta's laugh was warm and genuine.

"Make yourself comfortable. I'll be back in a few."

Julia had to concentrate to not drop the tray of food and the bottle of wine when she returned. The sight of her movie idol in her restaurant was one thing, but up close, Julia now wondered why they always made her look so much younger on-screen. *You're so much more beautiful like this.*

"That lasagna smells fabulous. My stomach just growled."

"Wait until you taste it. Grandmother Lucia was no pushover in the kitchen. This wine is a Sancerre that I've been saving for a special occasion, Miss Verralta. And special occasions don't come any more special than this out here in the desert—especially on a rainy Tuesday night."

"Pull up a glass, Julia. My friends call me Rina. Do you know of a hotel nearby? I've been on the road for hours and I think driving in the rain has exhausted me."

Julia joined her and took a sip of the Sancerre. "I'm afraid up near Palm Springs is the closest you'll find, and that's another long, dark, hour and ten—longer in the rain." She poured Rina more wine. "However, I have a little casita on my property. It's actually my sculpting studio. It's clean, has a good bed and you're welcome to it. I'm on private property so no one will disturb you there."

"Oh, no. I couldn't."

"Don't think twice. It's really the only game in town. By the look of tonight's sky, the rain's going to get worse before it gets better."

"Really, Julia? I'd be so grateful. I can drive you home and you can deal with your car tomorrow." She took another steaming forkful of lasagna. "This is so delicious you could patent it. You are an angel."

The next time Julia left the Starlight Diner, Nicki didn't even cross her mind.

CHAPTER ELEVEN

A torrent of sensation flooded Julia each time she stole a glance of Rina by dashboard light. Working hard to act normal, she called out the occasional turn. "Go slow around the bend. Take the next right." Finally, midway down the second dark country road she said, "Get ready to stop…right here." Julia hopped out of the Jaguar and unlocked the gate beneath the arch standing guard above it with the words "Y2 Ranch" scrolled on it.

"A real ranch?" Rina said when Julia got back into the car.

"It's not a working ranch anymore, but I still keep a couple of horses here. That's the main house up ahead. The casita is next to it on the right."

Rina parked between the two buildings.

"I'll get some lights on. Follow me." Julia flicked the switch on the side of the house and lit the path. She picked up Rina's suitcase and led her inside the sculpting studio.

The delicate glow from the wall sconces buffered the light trailing down from the loft as its beam settled into the dark-sand-colored walls. "Welcome to the Y2, Miss Verralta."

"This is beautiful," said Rina as she came through the arched wooden doorway and took stock of the room. "Look at all these horse sculptures! Did you make these?"

"Yes. I've been riding since I could walk. So I sculpt what I know, in addition to the things I find most beautiful."

"You're more talented than the artists selling in Beverly Hills galleries."

"No." Julia paused. "Really?"

"Yes, really. I've spent a minor fortune on my art collection." Rina toured the horses, running her hand along the mane of an Arabian forever poised to gallop. She approached the only piece covered by a tarp. "What's under here?" she asked, reaching for it.

Julia leapt across the room and placed her hand over Rina's to keep her from revealing it. "Sorry, you can't see it. It's a work-in-progress." She felt like she was standing on pillows, unable to quite feel the floor beneath her feet, when she touched Rina's hand and looked into her eyes. *Those eyes.*

"Julia, I haven't even paid you for dinner. And please allow me to pay for the accommodations."

"Oh, no. I wish the place was more fitting for someone like you. Clean and comfortable is all I have to offer."

Rina held out a few hundred dollar bills. "Please take it."

"No way. You haven't any idea how many times your movies have lifted me out of this small town. Taken me to places I didn't even know I wanted to go."

Silent, Rina stared at her.

"A-Are you blushing?" Julia asked.

"It sure feels like I am. My cheeks are suddenly very warm."

"Imagine that. A big star like you blushing," Julia chuckled. "Who'da thunk? Upstairs in the loft is the bed and bathroom, and there's water and snacks down here in the mini fridge." She pointed to the other side of the room. "I'll leave the back porch light on in case you want to raid the kitchen, but if we lose power from the storm, there's a flashlight by the casita's door."

Rina's eyes smiled at her. "What have I done to deserve you, Julia Dearling?"

"I'm certain you deserve a lot better than me."

Rina tossed back her hair and caught Julia's eye. "I don't know that they make them any better than you." She yawned.

"I'll go so you can get some rest. Make yourself at home and sweet dreams."

Too excited to go to sleep, Julia entered the house and lit a fire in the great room. When she finally made it upstairs and climbed into her bed, she tried counting sheep; then she tried counting Katarinas.

She tossed and turned, thinking about the goddess-at-large who was occupying her casita. *I might never wash those sheets again.*

Somewhere around her hundredth toss—or maybe it was a turn—she dozed off while replaying the evening yet again in her mind. She'd give anything to awaken to those shimmering sea-green eyes, to have those soft hands glide down her back. The fantasy jarred her awake again. That thought was over-the-top—even for a romantic like herself.

It was no use. She couldn't sleep. According to her clock, her longest stint of unconsciousness had lasted only fifteen minutes, and that had been an hour earlier. At two a.m., she got out of bed with a groan, poured a glass of wine, and rebuilt the fire until the room glowed a roaring orange. She piled pillows on the floor, warmed herself by the fire, and eventually dozed off. Minutes after she fell asleep, though, she awoke to a full-blown thunderstorm. Julia listened to the rain thrash the windows and took solace in the irregular flaming spikes in the fireplace.

When she heard the kitchen door squeak, she wiped the speck of sleep from her eyes and stood. The fireplace's golden orange glow reached clear across the room to illuminate the long-haired beauty standing in the archway.

"I'm sorry if I woke you, Julia," Rina said softly. "Big thunderstorms scare me."

To Julia, the room's glimmer exposed the chiseled beauty of Rina's age—made her eyes appear phosphorescent. Incapable of producing a coherent thought, Julia strode silently to where Rina awaited her with sleepy eyes, behind which Julia knew burned a passionate woman. She could feel it. The look in those eyes ignited in Julia all the desire she had ever wanted to feel, had ever wanted to express, but never had. The movie star averted her eyes. Julia's fingertips barely brushed the skin of Rina's cheek, then tilted the woman's chin upward until their eyes met again.

Without so much as a sigh, Julia pressed the actress back against the wall and kissed her passionately. Took Rina's breath away. Her lips trailed down Rina's neck while her hands pulled the woman from the wall and firmly against her body. With shallow and ragged breaths, Rina glided her hands down Julia's back.

"I haven't stopped thinking of you for a moment," Rina whispered in her ear. Then she shuddered at a thunderclap.

Julia spoke between kisses, leading her toward the pillows by the hearth. "Come with me," she said as they sank to the floor.

Rina moaned when Julia laid her back, thick waves of hair spilling away from her face. Julia straddled her, her fingertips tracing the woman's neck, the hard nipples under the silk nightgown she was wearing. Julia stripped off her oversized sleep shirt, then, looking deep into Rina's eyes, she tore the silk gown from her body. Thunderclaps crashed, then echoed through the walls, and Rina pulled her against skin made hot by the fire and the scorching rush between them. Julia drowned herself in Rina's stare, sliding her naked body deliberately along Rina's length, allowing every inch of their skin to meet in an avalanche of yearning.

Julia tried to hold back, tried to be gentle with her passion, but she lost every ounce of self-control for the first time in her life. Her coarse and pent-up desire broke free all over the woman beneath her. Here, now, there was no difference between them. One was much older—famous, the other seriously younger—unknown. None of it mattered naked in front of the fire.

"Oh, my god, Rina."

There would be no settling for merely pleasant or enjoyable—the way she had with Nicki and every other girl she'd known. This kind of sex reeked of raw midbrain, that sensory, there's-a-meteor-headed-for-Earth kind of passion. Rina rolled on top of her, her chestnut waves spilling onto Julia's skin as Julia opened herself to receive the woman's touch.

"You're unbelievable," Rina whispered, her body locked against Julia's—her velvety hands touching Julia in ways she'd always longed to be touched.

Julia breathed in her lover's scent, swallowed Rina's every need, and then relinquished to Rina everything inside of her. Their bodies intertwined, Julia became acutely aware of every sensation—from the incessant pounding of the rain on the roof to the irreverent craving coursing through her. She felt fully awake for the first time in her life.

To this woman whose touch set Julia's skin on fire, Julia surrendered her entire inner world. Rina's full lips and adoring mouth transported her into a new world, where each level of desire welcomed her home.

In their final moments of abandon, long after they'd begun, Rina's gorgeous glow-in-the-dark eyes rolled back in her head and a groan erupted from deep inside her. Julia gave her a minute to recover, then pulled the blanket from the couch and covered them both.

"I'm sorry about your nightgown," Julia whispered with a hint of a smile. "I'll be happy to replace it."

Rina laid her head on Julia's shoulder and sighed. The fire crackled, and rain now overflowed the gutters and washed down the windows. "Not necessary, but I'd prefer not leaving here naked."

"Take anything you want—just don't go."

With each minute that passed, they held on a little tighter, kissed a little longer—sighed deeper.

"I want to tell you how beautiful I think you are, Rina, but I can't even imagine how many times you've heard that...how meaningless it must be to hear it."

"It wouldn't be if you said it, Julia."

"Do you mean that?"

"I'm lying here thinking how I've waited a lifetime for fate to intervene—to feel what I'm feeling with you right now. But now that it's happened, I'm totally unprepared. I don't even know what to do with this."

Julia chuckled. "Clearly, you know what to do with this. I'm sure a lot of women would say the same."

"I think you have the wrong idea about me."

"Meaning?"

"I live a very isolated existence."

"Because you're so famous?"

"There's that obstacle. But I haven't been with anyone in a long time. In fact, I've been away on a soul-searching journey for the past month."

"Did you find it? Your soul?"

Rina kissed her and gazed into Julia's eyes. "I'm thinking I'm staring straight at it. If not, I'm definitely soul-adjacent. Right now, all I want is to stop time—to stay like this with you."

"Um, are you acting right now?"

"No. This is a first for me. I really don't know what to make of meeting you. Touching you this way." She sighed. "I can't get enough of you."

Julia stroked Rina's hair. "You? *You* don't know what to make of it? I'm thinking I'm in some drug-induced dream."

"What if I've been alone so long because I had to wait for you to grow up? I don't even want to know how old you aren't."

"I won't be indelicate by asking your age, Rina."

"You can find it on *Wikipedia*, if you're interested."

"I don't care about our age difference."

Rina hesitated. "I do," she whispered.

Julia shifted up onto her elbow and gazed down into Rina's now yellow-hazel cat-eyes. "Why?"

"Because it doesn't make my aging crisis any easier. Our age difference isn't measured only in years, it's more like generations."

"So what?"

Rina smirked. "That's what everyone who enters into an inappropriate liaison says in the beginning."

"Rina, look into my eyes. I. Don't. Care."

"But the difference in our bodies, in the lines on our faces—"

Julia shut her down with a steamy, lingering kiss. "I don't care," she repeated softly.

"But I do. It's okay. After all, we're just two people whose paths crossed on a rainy night. Right?"

Julia gently touched Rina's cheek and then traced the lines next to her eye. "I wouldn't know. I've never had a one-night stand before."

Julia awoke with a slow stretch. As she slid into consciousness, she wondered if it had all been an outrageous dream—until she breathed in the scent of Katarina doused in Dior. She reached out for Rina but felt only empty space. Naked, she bolted to the window, but the Jaguar was gone. She pulled the blanket around her and fell back onto the sofa.

"Not even a goodbye?"

For all that Julia had felt—had done with this woman all night long—Rina hadn't even woken her to say goodbye. A sliver of dread crept in and then widened, and through that gaping wound, her emotional lifeblood seeped out and pooled around her. She didn't think she could feel more alone than she did in that moment.

Dumped twice in one night! First by a woman I don't love, then by a woman I'm already in love with. Julia put on a pot of coffee and resisted the urge to go into her studio and throw a mound of clay against the wall—her work-in-progress even—and destroy it. Rina had been inside the casita. Rina had been inside the house. Rina had been… inside her.

She picked up the phone and called Cass. "Can you pick me up on your way in today? I want to work, but my car died at the diner last night."

"But it's your day off," said Cass. "Why would you want to work on your day off?"

"Because I do, Cass!"

"This is about that call from Nicki last night, isn't it?"

Julia rolled her eyes. "I can honestly say it isn't."

"Yeah. Sure."

"It isn't, Cass. Really." Julia felt a rush of warmth at the thought of Rina.

"I'll be there in half an hour."

CHAPTER TWELVE

Rina exited the interstate and hid behind her sunglasses at the drive-through where she bought coffee and a breakfast sandwich. No matter how she tried, she couldn't steer her mind in the direction of the meeting she was about to have with A-list director Reese Collingworth.

Julia's imprint remained—indelible from the moment her soft warm lips had met hers for the first time. She shivered from the sensation that had yet to fade.

Rina glanced into the mirror to confirm what she already knew. *If you think you look old now, just look at yourself next to her.*

She took one bite of her food, realized she wasn't hungry, and tossed the remainder into the car's trash bag, then drove the final half hour into Palm Springs. Like a drone, she followed the orders from her GPS, absentmindedly making one turn after the next until the voice said: "The destination is on your right."

Did last night happen? Is that girl for real?

Rina pulled up to the gate and touched the button on the speaker. As the gate peeled back, she repeated her new mantra: "Breathe." Then she updated it. "Focus!" She pasted on a smile, got out of the car, and rang the doorbell.

"Welcome, Ms. Verralta. I'm Mr. Collingworth's assistant, Zee," said the woman who answered the door. She led Rina into the sprawling desert estate. "May I bring you a beverage?"

"Coffee—medium light, one packet of stevia. And some water please."

"Right away. Straight ahead through the double doors."

Rina slowed in the hallway to peer into the atrium through the glass walls in the center of the home. Surrounding the large fountain sculpture, a micro forest displayed cactus and deciduous trees laced with billowing bougainvillea in splashes of purple, orange, and white, all landscaped with precision. The double doors just beyond it opened.

"Katarina." Tall and square-jawed with thick gray hair, Reese Collingworth reached for her and kissed her on the cheek. "I'm so glad you could make it."

"Reese, it's good to see you," she replied with a wide smile, returning his hug. "You look terrific."

"Come in, make yourself comfortable."

Beyond the sleek Natuzzi couch, an imposing wooden captain's desk displayed Reese's trophies and highest industry honors.

"I love your display." She sauntered over to the Golden Globe statues, Critics Awards, and the highly coveted Oscar figurines—six of them, counting the new one for directing *Allies of Night*. She'd reserved a space in her display case for a matching one, but it had gone to Britney Cavell instead.

"Thank you. I was beginning to worry," he said. "When I called the Ritz this morning, they said you'd never checked in. Are you okay?"

"It's a long story. I didn't make it all the way here last night because of the weather."

"Where were you coming from?"

"I drove from Phoenix."

His face contorted. "Why on earth were you in that cow town?"

"I was at a spa in Scottsdale. Last night, however, I wound up staying in a little town in the outer desert on the California side."

Reese showed Rina to the sofa and sat opposite her. "One of those little dust bowl places?"

Rina endured a lightness of being so surreal, she thought she might float away. She conjured up her last vision of Julia, tangled in the blanket, on the floor by the fireplace—the long brown hair draping the pillow. In her mind, she again tasted the entirety before answering. "It wasn't so bad really."

"I'm glad you made it safely. Ah," Reese said when his assistant entered. "Thank you, Zee."

The woman placed the coffee and water on the coffee table between the sofas. Next to them sat a small juice glass filled with green liquid.

Rina smiled. "What is that?"

The man rolled his eyes. "Layla insists my staying power has increased since she started me on this designer drink." He grimaced and then chugged the whole glass. "I figure if it makes her happy, I can deal with it."

Rina laughed. "That's adorable. Twenty years and it's still the little things, huh?"

"Twenty-two years."

Rina sighed. "I envy you. I'm happy for you, but I envy you."

"When are you going to settle down, Miss Movie Star?"

"I think the challenge has been settling down without settling. In case you haven't noticed, the women in LA aren't exactly homespun. For that matter, neither am I."

Reese nodded. "No one lassos you for long. Maybe coming out would increase your options. Surely there must be someone out there for you. I do believe there's a lid for every pot."

She inhaled Julia. "Maybe."

"Then the timing for this role is good. It will get your head into something you can really concentrate on. This part is so you—a powerful and beautiful woman fighting the corporate machine in the world of horse racing. The lawyers have looked over the contract, and there isn't anything Clay has asked for that we wouldn't happily accommodate. It's the role of a lifetime, Rina."

"That's exactly how Clay referred to it."

"You've read the script. What do you think?"

"It's a great script." Rina took a sip of coffee followed by a long drink of water.

"Can you ride a horse?"

"By ride, do you mean sit on top of one?"

Reese laughed. "Don't worry. We'll set you up for some lessons before we begin shooting. The stunt double will be doing the hard things. Guess who I got to play opposite you?"

"As my nemesis?"

"Yes. Britney Cavell!"

Rina choked on her water, coughing until her eyes teared.

"My god, woman! Are you okay?"

Rina composed herself. "Cavell?"

"She's the only actress who's strong enough to equal your screen presence. After this year's Oscar win, she's a hot property."

"Yes, I recall the evening with clarity."

"I'm sorry. I didn't mean to imply you weren't worthy of beating her for Best Actress. You got my vote."

"It's okay. I'm over it."

Reese pointed his stare at her. "Are you?"

"Yes. Once I exhausted the entire imported chocolate supply of Southern California, everything was perfect."

"I thought you gained a little weight, but you look refreshed compared to how you looked at the awards ceremony."

Rina cringed. "Is this you wooing me, Reese?"

"No, all I meant was that you really do have a little glow about you."

Rehab? Julia? "Thank you?"

"You can tell me, Rina. Did you have a little work done? Is that where you've been?"

Rina's jaw dropped open when she laughed. "Here we go—just when I thought it was safe to go back in the water. No, I'm *au naturel*. Well, Hollywood *au naturel*."

"Sorry, I don't intend to be an ass. I'm trying to say you look really good. You know I love you and that's why I want you to take this role. I think it'll do wonders for your career. It's a solid role for a strong older woman, and no one could play it better than you."

"Ugh, that word seems to be everywhere these days."

"What word?"

Rina wrinkled her nose at the stench: "Older."

Reese's tone bent toward conciliatory. "At least you're not playing the manic grandmother—and there are no perky ingenues in this film."

"You sure Cavell doesn't think she's the perky ingenue?"

Reese chuckled. "That was funny. The two of you on-screen in a film like this? It's a total win."

"With Cavell." On the spot, Rina invented Just Shoot Me Now *Numero Uno*—wide-eyed horror with a dash of You've Got To Be Fucking Kidding Me Number Eight.

"Yes. Don't let that self-absorbed child get inside your head. She's a terrific actress, and even though both roles are leads, you'll be the star. I'm the director and that's how I plan to shoot it."

Rina stood and meandered over to the desk. She ran her fingers along the Oscar statues as she thought about it. *Hmm. Freshly dusted. I didn't win for* Allies of Night, *but that was my fault, not Reese's. It would be foolish to pass up this opportunity. Or would it?* "I don't know. I need to think about this."

"What is there to think about?"

"Seriously?"

"Yes."

She turned back toward him. "I'm concerned about waking up every day between now and the wrap party knowing I have to do scene after scene with that woman."

"In her defense," Reese began, "when she heard you might be coming on board, she was ecstatic."

"I'll bet."

"Meaning?"

"The only reason that would excite her is because she's plotting to steal my scenes. Or my life. Or anything that serves her latest scheme."

"You two were over a while ago. I didn't realize the after-relationship was so contentious. She never let on."

"She didn't point her little Oscar at you and make demands?"

"No. But if she ever does, I'll see her her Oscar and raise her five."

"Do you already have the locations locked down?"

"We've been negotiating. Right now it looks like Vancouver. And some of the French scenes we'll film in Paris. I'm guessing six to eight weeks of rehearsal. I'm not sure of the shooting schedule yet. So what do you say, Rina?"

"I need to consider it carefully. If this is going to work with Cavell, we're going to need to set some boundaries in stone. Signed and sealed."

"Like what?"

"Let me think about it, Reese. I haven't been home in over a month, so I need a few days to get settled and discuss it with Clay."

"He's worked hard on your behalf for this."

Rina nodded. "Clay's my ace."

"Answer me honestly. If Britney Cavell wasn't in the film, would you be less hesitant?"

"Yes, but I still need to think about what I can bring to this character. She needs life and passion. If I can't give her that, I have no business accepting the part."

"That's what sets you apart from the rest."

She smiled. "I love your integrity, Reese. I know you wouldn't be offering me this if you didn't believe in me."

"Then come on board, Rina. We'll reach for that Oscar. We've already gotten one together."

"Yes, we certainly have."

"Together, we could show the Academy that they got it wrong last time around and give them a chance to redeem themselves."

She walked to where he stood. "Can you give me until next week?"

"Sure," he said. "Come on, I'll show you out. You can relax at the Ritz and Layla and I will see you later for dinner. We can talk more then."

"As much as I would love to, I've been dreaming about sleeping in my own bed for weeks now."

"Aww, poor baby." The director slipped his arm around the actress's shoulder.

She stopped in the hallway. "I love the renovations by the way. This atrium is magnificent."

"Thank you. It's very Zen. I love working out there, as long as it's not a hundred-and-eleven-thousand degrees."

Rina laughed. "How hot the desert can get!" *Julia. Updated mantra—focus!*

They ambled toward the front door.

"But I think we're going to start spending more time at the beach house."

"It would be wonderful to have you and Layla in Malibu."

Reese opened Rina's car door and hugged her. "Give Clay my best. We'll talk next week—and I'll see you at the table read!"

Rina smiled. "Working with you again would be a dream, Reese."

"So then, say yes right now."

"And working with Cavell could be a damn nightmare—for everyone."

As the actress pulled out onto Palm Canyon Drive, her insides twinged. She reached for her phone—then realized she didn't have Julia's number. *Perhaps it's better this way*, she thought, even as she reminded herself she could try to get her at the Starlight Diner if she had to.

Rina swayed gently to the right and back again when her car hugged the bend in the desert road. She merged onto the I-10 under a patch of blue sky the color of Julia's eyes, wishing she was heading back toward where she had started that morning. Instead, she pointed the Jag toward LA. The rolling hills in Riverside reminded her of the soft slope of Julia's curves—of her breasts. An hour outside of LA, she did a double take when the woman in the car next to her had hair like Julia's. To distract herself, she turned on the radio—only to immediately hear the song "Brave" by Sara Bareilles that had been playing when she left the ranch. She sighed.

"What have I done? I already have a song for her. I'm in trouble." She repeated along with the Therapy Brittany in her head: *"Breathe, Rina. Breathe."*

* * *

It wasn't until she pulled into her garage two hours from Palm Springs that Rina realized her every thought during the drive had been about the girl from the night before. She shocked herself back into reality, plummeting back to earth in a parachute made of Gigi and Clay.

"There's our girl!" said Gigi. Clay followed behind her as they came to greet Rina at the car.

"I really missed you," said Clay before he hugged her. "Oh, and thanks for calling me after the meeting!"

"Oh shit," said Rina, handing them each her belongings from the trunk. "I knew I forgot something. I'm sorry, Clay. I'm tired and I needed to concentrate on the road."

"I figured," he said with a smile. "Well, let's get you inside and I'll make you a Welcome Home concoction, and you can tell us all about it."

"Yes," Gigi said excited. "Where are we filming?"

"Let's not get ahead of ourselves." Rina followed them with her arms full.

"What are you talking about? You and Reese met," said Clay.

They entered the house, left everything in the foyer, and stopped two flights up in the kitchen.

"You look different," said Gigi, taking her seat.

"You just haven't seen me in a month," Rina replied from the chair opposite Clay.

"Nooo," Clay chimed in. "There's something very different going on here." He swirled his hands in the air like some Bob Fosse-choreographed finger painting air-masterpiece. "It's your energy."

Gigi nodded. "Exactly. What did they do to you?"

Again, Rina flashed on the night before. "Whatever it was, I'd like to do it again right now."

"Well then, while it's fresh in your mind and before you crash, how did the meeting go with Reese?"

Rina hesitated. "You know Reese. He's wonderful."

Clay stared at her. "What's that inscrutable expression I'm reading on your face?"

"I don't know about doing this project, Clay."

"Are you kidding me? You'd be out of your mind not to, Rina. You've read the script. It's meaty—Oscar worthy. Reese knows how to win an Oscar—or six—and you've already won one together."

"Did you know that Reese has already cast Britney Cavell in the role opposite me?"

"Not Bitchney Cavell!" said Gigi.

Clay stared at her slack-jawed. "He did *not* hire that woman. Why would he do that?"

"He said she was a hot property coming off her win and that she was the only actress who was strong enough to play opposite me."

Clay shook his head. "'Opposite' is the key word there."

Rina stood and moved toward the stairs to her suite. "Maybe you need your concoction more than I do, Clay. Your face has suddenly turned a brilliant shade of red—and is that steam coming out of your ears?"

CHAPTER THIRTEEN

The three days since Rina's departure had seemed more like three weeks to Julia. She had no idea that time could pass so slowly or that boredom and confusion were a family of co-conspirators.

"Lightning," she said to her horse, "I can't stand this funk I've been in and I need to do something about it! But what?" she added in a defeated tone.

While she'd managed to remove the traces of Rina from the great room, she couldn't shake the images that flooded her mind—or the sensations that coursed through her body, breathing in her regardless of where she was or what she was doing.

Tossing and turning had become her nightly ritual. Julia headed into work earlier each day—came home later every night. On the third night, her heart pounded when she at last mustered enough courage to enter the casita to check for leaks from the storm.

Listless, she flipped on the light switch.

"No!"

Right there, out in the open, her work-in-progress lay uncovered. Hastily, she rushed to replace the tarp over the unfinished sculpture— the bust of Katarina Verralta. She stopped and stroked the long waves of clay-hair first. She didn't notice the note lying on the table until it fell off the tarp and onto the floor by her foot. She sat and unfolded the paper.

Dearest Julia, the note began. And in Julia's mind, she heard Rina call her *Zhooliaah.*

You were sleeping so peacefully, I didn't have the heart to wake you. I had to leave early for a meeting in Palm Springs. It took all of my resolve to leave you. I won't stop thinking of you, of us, for a second. My cell number is below. If you choose to not call, I'll understand. After all, our age difference is more than just any obstacle. Know that in my heart, I'm grateful for you and I'm humbled by this magnificent sculpture.

The note had been signed, "Love, Rina," and there was a phone number beneath the signature.

Julia shook her head and stood. "Are you kidding me! I've been walking around despondent for the past three days while this note was sitting here the whole time! Aagh!" She dashed back to the house clutching the note and grabbed her phone. Her hands shook such that she had to enter the number three times before getting it right. When the call went straight to voice mail, Julia didn't know what to say and so she hung up.

Over the next week-and-a-half, she tried calling, leaving voice mails each time. Then she left messages with the unnamed woman who had answered "Miss Verralta's phone."

Julia left her name and number again, but Rina still hadn't returned her calls. Thoughts of Rina consumed her. *How many messages am I supposed to leave before I get the message that she's not calling back?*

"Julia!" said Isabella. "What are you doing?"

Julia's distraction crashed into reality. "Damn. Did I just pour a mound of sugar into the lasagna?"

Isabella handed her a new lasagna pan. "You have to start from scratch."

By the time this particular Tuesday night at the diner was over, Julia was no longer the orderly creature of habit she had always been. She hung the CLOSED sign, couldn't care less about counting her tips, and left most of the cleanup for the morning crew.

She flipped off the lights and locked up, expecting to see her Fiat the lone car in the parking lot. Tonight, however, a snazzy red convertible was parked next to it. "What the—"

Before she could complete the thought, the car door opened, and Rina stepped out into the night. Julia dropped her knapsack on the ground, locking onto Rina's gaze as the woman approached.

"Hello, Julia."

"Rina, w-what are you doing here?"

"Hmm. That depends."

"On what?"

"On you, Julia."

Julia's hand found its way onto her own hip. "Why haven't you returned my calls?"

"What calls?"

"My voice mails. And the messages I left with the woman who answers your phone."

"I never got any messages."

Julia's eyebrows arched. "It took me three days to find your note. But when you didn't call back, I'd assumed you had changed your mind. I mean, I knew how you felt about the age thing."

Rina closed the distance between them and stroked back the hair from Julia's eyes. "That's Gigi, my personal assistant. Her job is to filter my calls, protect me. I can't believe she didn't tell me you'd called."

"Maybe you should let her do her job. You were right, Rina. You couldn't possibly need someone like me—to mess up your life."

Rina touched her cheek. "No, Julia. I drove for hours to tell you I was wrong. You were right. I've done nothing but miss you. When it came down to it, I took a chance coming here because I can't let you slip away without trying to win you—if you're in the game." Rina shifted her weight, looked away and then back at Julia. "I mean, you did say in the throes of passion that you didn't care about the age thing."

Julia smiled. "Not true. I said it afterward."

"I haven't been able to concentrate on a damn thing since I left here. I even lost a shoe! Not a pair, mind you, but a single shoe from a pair that's worth a small fortune. Julia? Who loses *one* shoe?"

Julia laughed. "You didn't."

"I did."

"Right or left?"

"Right. And I've been sleepless. Have hardly eaten. All because I thought you hadn't called me. Honestly, I've been a bit of a mess."

Julia put her arms around the woman, pulled her in, and kissed her ardently before speaking another word. "Why are we kissing in the parking lot? Why don't you follow me home in your car?"

Rina chuckled. "It's not my car."

"What?" Julia looked beyond her. "Is someone with you?"

"No. It's your car."

"Huh?"

"You wouldn't let me buy my own dinner or pay for staying in the casita…"

"So you bought me a car! Are you crazy?"

"But it's an Italian car—a Fiat, just like that old wreck of yours, but, you know, dependable and with airbags. And lasagna is Italian. *I'm* half Italian—maybe a little more than that since the lasagna."

"I can't accept it."

"If it will make you feel better, you can pay for it."

Julia laughed. "I would if I could afford it."

"Oh, but you can."

"What are you talking about?"

"I took pictures of your sculptures before I left—showed them to some gallery owners I know in Beverly Hills. You're about to kick off a bidding war for two of the Arabians, and they want to see your work-in-progress when it's finished."

Julia felt her cheeks flush. "Hey, you weren't supposed to see that."

"But I did. And you're not selling it."

"I'm not?"

Rina stared at her. "Out of all the places in the world, I get stuck in the rain in the casita of a sexy young sculptress who happens to be creating a sculpture of *me*?"

"Yeah, okay, you're right. It's not for sale—and it still has a long way to go. Maybe it'll be your birthday present. Thanks to *Wikipedia* I now know when that is. Did you know you were born in Paris?" Julia winked at her.

"How about an anniversary present? I wouldn't expect something that beautiful—meaningful—for anything less momentous."

Julia smiled. "Follow me home in *your* car. I'll be driving the old Fiat."

"Julia. That car belongs in a museum."

Julia kissed Rina lightly on the lips. "Let's go."

"Come on. Don't you even want to drive it?"

"Definitely, absolutely not. Let's go."

"Not yet."

"Why?"

"Well, it *is* Tuesday night and I have driven an awfully long way. Grandmother Lucia's lasagna? I've been thinking about it the whole way here."

"You're lucky my assistant caught me ruining the first batch. You're not the only one who's been walking in circles, Rina. I know it's a long ride. Want to come into the diner and eat?"

"I was hoping you'd serve it to me in bed." She raised her eyebrow. "You know—afterward."

"You make me melt, Rina. If you don't touch me soon, I might evaporate."

This time, when Julia brought Katarina Verralta home to the Y2, they bypassed the casita and every room in the house except for the bedroom.

Julia pulled Rina on top of her, wound a shock of her chestnut waves around her hand, and gazed into her eyes. "You realize we're already in this—whatever it is."

"Thank you for saying it. I think I just took my first breath in two weeks."

"What time do you have to leave tomorrow?"

Rina grinned. "I don't have to be back for two days."

"Really? Really?"

"Yep."

"Tomorrow's my day off," said Julia. "Want to go riding with me? I'll pack a picnic."

"A picnic on horseback? Did I sign on to do a Western?"

Julia chuckled. "Yes. And as it happens, I'm your leading lady."

"Then it's a date."

"Not just a date, Rina. Our first date."

"You don't count having hot sex all night long as our first date?"

"No, I don't."

"Great. Glad there's no pressure." Rina kissed her. "We're already so good together."

Julia rolled Rina onto her back and gazed into her eyes. "Remind me."

CHAPTER FOURTEEN

Rina wound her way up the hill in the scorned red convertible and coasted into her garage. She rolled her suitcase into the house and stopped in the kitchen when Gigi came bounding down the stairs.

"I thought I heard the door. I'm glad you're home—since you weren't answering your phone for the past two days. You okay?"

"I'm great, Gigi. Everything all right?"

"Yes, except you haven't been preparing."

"What makes you think that?" Rina took a bottle of water from the fridge and turned toward the stairs.

"Shouldn't we be running lines? Let me get your suitcase." Gigi followed Rina up two flights to her suite. "Normally, at this point you're stressing and making all kinds of demands regarding the script."

"Are you saying I'm high maintenance?" Rina tossed her purse onto a chair in her living room and sat back on the Roche Bobois sofa facing Catalina Island. Gigi sat opposite her, staring.

"I'm just not stressed about the script." Rina twisted open the water bottle and drank.

"Okay. Want to tell me what's going on—where you've been disappearing to?"

Rina sighed. "Horseback riding lessons."

"Then why the secrecy?"

"I didn't want to say anything until I was sure of my feelings."

"Feelings? For horses?" Gigi scraped back her short hair. "What feelings?"

"I've met someone."

Gigi's eyes opened wide. Her mouth resembled a door left slightly ajar. "Where? Who? Is this your friend from rehab that you told us about? The writer?"

"No. She's not in the biz."

"Where would you even meet someone who's not in the biz?"

"It's simply one of those things. Fate, I suppose."

"Since when do you believe in fate?"

The actress smirked. "Since now."

"Tell me right now, Rina."

Rina laughed. "All right. I've met someone."

"You already said that! And?"

"I'm crazy about her." Rina still felt the imprint of Julia's body against her.

Gigi laughed. "What? You?"

"Yes. Why is that so hard to believe?"

"Because first of all, you don't fall for anyone. And I don't know who this woman is—where she is—how you met…"

"Perhaps if you'd given me any of her countless messages, you would know."

Gigi raised her eyebrows. "Is it that Julia person who's been calling?"

"Yes. Why didn't you tell me?"

"I thought she was some troll who somehow got your number. Usually if you're waiting for someone new to contact you, you let me know."

"I didn't hear from her immediately after we met so I didn't think she'd call me."

"Are you serious, Rina? Who wouldn't want to be with an A-lister like you?"

Rina sat up and leaned forward. "Not everyone is as infatuated with Hollywood as you are. Has it occurred to you she doesn't see me that way?"

"Honey, it's not a matter of opinion that you're a Golden Globe- and Oscar-winning movie star."

Rina's gaze drifted toward the sunset and then back to Gigi. "Yet somehow, right now, those things feel like a distant second."

"Since when does your ambition take a holiday?"

The actress sighed.

"Details please."

"Her name is Julia Dearling, and she lives in Desert Bluff, a small desert town out past Palm Springs."

"How in the hell did you meet someone like that?"

Rina's eyes searched in the direction of Catalina Island. "What do you mean 'like that'? She walked into my life—or rather, I drove into hers."

"If you're becoming intimate, I need to vet her—have her sign a nondisclosure agreement."

Rina waved the words away. "No. I don't need to do that."

"Yes, you do! Look at what happened with Bitchney Cavell—you didn't want her to sign anything either. Aren't you glad she did?"

"It'll ruin things. Julia's nothing like Cavell."

"What does she want? We'll give it to her up front so that nothing winds up in the tabloids that could out you."

"No."

"Yes. You're not thinking clearly." Gigi stood to leave. "I'll let you get settled in. Maybe Clay can talk some sense into you. Are you hungry? It's almost dinnertime."

Rina shot to her feet. "Thanks for reminding me. Julia sent me home with a pan of her famous lasagna. I left it in the car. Would you be a dear and bring it into the house?"

"What's with the red convertible?"

"Long story."

Gigi walked toward the door. "Lasagna? Since when do you eat carbs before shooting a movie?"

"Since I met Julia. You're going to love it. It's her Grandmother Lucia's recipe."

"Grandmother who? I'll make you a salad and have Clay mix you a vegetable concoction."

"No. I want the lasagna. And Gigi, from now on when Julia calls, give me the phone—right away."

"What if you're busy?"

"Unless a camera is on me, interrupt me."

Gigi groaned and closed the door behind her.

* * *

The incessant knocking on his door sent Clay dashing into the living room of Rina's pool house.

"Come in, Gigi. What's up?"

She stomped across the beach-themed living room. "You need to have a talk with her."

"Rina's back?"

Gigi scoffed. "She's back. And she has a new girlfriend."

Clay smiled. "Really? Now there's something you never think you're going to hear."

"Yes. She doesn't want her to sign a nondisclosure."

"Why?"

"She says it will…" Gigi put air quotes around "ruin things."

"Who's the woman?"

"I don't know. Some girl she met."

"Rina doesn't meet just 'some girl.' Is she the rehab friend?"

"That was my guess, but no."

Clay picked up his phone and called the main house. "Welcome home," he said when Rina answered. "Yes, she's here." He glanced at Gigi. "Okay, what time?" He paused. "Sure, that works." Clay hung up and turned to Gigi. "Rina said to remind you about the lasagna in the car, to heat it in the oven on 375 degrees, and that she'll meet us for dinner in thirty minutes."

"Clay, wait until you see her. Something's off."

"Like when she came home from chocolate rehab?" He snickered. "I'll never get used to putting those two words together."

"Yeah. She has that same eerie calm—like *namaste* but on steroids—or not. You know what I mean."

"Well, first things first. We need to vet whoever this woman is. On the other hand, you know how Rina gets once she starts filming."

"Good point," said Gigi. "She won't make time for anything or anyone for months until the film wraps."

"So, we'll do our due diligence and let Rina's nature takes its course."

"All the more reason we need a nondisclosure signed. If Rina dumps her…"

"Maybe it'll just fizzle out," said Clay.

"Yeah. No! She's all sizzle, no fizzle. You'll see."

* * *

Gigi sat at the kitchen table tapping her fingers as she and Clay awaited Rina.

"Stop that." Clay placed his hand over hers.

Gigi lowered her voice. "We have to get out in front of this."

"I know, but take it easy. You're making me nervous."

Clay stood when Rina entered. "There's my girl." He gave her a peck on the cheek, then stared at her.

Rina glanced between him and Gigi. "Look at you two! I feel like a teenager who's about to get lectured for coming home after curfew."

"Welcome home," Clay said taking his seat. "Gigi said you have news. You want to tell me what's going on?"

"Not really. But we all know that's not a possibility."

Rina took the lasagna out of the oven and dished it out. She sat down, closed her eyes, and inhaled the aroma.

"I love this!" She stuffed a forkful into her mouth.

"Honey," said Clay, "you don't…you can't eat this way before you begin shooting."

"Watch me." Rina took another bite. "I start my boring regimen and workouts with Maribelle tomorrow. But tonight, there's lasagna."

"This is so good." Gigi reached for another bite.

"So, who is she?" Clay sampled the lasagna. "God, this *is* good."

"You don't know her."

He stared at Rina. "Neither do you. We need to vet her."

"No! Not going to happen."

"What if she outs you in the press? Or tells them secrets or lies about you?"

"She won't, Clay."

"How old is she?" he asked.

Rina gulped. "Why does her age matter?"

"Is she…mature?"

"More mature than I am."

"Does she have kids? 'Cause if she has kids it'll give me leverage if she turns out to be a psycho."

"No kids, and I'm afraid she's a little too normal for any of us."

Clay stopped eating. "We need to check her out, Rina."

"Forget it. This isn't negotiable."

"Mmm, this is so good," said Clay.

"Her grandmother's recipe," Rina smiled. "Lucia. Grandmother Lucia," she said in her authentic Italian accent.

"What's up with you? Jesus, were you abducted by the Italian Amish?" asked Clay. "You walk around calm and—and happy. You let things slide that normally drive you crazy."

"What's up with me?"

"Yes."

"I gave up chocolate, Clay."

"This is all…chocolate?"

Rina swallowed her bite. "Not all. It's everything that was hiding behind my addiction."

"I still don't get it," Clay said. "How could anyone actually be addicted to chocolate?"

Gigi put down her fork and looked at Rina. "I hate to bring this up while you're eating, but Britney's manager called and said Britney wants to have a meeting with you sometime this week."

"Why?"

"She wants to discuss some of the scenes so that she can prepare for the table read and rehearsals."

Rina nodded. "Sounds reasonable."

"Aha! Who *are* you?" Gigi asked.

"What?"

"Rina, since when are you blasé about invoking the she-devil? Is this some kind of Zen-Jedi rehab thing?"

"Britney Cavell and I are going to be working together. We might as well get used to keeping it professional. I think it's a good idea—like a dress rehearsal before we actually have to work together. Call her manager and set it up. Take two hours out of my schedule and get us a table at La Cigale."

When Rina's cell phone rang, Gigi stood and retrieved it from the counter. "It's her."

"Cavell?"

"No. Julia."

Rina lit up and dropped her fork onto the plate from mid-air. "Really?" She stumbled from her chair and grabbed the phone. "Hello, sweetheart."

Gigi and Clay locked eyes.

Sweetheart? Gigi mouthed.

Clay shrugged.

"We're feasting on lasagna here, thanks to you," said Rina. "Everyone loves it." She stepped toward the family room and stopped in the doorway. "I miss you so much," she said in a hushed tone.

Gigi waited until Rina left the room. "Find her, Clay," she whispered. "She lives in Desert Bluff."

"Where the hell is Desert Bluff?"

"Out past Palm Springs."

"Don't worry. Get me Julia's phone number and I'll find her for you."

"Can you hear anything?" asked Gigi.

Clay stood and tiptoed to the door. A minute later he scrambled back to his seat. "Sounds pretty hot and heavy," he whispered.

Rina reentered the kitchen and took her seat. She slowly brought the fork to her lips, closed her eyes, and moaned when she swallowed the next bite. "Why are you staring at me that way?" she asked when her eyes opened.

"Because you just turned a bite of lasagna into soft porn," Gigi replied. "And you're not that good off camera."

Rina chuckled. "Oh? Evidently I am."

CHAPTER FIFTEEN

Vittoria Dearling made it to the Starlight Diner after the dinner rush. Julia's carbon copy, she could be distinguished from her twin primarily by her wardrobe—she had traded in her ranchwear for New York corporate-wear. The only other difference was Vittoria's stylishly layered, highlighted hair.

No longer the small-town desert dweller, she rented fancy cars when she visited and projected an air of success and city sophistication that made Julia tease her about becoming "New Yorkified."

Vittoria smiled as she came through the door. "I know she's here because that ugly Fiat is in the parking lot!"

"Vitty!" said Julia. They hugged hard and kissed on the cheek. "I can't believe you're finally here!"

Cass delivered the order she brought out from the kitchen and greeted Vitty with a hug.

"Cass, good to see you!"

"You too. Welcome home. It sure has been a while. Something up for you to make it all the way out here?" asked Cass.

"Can't I just come home for a visit to see my sister?"

"Sure you can," answered Cass, glancing at Julia.

Vitty looked around and exhaled a nostalgic sigh. "The diner has barely changed since Grandmother owned it. So, what's on the menu? I'm hungry."

"I made your favorite chicken dish," Julia answered proudly.

"Grandmother Lucia's cacciatore a la Julia?"

"Yep. Cass, would you mind fixing Vitty a plate?"

"Not at all. You want an iced tea with a slice of orange?" asked Cass.

Vitty smiled. "You remember."

"Of course I do. Your sister went nuts in the kitchen today. Wait until you see all the food you're going to have to eat before you leave."

Julia smiled. "All your favorites."

The sisters slid into the booth they had grown up occupying after school. The one where they had done their homework and where they had sat in anticipation of the special treats their grandmother gave them on all of their childhood birthdays—even the ones before their mother had left.

"This booth should have a plaque with our names on it," said Vitty.

"Isn't that the truth?"

"You're such a good cook, Julia. Do you realize you could be making a name for yourself in New York? It wouldn't be such a struggle like it is all the way out here."

"Any horse stables in your apartment building?" Julia laughed and reached for Vitty's hand. "I've really missed you."

"I've missed you too, Juju. You really need to come for a visit. I know you'd love New York."

"So you keep saying."

"Maybe there's a way to work it out. We'll talk about it later. How's my horse?"

Julia leaned back against the tufted Naugahyde. "You won't believe how good Thunder looks. At least three mornings a week we climb the mountain. But I'm afraid after all this time, he thinks he's mine. We'll take a ride in the morning so that you two can get reacquainted."

Cass placed Vitty's dinner on the table.

"Relax and eat," Julia began, "I'm going to help Cass clean up."

"If I finish before you're done, I'll see you at home."

"Good idea."

Julia got to the ranch balancing an armful of take-out containers stacked to her chin.

"Let me take that," said Vitty as she sprang from the couch. She followed Julia into the kitchen and placed the containers in the refrigerator. "I fed the horses. Thunder and Lightning were both happy to see me—not nearly as happy as I was to see them. Sometimes I forget how much I miss this ranch—the desert. I need to come home more often."

"If only! It's so weird to see you here. I'm used to coming home to an empty house."

"What about…Nicki, right?"

"That's dead and buried."

"Already? What happened?"

"Turns out she was more into herself—" Julia paused "—and a stripper than she could ever be into anyone else. Besides, I've moved on."

"So soon? I didn't know there were that many gay women out here."

Julia turned her chin toward one shrugged shoulder and gave Vitty what her twin had dubbed as her "girly smile."

"Oh," Vitty laughed. "You're blushing! Spill it, Juju. Who is she?"

"She's not from around here. We met at the diner when she was passing through."

"Well, where's she from?"

"LA. She's already been back to visit though."

"What's her name?" Vitty asked, excited.

"Rina. She's wonderful. Amazing. Beautiful. And she's very good to me."

"Any chance of meeting her on this trip?"

"She just left yesterday. We're pretty new so I haven't told anyone about her except you."

"Not even Cass?"

"Nope."

"So too soon to tell if it's going anywhere?"

Julia sighed. "For the first time in my life, I'm falling in love."

"You were with Nicki until recently. Are you sure this woman isn't just rebound therapy?"

"I couldn't be more sure. It's more like everyone before her was just practice. Of course I haven't told her that. I don't want to freak her out. But I knew in an instant."

"Don't be naive. There's no such thing as love at first sight."

"For me, there was."

"Just remember what Grandmother always said: 'No one can be perfect in an imperfect world.'"

"As long as she's perfect for me, that's what matters. But we do have a couple of challenges."

"Like what?"

"There's an age difference."

"How big?"

"Big enough."

"Why won't you tell me?"

"I'm not ready to say. It's bad luck."

Vitty snickered. "Now you sound like Grandmother Lucia."

"She did raise us. Something was bound to rub off."

"Then I'm glad it was you and not me who inherited her Italian superstitions."

"Anyway, age is just one challenge."

"There's more?"

"She lives a very different life from me. The woman has everything a person could want or need. I still don't know what she sees in me."

"She sees what the rest of us see. Have you visited her in LA yet?"

"No."

"So it could all be smoke and mirrors as far as you know."

"I doubt it."

"Why?"

"Because she tried to give me a new car."

"But you hardly know her. That doesn't seem suspicious to you?"

"Not if you knew why—which is a story for another time." Julia placed the last few containers in the refrigerator. "You'd love her. If things work out, you'll meet her. Just not yet."

"Why? We could hop in the car and drive to LA tomorrow if you want."

"Like I said, we're new. Frankly, my head's so far up in the clouds, I'm surprised I don't have a nosebleed."

"What does she do for a living?"

"She's in the film industry."

Vitty rolled her eyes. "Sounds positively fake. You know how LA people are—mansions without a stick of furniture inside, leased Rolls Royces, and not a dime in the bank. Be careful."

"I wouldn't care if she had nothing—because she's everything I could ever want."

"Then I have to meet her," Vitty said sternly.

"You don't have to protect me."

"I'm a city girl now. You wouldn't believe some of the shit I've seen. I hope she turns out to be who you think she is."

"She already has."

"So when do you think you'll see her in her natural habitat?"

"Soon I hope."

"Try to meet some of her friends. That's always revealing." Vitty smiled. "I really hope it works out—happy is a good color for you." She surveyed the room. "The place looks nice. I like the kitchen remodel."

"It really needed it. Good thing I have the diner, because this kitchen was out of commission for weeks. I was using the mini fridge in the casita."

"You work so hard, Jules. Don't you ever get tired of maintaining all of this—and the casita and the diner. And the horses?"

Julia shrugged. "Someone's gotta do it. I mean, for Grandmother Lucia."

"Sweetie, she's been gone for four years. I'm sure she'd want you to go out and make your own life. Find your own happiness."

"But this is what I know. It's what I've always known. And FYI, it does make me happy."

"There's a big world out there, Juju. Don't you ever think about selling the diner or the ranch—or at least part of the property?"

"I love being able to keep the horses and to live where we grew up. I need the diner to afford the ranch—and I need the ranch for those rides up the mountain."

"But is it what you really want out of life?"

Julia stared at her. "I don't know if I've ever considered there was an option. You should see what I've done with the casita."

"Show me?"

"Okay," Julia beamed.

They left through the back door, and Julia entered first and turned on the lights.

"Damn! It's gorgeous. Look at all your sculptures! I knew this was your hobby, but I had no idea how many pieces you've made. You've really come a long way since I was here last. Wow. Just wow." Vitty toured the room and studied them all. "I would love to have one of these."

"Really?"

"Definitely. I would display it proudly. I like this one." Vitty stopped before one of the Arabians.

"Sorry. That one is going to a gallery."

Vitty turned to her sister with a quizzical expression. "What?"

"Yes, thanks to Rina there are two galleries in LA that are interested in that one and the one next to it."

"Look at my baby sister, a known sculptress. I'm impressed."

"Not known yet!" Julia scoffed. "Baby sister? You're three minutes older than me."

"Three minutes is three minutes."

Julia retrieved a small horse sculpture from the shelf and handed it to Vitty.

Vitty studied it. "This is Thunder!"

"Yes, it is. Take him home so that your horse is with you every day."

"Thanks, sis!" Vitty held the horse close to her chest and continued the tour. She lifted the tarp from the work-in-progress and laughed. "A human? Since when! You don't even like humans."

"My first. It's barely halfway finished. I'm sure it'll look much better once I finish carving the details."

"She looks familiar. Who is she?"

"You'll know once it's done." She scratched her head. "At least I hope you will."

"I'm so proud of you, Jules."

"Thanks, but you're the successful one, remember? I'm just the cook and the rancher."

"And the talented sculptor!"

"You mean that?"

"Are you kidding me?" Vitty looked around the room, shaking her head. "Yes, I mean it."

"You must be tired after that long trip."

"I am."

"Let's go chill, and I'll get a bedtime snack ready for you."

Vitty put down the sculpture and threw her arms around her twin sister. "Gosh, I miss you."

* * *

At first light, the girls mounted their steeds and walked them until they took off toward the mountain.

"Attaboy, Thunder!" said Vitty.

A second later, Julia and Lightning came to a halt beside her sister. "We beat you, Jules."

"You mean as usual we let you win."

"It's quite a workout for them—climbing the hill." Vitty looked out over the mesa. "It's good to be back. Weird to see wide-open space after living in Manhattan. I pay three thousand a month for a tiny one-bedroom, and I lucked out."

"You should bring David with you next time. Does he ride?" asked Julia.

"I love my fiancé, but he's such a city boy. The closest he gets to riding is the subway or in taxis."

"Any chance you can come for longer than a weekend?"

"I can probably take more time off soon—when the New York executives have their week in the Hamptons."

Julia turned Lightning around. "Hey, wanna race across the mesa?"

"I thought you'd never ask."

Like when they were kids, they raced, teased one another, and then laughed as they walked the horses on the way back to the barn.

"I'll take care of the horses," said Vitty. "Then I have a surprise for you."

"What kind of surprise?"

"We're driving into Palm Springs."

"Why?"

"I made an early afternoon hair appointment for you. It's time for you to get a little style, maybe some highlights. Then we can go out for a nice meal. All my treat!"

"Aha! So that's why Cass pushed me out the door of the diner last night."

"Yes, we conspired against you. Hey, what do you think about David and me having the wedding here?"

"I'd love it. We can cater it from the diner. I do that now for big parties."

"I'm so happy you feel that way! We're not so far from LA—your girlfriend can come to the wedding."

Julia stared into her twin's eyes and feigned enthusiasm. "Yay!" *How ever can I ask Katarina Verralta to be my date at a desert ranch wedding!*

Vitty took Lightning's reins from Julia. "Go ahead. Shower. Get ready! We're leaving in an hour."

"Okay!"

CHAPTER SIXTEEN

Rina pulled a fast one on the gaggle of paparazzi by zipping past them in the rejected red sports car instead of the Jag. She smiled for two photographers outside La Cigale restaurant on Robertson Drive, left the car with the valet, and entered.

"Right this way, Miss Verralta," said the maître d'. "Miss Cavell is already seated."

"Thank you, Martin."

Rina followed him to the section reserved for people of her status. All decked out in a severe case of tasteful burgundy, La Cigale welcomed its guests into refined and formal dining. From the embroidered crests on the overstuffed high-backed chairs to the rose-filled centerpieces, it was the kind of place where gold-rimmed goblets matched the china and tablecloths. Rina nodded at the people who smiled at her.

She spotted Britney as she rounded the corner, and at first glance she couldn't help noticing what had first attracted her to the younger actress. Her short dark hair provided a dramatic frame for the expressive brown eyes that spoke a million emotions—all on demand. Depending on what she wanted and whom she aimed to lure into her lair, Britney always had a matching expression. She was nothing if not a talent-wielding, attention-commanding vixen.

Martin pulled out Rina's chair and unfolded her napkin.

"Rina," Britney said warmly.

Opportunist Smile Number Six. Sugar sweet with a dash of charisma.

"It's good to see you." Britney reached across the table to take Rina's hand.

Rina rested her hands on the napkin in her lap. "Hello, Britney."

The waiter placed a fruit plate and a small salad in front of Rina. "As you requested, Miss Verralta, no cantaloupe."

"Thank you."

He replenished Britney's glass of wine from the bottle in the ice bucket. When the waiter stopped pouring, Britney placed her hand gently on his arm.

"Keep pouring," she said. "And come back soon."

Rina waited patiently. What they knew about each other could sell a year's worth of tabloids. More importantly, Rina knew how to read between the lines—and knew that waiting for Britney to speak first always put Rina in the driver's seat.

"This is something, isn't it, Rina?"

"What?"

"A Reese Collingworth film—the director's director. I can't believe we have the opportunity to finally work together."

"Yes." She met Britney head on. "No one knows better than I do how you worship opportunity."

Britney leaned back, stared at Rina as though sizing her up. She slowly raised the wineglass to her lips.

"Be careful, Brit. The wine's starting to dry you out. You don't want to look haggard and bloated when you're playing younger."

As slowly as she had raised the glass, Britney lowered it unsipped and set it on the table. She smiled. "So, Rina, have you recovered yet?"

"From what?" Rina bit into a slice of apple.

Britney leaned in and lowered her voice. "You know, from the loss?"

"Aww." Rina sighed. "That's so sweet. But how did you hear about my cook taking ill?"

"What?"

"Silvia had to take an early retirement. She's been with me so long and she's been hard to replace."

"No! That's not what I meant." Britney took a big swig of wine.

"Loss?" Rina paused. "You're talking about the Oscar?" Rina finished the apple and fished around delicately with her fork until she stabbed clear through an artfully carved hunk of watermelon. "This

watermelon is delicious. Care for a bite? It will help detox your liver—
you know…" Rina pointed to the wine. "From all the drinking."

"Yes, the Oscar! I can't imagine how hard that was for you—
losing—to me of all people."

Rina raised her eyebrow and finished the melon. "What's past
is past," she said graciously. "Onto bigger and better things, right?
Speaking of which, how *is* Linnie?"

"We broke up."

Rina stopped eating. "Well, who could've seen that coming?"

Britney took a longer sip of wine. "She turned out to be halfway up
the psycho ladder. I should have never let you go—left you for her."

Rina placed her fork on her plate. "You can't let go of someone you
never really had, Brit."

"Huh. It sure seemed like I had you. We were good together. A real
Hollywood lesbian power couple."

Rina smirked. "Hard to be a lesbian power couple when neither
partner is out."

Britney laughed. "I suppose that's true. So, Rina, are we done
sparring about the past?"

"I don't know—I thought we were just getting warmed up. But
we do have a big film ahead of us. I want your word, Britney—utmost
professionalism."

"Of course, Rina."

"Swear."

"My god, what do you think I'm going to do, create a scene?"

"Yes. Isn't that what you do best? You and I have no relationship
anymore. None. Our characters, however, have a contentious one."

Britney smiled from the corner of her lips. "Then it won't be that
big a stretch, will it?"

"I'm giving you fair warning that I've written it into my contract. If
I feel you trying to undermine me and it affects me doing my job, then
I'm out. And you'll be left hanging."

As Britney polished off the glass of wine, the waiter stood nearby
to replenish it. "I promise. It'll be fine, but I have one request."

"What?"

"Once we're on location, you have to have dinner with me one
night. No managers, agents, or personal assistants allowed. Just you
and me."

"Why?"

"Consider it an olive branch. A way of keeping the peace."

Rina stared straight at her. "Like this olive branch?"

"Better than now."

"Are you capable of 'better than now'?"

"Yes."

Rina took her time considering it. "Dinner? Just dinner?"

"Sheesh. We have to eat, don't we?"

"You'll be civil? Professional? Not like now?"

Britney crossed her heart.

"Hope to die?" said Rina.

"Fine." Britney rolled her eyes. "Want to shake on it?"

"Not really."

"A kiss then?"

"There'll be no kissing, Britney."

"Maybe not here," the vixen smiled.

"Read the contract," said Rina.

"Yeah, whatever you want."

"What scenes did you wish to discuss?"

"The scene where you squash my character in the boardroom," Britney answered.

"You're talking about the hostile takeover scene?"

Britney sat up straight. "Yes! That's the power scene of the film, don't you think?"

"I think there's a lot we can do to show the conflict there. Also, in that horse scene on my character's ranch—that's a real good one."

"Exactly." She smacked her hand against the table. "See? I knew we were still on the same page. We're going to knock it out of the park with that horse scene."

Rina stared at her. "It's not so different from the night you bolted from my house at three in the morning—after taking a swing at me and destroying my favorite vase. I'd be happy to never have to see *that* mood again."

Britney sighed. "I'm sorry."

"Pardon me? I've never heard you apologize for anything."

"I am sorry, Rina. Looking back, it was a bit overdramatic."

Rina chuckled. "Gee. Ya think? For the record, the only drama I do these days is on-screen."

"You must hate me."

"I did. I don't now. I don't really feel anything for you. Although, sometimes I wonder how you manage to persist with all that toxicity. It's old—predictable."

"Okay. I know I can get a little crazy sometimes."

"Sometimes? A little?"

"You didn't deserve having me mock you at the Academy Awards. But I was hurt, too. Especially when you refused to take my calls after we broke up."

For that one moment, Rina saw the two percent of Britney that hadn't succumbed to the dark side. The sweet girl she had once known—the girl who wasn't yet famous—who displayed vulnerability and love. The one who had adored her.

Rina steeled her resolve. "It's history, Brit."

"So, there's no chance of us ever…"

"Stop right there. No. There is no 'us' and there isn't a chance."

"I know that look, Rina. There's someone else now, isn't there?"

An impulse to grin at the thought of Julia escaped in an uncontrolled burst. She said nothing.

"Who is she?"

"No one you know or ever will."

"Maybe by the time the film wraps you'll see how I've changed and you'll have a change of heart."

Rina chuckled. "No one ever really changes, Brit. If we work hard at it, maybe we evolve." She flashed on her time at the rehab. "The thing is, I know how good an actress you are. You have an Oscar to prove it."

"Truth be told, the Oscar doesn't keep me warm at night."

"But I bet it's one helluva chick magnet."

Britney signaled the waiter. "Check, please."

Rina grinned. "Don't bother. I've got it."

Before Britney stood to leave, she stared longingly into Rina's eyes.

Rina stared back. "I've missed Caring Gaze Number Ten. But it needs a little work."

"I'm flattered you'd notice. See you soon, Rina."

"I'll count the hours."

Britney rose, plastered a fake smile on her lips, and made a high-profile exit that rivaled what most assuredly had been a high-profile entrance.

"Will there be anything else, Miss Verralta?" asked the waiter.

"God, let's hope not."

CHAPTER SEVENTEEN

Julia stood in the bedroom doorway holding two mugs of steaming coffee. She leaned against the jamb, lightheaded at the sight of Katarina Verralta's curves tangled in her sage-colored sheets. Intoxicated still from Rina's touch, she breathed in a fresh dose of the scent to which she had become addicted, the one now embedded in her senses every day whether Rina was there or not.

Lying on her side with a stray chestnut-colored wave settled along her prominent cheekbone, Katarina breathed silently in the early morning light. Julia mentally traced the woman's outline, gliding her gaze along the slope of her shoulder, fixing the curve in her mind, knowing that if this dream ended, she would remind herself of it by sinking her hands deep into amorphous clay and molding it into the vision before her.

Julia crossed to the bed and looked down at her before placing the cups on the nightstand. Though it was only their fifth time together, already they had a ritual. She sat beside Rina and kissed her bare shoulder, lifting Rina's hair and bringing her to consciousness with soft lips against a smooth and warm neck. The beauty's eyes fluttered open.

"Mmm, am I still dreaming?" Rina stretched into a yawn. "Good morning, Julia."

Julia grinned at the way Rina spoke her name. It reminded her of the first time she'd heard it leave the woman's lips—*Zhooliaah*.

When their eyes met on this morning, Julia felt her world transform suddenly from a black-and-white silent film into a big-budget, A-list Hollywood musical. With Cinemascope. Dolby Sound. Lyrics dancing on notes. And the star splashed with flattering ambient light.

Julia gazed into her lover's eyes. "There should be a lottery to guess which color your eyes will be in the light of any given morning."

Rina smiled. "What color are they right now?"

"My favorite color."

"Which one is that?"

"The color of how you look at me. Whatever that one's called."

Rina rolled onto her back and pulled Julia into a kiss. Julia's body melted into her when their warm lips touched.

"Do I smell coffee?" Rina asked.

"You know you do."

Rina sat up against the cushioned headboard, the sheet wrapped loosely around her naked form. "If we had stopped kissing for an instant last night, I'd have told you I love the new hairstyle and highlights."

"Thank you. I wondered if you'd noticed. Here." Julia handed her the cup. "Medium light with fresh cream and that sweetener you brought with you."

"You're so good to me." Rina took a sip. "Have I told you how much I love your coffee?"

"Repeatedly. And I love your—everything."

Rina chuckled. "What does that mean?"

"It means I'm in, Rina."

"In what?"

"In this—this thing—whatever it is. I'm in love with you."

Rina's cup tipped, spilling a little coffee. "Shit!"

"Not exactly the response I was hoping for," Julia said softly.

Rina set the cup on the nightstand. "No, that was for spilling the coffee." She stroked Julia's cheek with her warm hand.

"You look shocked," said Julia.

"How can you be so sure of your feelings so soon?"

"Also not the response I was hoping for. I'm not asking anything of you, Rina. Take it. Leave it. Believe it or don't. I'm certain that I'm in love with you. I've never said that to anyone before—because I've never been in love until now." Julia fidgeted with the edge of the blanket. "And good morning," she added nervously. "H-Have I said good morning yet? No, I-I don't think I have."

When Rina stared at her, Julia could hardly catch her breath. The yellow-green cat-eyes bore right through her. She bit her lower lip and in the awkward silence turned her head and reached for her cup.

"Put that down, Julia. Look at me."

Julia needed an extra second to muster the courage to return to the gaze that held her a willing prisoner. *Dammit, I shouldn't have said it.* She inhaled—a junkie in need of her next fix—the scent of the woman in her bed. She wondered how and where she could lock this feeling away inside forever.

Rina peeled Julia's robe from her shoulders and allowed the sheet to fall away from her own body. She pulled Julia up against her and tasted her lips—kissed her hard, then soft, then lingered there, in the place where they met as equals. As lovers.

"Julia, do you have any idea what you're getting yourself into?"

Again, the woman's eyes made it difficult for Julia to speak. "I know that I love you, that I want you, and I don't care what I'm getting myself into—as long as you're in it with me."

"What if I'm not the woman you think I am? I fear that because I'm famous, you may have this unrealistic view of me."

"Or perhaps I see things in you that you haven't yet seen in yourself, Katarina."

Rina smiled just enough. "You called me Katarina. This must be serious. Such as?"

"You may be a lot older than I am, but…"

"Thanks for the reminder."

Julia continued. "But I see the girl in you. Not just the woman. The girl."

"You do, huh?" Rina said, still smiling. "So who is this girl you see?"

"Someone who deserved better early on—someone who needed more love than she got. So she used her amazing talent to get it from millions of fans instead."

"Excuse me? You know this how?"

"For one thing, you just stopped smiling."

"Hmm. Not bad. What else have you got?"

"I believe what you really crave is love from the one person who matters. I feel it every time we make love—in a connection that's so strong it defies age, culture, even lifestyle. I want to be that one person."

"What about when the day comes that you bring my morning coffee and you see an old woman lying in your bed?"

"Impossible. I only see the girl to whom my love matters. So, I guess the question is: Does my love matter to you? Don't answer that right now. I couldn't handle it if your answer was no."

"But you're young and I won't look like this forever."

"Do you really think I'm that shallow?"

"No, I'm just that insecure," said Rina.

"You? Insecure?"

"It's an occupational hazard."

Julia laughed. "You're the most confident person I've ever met."

"Don't confuse confidence with being secure." She paused. "Julia…" Rina's eyes first searched the reaches of the ceiling.

"What is it? I promise you can say anything to me."

"I've honestly never met anyone like you. Sometimes I wonder if you're for real."

"I'm for real."

Rina smirked. "I've been in LA for so long, I'm afraid a part of me has forgotten what real looks like."

"Maybe what you said before is wrong, and it's actually the other way around," said Julia.

"What is?"

"Perhaps you're the one who has an unrealistic view of me. You underestimate me."

They took refuge in the silence that followed, Julia craving the touch of the woman that destiny had literally driven to her door.

"Julia?"

"Yes?"

Rina pulled Julia on top of her and pierced her with her stare. "Make time stand still for me—again."

Julia ran her fingers through Rina's hair and gazed into the actress's now hazel eyes. With her lips but an inch from Rina's, she whispered, "I'm. In love. With you."

CHAPTER EIGHTEEN

Rina sauntered out to the barn wearing designer capri jeans, print sneakers, and a button-down pinstripe shirt tied at her midriff. Her hair still tousled from Julia's touch, her oversized sunglasses concealed her nearly naked face. Silent, she stood at the door, admiring Julia from behind. Her eyes drank in the sight of the long legs and narrow waist, the freshly layered hair that fell down her back. She held out a glass of lemonade when she entered.

"For my hardworking girl," Rina simpered. "The one who makes my knees weak."

Julia turned away from grooming Lightning. "Do you usually thank your women with lemonade?" She stepped over to Rina and kissed her lips. "Nice surprise," she said, taking the glass.

"Me or the lemonade?"

Julia set the glass on the wooden stand, slipped her arms around Rina's waist, and looked into her eyes. "You. Only you. *Always* you. Got it?"

Rina caressed Julia's cheek. "I missed you. You came out here twenty minutes ago and already it's been too long."

"I know."

"Even though I didn't say it back to you?"

"I meant it when I said I don't expect anything from you, Rina. Real love stands on its own—we are who we are. Who I am is the girl who has fallen in love with you. Whatever challenge that brings, I'll face it."

Rina's body froze in place—her face a snapshot of untitled panic. She forgot to breathe.

Julia tossed a glance at the stall. "If you need to bolt right now, Lightning here is pretty fast."

"I'll take my chances."

Julia nodded. "Smart girl." She glanced down at Rina's footwear. "Cute sneakers. Are you sure you want to wear them in here?"

"They're the only sneakers I have with me."

"I wouldn't want you to ruin a pair of two-hundred-dollar sneakers."

"Eleven hundred."

Julia raised her eyebrows. "Really? I didn't even know there was such a thing as thousand-dollar sneakers." Julia glanced at the sidewall. "There are some boots in the tack room—help yourself."

"Thanks."

Rina returned to watch Julia brush Thunder. "He seems to like that."

"We both do," said Julia. "It's relaxing. Very Zen. Come try it."

Rina took the brush and Julia stood behind her with her arms around the woman. She placed her hand over Rina's and together they brushed Thunder in long strokes along his shoulder, back, and flank.

The horse snorted.

"He likes you," Julia said.

"How can you tell?"

"He just snorted, his nostrils are relaxed, and when he takes a step back and forth like he just did, he's showing you which spots you're brushing that he likes. I wish I understood women as well as I do my horses."

"Hmm. You really do understand horses. You're right about the Zen thing. This really is relaxing. Or maybe it's the way you hold me."

"I'll make you a deal," Julia began. "If you'll do this, I can drive to the diner to pick up my small mixer and get dinner started early. That way we'll have plenty of time to…"

"You're trusting me with this?"

Julia kissed her shoulder. "I have complete faith that you'll bond with Thunder."

"Go. And hurry home, please. Twenty minutes without you was long enough. Take the convertible."

"No." Julia gulped the lemonade on her way out of the barn. She cranked up her Fiat and headed down the long dirt driveway.

* * *

Rina took her time brushing the horse. "Yes, I see you like that spot right here. You're awfully big."

The horse turned his head to look at her.

Rina smiled and met his eye. "Big and handsome, Thunder. While it's just us, do you mind if I tell you a secret?" She stopped brushing. "I really don't know what to do. I'm so afraid I'm going to screw this whole thing up. And I'm talking to you because I feel I can trust you."

The more Rina brushed him, the more her breathing slowed. The actress relived that morning—her skin still tingling from how Julia had made love to her. She marveled at how safe and protected Julia made her feel, as though Julia was the older one in this relationship. But her mind felt clear and calm for the first time ever, divorced from the assaults that her regular life made on her sensibilities, the paparazzi, publicists, managers, agents, assistants that were all integral to maintaining her "brand." She exhaled and continued brushing.

Rina took a deep whiff of the thin, cool, freshly washed desert air. The rain of the previous night had left the cactus alert, the sagebrush scrubbed greener than its usual gray, and the horses with newfound spunk.

Rina told Thunder and Lightning all about herself. Then she sang Roy Rogers's "Happy Trails," just so she could watch their ears twitch. "I like talking to you, Thunder and Lightning. I'm a very good judge of character, I'll have you know. After all, I'm fall…"

The crunch of tires on rocky dirt interrupted her. "Is that Mommy?" Moving to peek outside the barn, she saw a Mustang headed toward the barn. "Oh no! Visitors!" She grabbed a cowboy hat that was hanging on a nearby hook and smashed it onto her head, slipped on her sunglasses, and pulled Lightning into his stall. As she positioned herself on the big horse's far side, she heard the Mustang's tires slow and stop.

"Julia?" a woman called out. "I saw the barn door open. It's Nicki. Hello?"

Rina lowered the register of her voice and mustered something akin to the Southern accent she had mastered for her movie *Night Shades*.

"Julia ain't here right now."

Nicki's voice drew closer. "I'm sorry. I didn't see you back there."
Rina kept her back to the visitor and brushed Lightning's neck.
"I'm Nicki." The woman stepped toward the opposite side of the
stall and stopped a few feet away. "Are you Julia's mom?"
Rina cringed. "Nope."
"Her aunt?"
"Just here for the horses."
"Oh. What's your name?"
"Rin…" She halted her automatic response.
"Good to meet you, Reen. Do you know when Julia will be back?"
"Not really." Rina leaned down and rubbed Lightning's forearm
and knee, hiding her face behind his shoulder. The horse neighed.
"Maybe I'll just wait for her," Nicki said.
Rina threw a Hail Mary pass. "She said she wouldn't be back until
later."
"I thought you said you didn't know when she'd be home."
"All she said was not to wait for her."
"Well, if you see her, would you tell her that Nicki stopped by?"
"Sure thing."
"Thanks."
Rina heard the car door close and the engine vroom down the
driveway, but her heart was still racing.
"Whew!" She leaned back against the stall and ripped off her
sunglasses and hat. "Lightning, have I told you how happy I am that
you're so big? Who's Nicki?" She paused. "I see you're tight-lipped
about these things."

* * *

When Julia returned, she strode into the barn without pause,
swept Rina into her arms, and, before she could say a word, kissed her
passionately.
"You take my breath away, Julia."
Leading her by the hand to the clean stall full of hay, Julia gently
pushed her back into the pile. She stared down at Rina.
"There's that fire in your eyes," said Rina.
"Now. I have to have you right now." Julia got down on her
knees and kissed the woman deep and slow. Then deeper and slower,
sensuously nibbling Rina's lip. Grasping a fistful of hair, she kissed
her way along Rina's neck and followed her moans downward into her
lover's cleavage and the outer edges of her warm voluptuous breasts.

Julia's fingertips traced the hardened nipples and womanly curves with gentle adoration, then gripped her hips with strong, sculptor's hands.

With labored breath, Rina reached down and unzipped Julia's jeans, tugging desperately at them until Julia stripped them of their clothes and tossed them into a pile. Drenched in expectation, Rina wrapped her legs around her lover.

Drawn in by the shimmering beam from the luminescent eyes and savoring her intoxicating scent, Julia seduced her again, peeling away the layers of fame beneath which lived the tender girl she had fallen for—hard. Teasing, tasting, she delivered Rina into every pleasure she ached for, meeting her at every turn in a place she had only ever imagined.

Their eyes locked when Julia hovered over her, slowly lowering herself as Rina hungrily received her.

Power oscillated between them; pleasure forsaken for ecstasy and mediocrity crushed by a once-in-a-lifetime love. Over weeks, not years, they'd filled the voids that life had deposited in each of them.

"Oh God, I can't get enough of you," said Rina. She rolled over, pushed Julia down into the hay, and laid on top of her. She caressed Julia's face, her breasts, one hand coming to rest on Julia's slim naked hip. "I need you, Julia. I want you—all of you."

"Be careful, Rina. I'm the kind of girl who will believe you."

Rina moaned and pulled Julia hard against her. "You're the most beautiful woman I've ever known," Rina whispered into her ear.

Speechless, Julia pulled back to gaze into into her eyes.

Rina rolled onto her back.

Julia's hands and lips pledged devotion to Rina's every desire, raising the stakes and heightening the hunger with every stroke of her tongue and hands. She slid her body along Rina's. "You're exquisite."

"Take me now, Julia. Take me everywhere there is to go."

Julia reached deep. "We're already there."

This time Julia looked down into eyes that were now emerald green as she received Rina's breathless surrender. She made her lover teeter on the edge until she was certain she had taken everything but her need for more. Julia once again owned that precious moment when all Katarina would feel was her.

Wrapped in their naked truth, Julia noted how time had succumbed to the desert stillness in what was now a subtle shade of dusk. Like the relinquishing of day to night, Julia and Rina fused in a moment of twilight: neither day nor night but instead the inevitable melding of the two.

"I feel so safe with you," Rina said when she finally could speak. Julia held her tighter.

"I know the world is still out there, Julia. But here, behind the gate of the Y2, I know that nothing can harm us. No paparazzi. No tabloids."

"You are safe with me, no matter what happens down the road."

"I've never made love in a barn before," said Rina.

Julia pushed herself up on her elbow and teased her lover. "You're telling me I created a first for the worldly Katarina Verralta?" She flicked a piece of straw from Rina's hair.

Rina slapped her arm. "This hasn't been my first first with you."

"Really? What else?"

"I'll tell you another time."

"Why not now?" Julia stared at the woman, waiting for an answer. "Oh my God."

"What?"

Julia laughed. "You're blushing. Just like on the night we met—in the casita when I complimented you."

Rina turned to look away, but Julia wouldn't let her. "Okay. Yes, I can feel I'm flushed."

"Why, baby?"

Rina's now golden eyes filled. "I feel like I'm about to bungee jump off the Golden Gate Bridge—and there's not even a camera rolling to catch it."

Julia chuckled. "What does that mean?"

Rina's eyes first danced away from Julia's. Caught in the spellbinding gaze that returned to her, Julia fell in love again.

Rina sighed hard. "It means I'm taking the leap. I'm falling in love. Crazy, wild, once-in-a-lifetime love…with you, Julia Dearling."

Julia froze. "Y-you said it. I don't want you to feel obligated to say it just because I did."

"No, sweetheart. You're not the only one who's never felt this way before."

"I can't even believe this is happening. Tell me it's real, Rina."

Rina nodded. "More real than I've ever thought possible for me."

"Oh great, now I guess I *have* to make you dinner." She kissed Rina's lips, aware of her every breath and intoxicated by the scent of Rina doused in Dior—of Rina doused in her. "So much for an early dinner, huh?"

"I wish you would make dinner. I've worked up quite an appetite today."

"And you'll need your strength for later on."

"Are you trying to kill me?" asked Rina.

"No. Just making up for lost time."

"What lost time?"

"All that time you've complained about having to wait for me to grow up. Are you ready to go back to the house?"

"In a minute. I don't think I can stand up yet. My legs are limp."

"Good. So, did you bond with Thunder in my absence?"

"Thunder, Lightning, and I had a good talk." Rina sat up and pulled on her jeans.

"I'd like to hear all about it once I float back to earth." Julia dressed and pulled on her boots.

Rina put on her shirt and pulled Julia into one last kiss before they ambled back toward the house, Julia's arm tight around Rina's waist, Rina's head resting on Julia's shoulder.

"In all that passion, I forgot to tell you. You had a visitor."

"A visitor?"

"Who's Nicki?"

Julia halted. "Did she recognize you?"

"No. Luckily I was able to hide behind Lightning in his stall. So? Who is she?"

"Nobody."

"Tell your face, Julia."

"Fine." Julia shifted her weight to one foot and sighed.

"Well?"

"Moments before I left the diner on the night we met, the girl I was seeing dumped me. Anyway, that's her."-

"I wish I'd known!" said Rina.

"Why?"

"I'd have thanked her. She did me the biggest favor of my life."

"I left here in such a hurry to get back to you I forgot to lock the gate. What did she want?"

They strolled a few more steps.

"Perhaps she came to tell you she wants you back."

"Is that your way of asking if I'm interested?"

"Maybe."

Julia stopped walking when Rina did.

"Julia, she asked if I was your mother!"

"I'm sorry, honey. Forget about her."

"Have you?"

"Forgotten about her? What did I say before I left? You. Only you. *Always* you. Got it, Rina?"

Rina smiled and started walking again. "I think I'm beginning to."

"Someday, Ms. Verralta, you're going to wonder how you could have ever doubted yourself."

"Don't you mean I'm going to wonder how I ever doubted *you?*"

"No. No, I don't."

CHAPTER NINETEEN

After dinner, Rina cleared the table. "I feel like I'm floating on a cloud. Between all this torrid sex and great food, I could just curl up with you—forever." She sighed and placed the dishes in the sink.

"Go relax by the fire. How about if we watch a movie?"

Rina lit up. "Great. What did you have in mind?"

Julia shrugged. "Whatever you want. I have some DVDs in the living room, or we can stream something off of Filmnet.com."

"I'll go see what you have."

Julia finished up and brought Rina a decaf cappuccino. Cuddled up on the sofa, Rina smiled up at her. "What is it? You look like you want to say something."

Julia placed the cup on the coffee table. "You know, I don't think I've ever seen you look more beautiful than you do right now."

"What? With no makeup and my hair a mess?"

"More beautiful than when you're on the red carpet."

"You're saying that to feed my fragile ego. But…go on."

Julia laughed. "Ego? You?" She sat next to Rina and handed her the demitasse.

"How did you know I wanted this?"

"I saw you glance at the espresso machine."

Rina took a sip. "Honestly, I don't think I've ever met anyone as attentive as you. You've already spoiled me."

"What's the point of being in love if you don't spoil your lover?" Julia reached for the small stack of DVDs that Rina had left there.

"You say it so easily."

"What?" asked Julia, flipping through the films.

"You know."

Julia looked up. "Being in love? You lovely, lovely, lovely woman! There, take that." She paused. "I can't believe you're blushing again."

"Sometimes the age difference strikes me—hard."

"And?"

"Then I remind myself that you're the grown-up in this relationship."

"All right. I'll change the subject—because you can't stay that red forever. Did you find something you'd like to watch?"

"Did you do it on purpose?"

"Did I do what on purpose?"

"You have every film I've ever made on that shelf."

Julia stroked back the hair from Rina's cheek. "I love those films, mostly because you're in them. I've seen them so many times, I can recite dialogue."

"Answer me truthfully, Julia?"

"Always."

"Is there even the slightest chance that what you're feeling for me is infatuation?"

"Yep. A big fat chance. The film star?" Julia held up her hands. "Handcuff me now. Guilty of lock-me-up, first-degree infatuation." She let her hands fall. "But I also happen to be in love with you. When you're with me, in me, and asleep next to me—your lips against mine? Hardcore in love with every breath. See the difference? As for the films, I've loved those movies since I was merely infatuated with you."

"Did Clay tell you to say that?"

"Who's Clay?"

Rina set down the cup and took Julia's hand. "Honey, it's time you met my crew."

"What crew?"

"The crew that handles my life and occupies it with a vengeance."

"Like Gigi? The woman who wouldn't give you my messages?"

"Yes, but that was before she knew to tell me."

"No. It wasn't."

"Well, she knows now," said Rina. "My daily life includes any or all of the following: a publicist, an assistant, lawyers, a personal manager, an agent, personal trainer, and friends. Then there are the stylists, directors, writers—well, just a lot of people. Think you can handle that?"

"That depends. Are you in it with me, Rina?"

The actress's eyes flared. "Deep in it."

"Okay, then whatever it is, whoever these folks are—I'm ready."

"Terrific. They're going to love you."

"But will I like them?"

Rina sat up and slung her arms around Julia's neck. "Do you like me?"

Julia smiled. "You know I do."

"Then you might like them too. I'll throw a small dinner party so that you can meet everyone at once—unless that's too overwhelming."

"If this was a movie, we're in the scene where the guitars start out with a soft romantic hook…and violins become louder and surround the guitars, then a piano joins in with some cheeky melody. And we're supposed to kiss."

Rina laughed so hard her eyes teared up. "Aren't you being a tad melodramatic here?"

"No. This is a 'falling in love with you harder' scene. There are always violins in the 'falling in love with you harder' scene."

"Wow! You're right."

"I am? I made it up," said Julia.

"I'm starting to hear the cheeky melody. Yes, I'm definitely falling in love with you harder."

"So it's a done deal? We're getting my debut over with?"

"Yeah…great. Uh…good." Rina flopped back on the sofa pillows.

Julia chuckled. "Are you sure?"

"Can you make it up to LA for a couple of nights?"

"I think so. I'll talk to Cass to see if she can cover for me at the diner, and I'll get someone to feed the horses."

"Who's Cass?"

"My best friend since Desert Canyon Junior High and my manager at the diner."

"Have you told her about us?"

"No. But she knows something is up. I can barely contain myself and keep a straight face. She keeps hinting at changes in me. I've only told my sister."

"You haven't really told me much about your family."

"You never talk about your family either," said Julia. "You go first."

"There's not much to tell really. I left home when I was pretty young to come to the US alone, and I started modeling soon after I got to Los Angeles. My mother and my brother and his family still live in Italy. I speak with them often, but my mother is not the easiest person for me to be around so I don't visit much. And you?"

"I have a mother out there somewhere. My sister is really my only family, except for Cass and Isabella—an old family friend. Vittoria, my sister, flew in from New York for the weekend after you were here. We haven't seen each other in about a year and I couldn't help telling her about you."

"What did you tell her?"

"That I had met someone from LA and that I was falling in love with her—madly in love with her."

"You honestly knew that soon?"

"Standing out in the rain that first night, I knew in an instant that I would fall in love with you."

"So you believe in love at first sight?"

"I believe in you at first sight. Or maybe I've always loved you. Hard to tell."

"Julia?"

"Hmm?"

"Make a pass at me, because I can't keep throwing myself at you and maintain any sense of dignity."

"Good enough reason for me, Katarina." Julia moved close, leaned in, and kissed her lover's neck.

Rina tilted her chin upward and moaned. "I love when you say my name that way."

"I know," Julia whispered, her breath next to Rina's ear causing the woman to shudder. Their cheeks grazed one another's as Julia pulled back to kiss her lips. "Are you certain *you're* ready for this, Rina?"

"I couldn't be more proud to be with you."

"What if your crew doesn't like me?"

"Whether they do or don't, I didn't wait a whole lifetime to fall in love just so they could ruin it."

"A whole lifetime? You just said 'it' again, ya know."

"I did, didn't I? Yes, Julia, a whole lifetime. I'm so completely— yours. I'm walking a tightrope with no net and I don't care. I've been famous for so long, I think I learned to settle for so much less. And then—thank God, there you were."

"You settled for less than plain?"

"Honey, I would never call you plain. You're crazy-sexy. You dazzle me with your abandon, your sculpting talent…and oh my god, you're a culinary vixen." Rina's gaze drifted to the fire and then back to Julia. "We laugh, we love—we talk like two old friends—" Rina moved the bangs from her lover's eyes, "—and I'm experiencing myself in a whole new way for the first time. You opened me to real love when I least expected it." She smiled. "Look who's blushing now."

"I thought it got warm in here. Okay, then I suppose it's time to throw myself to the wolves in your honor."

Rina slapped Julia's arm playfully. "I promise I won't let them devour you."

"Set it up." Julia grabbed a couple of DVDs and held them up. "So, which movie?"

Rina bore into Julia with her naked stare—camera-ready, almond-shaped. "Take me back to bed."

Julia stood and offered Rina her hand. "Right now, your eyes are transparent. And the way you're looking at me…"

"What about it?"

"Each time is like the first time you looked into my eyes. I remember thinking that I felt like I was standing on pillows—couldn't even feel the floor beneath my feet."

Rina stood and held Julia's gaze. "Make sure it stays that way."

"Why would you say that?" Julia led her upstairs by the hand.

"There's something I've been meaning to tell you, but we haven't been off of each other long enough."

Julia snickered. "What is it?"

"I'm starring in the new Reese Collingworth movie."

Julia stopped on the step and turned to Rina. "When? Where?"

Rina tapped her temple with her index finger. "Don't worry, I've thought it through and have a plan to see you. But honestly? Right now that's all the blood my brain has available."

Julia led her the rest of the way and turned to her. She sensually stroked her lover's neck, kissed it, teased her with warm lips and hot breath. She coaxed Rina back onto the bed.

"There's that fire in your electric blue eyes, Julia—like when you took me in the barn."

Julia stared at the woman under her. "There's only one way to put that fire out, Ms. Verralta."

"Don't look to me for help—I'm only going to fan the flame."

"I'm counting on it."

CHAPTER TWENTY

Two nights later, Cass stumbled through Julia's front door juggling everything they'd need for their long overdue movie night. "Hey, Jules, I'm here," she called out excitedly.

"I'm on the phone. Be down in a sec," Julia answered from upstairs.

Cass didn't even care that Julia had suggested a Katarina Verralta movie—she could have guessed that. Happy that things finally seemed to be getting back to normal, she carried the bag of snacks into the kitchen and set it down on the island. One deep whiff of the exotic flower bouquet wafting from the table throughout the kitchen caught her attention. Taking a step toward it, she listened for Julia in the hallway before she peeked at the card on the spike in the back of the arrangement.

Under her breath she read: "Thinking of you every minute. Remember how much I love you. R." *What?*

Cass hastily stuffed the spike back down into the arrangement when she heard Julia bounding down the stairs.

"Hi, Cassie!" Julia kissed her on the cheek.

"Hey. You're in an awfully good mood."

"I'm glad we're finally back to movie night."

"You're so busy all the time. Wait till you see what I brought."

"Popcorn?"

"Yes, and your trail mix experiment from the diner. There's chocolate and," Cass fished through the bag and pulled out a bottle, "wine."

"Great! Do you mind watching the Verralta movie or did you have something else in mind?"

"That's fine. I haven't seen it and I know how you love her."

Julia grinned. "I do. I love her."

"What's the title again?"

"*Allies of Night*. I have to tell you though, the small screen won't do some of the scenes justice. I'm glad I saw it in the movies."

"So—who are the fancy flowers from?"

"I did a favor for someone, that's all." Julia shrugged it off and took her corkscrew from a drawer. She twisted it down into the bottle and eased out the cork.

Cass set two glasses on the counter and deliberately waited for Julia to begin pouring before she asked. "Where have you been disappearing to on your days off?"

Julia missed the glass, splashing wine on the counter. "Shit." She reached for a rag. "I haven't even had any wine yet!"

"So? Where've you been going? I've hardly seen you and neither has anyone else."

This time Julia carefully steadied her hand. "You know—in the studio. Riding. Just busy."

"Uh-huh. Do you want to tell me what's really going on?"

"When?"

"Like every time I call when you don't pick up and then don't return my call until a day later. Or the phone calls you make from outside on your breaks? How about when I call to come by and ride with you and you tell me that both horses have already been ridden?"

Julia took a long sip of wine.

"Who is she, Jules?"

"Who is who?" Julia answered wide-eyed.

"Don't insult me. You're a bad liar, and I know every guilty expression you have. I'd much prefer you say you don't wanna talk about it."

"Okay. I don't want to talk about it."

"You *have* to talk about it!"

"Why?"

"Because I'm your best friend and I have a right to know."

"Why do you need to know right now?"

"Because face it, you're acting weird."

"How?"

"For instance? You don't usually store baking dishes in the cooler."

"I did? I'm sorry."

"I haven't even had the opportunity to tell you that Nicki has been coming into the diner the past couple of weeks when you're not there."

"Why?"

"She's been asking about you a lot. But after I saw how she had treated you at her birthday party, I told her she blew it."

"Glad she didn't come when I was there."

"Then you're going to be extra un-glad when I tell you she's acting like she wants you back."

"What! No way."

"She asked me about the woman she met in your barn."

"Nicki had no right to ambush me that day. My fault for leaving the gate open. Since when does she talk to you about me?"

"Perhaps you haven't noticed, but we've been selling out of humble pie at the diner. Anyway, she keeps coming in and asking about you. You're not interested—" Cass's nose crinkled. "Are you?"

"No."

"Then back to the lady in your barn. Nicki said you'd hired some barn help and asked me if I knew her. Somebody named Reen? She admitted she was jealous until she thought she might be older."

"Big deal, I needed some help."

Cass thought of the card on the flowers, signed 'R.' "Who's Reen?"

Julia groaned. "I'm not ready to talk about her."

"I know whoever she is, it's a big deal or you'd be gabbing away by now. I have one question. Why won't you tell me?"

"It's complicated, Cass."

"How so? She's not married, is she?"

"No!"

"What then? She's older—is that it?"

Julia downed her wine and picked up the DVD off the counter. She stared down at Rina's picture on the cover and slowly lifted her eyes to meet Cass's stare. She held out the DVD.

"What?"

Barely audible, Julia replied, "Her."

"Her what?"

"Her, Cass. It's *her*."

"No more wine for you."

"Reen is Rina—which is short for Katarina. Katarina Verralta is my lover."

Cass burst out laughing. "God, I miss you. That fucking dry sense of humor." Then Cass laughed until tears came to her eyes. She picked up the wine bottle and turned toward the living room. "Come on, goofball, get the popcorn and let's start the movie. Hahahaha. Her," she mocked. "Her!"

Julia ran her finger lightly over Rina's picture when she took out the DVD.

A huge party bowl of popcorn and almost a bottle of wine later, Julia's phone rang. Cass reached for it on the coffee table before Julia could get to it. Her jaw fell open when she read the name on the caller ID. "Rina?"

"Give me that!" Julia swiped the phone from her hand and fumbled it trying to answer. "Hi, what a wonderful surprise." Julia paused. "Yes. Cass is here for movie night. *Allies of Night*." She paused again. "No, really. It was Cass's pick." Julia winked at her friend. "Any chance I get to see you is good, even if it's only on film. Thank you, the flowers are gorgeous." Pause. "I miss you, too. Yes, a lot. Yes, more than that. And that. That too. May I call you later?" Julia smiled and uttered a phone kiss before hanging up.

Cass paused the film and filled their wineglasses to the top. "Julia Dearling, you tell me right now, girl!"

Julia chuckled. "I tried to, but you wouldn't listen."

Cass glanced at the frozen image of Katarina on the TV screen, then she turned and stared at Julia. She repeated the ritual three times. "Seriously?"

"Very seriously."

"You? And, and, and, *her*?" Cass stared at Julia head on.

Julia nodded for what seemed like fifteen times before Cass could speak.

"How? When? *Where?*"

Julia inhaled deeply, exhaled forcefully, and began. "It happened the night Nicki and I broke up. Right after you left me at the diner. When my car died."

"You mean if I hadn't left you there I'd have met Katarina Verralta?"

"Yes. But as a straight girl, I doubt you'd have been the one to sleep with her."

"Guess again! I'd make an exception—she's drop-dead gorgeous. I'm dumbfounded. I don't even know what to say."

"You're the first one to know. That means if anyone around here finds out, I'll know it came from you."

"I'm the first to know?" Cass smiled.

"Well, yeah! You *are* my best friend."

Cass bounced up and down twice on the sofa. "This is so exciting."

"Settle down. Rina wanted me to ask a favor of you."

"She knows my name!" Cass beamed.

"Yes."

"What's the favor?"

"She wants to have a dinner party to introduce me to her friends. And she needs to do it on a weekend."

"You need me to work for you?"

"Would you mind terribly? I'd ask Jimmy, but we all know he'd need supervision."

"You've got it, on one condition."

"What is it?"

"I want details. A blow-by-blow of the party. Everything."

"Duh! Who else am I going to tell?"

"Vitty doesn't know?"

"She knows I'm seeing someone but no details other than the woman is from LA."

"Back up. Tell me how you met. I want to know everything."

Julia and Cass pulled their feet up under them, tailor style, and leaned in to share their secrets the way they had when they were teenagers. Only now, there was wine. Lots of wine.

"Where do you want me to start?"

"Wherever you want, as long as you don't leave out the best parts."

Julia took another sip of wine and placed the glass back on the table. Her gaze drifted to Cass, and she waited a beat before speaking. "Cassie, I'm gonna marry that girl."

Cass cocked her head. "Don't you mean that woman?"

"Her too."

CHAPTER TWENTY-ONE

So this is Malibu, land of dreams both made and broken, Julia thought. She rolled to a stop before the scrolled wrought-iron gate, then reached out and pressed the Call button. She swiped back her wind-blown bangs when her image appeared on the camera screen.

"Ms. Verralta is expecting you, Julia," said the disembodied female voice. "Follow the drive, stay to the right past the guest house, then drive up the hill."

"Thank—"

Click.

"—you."

The old Fiat convertible strained as it ascended the winding drive in second gear, first curving past floppy webs from elderly sycamores, then beneath palms that stretched to the peacock-blue sky, their fronds towering above the lush grounds. Julia inhaled the mingled scent of eucalyptus trees and ocean that replaced the fumes she had left behind on the traffic-bloated Pacific Coast Highway. The vehicles that had raced behind her there faded from her consciousness the farther she traveled toward the curious new world ahead—the world where Rina really lived. Not the ranch where the woman came to have clandestine trysts with her simple landlocked girlfriend. A sudden quiet enveloped her and she took a full breath, forcefully exhaling her jitters—and the car lurched forward, responding to the unsteady foot hesitating on the clutch.

Julia slammed on the brake to let a coyote pup cross into the hillside. He seemed out of place to her—strangled in civilization.

Around the next bend, the brilliant cobalt ocean below filled the trough between her and infinity—a vibrant but startling contrast to the burnt umber and earthen hues of her desert world. So bright was the reflection of the sun glimmering on the waves, she envisioned a gazillion sparkling diamonds floating on a bed of sapphire. Malibu was hyper-chromatic Technicolor in her eyes—green never greener and the richness of the water bluer than the sky. She sighed, as though until this moment she had lived her life in sepia or worse, in beige— the color of dust.

This place was like nowhere she had ever been or imagined—the manor of Katarina Verralta. Movie star. Girlfriend.

What does Rina see in me? What happens when she sees how out of place I am in her world? What if I see it? She groaned. *I already see it.*

At the next turn, terra-cotta rooflines of Spanish Mediterranean architecture came into view—several, as though this were two or maybe three really big houses instead of one. Nestled in the hillside, beyond the terraced gardens, Italian cypresses guarded the pool and spa and, beyond that, the endless sapphire jewel. As she neared, Julia's stomach rumbled louder than the Fiat in neutral. Looking down at her attire, she suddenly felt too plain, so ordinary.

"What am I doing here?" She scraped her long wind-blown hair back from her face, then paused to reassure herself. "For chrissakes, it's just Rina—the woman you're in love with. The one who told you she's in love with you. The same Rina who sleeps in your four-poster bed on the ranch and who took you for hours in the barn."

Her mind raced. She tried to sigh away the anxiety. The idea of diving into this foreign world whose inhabitants were rich and famous unnerved her. These people were refined. Successful. Older.

Then her heart fluttered, and she shivered at the thought of Rina's touch. They were so safe on the ranch, locked away behind the gate of the Y2. Julia stopped and tilted her rearview mirror to check her makeup. She swiped some gloss onto her lips and coasted to the main entrance.

The instant she caught sight of Rina, Julia's entire inner monologue flew out of the convertible and onto the cobblestone driveway, where her tires promptly squashed it. A thought-free flood of longing rushed through her body and all her fears melted into amorphous blather.

The actress stood waiting in front of the grand double doors of the estate. A gentle ocean breeze made the silk fabric of her off-white flowing shirt and pants ripple as Rina stepped toward the semi-circular driveway.

That's her I-won-the-Oscar smile! Oh, god. She's aiming it straight at me. The Fiat engine grumbled for a few seconds after Julia turned it off, but she hopped out of the car anyway and reached for Rina's embrace.

Rina squeezed her tightly and then placed her warm lips against Julia's. "I'm so happy you're finally here, Julia."

Julia tried to respond, but it was all she could do to remain on her feet when the woman with those incredible almond-shaped eyes looked right through her. She wrapped her arms around Rina and nestled into her neck.

Rina pulled back. "Honey, you're trembling. Don't tell me you're nervous."

Julia finally caught her breath. "Of course I'm nervous. Aren't you?"

The actress hugged her. "Welcome to my home."

"It's beautiful here, Rina. I'm awestruck."

"Awestruck. That's exactly how I feel every time you're near me." Rina grinned. "Let's go inside so I can throw myself at you."

Julia laughed.

"Thank you, Julia. For a moment there I thought I'd lost you to awestruck."

Julia turned back to her car. "Let me grab my stuff."

"Maybe you'll learn to like it here as much as you like the desert," Rina said as she reached for Julia's purse on the passenger seat.

"Wherever you are is where I like it best. Like, you could live in a yurt and I wouldn't care," said Julia, hoisting her suitcase out of the convertible.

"What's a yurt?" Rina stared at the Fiat and then looked at Julia and shook her head. "Would you please accept the sports car already and give the Fiat a proper burial?"

"No."

"Why won't you take the car?"

"Because I wouldn't want you or your friends to think I'm some kind of gold digger."

Katarina rolled her eyes. "Come on, it's not like I bought you a Ferrari. Besides, it's only a car and I can pay for a fleet with my pocket change. Are you always this stubborn about everything?"

Julia's smile broadened. "Only the things that matter. While I may not always be flexible, I *am* very adaptable."

"Well now, Miss Dearling, that's a side of you I can't wait to know better."

Julia followed Rina inside and stopped as she crossed the first threshold. Rina had almost reached the staircase across the room before she noticed Julia hadn't moved past the door.

"What's wrong, Julia?"

Julia stared at the perfectly lit display case against the wall next to the picture window. "I've never seen a real Oscar, let alone four of them."

"The Oscars are lit just to impress you—in case you've forgotten how much you like me."

"That view of the ocean doesn't even seem real. Framed by the windows it simply looks like…art."

Rina doubled back to where Julia stood. She eased the suitcase from Julia's grip and set it on the floor. "Look at me. It *is* art. And it's real. We're real. I don't know about you, but I've counted the minutes until you arrived."

"Every minute," Julia added.

"Do you want to take the house tour now or later? Would you like something to eat? Or drink?" Rina sighed and leaned on her right leg, placing her hand on her hip. "You know. I think you had a point. On second thought, I am a little nervous. Let's go up to my private suite. I have food and drinks there and you can get settled in."

Julia gazed at her lover. "I'm hoping that 'settled in' is some kind of euphemism for 'I want to rip off your clothes and make savage monkey love to you in every possible way, right now.'"

"In case you haven't noticed, this is me throwing myself at you yet again."

Julia picked up the suitcase and delivered the line in the way she knew would garner her lover's adoration. "Lead the way, *Katarina*."

They crossed the room and Rina led the way upstairs. "You *know* I love it when you say my name that way."

"I'm counting it as foreplay."

"Julia, just to remind you, we have dinner with Clay and Gigi in a couple of hours."

"I'm counting that as foreplay also."

CHAPTER TWENTY-TWO

The next day, before Julia began getting ready for the big dinner party with Rina's friends, she came upstairs to Rina's suite from the kitchen. "Where are you?" she called out.

"In the dressing room."

Julia leaned against the doorway and watched the woman argue with a zipper.

"Dammit! Come on," she spat while struggling to close the zipper two teeth at a time. "These feel so tight around my waist! Julia, why do you have to be such a good cook?"

"We just need to ride more when you're at the ranch."

"And eat less." Rina glanced at her in the mirror. "This is depressing. These were cut perfectly for me."

Julia went to her. As gentle as a Southern breeze, she lifted Rina's hair from her neck and kissed the soft skin. "I didn't notice they were tight."

Rina leaned into her lips. "Stop trying to humor me."

"I'm not. I'm in love with you. And I couldn't care less if you gained a pound, lost a pound, ate a cookie, didn't eat a cookie."

Rina turned and put her arms around Julia and stared at her dead-on. "You are so not LA."

"You say that like it's a bad thing."

"It's not, but how can I count on you to tell me when I don't look right? Where's Gigi? I can't get dressed without Gigi!"

"When you're naked in bed—my bed, your bed, rolling on hay in the barn—you look perfect to me." Julia stepped back. "Anything I can do to help?"

Rina turned back to her rows of hangers and shuffled through them like a deck of cards. "No." Slide. "No." Slide. "No, no, no." She continued to slide each rejected contender along the rack. She stepped out of the pants and left them on the floor.

Julia stared at a panorama of designer jeans, shelves full of cashmere sweaters, racks of shirts in every shade. She reached around Rina and selected two silk outfits with loose-flowing pants. Holding Rina's hand, she led her into the bedroom and laid the clothing on the bed.

"Try those." Julia sat in the upholstered armchair and leaned back, admiring the woman standing before her in the bra and silk boxers.

Rina stared at her girlfriend with an amused upward turn of her lips. "Fine, Julia, just to accommodate you." The actress held up each outfit on its hanger under her chin and then switched them back and forth. "Well?"

"The green one," Julia replied. "It makes your eyes electric and creates a soft contrast with your auburn highlights."

Rina chuckled. "A soft contrast? You're just full of surprises, my little artist." She laid the clothes on the bed and sat on Julia's lap. She stroked her lover's face and gazed into her eyes. "Kiss me, Julia, and don't smear my lipstick."

The sculptress's hand delicately traced the length of Rina's thigh up to her silk boxer-covered cheek. Her fingertips molded Rina's kinetic reaction to her touch—an anatomical binding of art and life, without the sacrifice of one having to imitate the other. "Right now, looking into your eyes makes sex appear closer than it really is."

"Be a good girl. I'll be counting the minutes until we're alone tonight. Know that every time I touch my earring, like this," Rina tapped her earlobe with her fingertip, "it means I love you." She stood, tried on the green silk outfit, and walked to one of her mirrors. She inspected herself from every angle. "You're absolutely right, Julia. Huh! I'll have to remember to buy more outfits in this color."

Julia laughed. "Just what you need—more clothes to be unable to decide between. You look drop-dead gorgeous, Rina. Too beautiful to have a ranch girl slash cook slash sculptor as your dinner date."

Rina flicked a glance at Julia in the mirror and then went to her. "Stand up."

Julia stood and let the woman lead her to her favorite three-paneled mirror—the one positioned for Rina to make her final once-over before walking out the door. She stepped behind Julia and wrapped her arms around her. "Look at us, Julia. This is *us*, remember? We made a deal on the ranch."

"Which one? We've made a few."

"We're not going to let anyone else define us. Who we are together is ours and ours alone."

"I'm nervous about meeting your friends. Well-known actors, important Hollywood folks, Reese Collingworth! And who am I?"

Rina's eyes captured Julia's in the reflection of the mirror and she wrapped Julia even tighter in her embrace. "You, my love, are everything."

Julia held her gaze. "You mean that, don't you?" She turned around in Rina's embrace and kissed the woman. "I'm beginning to know when I'm talking to the real you."

Rina took a step back. "Go get dressed and come get me when you're done. I want you on my arm when we make our entrance."

"All right. But do you ever tire of making an entrance?"

Rina chortled. "Oh my God, no. Never. You'll get used to it."

"Sure, as long as you can get used to someone who hasn't a clue and couldn't care less."

"That's why you have me. Get dressed. We can't be late for our own dinner party."

"God forbid." Julia retreated to her bathroom and adjoining dressing room.

When Julia returned, she was wearing the outfit that Rina had left for her. She didn't even want to guess what this trendy little number she was wearing cost. All Rina had asked her for were her measurements and favorite color.

"I'm really not used to wearing off-the-shoulder silk knits, Rina. It makes me worry about a wardrobe malfunction."

"Let's see. Turn around."

Julia did a spin.

"Oh, Julia! You're not only beautiful, right now you're upstaging me. Makes me want to rip off your clothes the way you did to me our first time together."

"So, rain check on the dinner party?" Julia teased.

"I've never seen you wear makeup that way. You look stunning with your hair down."

"I know what you're doing. You're trying to boost my confidence, aren't you? You're not *that* good an actress."

"Don't be ridiculous, of course I am. But I'm not acting. Come here."

Julia groaned. "Again with the mirror?" She crossed the room to join Rina.

"Stop right there. Now close your eyes. Go ahead, do it."

Julia closed her eyes.

Rina counted to five. "Now, when you open your eyes, look straight ahead."

Julia did so. "This *does* look nice on me."

"Not just nice, honey. You're a knockout. The vultures are going to swoop in on you." Rina tickled her.

"Now you're scaring me."

"We have to get out of here. Being alone with you makes everywhere else negotiable."

"Promise me something, Rina?"

"Anything, love."

"Don't let them eat me alive downstairs."

"I told you, they'll only respect you if you push back."

"But that's not my style."

"Julia, this is about survival, not style. Survival is pushing back. Style is about how you take them down. I'm confident you'll show them your boundaries."

Julia exhaled hard. "If you say so."

Rina held out her hand. "Shall we?"

Julia took her hand and walked through the sitting room toward the front door of the suite.

"Remember what I told you about everyone and you'll be fine," said Rina. They descended the stairway and turned toward the party room. "Enter slowly, like you own the place. Shoulders relaxed, head high. Smile. Take a deep breath. Exhale. Enjoy yourself." They took another few steps.

"Jesus, Rina, am I about to make my first entrance?"

Rina laced her arm through Julia's and stepped across the threshold. "Darling, you already have," she whispered.

CHAPTER TWENTY-THREE

"Reese. Layla," Rina said joyfully. The director kissed her on the cheek. Reese and Layla Collingworth, I'd like you to meet my lover, Julia Dearling."

Julia froze. *Lover.* She shook their hands. "Hello," she mustered. "A pleasure to meet you."

"And this is my publicist and friend, Susie Blank."

"Hi, Julia. Welcome to LA." The woman gripped Julia's hand and stared into her eyes.

Julia tried to avert her stare from the too-perky breasts on either side of the canyonesque cleavage. *Those have to be fake.* "Thank you. Nice to meet you, Susie." She slid a little closer to Rina.

Rina looked out at her small gathering. "We're so happy you could make it to the first of our many soirées as a couple."

Julia gulped. *Soirées? Couple!*

"Rina!" came one voice after the other. The hawks swooped in, and with each greeting, the flock subtly moved Julia another step farther from her date.

Julia absorbed the scene as Rina greeted her friends. She wasn't sure where to stand or what to do with her arms so she let them hang by her side. With every person that Rina greeted, Julia's breathing became more shallow. The pang of lack-of-accomplishment hit her when she surveyed the room. By these standards she might have been the least accomplished person in the entire galaxy.

Each person's handshake upon meeting her was no doubt an assessment—a once- over—over and over. She smiled anyway. *Everyone is exactly as Rina described them.*

Rina reached for Julia's left hand and stepped through her guests to close the space between them. "Have you met Pinna, Julia?"

Julia smiled the good-to-meet-you smile she'd rehearsed with Rina. "Pinna Goddard? From Voice of Hollywood?" The woman's talonesque manicure only reinforced Julia's fears of being torn to shreds by the end of the evening.

"I like her already, Rina."

Rina introduced the rest of the small circle—not that most of them needed an introduction.

Julia swallowed every silent "Ohmigosh." Her stomach flip-flopped every few seconds, especially when she met actor Monty Callan. But clinging tightly to Rina's advice—and her hand—she just relaxed and let it happen.

"What would you like to drink, Julia?" asked Gigi.

Not exactly the beer and peanuts crowd. "I'll have a water, please."

"Ah, are you in the program?" asked the Emmy-winning Monty.

"Program?" Julia repeated.

"You know, AA? Or rehab, like Rina did?"

"Oh. No, it's nothing like that. I'm parched." *Rehab like Rina did?* "I was a big fan of your show, Monty—and so disappointed when it was canceled."

Monty stared at her, expressionless. "Yes," he said, allowing his "S" to hiss.

Rina cleared her throat, and Julia gathered she'd already made her first *faux pas* of the evening. "Honey," said Rina, "I have that white wine you served me the night we met. Join me in a glass?"

Julia smiled. "You remembered the vintage?"

"How could I forget? Gigi, would you please have the waiter pour us the Sancerre?"

"Sure." Gigi flagged down the server.

"Sancerre." Pinna nodded her approval. "I'd like to hear more about the night you met. Julia, have you met Gil Garrish?" Pinna held out her hand to welcome Gil to the circle.

Julia raised her eyebrows. "Garrish Productions?" she asked.

Through a beard a little too black for his age, Gil smiled. "See, Pinna, I told you audiences read the credits. Or did Rina put you up to this, Julia?"

Julia felt her face flush. "Nice to meet you!"

Rina chuckled. "No, Gil. Julia is a movie buff. However, you may be out of your league with her. She can quote dialogue."

"Adorable," said Susie before she tossed back her shot of tequila.

"Isn't it?" added Gigi.

In the far corner of the room, the DJ spun from his eclectic repertoire of cocktail party music.

"I'm impressed how you've managed to keep this relationship quiet," said Pinna. "How long have you two been together?"

Julia heard Rina in her mind. "*Let me field any questions from Pinna. I love her dearly, but she is the actual voice of Hollywood.*"

"It feels like I've known Julia forever." Rina put her arm around Julia's waist.

"Four months," Julia blurted out.

Pinna laughed. "Honey, in Hollywood every month counts as a year."

Breathe. Julia exhaled and turned to the waiter who approached. "Thank you," she said as he served the wine.

Rina raised her glass and gazed into Julia's eyes. "To you, my love."

Gigi raised her glass. "Congratulations, Rina. This is certainly a side of you no one ever sees. Not even with Brit…"

Rina cut her off. "Thank you for your good wishes, Gigi."

"Not even with…?" Julia began.

"Not important," Rina interrupted.

Julia drank a long, unsophisticated dose of Sancerre and set the glass on a table. "Let's dance, Rina."

"To this? I thought you didn't like to dance."

In the silence that followed, Julia felt eyes awaiting her response. "Name what you'd like to dance to and I'll ask the DJ to play it."

"How about Madonna or some Eighties techno?"

"You're kidding, right?" Julia's expression was dead serious. "How about something from this millennium?"

Pinna coughed and turned away. Susie the publicist seemed struck with the same *schadenfreude* that made people stop to watch train wrecks, and Clay simply smiled at her.

Ugh. I can't believe I just said that in front of Rina's friends. She must hate me right now!

"Surprise me, Julia. But not before you kiss me."

Julia delivered. Rina gazed into her eyes and touched her earring. Suddenly she was grounded again. In her mind, she heard Rina say *"I love you."* She felt her shoulders drop three inches back to their normal height. "Excuse me," she said before leaving. *So this is what it's like to be examined under a microscope. Glad I flossed my teeth.* Even from behind her, she could feel the furtive stares.

Julia had known she'd be the subject of scrutiny that evening, that many in the group had probably been taking bets on how long it would take for her to make an ass of herself. She sighed. Well, they didn't have to wait any longer. She already had. *Poor Rina. She has to put up with my lack of sophistication. Then again she also has to put up with the snobbery of these so-called friends.*

As familiar as she was with the kind of odors that were part and parcel of mucking out stalls, Julia discovered that the pungent stench she now connected with human disdain offended her far worse.

"Hi," she said to the DJ. "Do you have that Rihanna and Calvin Harris song, 'This Is What You Came For'?"

"Sure do," he replied. "A little dance music coming up next."

Julia turned to see Rina speaking with Susie and Pinna. Susie, the more animated of the two, expressed herself with grand gestures, enough to fill in any missing syllables that Julia missed on her return approach.

"It's going to take a lot to keep this quiet, Rina," said Susie. "Julia seems nice, but she's—"

"Well, I think you've never looked more radiant, Rina," Pinna interjected.

Julia waited a beat before speaking when she arrived. "You were saying, Susie? Julia is…" said Julia.

Susie stared at her blankly but remained silent. Julia stared back with her best poker face. "Pardon us, ladies, but Rina owes me a dance. It's a special request." She turned to Rina. "Just for you, babe."

Susie hid her quiet huff with a smile while her eyes darted elsewhere.

"This one that's just starting?" asked Rina.

"Mm-hmm."

"I like it," said Rina.

Julia took her hand and led her onto the dance floor out of eavesdropping range.

"Julia, that was a little rude confronting Susie that way."

"Aren't you curious to know what she thinks I am? 'Julia is…'?"

"I don't care what she thinks. And neither should you. Her job is to plan my strategy to maintain my brand. It's what she's paid to do."

"But you said to push back. This is me pushing back."

"You're very cute." Rina chuckled. "You're right. Susie can be a bit of an ass."

"Gee, ya think?"

They began to dance in the middle of the room. When Rina fell a little out of step, Julia pulled her close and pressed against her. She gazed into Rina's magnetic green eyes and leaned toward her ear. "Honey, just pretend I'm on top of you."

Rina regained her rhythm. "You're right, that makes it much easier. You may not like to dance, but you're very good at it. If it helps to know, I'm a little nervous too."

"About what? You're so totally in your element—and I'm so totally *not*."

"I'm nervous that you won't have as good a time as I want you to have or that you won't like me as much after this."

"Truthfully, I'd like to hear more about rehab. I mean, no offense, but should you be drinking?" Julia whispered.

"Chocolate rehab," Rina whispered back.

"What?"

Rina nodded. "I went to rehab for a chocolate addiction."

"No wonder you wouldn't do that thing…with the chocolate."

"In bed?" said Rina.

"Yes."

"I'm sorry. I should have told you about rehab then, instead of making you feel bad about it."

Julia pulled her closer. "How could anything ever feel bad with you? I love you, Rina. I *love* you," she smiled.

"Look into my eyes."

Julia leaned back and looked at Rina.

"Ms. Dearling, mess up my lipstick."

"Here? Now?"

"Right here. Right now."

"But…"

"I don't care."

Julia kissed her gently, longingly. In that moment she couldn't have cared less about the furtive stares or the snide suppositions about her. She had everything she needed—from the core of her existence right out to the far reaches of the universe. Suddenly, her fears of galactic inferiority vanished, and all that remained was Rina up against her.

"What *is* this music?" asked Rina.

"Rihanna is singing about how everyone in the room is watching you, but you're watching me."

Rina laced her fingers around Julia's neck. "Subtle. I'm seeing an interesting new side of you tonight. You're a little fierce when left to your own devices, Julia."

Julia drew Rina in. "I grew up on a ranch wrangling animals that weigh up to a ton and I cook with high flames. Need I say more, Ms. Verralta?"

"Any one of them could move in for the kill at any moment," Rina teased.

"They already have. How do you do it, Rina? We've just started and already I'm exhausted."

Rina smiled the sweet smile, the one Julia had become used to seeing when she was being polite. "They're very accomplished and talented people. And they're my famous friends."

"Who are your not-famous friends?"

"You. Except that we're more than friends."

"Do you hold your friends to the same standard you hold me?"

"Meaning what, Julia?"

Monty and Pinna joined them on the dance floor. "Good song, Julia," said Monty. Then he leaned between them. "Nicely played with Susie." He winked at her before dancing Pinna across the floor.

Julia cocked her head to the side. "See? Monty gets it."

Rina laughed. "Point taken. Give them a chance?"

"I'll give them the same chance they give me. I already like Monty. Who knows, with any luck maybe he'll forgive my cancelled series remark."

"He's over it. He's already producing a new show."

As she and Rina danced, Julia saw from the corner of her eye expressions of scrutiny. She'd been whispered about before, and she understood what those looks meant. It was just a matter of time before all those martinis the guests were emptying from the pitchers kicked in and Julia could see who she was really dealing with.

It hardly took any time before everyone had their turn on the dance floor, laughing and chatting until an air of levity permeated the room. Even Susie smiled at her once—although it could have been something amusing that Gil had said. Monty asked her to dance, which she did. Reese Collingworth shared his love of the desert with her and even told her that in the years he'd known Rina, he'd never seen her look so happy.

"Excuse me, Reese," said Rina. "Julia, will you ask the DJ to lower the music?"

"Sure."

Rina waited until she had everyone's attention.

"You're all in for a treat tonight. My chef has outdone herself. Dinner is served."

CHAPTER TWENTY-FOUR

Rina slipped her arm around Julia's waist, and together they led the way toward the formal dining room.

"It's odd not being the one doing the cooking," said Julia.

"You're my favorite chef, but tonight you're my guest," Rina whispered.

They entered the wide, square room with the ocean view. Now that the sun had set, the modern bridge chandelier illuminated the room. Below it, a trail of candlelight glowed along the gray marble dining table. Rina sat at the head with Julia to her left and Clay to her immediate right. Monty held Pinna's chair and took the seat next to her. Reese and his wife Layla, Susie the publicist, Gil Garrish, and Gigi, trickled in.

Relieved to finally have Rina by her side for longer than a nanosecond, Julia took a breath and watched as the rest of the group took their seats. She still didn't know if any of the eight guests were worthy of the trust that Rina seemed to place in them. Except perhaps for Clay. Maybe Reese. On the other hand something about Gigi was still giving her voodoo vibes. Clay had made her feel welcome during dinner the night before, but Rina's personal assistant had practically interrogated her. "It's a little unusual with the age difference, don't you think, Julia?" And then, even more snidely, "Whatever *will* you do with yourself while Rina is off shooting in exotic locations? You don't expect to come along, do you?"

Julia wondered how long it would take for Rina to get bored with her. *I'm so out of my league. They must be wondering what she sees in me. I know Gigi is.*

"I still think the Academy got it wrong," said Clay. "I'm happy you won Best Director for *Allies of Night*, Reese, but Rina was every bit as deserving of the Oscar for Best Actress for it."

"You're preaching to the choir, Clay," Reese replied.

"What was the Academy thinking, giving it to Britney Cavell?" Susie said, shaking her head.

"I agree," said Julia.

Everyone stopped and looked at her.

"I'm sorry," said Julia, "but I saw that movie before I even met Rina."

Gil Garrish placed his wineglass on the table. "Julia, earning an Oscar depends on politics, popularity, and how much money is spent on the campaign to win."

"Thanks for educating us, Gil," Rina said.

"I'm not telling you anything new," he replied.

Reese put down his utensils and took a sip of wine. "Let's get the opinion of a moviegoer. A plain *not-old*, not-in-the-biz moviegoer. Julia, would you share your thoughts about *Allies of Night*?"

Julia's eyes widened. "Me? You want *my* opinion?"

"Yes, Julia," said Reese.

Everyone waited while Julia glanced at Rina, who nodded at her.

"But I don't know anything about making movies. I just go to the theater and buy a ticket and popcorn."

"How quaint," said Susie.

Reese continued. "Rina tells me you're quite the movie buff. So, let's have it. We're all friends here. Give it to us right between the eyes."

What next? Spielberg wants to know if I liked E.T.? Julia dabbed her lips with her napkin. "Honestly, the film reminded me of the Hollywood classics." She took a sip of wine and said nothing else.

"Come on, Julia, don't hold back. Tell us," said Gil.

"I thought Miles Blaydin was dashing in that role—debonair, like Cary Grant in *An Affair to Remember*."

"And?" said Reese.

"You want more?" asked Julia, reaching for Rina's hand under the table. She glanced at her lover. "Rina played the character flawlessly. When I saw the movie…"

"Where did you see it?" Gil interrupted.

"At the only theater near me, which is about a twenty-five-minute ride down a dark desert road from where I live. It's actually in the next town over."

"So you drive all that way just to see a movie?" Layla asked.

"Either that or wait for the DVD. But I see *all* Katarina Verralta movies on the big screen."

"Aww," said Monty. "That's freaking adorable."

Rina nodded. "You have no idea just how adorable, Monty."

"Please, Julia, continue," Reese said, motioning with his hand.

She took a breath and another sip of wine. "*Allies of Night* is a modern classic in every sense. It had all the elements of old Hollywood put together in a new way. The opening scene is breathtaking. I was hooked from that instant. Of course the score had a little something to do with that. No offense, Reese."

"See, Rina?" said Reese. "I told you that window shot would set the tone. And no offense taken, Julia."

I want to be in that bed in Paris with her right now! In the rain! Julia gulped more wine. "You had me from the instant the camera panned the rainy Paris rooftops at dawn, then homed in through the bedroom window to where Rina's character lay sleeping."

"What did you like or not like about the story?" asked Gil before he shoved another forkful of sea bass into his mouth.

Julia continued thoughtfully. "I think what grabbed me most was how the hero and heroine fall in love under the worst possible circumstances of war behind enemy lines. I mean, right there you know there's gonna be trouble, especially with that score—that music had me on the edge of my seat. And the cinematography—those looming European skies confusing day with night, light with darkness. Like, I've never been to Paris, but in the opening scene I swore I could *smell* that rain."

Rina chuckled and took a sip of the martini that she'd switched to after the Sancerre was gone. "I'm sorry, darling, continue."

Julia hesitated. "Um, so they fall madly in love, right? And she has no idea he's a double agent. But he has no idea that the information he gave to the other side is going to put her in danger. Thankfully, he figures it out, then puts his life on the line to save her! She of course has it all figured out by the time he does that, but she would die to save him. When she sees him get shot trying to help her, she risks her life and comes back for him, and she gets shot. Now *that's* a story. Passion. Loyalty after betrayal. I really didn't know what was going to happen to them! I knew he wasn't a good guy from the start, but her love redeems him. It's one of those stories that sticks with you when you leave the theater." Julia emptied her glass.

"Great synopsis," said Monty.

Julia continued. "I couldn't stop thinking about them—I mean, like, for days afterward." Then Julia added as an afterthought: "The next morning on my horse I was still thinking about the movie— wondering what that Paris rain smelled like, loving the metaphor of it washing away their sins before the movie even started."

Rina stroked Julia's cheek and then touched her earring. "The morning after—were you with Thunder or Lightning?"

"Lightning," Julia answered.

"You know, I think he's a much better listener."

"Who?" asked Reese.

"One of Julia's horses," Rina replied. "I'm partial to Thunder, though, ever since we bonded in the barn."

Julia's cheeks flushed at the memory of their hours of lovemaking in the hay.

"You? In a barn," Monty teased. "Since when does Versace make barn-wear?"

Gigi and Pinna laughed.

Julia turned to Rina and shook her head. "You deserved that Oscar, Rina," she said innocently.

Reese applauded. "Buy this girl a drink. Well done, Julia! Maybe you should be a movie critic instead of that hack at *Behind the Set.*"

"So," said Susie, "Rina tells me that you have a little food stand in the dust bowl."

"Stop it, Susie, I said no such thing," Rina chimed in.

"It's a diner actually—in the desert. I took it over when my Grandmother Lucia passed."

"And you live on a ranch?" said Monty with his affected tone.

"Uh-huh. Yes."

"With Thunder and Lightning," he reiterated.

"Yes. Then there's my sculpting studio. I don't make much time for anything other than that and cooking. And Rina."

"Rina mentioned you had quite the meet-cute out your way," said Reese. "I'd like to hear that story sometime. She was on her way to a meeting with me the next day, you know."

"No, I didn't know," Julia replied. She reached for her wineglass, discovered it was empty, and stretched her arm in front of Rina, snaring her lover's martini instead. Taking a swallow, she remembered their first night together in front of the fire and when Rina had left Julia sleeping and she had believed for three days that the actress had abandoned her.

"I'm looking for some new ornamentals." Susie smiled. "Do you make vases?"

Rina stepped in front of Susie's poison dart. "No, Susie, Julia is a sculptress." Rina held her gaze dead-on.

"Where is your work showing?" asked Monty.

"At the Y2," Julia replied.

"The Y2..." Pinna's voice trailed off as she gazed up at the ceiling in thought. "I'm not familiar with that gallery."

"The Y2 is the name of Julia's ranch," said Gigi.

"How do you know that?" Julia asked her.

"I know everything where Rina's concerned, sweetie. Every little thing."

Julia mentally shuddered.

Rina turned to Julia. "I keep forgetting to ask you why the ranch was named Y2."

Julia dabbed her lips with her napkin. "It was renamed for me and Vittoria. Get it? Why Two?" She looked back to the dinner guests. "Enough about my unexciting life. I'm sure what you're all working on is much more riveting."

"Yes," said Susie. "Tell us about this next film, *The Big Picture*, Reese."

"Rina is perfect for the part," Clay interjected. "The role of a lifetime, right, Reese?"

"Without a doubt," Reese replied. He chuckled, "I can't wait to see Rina shoot the scenes on horseback."

"I'll have you know Julia is teaching me to ride like a pro."

"Out on the ranch," Pinna said, two parts sarcastic statement, one part question.

"Yes," said Rina. "I've had a lot of time in the barn. And in the saddle." She made googly eyes at Julia.

"I'll bet you have," said Gil.

Julia stared at her lover, her lips parting, without words to fill the gap. Her face now warm, she wondered how deep the shade of red played to the crowd.

"Interesting that no one out there in the desert has recognized you yet," said Layla.

"We pretty much keep to ourselves," said Julia.

"It's so far from here. I imagine that can't be easy for either of you," Layla added.

Rina squeezed Julia's hand under the table. "We have some logistical challenges to solve."

"Are you ready to come out in the press, Rina?" asked Pinna.

"Don't be a dolt, Pinna. However, you're more than welcome to write a story about an up-and-coming sculptress whose magnificent Arabian horses are currently sparking a bidding war from some notable galleries in Beverly Hills."

"Really? A bidding war?" asked Susie.

"I'd like to see them sometime," Clay said in earnest.

Julia looked into Clay's kind eyes and smiled an unspoken thank-you. "I have some pictures on my phone if you'd like to see them before I leave."

"Cool, I'll look forward to it."

"So, Rina," Pinna began, "how do you feel about working with Britney Cavell? Especially with your history."

Rina's hand tightened on Julia's in response to the question.

"History?" Julia said.

"All I can say is that Reese has assured me, as has Britney, that she'll behave like a normal person."

Pinna chuckled. "Good luck with that!"

Julia's heart sped up and she strained to keep her tone normal. "I didn't know you were doing this film with Britney Cavell." *Why hasn't she told me that?*

"Come on, Reese," Monty began, "you really hired Cavell after all that she did to Rina?"

Rina's eyes danced far away from Julia when she stared at Reese, awaiting his answer.

"We've been very specific in the contracts about the do's and the don'ts," said Reese. "I promise you I can keep her in line."

Julia glanced at Rina. *Keep Britney in line? Why would he need to?* she wondered.

* * *

"At last," said Rina, falling back onto her bed beside Julia. "What a fun night. How are you?"

"I'm exhausted, Rina. And I'm worried."

"About what?"

"That I'll never fit in—that I embarrassed the hell out of you tonight. What's worse is that I don't even know when and how many times I did it."

Rina rolled over. "You did no such thing. You were wonderful." She pushed herself up on her elbow and kissed Julia's lips. "I know it wasn't easy for you, but you seemed to become more comfortable as the evening progressed."

"Thanks to your martini. But, really, I wish you would have intervened a few times."

"When?"

Julia mindlessly played with Rina's hair. "Susie was so condescending."

"I spoke with her about that. Ignore her."

"Why is she your publicist?"

"Because she's the best there is."

"And Gigi. She's used every opportunity since I've gotten here to let me know my place. I think she has it out for me. Did I offend her in some way?"

"No. She's the layer between me and the world. I'm afraid her reflex to protect me can be overwhelming. I'll have a talk with her."

"I don't want her to think I was whining to you about her."

"Don't worry, I'll take care of it, Julia."

"I hope you'll be as forgiving of my flaws as you are of those of other people."

Rina stroked back Julia's bangs and smiled at her. "Now that everyone is gone, do you know what we need?"

"Don't say more food."

"I wasn't going to. How about a relaxing hot tub?"

"I didn't bring a swimsuit."

"Honey, no swimsuits needed—or allowed. It's around the corner on the bedroom terrace." Rina pointed to the French doors.

"I'm confused. I thought I saw the hot tub downstairs by the pool."

"Yes, that one is for guests. This one is private. For you and me."

Julia grabbed a handful of chestnut locks, pulled Rina down to her, and kissed her deep and long. "So why would there be a problem between you and Britney Cavell on location? What's the bad blood?"

"We used to be lovers."

Julia stared at her dead-on. "What?"

CHAPTER TWENTY-FIVE

Julia awoke to the addictive scent of Rina on her skin and on strands of her hair. She kissed the bare shoulder of the sleeping elegance draped across her. Unable to tell in the blacked-out room if it was day or night, she slid out from under Rina's arm and reached for her phone on the nightstand.

Since when do I sleep until ten a.m.? She yawned. *Rina's going to want her coffee soon.*

Silent as a Sunday sunrise, Julia stood and slipped into the robe she had worn to the hot tub, then tiptoed barefoot out of the suite. She rubbed her sleepy eyes on the first flight of stairs. Midway down the second flight, she stopped to listen to the voices trickling out from the kitchen.

"I still don't like it," said Gigi. "She's all wrong for Rina."

"Give the girl a chance," said Clay. "Considering she's young and an outsider to our world, I think she held her own last night. I like her. I mean, she's such a refreshing change from the vultures in Rina's past. Didn't you see how they treated each other?"

Outsider? Vultures? Was Britney Cavell a vulture?

"I don't trust her, Clay. She must want something, and I'm here to make sure Rina doesn't get blindsided. As for how Rina acted toward her—she's an actress. Have you ever seen her *not* act with a girlfriend?" She paused and then chuckled sardonically. "Did you hear what Julia said to Monty about his show being canceled? I thought his claws were going to come out. Then she was positively rude to Susie."

"Come on. Monty knew it was an innocent remark. Julia was being conciliatory, and by the end of dinner, Monty was quite taken with her. As for Susie, she had way too much to drink last night and acted like an ass. You need to stop worrying."

"You know what, Clay? You're right. I'm not gonna worry—I'm not. Nope. You know how Rina gets when she's filming. This little fling will fade away like the others, especially once Rina goes on location."

"You mean once she's on location with Britney."

"That too."

Fade away like the others? Britney! Ugh. How do I compete with this? Julia pivoted to creep back up the staircase, climbed two steps, and stopped. *Push back. Rina told me to push back. How do I do that with the person closest to her?* She descended the rest of the steps and entered the kitchen with a smile and a bounce in her step. "Oh! Good morning. I didn't know anyone was here."

"Good morning, Julia," said Clay. "I take it Rina is still sleeping?"

"Yes, she is. I know she'll be up soon so I came down to make her coffee."

Gigi stood from the table, moved to the counter, and picked up the coffee pot. "I'll do it. I know how she likes it."

Push back! "That's okay, Gigi. We kind of have a special morning ritual."

Gigi stared at her.

Julia shrugged. "What can I say? The woman loves how I serve her my coffee in bed." She held out her hand and took the coffee pot from the assistant.

Gigi winced when she handed it over.

Clay snickered.

* * *

Julia set the tray of coffee, fruit, and croissants on the counter of the kitchenette in Rina's suite. Time skidded to a halt when she entered the dark and serene bedroom. Except for the echo of Gigi's comments, which she was unable to leave at the door, Julia had never been filled with such deep insight. For the first time, she understood that this ache, this craving for another, was more than an idea or a fantasy. It lived a full life inside of her. Her stomach fluttered with a short growl.

She touched the wall switch and raised the automatic blinds just enough for an oblique shaft of light to pierce the darkness low to the floor. The scant light that filtered upward left her admiring the outline of Rina tangled in the sheets, asleep with her thick hair tossed across the pillow and her head turned to the side. The vision flooded her with longing—a cascade of chills chased by heat, followed by another chill down her back and goose bumps along her arms. Julia's lips went dry, then they parted. A continuous loop played in her mind of how Rina had taken her in her own bed for the first time. She gasped to restart her breathing.

Sonofabitch. This is what true love really feels like.

Thoughts of what Clay had said invaded her peace. *"Vultures in Rina's past."* Next, she replayed the ugly words spoken by Gigi—every single one of them—and her conversation with Rina the night before, when she'd asked her about Britney Cavell. *"We used to be lovers."* She still couldn't get that thought out of her head.

Suddenly nauseated by the thought of Rina having been with Britney Cavell, Julia didn't know how to deal with it. *Should I bring it up? Or do I wait for Rina to tell me about it?* She had tried in the hot tub the night before to ask about that, but Rina was clearly intent on making love. Still, she had no idea what to do with this information. *How could Rina want to be with me after being with a gorgeous woman—an Oscar winner!—like that?*

Julia retrieved the tray from the counter, walked into the bedroom, and placed it on Rina's night table. She sat quietly beside her lover, leaned forward, and placed her lips lightly on the softest lips she had ever tasted. Lips that were full and smooth—not chapped by dry desert winds. In the stillness, Julia had no words except for the ones she whispered. "I love you, Katarina."

The actress stirred before opening her eyes. Julia always prepared herself for that moment, never knowing exactly what color Rina's eyes would be, only knowing that she couldn't wait another second to look into them—to be seen by them—to be adored by them.

"Good morning, Julia," Rina whispered. "Did you just tell me you love me or was I dreaming?"

Julia smiled at her. "Yes."

"Is that your amazing coffee I smell?"

"You know it is, baby."

"I love it when you call me that."

Julia stood, fluffed Rina's pillows, and positioned them the way she liked them for coffee in bed. Their custom had fast become ritual.

Julia poured her a coffee from the carafe, mixed in the cream and sweetener, then set the tray on the bed.

"What's all this?" Rina asked after taking her first sip.

Julia let her robe fall to the floor and stood naked before her. "Breakfast in bed."

Rina devoured her with one stare. "I never tire of seeing you this way."

"That's what you said in the hot tub."

"Was that before or after you fucked me into oblivion? No wonder I slept like the dead."

Julia climbed onto her side of the bed. "What are we going to do, Rina?"

"When?"

"When you leave."

Rina placed her cup on the tray and cradled Julia's cheek. "Why are you asking that right now?"

"Truth?"

"Always."

"I overheard Gigi and Clay talking. Gigi had said that once you start filming, you'll forget about us. I think what she actually said is that our fling will fade away just like the others."

"That's ridiculous."

"Is it?"

"Yes. First off, you're not a fling. Secondly, there are no longer any others."

"Rina, I'm head over heels, madly…crazy in love with you. So, if there's even a chance that what she said is true, you need to tell me. Now."

Rina picked up the tray and placed it on her night table. She tossed back the sheet, turned to Julia, and opened her arms. "Come here."

Julia crept across the sheets, an inch at a time until her body was up against Rina's. She shivered at Rina's touch, at the slow sweep of her hand as it tickled her back. The actress pulled her tight against her own naked body until they were nose to nose.

Rina sighed. "I never want to forget this moment with you. I'm not awake enough to throw myself at you again, so I'll just come out with it. Make love to me."

Momentarily disabled by the mutable green stare, Julia anchored everything about this moment into her mind so that she could replay it forever, whether or not Rina was with her. Rina's scent. The timbre of her lover's morning voice. Her soft skin and ample breasts pressing against her own. The way the morning light fell on the fine lines next to her eyes. The siren's breath on her lips; the bouquet of Rina mixed in with Dior—an essence that permeated her own bed for long afterwards each time that Rina left the ranch. All, all, *all* of it!

"I will, as soon as you promise we can talk afterward." Julia teased her with her lips on Rina's neck, then she kissed every spot that made the woman groan.

"Um-hmm, we'll take a walk on the beach…and we'll talk."

Rina's nails lightly traveled along Julia's back as she slid down and coaxed Julia on top of her. The sculptress traced the outline of the woman beneath her again and again, her hands learning it by heart and marking how their bodies differed; she wanted desperately to sculpt that difference—to make tangible the shape of time. Sleep had only served as an inconvenient intermission—an interruption of the craving that rarely left them. Julia's hand stroked the heat of Rina's thigh up to its source. She whispered in Rina's ear. "The beach is a long way off."

Rina moaned. "I'm in no rush."

Their bodies entwined, their tongues played against each other's, and Rina pulled her in until even the coffee in the insulated carafe grew cold—until her head whipped back and her nails gored the sheet. Until that exquisite instant when Rina called Julia's name—and every stray nuance coalesced.

The stark silence that followed filled Julia with a hollow deafness—a dread that was not an absence of sound, but a confluence of unanswered longing for permanence in her life. She told herself she knew better—permanence was a temporary condition.

Rina wrapped her legs around Julia's. "I want you, Julia. I want us."

Julia pulled back to look at her. "How can I be sure?"

"You're here with me, aren't you?"

"But I barely survived your entourage. Do you really think we have a chance of making it through being apart when you're on location?"

"Why do you say that?"

"Because, as I figured out last night, there's so much about you I don't know."

"Ask me."

Julia rolled to Rina's side, stroked her cheek, and wondered how she could ever make it through a day, let alone a lifetime without looking into those dreamy eyes. Even the thought was painful.

Rina smiled. "Let's walk on the beach and we can talk about whatever you'd like."

"Right after I have coffee."

Rina laughed. "I'm so glad you said that. Not that the sex isn't amazing, but I feel a little cheated out of our routine." She glanced at the untouched breakfast tray and reached for a strawberry. She lightly traced Julia's lips with it and then pressed the fruit against them until Julia took a bite. Teasing with her most alluring expression, Rina took a long sensual lick before she finished it. "So then…your fabulous coffee?"

CHAPTER TWENTY-SIX

Disguised beneath a wide-brimmed hat and large sunglasses, Rina strolled alongside her lover at the brink of the ocean. A set of waves had broken before she snuck in a sideways glance. The midday sunlight poured through Julia's long, highlighted layers as the breeze blew them gently back.

I can't lose her.

A bank of cumulus clouds offered patches of shade, distorting the light over an endless navy horizon. Rina had never wanted to hold anyone's hand as much as at that moment, but she knew better. Photos, conjecture, outing—it was devious luck that nothing had ever stuck to her. She flashed on Cavell. *Amazing how that escaped the press.*

But none of that changed the fact that until now, she had never been in love before or felt this vulnerable. Never had she wanted anyone in the way she wanted this young woman who often enough made her call her own wisdom into question. Julia made her feel protected and safe—wild and free. Loved.

The ranch girl shoved her hands into the pockets of her jeans, her eyes darting in every direction except Rina's.

"What is it you're not saying, Julia?"

Julia stopped and turned. Rina waited. "How can I compete with your life? With the people in it? How is it I didn't know about rehab or your relationship with Britney Cavell?"

"In all fairness, neither of us has been very forthcoming about the details of our pasts. You still change the subject every time I bring it up."

Julia waited for a runner to pass them before continuing. "How can you feel about me the way you say you do? I mean, I feel it, but then I remind myself that you're an Oscar-winning actor, and that makes me question if this is as real as I think it is." She shifted her stance to let the breeze blow the bangs out of her eyes.

"Sweetheart. Do you think I let everyone, no, anyone ever see what I've shown you?"

"I believe every character you throw at me on-screen and off. Then once I get through all of that, I'm faced with the fear that you'll get bored with me…that I won't measure up. Really, Rina. Look around you." She nodded at the estate on the cliff.

Rina exhaled. "Honestly, I don't have a choice about what I let you see. Feelings I've never known gush out of me, and I can no sooner control them than I could control riding Thunder at full speed down the mountain."

They began walking again.

Julia smiled. "You know, you look pretty damn hot on that horse."

Rina playfully poked her arm. "When I'm not with you, all I want to do is be with you. I can't think or be around anyone else—including my entourage."

"How is that possible?"

"From the first time you touched me, I knew I'd been lying to myself for a long time. I'd told myself that my past relationships didn't work because of one reason or another—that always boiled down to what was wrong with those women. But in retrospect, there was something wrong with me—something broken that I didn't even know about until you fixed it. They weren't right for me because I'd settled for 'not-you.'"

Julia stopped again, looked out to sea and then sat on the sand. Rina joined her.

"See?" said Julia. "You say something like that and my whole world upends. Every cell in my body believes you, and then later, I wonder…"

"If it's true? I'll tell you what's true for me," Rina began. "My fear that you don't love me as I do you, that you'll want someone else when you're a little older—someone younger when I look old."

"What? You can't be serious."

"Oh, but I am."

"I wouldn't leave you unless you did something awful to me. I'm not that kind of girl."

Rina lowered her glasses to meet Julia's eyes. "No. You're not, are you? When I told you I've never felt this way, I wasn't being dramatic. You're the only woman who's ever known how to love me—who makes me feel the way I've always wanted to feel. I'm lost in your eyes right now."

Julia lingered there, in that magnetic pull, until her expression dulled. "Seriously, what do I have to offer you? You have fame and a mansion. I have lasagna, horses, and a banknote on a ranch."

"You love so hard, and deep. Sometimes I think you're the grown-up while I'm—some older woman, making a fool of herself."

"But I could never offer you…"

"You have everything I want." She chuckled. "Including those horse sculptures. Hey, don't look away."

Julia turned back toward her.

"The way you cared for me, protected me at the party? Only made me want you more. I loved watching you step in each time someone crossed a line or made a snide inference about our age difference. What was it you said to Susie?"

Julia's eyes brightened. "The nine-hundredth time she made a disparaging age remark, I couldn't help myself. I told her: 'Unlike most of us, only love and wisdom are timeless.'"

Rina laughed. "She didn't say another word about it. It took everything I had to keep a straight face."

"I felt bad after I said it. It was rude."

"She was rude! I'm glad you put her in her place."

"You're not just saying that to make me feel better?"

"No. No one has ever stepped up for me the way that you do." She playfully pushed Julia sideways. "Susie was nasty to you because she's jealous."

Silent together in front of the crashing waves, Rina smiled shyly. "I feel so exposed right now." She drew little circles in the sand between them. "Don't ever wonder how you'll fit into my world—" her gaze drifted up into Julia's "—because you've become my world. I worry more about how I'll fit into your world. Obviously I'm way out of my league on the ranch—in real life. But it's the craziest thing…" Rina stared into the distance, "…being with you makes me—more me."

"'You've become my world? Being with you makes me—more me?' Damn you can deliver a line."

While she couldn't remember the exact scene from which it had come, Rina conjured up Poker Face Number Four—blank emotion tinted with embarrassment. As soon as she'd done it, she knew she should have gone with Matter-of-Fact Number Two.

"Yes. More me."

Julia held back a teasing grin. "You want to tell your face, Rina?"

"Crap, I knew that expression was *all* wrong when I did it."

They both laughed and settled for the warmth in each other's eyes.

Julia's blue eyes danced across the seascape before coming back to her. "I love your laugh. I love us. We're so hot together."

"I suppose."

"Suppose!" Julia said, incredulous.

"Don't judge, but I'm outmatched. I always need a day to recover when you're done with me."

"Really?"

"Uh-huh. Then I have to suffer all the teasing from Gigi and Clay and anyone else who knows me. They keep telling me my head's in the clouds or that I need to pay attention to whatever." Her lips curved into a telling smile. "The fact is, at those times all I think about is when are you going to call. Or when I'm going to see you again. Or... why can't I just jump into the car and show up at your door—forever."

Julia leaned over to kiss her and Rina pulled back. "Not here."

"Do you think there will ever come a time when you'll live openly? When you'll come out?"

"I...I can't."

"Can't or won't?"

"Until you, I'd never even considered it."

"And now?"

Rina lowered her eyes.

"I live an honest life, Rina. It may be a humble life, but it's an honest one. Even if I wanted to, I don't know how to live differently. It's why my mother left me to Grandmother Lucia and moved to New York for a job."

"Your mother left? That's how you wound up with Lucia?"

"Yes, but that's not the point." Realization colored her stare. "How long will it take before I feel like a Katarina Verralta ornament—a hanger-on hiding in the shadows. Watching my every move to keep your secret. I heard loud and clear what Gigi said about me this morning. I wonder how long it will take before I start to believe her."

Take the leap, Rina told herself. *Kiss her right here, right now! Don't let her leave this way!* She sighed. "I understand. It's getting late—shall we head back?"

Julia stood and offered her hand to Rina to pull her to her feet and withdrew it just as quickly. "I'm sorry, I didn't mean to…"

"It's fine," Rina said, standing and brushing the sand from her pants.

Quiet suffused their footfalls as they climbed the long stairway from the beach to the house. Gigi was waiting in the garden.

"Rina, you have to…"

"Not now, Gigi."

"But…"

"Not now. I'll call you after Julia leaves."

Gigi smiled at Julia. "Well, it was nice to finally meet you, Julia."

"Was it, Gigi? Is that what you say to all of Rina's 'flings' before they fade away?" She stood there long enough to see Gigi's jaw drop open but not long enough to give her a chance to respond.

Rina followed Julia upstairs to the suite, where Julia immediately tended to her belongings—tossing them haphazardly into her suitcase. Rina sat on the bed watching her, haunted by the ghosts that still kept her from living her truth. *"The better an actress you become, the less chance anyone will know. You can't ruin your image."* The harsh words, the judgments she had suffered for decades now, still rang in her head—spoken by a mishmash of voices. Her mother. Agents. Directors who'd had her career in their hands. Studio execs who had tried to grope her. Somewhere along her rise to fame, she'd decided they'd been right. She couldn't be her generation's Sophia Loren *and* be gay.

In that moment, Rina was struck by the still-unanswered question that Therapy Brittany had posed to her at Namaste. *"Do you use chocolate to cover up your feelings about all of your relationships with women or only the bad ones?"* For all the time she had contemplated the question, watching Julia prepare to leave provided a valuable insight. *There isn't enough chocolate in all of Belgium that could satisfy my craving for her.*

Rina's insides tightened at the thought that in only minutes her lover's presence would be but another mind-bending memory. She pulled to her face the pillow on which Julia had slept—inhaled deeply, then fell back on top of the tangled sheets that would have to comfort her in her lover's absence. Already, her breathing was shallow, and with each item that Julia placed in her suitcase, the void inside her expanded. She sat up and looked at Julia. "Don't pack your love," she said, only half kidding.

Julia stopped and turned to her. "The problem is, I can't pack it. You always take it all."

"Please understand."

"I do understand. Really, I do. I just don't know what becomes of us when we're forced to live by everyone else's rules. How does love even survive when it gets kicked to the curb—repeatedly—for a photo op, for an hour—for a lifetime?"

"I would never kick your love to the curb." A shudder coursed through her and chilled her.

"When the cameras are on or when you're surrounded by your famous world, where am I then?"

"Don't." Rina's lips tightened.

"Don't what, baby?" Julia's knowing expression left Rina motionless.

"Do we really have to think about logistics right now? Can't we just revel in your first visit and all the amazing things we've felt and discovered together?"

"I can, but can you?"

"Of course I can. I'm reveling right now."

"Then we define revel differently."

"How so?"

"I'll continue to do it when I walk out that door and back into the world. It will be with me everywhere. Can you say the same?"

Rina stood and went to her. She enveloped Julia in her embrace from behind and kissed her neck, held her tightly. "Can we let it all rest for right now? We'll talk more this week when I come out to the ranch for my riding lesson."

Julia turned around and embraced her lover. "Sure. Take all the time you need. You know where I'll be."

"That I do." Rina wanted to scream, to throw her body in front of the door and not let Julia leave. The thought of Julia slipping away—not from her love but from her closeted life, something that had never presented a problem until now—chilled her to the bone. She would never have guessed that her greatest challenge in this relationship would be herself.

Julia's right.

Rina escorted her lover to the garage, kissed her for the seven-thousandth time, and waited for her to start the dilapidated Fiat.

Chug.

Click.

Julia tried again.

Chug.

Click.

"Dammit!"

Rina opened her car door. "That's it, Julia, I'm putting my foot down. You're leaving that death trap here and driving home in the car I bought you. End of discussion."

Julia's eyes narrowed when she looked up at Rina. "Fine! But I'm coming back for the Spider."

Rina smiled Passive Coup Number Six—the one with the dreamy eyes and the *coup d'etat* raised eyebrow, subtly followed by a gently curled smile. "Whatever, darling."

CHAPTER TWENTY-SEVEN

In the outer desert beyond Palm Springs, Julia tapped the accelerator of the sports car and zigged around a truck. She checked her rearview mirror for cops, then without any traffic ahead, she floored it. *I could get used to this! Ugh, exactly what I was afraid of.*

At this rate she'd be home in no time. But she wasn't ready to admit her lust for this car to anyone—especially not to Rina. Where she came from, a car like this stood out. She couldn't imagine her life without the Fiat Spider. Grandmother Lucia had given it to her for her sixteenth birthday, and a day hadn't passed since then that she didn't think of Lucia when she drove it. It was once a nice car. But how would she fend off comments from all the nosy friends and neighbors who might ask her about this sexy beast? Whatever she came up with, it would have to be something that Cass would back her up on.

She zagged back into the other lane. *I've got it! I'll just say that Vitty bought it.* She smiled at her ingenuity. *Note to self: remember to tell Vitty she bought a car!*

In the waning of the day, Julia inhaled the wide-open space, the stillness that lay upon jagged mountain faces along which the last light dripped down through fissures, illuminating dark breaches. The desert's hush was such a stark contrast to her experience of Malibu's chronic perpetual waves.

Interspersed in her thoughts were flashbacks of the weekend. Waking up to the indigo Pacific. Waking up to Katarina in her luxurious bed. The sensation of her lover's arms wrapped tightly around her—her hands everywhere on Julia's body—as they stared out to sea together, their silent ballet a feast of taste, of touch...

The recollection unlocked her sensation of longing and made the tiny fine hairs on the back of her neck rise.

The talk they'd had on the beach had stuck with her. Being with Rina was easier than anything she'd ever experienced, but she couldn't shake the notion that existing in Katarina Verralta's world wouldn't be easy. Not that she expected easy. She wasn't yet sure, however, that she had what it would take to meet the challenge.

The morning of their dinner party, when they had left Malibu to shop on Rodeo Drive, Clay and Gigi had accompanied them. "Come over here," Clay had said, taking her hand when some of the tourists started turning their cell phones in their direction.

God forbid anyone would assume Rina and I were together.

She asked herself what it would take to walk away from this before they became even more involved—before she fell in love any harder. *Too late on both counts!* She squashed the demon-thought of ending things like a bug hitting the windshield of the sports car, which was now cruising at ninety. *Splat!*

Julia coasted through the unlocked gate to the Y2, parked next to Cass's car, and stopped in the barn. "This is a nice surprise. I didn't expect you to still be here."

"Welcome home, Jules. I didn't hear your car."

"There's a reason for that."

"So? How was it?"

"I could start with magical and go downhill from there...or maybe it's uphill. Depends on how you see it."

"Downhill, uphill. Uh-huh."

Julia fanned out her arms in excitement. "It was fine. I mean good. It was *really* good. I think."

"Okay, so far I'm hearing magical, downhill, uphill and fine-borderline-good—no, *really* good."

Julia chuckled. "I'm running on fumes. I stopped for two cups of coffee on the way home to stay awake."

"Somebody didn't get much sleep."

Julia laughed.

"Look at that grin on you, you bad girl. You're blushing." Cass went to the door. "Where's your car, and whose car is that?"

"The Fiat died when I left LA so Rina made me drive this one home."

"'Made you'? Did your sugar mama give you that?"

Julia cringed. "That's so not funny. It was a safe ride home. But if anyone asks, tell them Vitty bought it."

"Does Vitty know she bought a car?"

"She will."

Lightning neighed at her. "Hi, guys, did Auntie Cass take good care of you?" She entered their stalls, patted both horses, and gave them each the carrots she had left over from the ride home. The ride that took half an hour less than it would have in the old Fiat.

A sudden urge to beat out the wind overtook her, but it was too late—too dark for her to hop onto Lightning bareback and let him run full-out while she held on to his mane. Then she reminded herself she couldn't outrun her feelings—she hadn't been able to out-drive them either! No matter how fast she had gone.

"I'll see you guys in the morning. You coming inside, Cass?"

"Depends on whether or not you're going to give me all the sordid details—which by the look on your face tells me no."

Julia's half-assed smile matched the slow shake of her head. "Mind if we talk tomorrow?"

"No, I figured you'd be worn out by the time you made it home. I brought you some stuff to eat from the diner. It's in the freezer."

"You're an angel."

"Are you okay?"

"I need some sleep."

"You should see you right now."

"Why?"

"I've known you for how long?" Cass said rhetorically. "You're in love, Julia. You know how I know?"

"How?"

"Not only have I never seen you this way in our whole lives, but you actually look different."

"I do?"

"Yes." She hugged her friend and picked up her purse. "Get some rest and I'll see you bright and early."

"Thanks for everything, Cass. I don't know what I'd do without you."

"Just don't go all Hollywood on me. I'd miss my best friend."

Julia dropped her suitcase in the bedroom, changed into her sculpting clothes, and entered the casita. The bust of Katarina Verralta stared at her with eyes not yet filled with the passion that made Rina who she was—not yet engraved with every detail that Julia had come to love in the early morning light while Rina slept.

When her text message alerted her with Rina's special ringtone, she pulled the phone from her pocket and smiled.

Are you home yet? Rina asked.

I got home a while ago. You didn't tell me that car had a jet engine and wings!

Thank you for a wonderful visit. I can't stop thinking about you. About us.

"How do I get through tonight without you?" Julia asked the likeness of Rina before her. *I miss you* was all she could text.

How was the drive?

I didn't stop feeling your touch or thinking about you for an instant.

Good! Rina replied. *I don't want you to worry about us. I know in my heart it will all work out. Okay?*

I hope you're right. I've never felt so vulnerable. But then, I've never known this kind of love.

Seconds after she pressed Send, the phone rang, turning it from a flat and lifeless object into a lifeline.

Rina whispered in her sexy alto voice with the Italian accent: "I don't know if I can wait until Tuesday night. I crave you more than chocolate." Julia heard the slight catch in her throat.

"Katarina?"

Julia could tell she was smiling when the woman replied. "Yes?"

"It's only two days away."

Rina sighed. "Or a lifetime, depending on how you feel."

"How *I* feel? I miss you so much it hurts inside. I didn't want to leave you."

"Do you mean it? After our conversation on the beach, I wasn't sure."

"Have I ever lied to you?"

Rina chuckled softly. "Never. Not even when I wanted you to."

"When have you wanted me to lie to you?"

"Twice. Once when you told me I looked tired, and the other was when you told me I could end things between us and you would understand—that you'd let me go."

"I was trying to give you a chance to make a graceful exit." Julia traced the long strands of clay hair.

"Don't stand in the middle of a theater and yell 'Fire!' unless there is one."

"There is one."

"We'll work it out, sweetheart."

Sweetheart. The timbre echoed in Julia's mind, reverberated through her body, right down to the place where Rina had touched her when she came.

"I can't believe you were here only a few hours ago. It seems like a lifetime."

"I know, but I'll bet you suffered some aftermath from Gigi."

Rina paused. "No."

"Katarina?" Julia waited.

"It wasn't that bad. Really."

"Want to try that again with a little conviction?"

"It's nothing. Gigi is just concerned about me."

"I get that, Rina. But why is she concerned about us? Does she have a thing for you or something?"

Rina scoffed. "No! Why would you ask that?"

"Because she acts more like a jilted lover than a personal assistant."

"She's never seen me the way I am when I'm with you. Both she and Clay told me that."

"But Clay likes me. Gigi doesn't."

"Don't worry, Julia. It will be fine."

"Until it isn't."

"I didn't call to talk about Gigi!"

Julia smiled. "What *did* you call to talk about?"

"I got a call from Reese after you left. We're doing the final table read at the end of the week in LA, so I can only stay two nights. You'll be working Thursday, so I didn't think it would be a big thing if I left early. Besides, I'm learning lines, but we both know what happens whenever you enter the room."

Julia didn't respond.

"What's wrong?" asked Rina.

"Nothing."

"Are you sure?"

Julia shrugged. "I can't get the fact out of my head that you and Britney Cavell were lovers—and now you're going to be on lockdown together."

"It's called 'on location.'"

"You see it your way and I'll see it mine."

"Julia, listen to me. I have zero interest in her."

"Does she feel that way about you?"

Rina hesitated. "It doesn't matter what she feels. You're the one I want. How can I ease your mind?"

"I don't know. I hate that I feel this way. Worse, I double-hate that I just told you I feel this way. I really need to get some game because I can't act all cool and everything." She paused. "Damn! Now I've told you that, too!"

"Why don't I fly you in to spend a couple of days with me in Vancouver?"

Julia remained silent.

"You don't have to answer now—think it over."

"When on Tuesday will you be here?"

"By late afternoon. I have a car and driver bringing me so I can learn lines on the way. Did you like driving the new car?"

Julia knew Rina was smiling by her teasing tone. "It was different from the old Fiat—that's for sure."

"But did you like it?"

"Ugh. What do you think?"

"Good. Then you'll keep it," Rina said.

"We'll see."

"You can be so hardheaded!"

Julia sighed. "Honestly?"

"Always."

"I keep waiting for that other shoe to drop."

"I'm going to fix that."

"How?"

"By loving you more and better than you've ever imagined possible," said Rina.

"I can't wait to hold you."

"What are you doing right now?"

"Sculpting."

"I'll bet the first thing you did when you got there was to see Thunder and Lightning."

"Uh-huh."

"Then you went right into the casita."

"Am I that predictable?"

"Yes, thank god. I love that about you."

"Then you must already know I'm counting the hours until you get here."

"Does it bother you that I call in the middle of the night and wake you to tell you I love you?"

Julia smiled. "No. I love it."

"Then I'll say a *faux* good night in my most convincing tone."

"Faux good night back."

Julia put the phone in her pocket and opened the case of sculpting tools. She studied them before selecting the finest and narrowest blade. With the tiniest of precision strokes, she etched fine expressive lines next to Rina's eyes—the ones she had kissed in that morning's light. When she was satisfied that she had captured some of the expression, she closed up the studio and went home.

In the bedroom, Julia unpacked her suitcase. She pressed to her face the T-shirt she had worn on the beach and inhaled the commingling of ocean, Rina, and Malibu embedded in it. Her lover's words still rang in her ear: "*It means I'm taking the leap. I'm falling in love. Crazy, wild, once-in-a-lifetime love…with you, Julia Dearling.*" Then, as always in her mind, she heard Rina call her *Zhooliah*.

About to toss the shirt into the laundry pile, she instead changed into it and wrapped her arms around herself. It was the best she could do to keep from missing Rina all the more. Dinner consisted of a few sips of defrosted minestrone and three bites of a salad while she finished out her night watching her favorite Katarina Verralta movie, *Spinning the Light*. She was even able to spot the expression that Rina called Turbulent Aunt Zelda.

Rina had already ruined her for anyone else for a lifetime. Not because she was the famous Oscar-winning actress. Or because she was the most gorgeous woman ever created. Neither was it her extreme warmth and genuine nature. It was rather that Julia couldn't fathom being with anyone else—ever. In that moment, she understood how Rina's inner beauty far surpassed her good looks. Rina knew how to love her. That was all she needed to know. Still, no matter how predestined their paths crossing seemed, she couldn't quite envision a smooth road ahead.

Julia yawned and lazily climbed the stairs to go to bed.

Does love really conquer all, or does it simply vanquish those who get in its way?

CHAPTER TWENTY-EIGHT

Before the sun completely lifted the new day above the mountain, Julia raced the sports car down a back road on her way to work. She arrived at the Starlight with a bounce in her step, made coffee, and immediately began her prep work.

The photo Vitty had taken of Grandmother Lucia at her final birthday hung in the frame Julia had made for it—Lucia's eyes ever watchful from the wall behind the counter. She poured a cup of coffee and stared at the photo, lost in thought—wondering if Lucia was indeed watching over her; wondering if her grandmother would be proud of her and would have approved of the changes that she and Isabella had made to the diner. "I can't even imagine what you'd think of my relationship."

The few days Julia had spent in Malibu had been her longest vacation since owning the Starlight. While Rina occupied most of her thoughts, she was glad to be home and sporting her work ponytail and sneakers. She issued a sigh of relief and took great comfort in the fact that she didn't have to dress up today—or deal with Gigi's attitude and forbearing expression. Or pretend to like restaurants whose fancy presentation far outweighed the overpriced food.

Rina's world had drained her—but waking on this day to see her horses had repaired her. She flashed on Rina and their jaunt to Rodeo Drive in Beverly Hills. *Could our lives be any more different!* She scratched her head. *She shops at all the "Cheez"—GucCI, VersaCE, GivenCHY! I shop at Ronnie's Tack and Feed.*

By the time Isabella arrived, Julia had finished most of her work too.

"*Buenos dias,* Julia, you're here awfully early."

Julia beamed and hugged the woman with the short gray hair, who barely made it to Julia's shoulder height. "*Buenos dias, Tia.*" Julia had grown up seeing Isabella as her aunt even though she had been Lucia's friend and was not a blood relative. Tia Isabella had been real family to her—after her father had died and especially after her mother subsequently left Desert Bluff for a job in New York.

Christmas visits, birthday cards, phone calls she'd tried to avoid, and Lucia's funeral were all she really knew or wanted to know of the woman who had given birth to her. Maria—the woman who had decided to stop being a mother when her twins were twelve. The reason for her leaving remained unconfirmed, but Julia knew somehow that her attraction to other girls had figured into it. At the time, Maria had told her and Vitty that she needed to support them now that their father was gone and the opportunity to do that was in New York. Whatever the reasons, all Julia knew now was that she had left and pretty much stayed gone.

Lucia and Isabella were the ones who had thrown her and Vitty the birthday parties and baked the cakes, shopped for school supplies. She remembered her and her sister's art accomplishments tacked to the walls of the diner's kitchen. If it hadn't been for her grandmother, she and Vitty wouldn't have known what it meant to have a real mother after the age of twelve.

"Did you have fun in Los Angeles, *mija?*"

"I had a wonderful time. Thanks for picking up the slack for me so that I could go away."

Isabella flashed her warmest smile. "You should go more often. You look happy."

"I do?"

Isabella laughed nostalgically. "Yes, you have the same smile you had as a teenager when you got away with something!"

Julia acted innocent. "Like what?"

Isabella narrowed her stare. "Like when you and Cass stole Lucia's car to go joyriding in the middle of the night. Same smile."

Julia feigned shock. "I never stole Grandmother Lucia's car!"

Isabella shook an accusing finger at her. "Fine—borrowed it. She always knew what you were up to."

"She did?"

"We both did. But she always said you were the responsible one. You had her love of the ranch and the diner—always did your chores and got good grades. She said that Vitty was more like your mother—needed a bigger place and a more exciting life."

"That was never a secret. Vitty wanted different things than I did... *do*—than I do."

"But she didn't worry about Vittoria the way she worried about you."

"Why would she worry?" asked Julia while filling the omelette station containers with freshly chopped vegetables.

Isabella placed the omelette pans on the counter. "She said Desert Bluff didn't have much to offer a young beautiful girl who neither wanted nor needed a man."

"But I love sculpting in the casita and riding my horses and cooking."

"That's wonderful, *mija*, but you do it all alone. Do you think your girlfriend in LA would ever want to live in such a quiet place as this?"

"I doubt it." Julia felt a pang of guilt, not yet having shared with Isabella that her girlfriend was Katarina Verralta. She tried to picture it—Rina out here in the desert, without her driver, her entourage, and without the life-saving transfusions of Rodeo Drive. But the actress barely primped when she stayed at the ranch.

That wouldn't last for long! She told me I need to get more mirrors. And better lighting!

While Julia loved how natural it felt when Rina came to visit, she also knew she was kidding herself to think that a woman like that could be satisfied with this for longer than a couple of days at a time. *How long would it take for her to get bored with me? I already get bored with me.*

Now that she had spent time at Rina's, she understood how much of life didn't happen here in her little world. Still, she couldn't exactly see herself living the Malibu lifestyle either. There wasn't even a stable on the property! *That's probably because there's nowhere to ride.*

Isabella touched her shoulder. "Come look at the new item I made. If you like it, we can add it as a special."

Julia followed her to the walk-in cooler. "What is it?"

Isabella removed the pan, placed it on the counter, and opened the lid. She cut a square with the spatula, put it on a plate, and heated it in the mini-oven.

"Here, try it. It's a lentil, vegetable, and rice loaf. We've been getting a lot of requests for vegetarian dishes. Also, it freezes well."

Julia took a bite. "Isabella, this is delicious. I was a little skeptical when you told me what it is, but this is really good!"

"What do you think about giving out little samples of it at lunchtime?"

"Great. We can get some feedback, and if it's a go, we'll put it on the menu, pair it with a salad or soup. You know, I thought about what you said—packaging our food for retail. I like the idea, and with our catering, we could expand the business and make good money."

"I'm here! I'm here," Cass blurted out as she raced through the kitchen and dumped her belongings in the office.

"You okay?" Julia asked.

"Couldn't get out of my own way this morning!" Cass looked at the plate. "You tried the lentil loaf?"

"Yes. Love it."

"I didn't want to talk business with you when you got home—" She glanced at Isabella. "Poor thing was so tired last night." She looked back to Julia. "I picked up two catering jobs while you were gone."

"That's great. Gee, you guys do better without me here."

"Hardly," said Cass. "But the first job is next Sunday so we'll need to get the order in to the distributor today. Totally manageable, though—twenty-five people for a brunch birthday party. The other job is later this month. Also on a Sunday and it's a buffet, which will make it easier since it's for fifty people. I have both customers' requests, but we'll need to plan the menus."

"Fifty people? That will be our biggest party yet!"

Isabella interrupted them. "Someone needs to go out front. I heard the bells on the door."

"I've got it." Julia tied her apron and grabbed a couple of trays to leave by the coffee station. When she pushed open the swinging door and saw Nicki enter behind a group of women, she froze until the door swung back and whacked her in the noggin. "Hey, Cass," she said rubbing her head, "Nicki's here with some friends. Will you take their table for me?"

Cass picked up her order pad. "That girl has some kinda persistence—gotta give her that much."

"Persistence?"

"She stopped in again while you were gone, asking questions about where you were and what you've been doing."

"What did you tell her?"

"I told her to ask you!" Cass entered the diner.

Julia waited a few minutes for the usual crowd to filter in before Isabella pushed her out of the kitchen. She seated two parties as far from Nicki as she could get and took their orders. On one of her trips back to the kitchen, Nicki intercepted her.

"Julia, hi."

If Julia had learned anything during her time spent with Rina, it was the value of having the right expression to go with a reaction. All the better if it were natural. *Indifference it is, then.* "Hi, Nicki."

Nicki shifted her weight to her opposite leg. "It's good to see you. How've you been?"

"Good. Kind of busy right now, though."

"Oh, sure. Is there a time when we can talk?"

"I don't have anything to say."

Nicki tried harder. "I do. I want to apologize."

Julia tossed a pleading glance at Cass when she came out of the kitchen.

"Jules," Cass said as she passed by, "Isabella needs you in the kitchen."

She glanced back at Nicki. "Don't bother. It won't change anything. And as usual, your timing sucks."

"How about if I come out to the ranch?"

Julia didn't answer and left her standing there.

CHAPTER TWENTY-NINE

With the rush behind them and the tables cleared, Julia and Cass took their coffee break at the counter under Grandmother Lucia's watchful eye.

"So Nicki said she wants to apologize, but I wonder what she really wants," said Julia.

"My guess? She wants you back."

"I'm not giving her the opportunity to apologize for how she treated me. Now that I know what it's like to be treated well, I don't want anything to do with her."

"As you well know, Nicki is pretty persistent when she wants something."

Julia rolled her eyes. "Then I guess she's in for a surprise because, and I repeat, I don't want to have anything to do with her."

Cass poked Julia's leg. "I can't believe my best friend is dating you know who. Forget Nicki—when do I get to meet her?"

Julia giggled. "I don't know. Soon, I guess. She'll be here tomorrow night, but that's the last time we'll be together until who knows when." Julia fielded an imaginary bad taste in her mouth. "Ugh, she's leaving to go on location for her new movie with Britney Cavell."

"Britney Cavell? Why do you say it like that? Have you met her, too?"

"No, I haven't. But you don't know the half of it."

"Tell me!"

"Let's just say I've never met the woman, but I already despise her."

"Are you going Hollywood on me?"

Julia grinned. "Doubtful, but I could go a little bit Malibu from time to time." She sighed. "You should see Rina's home. I've never even imagined anything that beautiful. You wake up and the Pacific is staring at you from the other side of the wall. Hot tubs, private chef, entourages, and ohmigosh, the art on the walls! She has one of those built-in bookcases with spotlights showcasing her Oscars and Golden Globe awards—and ones I'm not even familiar with. She took me to one of those fancy restaurants in Beverly Hills—a place whose food has nothing on ours except that it's ten times the price. But the dinner party she threw?"

"Yeah?" Cass sat on the edge of the seat waiting.

"Reese Collingworth, Monty Callan, Pinna Goddard…"

"Get outta here!"

Julia nodded. "Then Rina thanked everyone for coming to," Julia made air quotes, "'our first soirée as a couple.'"

"Ooh. Fancy. A soirée!"

Julia shook her head. "Soirée was your takeaway there, Cass? Really?"

"Yeah, why?"

"I'm stuck on the word 'couple.'"

Julia glanced up when the bells on the door jingled. "I've got it. Enjoy your coffee."

Julia seated two tables of four and took their drink orders. As she stood filling the glasses behind the counter, Cass leaned in from her right side.

"So she's really coming here tomorrow?" Cass whispered excitedly.

"Yes, but she has to cut her time short on account of the new movie."

"Okay, but promise me I get to meet her even if you break up."

Julia flashed her pal the girly smile, loaded the drinks onto her tray, and served them. She felt her cell phone vibrate in her pocket while taking lunch orders. Walking back to the kitchen, Julia glanced at her phone and met up with Cass at the salad station. "I think you might be right. Nicki just called."

"Did you answer?"

"No."

"Be careful. I'm telling you she's not going to stop until you get it through her head that it's over."

Julia leaned in and whispered. "She can't be coming around over the next couple of days. I don't want anything to get in the way of my time with Rina."

Cass nodded. "If you're going to be busy this week, when do you want to plan out and order the food for the first catering job?"

"Let's do it this afternoon when we close between lunch and dinner. It's also time you and Isabella got a bonus for all the extra work and for keeping our doors open."

"Thanks, Jules! I'll go ask Isabella if she can stay after the lunch rush."

Cass flipped the CLOSED sign and locked the door. Two of the three diner masterminds slid into the large round booth in the corner. Isabella joined them toting her order clipboard.

"So...whose party are we catering?" Julia asked.

"Nicki's cousin," Cass replied.

Julia exhaled. "Great. I'm not having much luck keeping her away from me, am I?"

Isabella comforted her with a pat on the hand. "Don't worry about her. She's afraid of me."

The girls laughed.

"Afraid? Of you?" Cass mocked.

Isabella stared her down.

"Stop that," said Cass. "It makes you look creepy!"

Isabella nodded and laughed. "Exactly!"

Julia picked up a pen and slid the clipboard in front of her. "Let's see what you have so far."

Cass flipped the top page and pointed to the list. "I spoke with the clients and based on that, Isabella came up with this menu."

"Since it's a brunch," Isabella began, "I thought we would do an omelette bar, a taco station, then the cooked entrees and sandwiches."

"Did you give them a soft quote yet?" asked Julia.

"No," said Cass.

"Okay, we'll offer two kinds of sandwiches—customer's top two preferences from their list. What cooked entrees have they decided on?"

"Barbeque chicken and grilled salmon," Isabella answered.

Julia made some notes on the clipboard. "Got it. I'll call this in as soon as we're done. Isabella, I've already told Cass you're getting bonuses, but I want to thank you both for all you do. Let's talk about your vision."

"Vision?"

"Yeah, Cass. You know, that retail idea you and Isabella have been tossing around."

"The population has grown with all the new golf community retirees. There's a lot of business passing us by on this road and on the freeway," said Isabella. "If we carry some specialty items in addition to prepared foods and frozen ones, we would expand our business."

Julia nodded. "We have enough room in the freezer, and we could get a small refrigerated case in the diner for customers to buy meals to take home."

"I think it would help a lot to advertise on a freeway billboard," Cass added.

Julia didn't have to think twice. "You're right. I think you guys have a winner. So, in catering and retail we'll be equal partners."

Isabella smiled wide. "Really? You sure we can afford it?"

"Well, sure! You two have been picking up the slack for me for the past few months. And this is your idea—so you should be sharing the profits."

"Partners!" Isabella twisted to look over her shoulder.

"Are you looking at Lucia?" asked Cass.

Isabella turned back to her. "It's more like Lucia is staring at us!"

"All three of us will have to work the first party," said Julia. "But we need to start hiring for the catering side of the business—especially before the big party." She looked at Isabella. "We need to hire you some kitchen help to train."

"But that will really cost a lot," Isabella replied.

"It's not a cost. It's an investment—a good one," Julia said.

Isabella nodded. "Jimmy has really been a big help here. I'll talk to him."

"Great," said Cass. "We'll need him to do some of the heavy lifting and to help clean up."

"Maybe he knows some people looking for work," Isabella added.

"Good. Anything else we need to address?" asked Julia.

"No." Cass stood and removed her apron. "Can you give me a price today on the first party so that I can call the customer before the dinner rush?"

"Sure," Julia replied.

"See you in a couple of hours." Cass grabbed her purse and left.

When the diner phone rang, Julia answered it. "Starlight." She paused. "Hi, Vitty. Right. That weekend will work out great. I'm glad I'll get to spend some time with my future brother-in-law. Let me know David's favorite meal—I'd like to get on his good side before we're actually related." She laughed. "Love you too. Yes, I'll tell her," she said before she hung up.

"Hey, Isabella, Vitty said she can't wait to see you because she has an important question to ask you."

"Oh? You have any idea what it is?"

"Nope. Not a clue."

Isabella held open the kitchen door and turned to Julia. "Are you coming to help or are you just going to stand there staring into space with that silly grin?"

CHAPTER THIRTY

The saturated air at daybreak sank heavy in Rina's chest. Even the parched desert flora strained to sift the humidity from the gray and homogeneous breeze. Clouds splintered into Rorshach patterns, celestial angels, and chunks of dancing bears drifting away to the east.

Rina placed her left foot in the stirrup and hoisted herself onto Thunder. She swung her leg over him and into the other stirrup, the leather saddle creaking as she centered her weight.

Julia watched her. "You're getting good at mounting the horse, Rina. That looked real natural."

Rina smiled. "Thanks to you, at least I'll look good getting on the horse in *The Big Picture*." She held her reins the way Julia had taught her. "There won't be one take where I'm not thinking of being with you. Being here."

Julia led Lightning to where Rina and Thunder waited. She grabbed the saddle's horn and, in one fluid and seasoned move, seated herself on her horse. "Smells like rain." Her boots slid into the stirrups with the same familiarity as feet sliding into slippers. "We won't go all the way up the mountain just in case."

"Are my eyes open?" Rina pulled her sunglasses down to the end of her nose and sighed at Julia. "Remind me again why we left your comfortable bed before dawn to come out here."

"Because you have a riding lesson, Ms. Verralta." She clicked her tongue to get the horses moving.

"So now I'm Ms. Verralta, huh?"

"Where else do I get to call you that? You don't think I'm going to call you that in bed, do you? Right now I'm your riding instructor."

"Yes, Miss Dearling. After you."

"Well, of course." Julia winked. "Lightning always precedes thunder."

Lightning stepped ahead at Julia's urging, his hooves clopping lazily against the desert floor. When they began the slow climb up the mountain trail, the percussion of hooves tapped out a natural equine synchronicity.

For the next several minutes Rina listened to every footfall the horses made and from behind watched the gentle sway of her lover in the saddle.

"I've never seen the saddle you're in. Why does it have Cary Grant's name stitched across the back?"

"Back in the day, Grandmother Lucia boarded his horse and they became friends. The saddle and stirrups were custom-made—no adjustments. So when he sold his horse, he gave the saddle to her as a gift. Of all the ranch hands through the years, my legs turned out to be the only ones long enough to fit the stirrups."

"Cary Grant, huh? So the Y2 has a legacy and I'm not its first movie star."

"No, but you're the only one I have hot sex with."

"Julia!"

Julia laughed hard. "Look around, Rina. I could shout it from the top of this mountain and still no one but you would hear me."

"If it wasn't for us riding, I don't think there would be a single sound up here. It's so quiet. I mean really quiet."

"That it is. Sometimes I wonder how my sister Vitty lives in New York. I'm sure it's real exciting, but all that noise—all the time—day in and day out. No open space to get away."

Thunder neighed.

"I think Thunder understood what you said and he agrees."

Julia chuckled. "Thunder is her horse so I wouldn't be surprised. He misses her, and I'm glad you two have hit it off. He's liked you since the first time you brushed him."

"Yes, he has." Rina leaned forward and patted the side of the horse's neck. "You're such a good boy, Thunder."

They climbed past the large striated rock. When they reached the first plateau, Julia turned Lightning around and pulled up beside Rina.

She stood in her stirrups and leaned over far enough to get a kiss. "Good morning, lover. How are you feeling so far?"

Rina paused to gaze into Julia's warm blue eyes.

Julia stilled Lightning and waited. "When you look at me that way, I swear I could forget my own name."

"You're so beautiful, Julia. Everything about you."

"Each time we're together I fall harder in love with you. Does that sound crazy?"

"Not to me it doesn't."

"Katarina, are you blushing again?"

"I like it when you call me Katarina. Not as much as when you call me Ms. Verralta, though."

They both laughed.

Julia's eyes opened wide. "Honestly? You like it?"

"There's that certain way you speak it—different from everyone else."

"Hmm. Then we must be ready to take this thing we have to the next level."

"What's the next level?"

Julia pointed into the distance. "Literally, the next level. There's someplace special I'd like to show you."

Rina winked at the cowgirl. "Someplace you haven't shown me already?"

"I've been saving it for a special day with you—but they're all special, so now is as good a time as any." Julia glanced up at the cocktail of clouds that had swiftly coalesced. "By the look of that dark cloud to the north, we might not make it there before it pours."

Rina stiffened. "What if we get caught in a storm?"

"I reckon we'll just have to tree-up," Julia said straight-faced.

"Tree-up? Tree-up! Please tell me that's a euphemism."

"Nope."

"You mean ride out a storm under a tree?"

Julia laughed. "Don't worry." She clicked her tongue to get the horses moving again.

"No, really," Rina began, "you know how storms frighten me. I'm not spending a storm under a tree!"

"Then you'd better get a move on, woman."

Julia took off and Rina raced after her, going faster than she ever had. The wind lifted her hair, blowing through each strand and giving her a sense of newfound freedom—without fear for the first time. She let Thunder run full out to catch up to Julia.

Julia slowed down a little until Rina was beside her.

"I can't believe I just ran on horseback!"

Julia smiled. "How did it feel?"

"Like flying. Have I told you how much I love the view of you in front of me? You ride like you were born in that saddle."

"Sometimes that's how it feels. As soon as I was big enough, I started riding bareback or with just a pad since I was too small for any stirrups we had. I fell in love with that oneness of motion. Being so close to the horse taught me everything I know about riding."

"No wonder you're so good in bed."

Julia held her gaze with a deep stillness that made Rina need to take a full breath.

"You really think it will rain?" Rina asked.

"We'll get something, but you never know what. In monsoon season all bets are off. Sometimes it looks like this all day, and the air is even heavier than it is right now, but then the rain never makes it to the desert floor. Other times, it comes on with the wrath of an evil spirit."

They reached the next fork in the trail. "This way," said Julia. They climbed a short path that quickly leveled out.

"You okay back there, Rina?"

"Just fine."

"Do you feel safe going a little faster? I think we need to pick up the pace."

"Lead the way."

Julia glanced over her shoulder. "Follow me, gorgeous." Julia tapped Lightning's side with her boot and the horse loped across the open space. She looked back every few seconds to see how Rina was doing and slowed down when they reached the next vista.

"Look at that!" Rina sighed. "It's magnificent—like a painting."

"I'll have to bring you here when the end-of-day colors are deep rose, periwinkle, and gold. So vibrant—and the air is crisp and dry."

"Can I count on that?"

Julia looked up. "See that dark hovering cloud? We need to keep moving."

As they cut across the mesa, a violent thunderclap echoed off the rocks.

"I'm grateful my horses don't spook in storms." Lightning neighed. "Don't make a liar out of me." Julia eased up on the reins.

Four steps later, the heavens opened into a downpour.

"Follow me, Rina!" Julia let Lightning set the pace on the path in the pouring rain.

"Is that some sort of shack up ahead?" Rina called out.

"Come on!" Julia raced to a quick halt at the door of the tiny log cabin. She slid off the horse and hastily removed Lightning's saddle while Rina caught up. "Hurry. Open the door!"

Julia tossed her saddle onto the floor. "Get inside!" She returned to Thunder, removed his saddle, and laid it next to hers. "I'll be right back after I tie these guys to the lean-to."

A dendritic blue lightning bolt cleaved the smoke-gray sky from top to bottom. Julia raced to the side of the cabin, leading the horses. By the time she reentered the outpost, her clothes were drenched—plastered against her skin like spandex on a metal hair band from the 1980s.

"Damn, that came on fast!" She slammed the door against the blowing wind and horizontal rain. "You'd think a girl—born and raised here—would have known better!" She sat on the nearest kitchen chair and removed her slightly soggy boots.

"The temperature dropped like twenty degrees in a few minutes! I'm freezing," said Rina, her teeth mildly chattering.

"Hold on, I'm going to fix that." Julia opened the cedar chest in front of the old wooden and leather bench and tossed a towel to Rina, who wrapped it tightly around herself to stem the chill.

Julia pulled a plastic bag from her saddlebag. "Here," she said holding it out to Rina. "Put these on."

"What's this?"

"Sweats."

Rina shivered as she undressed.

Julia stood there, lips slightly parted, wide-eyed, watching. "God, you're gorgeous like this."

"Darling, is it sexy the way I climb into sweats? I haven't worn sweats since the 1980s! Since Jane Fonda's workouts."

"The eighties, huh?" Julia peeled off her wet jeans.

Rina scrunched her eyes closed and shook her head when she realized what she had said. Her eyes popped open. "Oh my god, you weren't even born yet. Aren't you freezing?"

"Maybe. But it's worth it to watch you look at me the way you are right now."

"Were you a Girl Scout?"

"Nope." Julia hastily stripped off the rest of her clothes. "I taught the Girl Scouts everything they needed to know about ranch life."

Rina raised an eyebrow. "I'll bet you did."

"Wanna like me even more right now?"

"Not possible. You're already naked."

Julia smiled. "I have snacks. But I need to put on some dry clothes!"

Rina waited for Julia to return from the tiny bedroom and laughed when she saw her. "A Big Apple sweatshirt out here in no man's land?"

"My sister gave it to me on her first trip home after she moved to New York." She retrieved a pair of jeans from her saddlebag and slid into them. "That feels much better."

"Talk about absolutely adorable," said Rina. "Could you be any more adorable?" She kissed Julia lightly at first, savoring the pounding of the rain, the sweetness of Julia's lips that fit hers perfectly. "I'm addicted to kissing you," she whispered. "I can never get enough."

"When you kiss me like that, Katarina, each time feels like the first time we ever kissed."

As unpredictable as the lightning strikes, Rina grabbed Julia, pulled her in, and kissed her until they gasped for air. Their tongues teased, and the more their hands stroked the more erratic their breathing became. Each irreverent sensation belonged to this moment that transcended any passion Rina had known—any hope she'd ever held that had yet to be answered. All of it—in one kiss.

Julia pulled away slowly and flashed the shy smile that Rina had come to love. She lit some oil lamps and led Rina by the hand to the old leather sofa. "Let's get comfortable. We're going to be here for a while."

Rina placed her head on Julia's shoulder and sighed. She gazed up at the ceiling and took in the view of the cabin from where they sat. "What *is* this place? A log cabin in the middle of nowhere, and I do mean nowhere. Honestly, I thought the Y2 was in the middle of nowhere, but compared to this, the ranch is like being in a traffic jam in downtown Los Angeles on a Friday at rush hour."

"Welcome to my cabin. I only bring special girls up here," Julia teased.

"This is yours?"

"Yep. We're still on my land."

"Really?"

Julia nodded. "Everywhere we rode today is part of the Y2. My dad built this place after he had kids as a sort of getaway. Once Vitty and I were old enough to ride up here on our own, well, let's say that some unlucky kids only get a tree house."

The open fireplace, old chairs, and tables added a minimum requisite charm to the basic two-room with the log walls. Rina stood and walked to the small window by the door. "I can feel your eyes on me from behind, Julia."

"With your hair wet, standing there by the door…" Julia rose and sauntered in her direction, "it reminds me of…"

"Our first night." Rina turned and let Julia press her up against the wall in a steamy first-kiss-redux. But this time, their lips met with a newfound hunger—in their secret getaway where rain pummeled and wind sheared, where bursts of thunder rumbled through the walls and from the floor up through Rina's wet body. In this place, where the only character she needed to play was herself—unscripted, where paparazzi had no access to all that cured her—she had an epiphany. *If I can't be in love here, I can't be in love anywhere!*

"Come with me," said Julia, leading Rina to the bedroom.

"Wait. Are Thunder and Lightning okay?"

"I love that you care about the horses."

"Should we bring them inside?"

Julia laughed. "They're not dogs, Katarina."

"Yes, but they're used to the barn. Maybe we should check on them."

Julia exhaled hard. "By 'we' you mean me. You're not going to let this go, are you?"

"No."

"Fine. Let me change back into my wet clothes."

"Be careful out there. I'll wait at the door."

Dressed in cold, soaked clothing with a parka tossed over her, Julia sprinted into the deluge. She sloshed back into the cabin within the long side of a minute. "They're fine," she said, dripping inside the door. "They're tucked away against the wind and rain on three sides and under the roof. Happy?" She hung the parka on a hook by the door and removed her now slightly soggier boots. "I'm freezing!" Hastily tossing some logs and kindling into the fireplace, Julia struck a long match and stood as close as she could to the growing flames while she dried off and changed into her dry clothes.

Rina sat on the love seat, watching her. "I feel much better knowing Thunder and Lightning are okay."

"How about a hot coffee?"

"That sounds perfect."

Julia connected a small propane tank to the two-burner stove. She reached into the cabinet, found the old dented percolator, and filled it with water and coffee from a generic can labeled "Coffee."

"You're going to have to drink it cowgirl style. I lacked the foresight to pack cream or that Beverly Hills sweetener you like," Julia teased.

Rina moved to Julia and from behind slid her arms around her waist, resting her chin on Julia's shoulder. "I think I can handle it, you know—'cowgirl style.'" She kissed the back of Julia's neck.

Julia turned around and slipped beyond Rina. She picked up the pile of clean horse blankets and dropped them in front of the hot fire, then stared into her lover's eyes. "Oh? You sure about that?"

Rina shot her her hottest Oscar-worthy come-on look. "Try me— Cowgirl."

The all-consuming fire had long been reduced to embers and ash. Rina rolled on top of Julia and kissed her again, savoring the warmth of Julia's breasts pressed against her own—the wool blankets haphazardly covering their naked bodies from the waist down. "The rain stopped an hour ago. Shouldn't we head back to the ranch?"

Julia grinned. "Damn, I was hoping you hadn't noticed."

Rina looked down into her lover's eyes. "I could stay like this with you forever."

"Careful, you're such a great actress, I'll believe you."

"You should believe me. I mean it."

"But it'll never happen."

"Why do you say that?"

"You'd miss your big life."

"My 'big' life?"

"Compared to mine? Compared to well, anyone, yeah, your life is very big."

"Hmm. You're right. It is a big life."

Julia sighed when Rina rolled to her side. "I can't believe you're leaving tomorrow to go home and then on location. I'm starting to feel withdrawal symptoms, and you were inside me until five minutes ago."

"I know what you mean. You go out to the barn and I'm jonesing for your touch. But once I'm on set and see the shooting schedule, I'll look for a time when you can fly in for a day or two. I had Gigi check flights from Palm Springs to Vancouver. It only takes a few hours."

"Are you sure that would be okay? To have me up there...you know, while you're working? With Britney Cavell?"

"I don't know how I'll make it through without seeing you. I really want you to come. Say you'll come to see me."

Julia tossed her lover her favorite grin—the sarcastic one. "I don't know, Katarina. It's an awfully long ride for a booty call."

"Oh you're a bad, bad girl, Ms. Dearling."

Julia lifted an eyebrow. "Ms. Dearling?"

"Yes. Oh! You mean hot sex in a cabin wasn't included in the riding lesson?"

"The lesson and the sex? Compliments of the Y2."

Rina stroked Julia's soft hair. "You always only give. Before you, I'd never been with someone who wasn't trying to get something from me."

"Who says I'm not?" Julia teased.

"Let's cut to the chase then. What is it you want?"

"You—all over me. Forever."

The shock of pure honesty—the sensation of Julia, and of being truly loved, momentarily caused Rina to stop breathing. She took a deep breath finally but remained speechless.

"Rina, I hate that by this time tomorrow you'll be gone." Julia stroked Rina's cheek—gazed into eyes that had mesmerized audiences around the world—eyes that in this moment were meant only for her. "Your eyes are a color I've never seen before."

"Which one?"

"Sad."

"What color is that?"

"Gray."

Rina stared at the embers before speaking. "I need to know that you won't leave me while we're apart."

"Have you not been paying attention here? Now why would I ever do that?"

"You're young, beautiful, and ridiculously sexy. I'm sure there are plenty of women who would say yes to you and that great ass without a second thought."

Julia frowned. "But I wouldn't be asking. I only want you. Then again, there must be stables of women I don't know about who pursue you." She paused. "You wouldn't string me along if you wanted to date someone else, though, right?"

Rina scoffed. "Why would you even think that? Why would I ever want anyone else when there is you?"

"I have a long history of trusting people I shouldn't—of not knowing someone's leaving until they do."

Rina wrapped herself around her naked lover and whispered into her ear. "It seems to me that we're ready to make some kind of commitment."

"You mean you want to…like…go steady?"

Rina pulled back. "What? Steady!"

Julia laughed. "Well, yeah. You're never going to put a ring on it—which became pretty clear from our conversation on the beach."

"Julia Dearling, I never said any such thing!"

"It's implied. If you never come out, how can you be married?"

"I never really looked at it that way. Don't change the subject. I want a commitment from you."

"You're so dramatic."

"Julia. We all play to our strengths."

"Really? A commitment?"

Rina chuckled. "Right now, you have the goofiest grin. I don't want you to feel pressured, especially if you're not ready. But what do you say, Julia? Want to 'go steady'?"

"I say our clothes are dry, and that it's time to mount up and head home."

Rina withdrew and went silent.

Julia kissed her lips. "Are you kidding me? I'd love to go steady with you."

"I can't believe I have to use the term, 'going steady.'" Rina squinted at her. "It's bad enough we have almost a thirty-year age difference."

Julia waited a beat. "Twenty-six."

Rina hesitated. "Right. Twenty-six."

"And a half."

CHAPTER THIRTY-ONE

Julia sat on the edge of the bed, and Rina allowed the awkwardness between them to settle into the desert stillness. With the window open, she inhaled the ranch essence that would have to last her for the next few months, savored Thunder's neigh from the hitching post off the porch. She glanced at Julia in the mirror and smiled into her eyes.

"I wish it was still yesterday—up in the cabin," said Julia.

"Where did the last twenty-four hours go?"

"They're where all memories of us go—locked away deep inside me for safekeeping." Julia leaned forward, her elbows on her knees.

"I don't know exactly when I'll be able to call, but I will as soon as I can," Rina said as she put on her earrings. "The call I got this morning? After all the table reads, they've decided to do some rewrites while we're filming—more lines to learn."

"Don't worry about it." Julia sat up and held her gaze. "This? What we have…was never supposed to have happened in the first place, let alone last."

Rina spun around to face her. "But I asked you to 'go steady' and you accepted. I know you, Julia. You're waiting for that other shoe to drop. But it won't. I simply won't have it."

"I'm saying that I'm not asking for promises, Rina. Life has a strange way of intervening no matter what we want. Asking me to go steady is a beautiful gesture on your part, but it's not like we're engaged. You'll be far away, spending every day with Britney—costar, ex-lover—and there's nothing I can do about that."

"Why do you have to be such a grown-up?"

Julia stood and crossed the room. "Because someone has to be."

"But…"

Julia interrupted her by placing her finger gently against Rina's lips. "I have a lot to do once you're gone. Besides my normal diner schedule, the catering business is picking up, your sculpture is in dire need of attention. There are also the horses and then my sister's wedding to plan."

"But you'll wait for me?" Rina asked softly.

"Will you come back to me?"

Rina sighed. "I told you, I'm not interested in Britney!"

"You never answered me when I asked if she was still interested in you."

"It doesn't matter. I don't care what she wants."

"Maybe you'll care after a month with her. She understands your world."

"But you understand me. I'm done talking about her." Rina fished through her case and pulled out the small square red box. She peeled back the lid and presented the delicate pink gold necklace to Julia.

Julia tilted the box and read from the inside of the lid. "Cartier?"

"I found the interlocking rings and chain so beautiful in pink gold." Rina turned the box so that she could remove the chain. "It's called the Love necklace. Appropriate, isn't it?" She put the box down and displayed the chain across both of her hands.

"I know you, too, Rina. You planned this, didn't you?"

Rina smiled from the corner of her lips. "I really wanted to give you a little token to make you smile before I left."

"But I have nothing to give you."

"Julia, what you have given me is worth more than all of these in the world." She unlocked the clasp.

"That's so beautiful—you don't need to give me that."

"Oh, but I do." She walked behind Julia, draped it around her neck, and hooked it together. "Will you keep it on at least until we're together again?"

Julia touched it gently and turned to face Rina. "Always…except when I'm afraid something will happen to it." She kissed her lover. "I love you with every breath and that's not going to change—except for the fact that when you're not with me…"

"Don't look down." Rina gently lifted Julia's chin until their eyes met. "What is it? You can say anything to me."

"I feel so empty without you. It's a god-awful feeling. Hollow—as if all that I am leaves with you every time."

Rina held her close. "I feel it too—it's called being in love. But we have phones, and FaceTime…"

Julia smirked. "And a shooting schedule, in addition to everything else I mentioned."

"It will work out, okay?"

Julia gazed into her eyes and then gathered Rina's belongings. "Your driver is waiting. Come on, I'll bring your suitcase downstairs."

Rina waited until Julia was halfway down the stairs. Her gaze danced slowly around the bedroom, snapping every mental picture she could catalogue. She picked up Julia's pillow and pressed it to her face. Her eyes closed, she inhaled deeply—then she did it again. The tear that escaped barely made it onto her cheek before she wiped it away.

Rina descended the steps slowly and stared into her lover's eyes.

Julia held up takeout containers from the Starlight. "I packed some healthy snacks for your ride home."

Rina panned the great room and the cold fireplace with the logs that had burned to nothing while they had made love in its warmth. She ached for more. The chill of saying goodbye ran rampant through her, and for a moment she froze in place—unwilling to go back to a life that Julia didn't inhabit. She slowly approached the sculptress, wordless, her breathing irregular.

"It's okay, Rina. I'm not an actor, so we don't have to say goodbye with awkward silences and dramatic pauses."

"Yes, we do. It's the dramatic pauses that make or break the scene. And in case you've forgotten…"

Julia touched Rina's lips. "I could never forget."

"Sometimes you're maddening."

"Why?"

"Because you're just letting me go. Scenes likes this one are supposed to contain drama and passion and tension."

"What makes you think this one doesn't? Or do you just not know how to play the scene?" Julia smiled into Rina's welcoming eyes. "I can still see our first hello and every single moment right up till now—our goodbye. Perhaps you've forgotten what passion and tension feel like in real life."

"It's more like—I've never known."

"Wow, you really *do* know how to deliver a line."

Julia cradled Rina's hand, closed the space between them and spoke softly into her ear. "Whatever happens, or doesn't, I'm in love with you, Katarina Verralta. Keep that with you in good times and not-so-good times."

Rina grabbed Julia and kissed her with all the passion she knew how to convey. She tried to say the words—she desperately wanted to say them. Inside her head, she screamed them. *Marry me, Julia.* Her lips parted, but only her breath escaped.

Julia smiled, her emotion causing a quiver to pull at her lips. "It's time." Julia walked outside and handed the suitcase to Rina's driver. He placed it in the trunk and opened the limo door.

"Give us a moment," Rina said to her chauffeur. She waited for him to get into the car.

"I'll call you when I get settled," said Rina.

"Baby, don't make promises you may not keep. You know how I feel about you, and you know where I live. Text me when you get home so I know you made it?"

Rina nodded, wiped a tear that escaped, and then smiled. "Leaving you is torture."

"Well, that's a whole lot better than if being with me was torture."

Rina chuckled. "Leave it to you to find the bright side." She touched Julia's hand and got into the car.

Julia closed her door, then unhitched Thunder from the post on the porch, and mounted him bareback. As they accompanied the limo down the long dusty drive, Julia smiled down at Rina, who stared up at her through the window. When they arrived at the gate, Julia dismounted to lock it and wave goodbye.

Rina's last view of her lover was of her closing the gate to the Y2, with Julia on the wrong side of the fence.

CHAPTER THIRTY-TWO

Three lonely weeks had passed before Julia smiled willingly. Each day since Rina's departure, she'd found herself making excuses for her lover when she hadn't heard from her. *Rina lives a big life, in an important world*, she told herself. *She's filming, learning lines, working for her next Oscar.* Then Julia would push it all from her mind to sculpt or cook or ride—whatever it had taken to keep her sane in the moment.

Julia jumped off the porch with her arms opened wide. "You made it!"

Vitty brought the rental car to an abrupt halt and hopped out to embrace her sister. "Hi, Juju!"

While they hugged with a vengeance, Vitty's fiancé David got out of the car and walked toward them. "Wow, it really is like I'm seeing double!" Tall and fit with a shock of pitch-black wavy hair and a bright smile, Julia's future brother-in-law leaned in for a hug.

"Great to finally meet you in person," he said.

"I'll say! You weren't kidding, Vitty. He sure is tall and handsome."

Vitty put her arm around his waist. "And smart and sweet. David, you're the real deal."

He leaned into her. "I must have something to have landed your sister, Julia."

"Well, welcome home, you two! How was the drive from Palm Springs?"

David raised his eyebrows and his eyes widened. "Your sister is a speed demon, so we made ridiculously good time."

"It's a family trait," said Julia. "We Dearlings grew up in wide open spaces, so we know what to do with them."

David laughed. "Vittoria reminds me regularly. White knuckles and all, I finally get to visit the famous Y2 and see what all the fuss is about."

Vitty pointed west toward the rose-colored twilight sky. "Just wait until tomorrow when I take you riding up that mountain."

"On a horse?" he asked.

Vitty turned to Julia. "He's nature-challenged."

"We'll fix that, David," Julia teased.

"I can see why you miss it, Vittoria. That's a beautiful sky." He took a deep breath. "And the Y2 smells way better than the subway."

Julia chuckled. "Until you hit the barn at the wrong time on a brutally hot summer day. Do you need help with your gear?"

David walked back to the car. "No, we're traveling pretty light since it's only for a couple of days." He lifted the two small suitcases from the trunk, closed it, and followed the girls inside.

"It smells great in here," said David.

"There's a reason for that," Vitty said. "What you're smelling is Grandmother Lucia's cacciatore a la Julia."

David smiled. "If it tastes as good as it smells, I'm prepared to eat whatever you place in front of me. Not for nothing, Julia, but I wish your sister had gotten the cooking gene."

Julia turned to him. "The beauty about my twin and me is that if there's something one of us didn't get, the other one probably did. Together, we make the perfect woman. So what did you decide, Vitty? Casita or house?"

"We didn't come all this way to not be under the same roof as you!" Vitty answered.

"Are you guys hungry?"

"Why? Is dinner ready?" asked David.

"I'll take that as a yes. Why don't you get settled and I'll have dinner on the table in—say—fifteen?"

"First things first," answered Vitty. "David, come meet Thunder and Lightning."

"I liked that sculpture of him that you gave to Vittoria," David said to Julia. "I'm guessing the real Thunder is a bit bigger?"

"Come on," said Vitty. "We won't be long—I know you're starving."

Vitty led David into the dining room. "Candles and vino and flowers? You went all out, Juju. I feel so special."

"I wanted tonight to be special and for David's introduction to ranch life to be a good one."

"It is!" he laughed. "I've already watched my almost-step-horse give my future wife a big welcome home, and I'm about to gorge myself on all this beautiful food. Look at this feast!"

"Don't be shy—I made enough to feed a small army."

"I see that."

Julia placed a hot baguette in the center of the table.

Once they were seated, David filled the wineglasses from the open bottle on the table. "I'd like to make a toast. To the two prettiest girls I know—one of whom I'm going to marry and the other who's going to have a frequent dinner guest. Thanks for doing all this, Julia."

"You're welcome. I'm glad you're here—I always wanted a brother."

Everyone dug into the meal that channeled the best of Grandmother Lucia. From the antipasti with the fresh roasted peppers, to the cacciatore, to the lasagna and sautéed spinach.

David ripped off a hunk of the freshly baked bread and dunked it in the cacciatore sauce. "Please learn how to cook this," he said to his fiancée. "I'm begging you."

"Or you could learn how to make it." Vitty laughed. "Um, that perfect woman Julia mentioned? Yeah, this is her domain, like finance is ours, babe. Julia, you'll be very happy when you see your returns this year. You made some good investments."

"If you say so." She looked at David. "See how that works? Which would you rather have—someone who can cook or someone who's so smart she can afford to take you wherever you want to go for dinner *and* pay for it?"

He smiled. "I don't know. I'd pay a fortune for this meal—it's that good."

"I keep urging Julia to come to New York and be a chef. I think she'd clean up in that town." Vitty savored her next bite.

"Without a doubt," David said.

"No," Julia said. "Really?"

The resounding "yes" captured the best of the guest duet.

"It sounds good, until the city strangles me, and what about the horses? And space. And…"

Vitty stopped eating and stared at her sister. "And?"

"And I'd be on the wrong coast to be with Rina."

"Oh?" said Vitty. "Is this still the same woman in LA?"

Julia felt her face flush. "Yes."

Vitty took another bite. "You know, now that you mention it, why haven't you been talking about her? It's not like you."

"There'll be time for all of that later. She had to go away for work, and frankly I'm missing her terribly. Right now, I just want to love the fact that you and David are here."

"What does she do that has her traveling?" asked David.

"She's away on location—working on a film."

"You never did tell me exactly what she does, Juju."

"You know me. If it isn't about the horses, cooking, or the ranch, it goes in one ear and out the other."

"When will she be back?" David asked.

Julia sighed. "I reckon as soon as she can come."

David chuckled. "You 'reckon'?"

"Yep. Why?"

"It's just cute the way you say that. Makes this New Jersey boy feel like a cowboy—on a ranch—chowing down with my woman."

Vitty laughed. "I think you've watched too many cowboy movies."

"Did you guys want to talk about the wedding tonight or wait until tomorrow?" asked Julia.

Vitty thought about it. "How are you planning on catering it and being my maid of honor at the same time?"

"The catering side is starting to take off and we've already started hiring staff to handle that."

"That's great, sis. I'm proud of you."

"I'll cook the lasagnas ahead of time, and Isabella and Cass will oversee everything beforehand. I don't know what I'd do without them. They came up with this great idea of packaging for retail and advertising on billboards. I made them full partners in that side of the business."

Vitty nodded with an approving smile. "You really think that'll work out here?"

"It already is. We've gotten very busy at the diner, and new catering requests are coming in every week. Isabella and I are creating some new dishes and it's bringing in a large dinner crowd."

Vitty looked at David and then back at Julia. "Remember when I called you at the diner and said I had something to ask Isabella?"

"I do. What was it?"

"I'd like her to be my matron of honor."

"Aww, Vitty, she's going to love that."

"I hope so." She took a sip of wine and then a deep breath. "On a very different note," she hesitated, "I heard from Mom again."

Julia remained silent and waited for Vitty to continue.

"I told her I'm getting married—here."

"And?"

"Well, she is our mother—and it is my wedding."

Julia bristled. "I really don't want to see her."

"She wants to come. She wants to see you, but she said she'd only attend if you were okay with it."

Julia downed her wine and poured another glass. "Maria is about a decade late, Vitty. I haven't even heard from her since last Christmas."

"Better late than never?"

"Look, I know you must see her from time to time in New York…"

"How do you know that?"

"We're twins. I know," Julia said sarcastically.

Vitty reached across the table and placed her hand on Julia's. "Maybe we could get the band back together? For my wedding?"

"So if I say no then I'll always be the bad guy for having deprived my sister on her wedding day. I'm in a no-win here. Oh, man!" She exhaled hard and stared at her doppelganger. "You actually want her here?"

"I do, Jules."

"Okay. It's your wedding, and if you want her here, then you should have that."

"Can I add something?" asked David.

The girls looked at him. "I've met her, Julia. She doesn't seem anything like the woman who left you two. I know she misses you terribly, but from what Vitty has shared with me, I can only imagine how hard this must be for you. If it helps to know, Maria's done a lot of therapy. Maybe she'll surprise you in a good way."

"I doubt it," said Julia. "The one thing Maria Dearling could never be accused of is a good surprise. I'm not going to pretend to be happy to see her because I'm not. I'm…not. But I won't get in the way of her coming to the wedding as long as she leaves me alone. And she has to stay at the motel with the out-of-towners. Fair enough?"

Vitty nodded. "If it's the best you can do, then that's all I can ask of you."

David fidgeted. "It wasn't my place to butt in. Sorry, Julia."

"It's okay—it's a sore subject. Let's talk about something pleasant. Like decaf cappuccinos and cannoli?"

"You don't have to ask me twice." David stood and began clearing the table.

Julia stood and smiled. "I've got this. Vitty, how about you and David build a little fire and I'll be back with dessert and those coffees?"

Vitty raced around the table and hugged Julia. "Thank you for everything! The one thing Mom did do right was to give us each other. It's so good to be home."

"Yeah, it sure is good to have you here."

David laughed. "Okay, side by side, now it's starting to freak me out how alike the two of you are. Forget that you look like carbon copies—but even your mannerisms…"

"Better remember which door is your bedroom, Davy," Julia teased.

"Davy? I look like a Davy to you?"

Julia winked at him. "Nah, I just wanted to see if I could get a rise out of ya."

"Yep," he said, "carbon copies."

CHAPTER THIRTY-THREE

Alone in her hotel room, Gigi answered her cell phone on the first ring. She listened intently when the man who called spoke.

"So, you're saying you've already sent me everything you have?" She paused. "Good, that will do for now. I'll be in touch."

She ended the call, picked up her purse, and rolled her carry-on suitcase down the hall to Rina's suite. She knocked once and used her card key to enter.

"Come on in, Gigi," said Rina. "Are you getting ready to go?"

"I'm leaving now. My flight's at eight-fifteen, so by the time I land and get to Malibu, it'll be too late to call you."

"That's okay. Make sure the contractor handles the tile issues first."

"No problem. He said everything on the list will only take a day, so assuming he finishes tomorrow, I'll fly back the day after."

"Good."

"Reese called. He wants you to stop by his suite on your way to dinner."

"He's going to make me late." Rina put her phone in her purse.

"I don't think so. He said he had a few notes for you that he wanted you to think about before tomorrow." Gigi checked her watch. "I have to get going. Text me if you need anything else."

"Thanks, Gigi. I'll walk out with you. I don't know what I'd do without you to take care of this stuff at home."

You'll never know the half of it. Gigi thought of the call she had just taken from the private investigator she had hired. She nodded at Rina. "Thanks." She grabbed the handle of her carry-on and they got onto the elevator together.

"What's Reese's suite number again?"

"Two-oh-nine," Gigi answered.

Rina got off on the second floor. "See you in a couple of days."

"Have fun at dinner with Britney," Gigi said, tongue-in-cheek.

*   *   *

Forty-five minutes later, Rina entered Les Nouveaux, the latest in French fusion restaurants on the Vancouver waterfront. Luxury dining at its finest. She was glad to be away from the movie set, even if it meant having dinner with Britney.

Filming with her has been fine—why shouldn't dinner go smoothly?

Britney was staring out at the water when the maître d' led Rina around the room's equator to the corner table. For an instant, her profile reminded Rina of a long time ago. Except back then, the restaurant was in Laguna Beach—and they were still together.

"Oh! Hi, Rina, I didn't see you coming."

"Hi, Brit." Rina sat on the cushy upholstered dining chair in the bright and trendy restaurant with the high ceilings and top-to-bottom glass. "I'm sorry I'm late. Reese wanted to see me before I left the hotel." She looked up at the waiter. "Sparkling water with lime, please."

"I'll have one also," said Britney. "Isn't this view great?"

Rina panned the waterscape. In the distance, the dome-shaped mountains of granite dipped into a trough—their arcs converging at the base into a low hammock written in stone. "Lovely. I've heard very good things about the food, too."

"I know. The fresh fish and seafood look spectacular."

"That's why Gigi had suggested it."

Britney relaxed into her chair. "I'm glad we're taking this break away from the set. From all those people."

Rina nodded. "Well, I did agree to have dinner with you once we were on location. We still have a long way to go, but you're right. It's a nice break."

The waiter poured two glasses of sparkling water and left the bottle. Britney raised her glass. "To a successful film." She smiled slyly.

"Who knows? We may both get nominated for Best Actress for this one. Maybe next time around you'll even beat me."

"I'll drink to that," Rina replied. "How do you think it's going?"

"Mixed feelings about that last take we shot today."

"I'm glad you said that. Reese wasn't happy with it either. He suggested you and I talk about our chemistry tonight so that we can reshoot it tomorrow."

"What was wrong with our chemistry? For better or worse we always have chemistry."

"I felt our timing was kind of lackluster," said Rina.

"It's good that we all agree it wasn't right. What do you think was missing?"

"You."

Britney raised her eyebrows. "Me?"

Rina returned to browsing through the menu. "Yes, you."

"What do you mean I was missing today?"

Rina looked up at her. "I don't know. It seemed like you were distracted. Are you okay?"

"Now that you mention it, I was a little distracted."

"What was up?"

"Nothing really."

Rina waited a beat. "You forget I know you better than you do."

"I used to resent that about you."

"And now?"

"Now I just find it annoying."

"Progress. Good for you." Rina focused on the menu. "Do you know what you're having?"

"Why? Are we on a time limit?"

"Actually, I am. I need to get a lot of rest to shoot the horse scenes tomorrow."

Britney chuckled. "Not as young as we used to be, huh?"

"In my riding lessons, I used to arrive early to breathe and slow down...and to talk to the horse."

"Talk to the horse?"

"Yes, I find it prepares us both to ride. There's this connection with a horse that can be special." Rina thought of the last time she had brushed Thunder with Julia's hand guiding hers. "Kind of Zen."

"Well, you sure have changed." She laughed. "Pardon me, but the thought of you in a barn strikes me as funny."

Barns are very sexy. Rina smiled. "Clay is with you on that. He can barely bring it up without laughing. But the truth is, you're right—I have changed."

They paused to order dinner and continued talking shop until it arrived. By the time they took their first bites, they had decided on how they wanted to reshoot the scene from earlier.

"We'll call Reese when we finish?" Rina asked.

"Sure. I think he'll like what we came up with."

"Me too."

Peacefully, they chatted about Reese and his vision for the tone of the film and their horse scene together the next morning.

"Hey, Rina, it's nice to be able to sit and just talk with you. I miss that. Look, I know it's long overdue, but I've really wanted to apologize for what an ass I was when we had lunch in Beverly Hills."

Rina stopped eating and stared at her. "Thank you, I appreciate that. Why were you being such a brat anyway?"

"You know why."

"Honestly, I don't. Was it because you had just broken up with Linnie?"

"No, it was because I had realized how fucked up it was to have left you for her."

"Water under the bridge, Brit."

Britney paused and searched the far reaches of the room, out to its most distant corners before her gaze came to fall on Rina. "You look very pretty tonight. The way that candle reflects in your eyes…"

"Stop right there," Rina said softly. "I know where you're going with this and it's not going to happen."

Britney stopped speaking until the waiter cleared the table and left. "Why not? You used to believe in second chances."

"Yes—six chances ago. I no longer have those feelings for you."

"I get it. You want to make sure I get a good dose of my own medicine."

"What? No!"

"Would you care to see our dessert cart?" asked the waiter.

"No!" they answered automatically.

"I'll have a decaf cappuccino," said Rina.

"Make it two," Britney added.

"Right away," said the waiter.

"No. I'm not trying to give you a dose of your own medicine. You must have us confused—that's your style, not mine."

Britney laughed.

"What's so funny?"

"I can't help remembering how pissed off I was at you when we had that little dinner party, and I put cayenne pepper in what I thought was your food…"

Rina issued a guffaw. "Poor Gigi. Oh my god, I thought her face would explode it was so red! It took a week for her taste buds to come back."

"I'll let you in on a secret. Being a bitch wasn't as easy as I made it look. I was a better actress than you gave me credit for."

"Oh, come on, honey, you were a natural! I've never underestimated your talent. It was your character I didn't trust."

They smiled into each other's eyes, Rina wondering what Britney was really like now. What it would have been like had she only gone to the dark side a little less often.

Britney took a sip of her cappuccino and gently placed the cup in the saucer. "Do you still find me attractive?"

"It's not a matter of opinion. You are attractive."

"That's not what I meant and you know it."

Rina sighed. "Brit, a part of me will always be attracted to you."

"Then why not us?"

"Because I know now what it's like to be attracted to who someone *is*, on every level. Someone who never feels a need to diminish me or compete with me—someone who knows how to love who I really am."

"I love who you really are."

Rina tried not to say it but lost the battle. "Sadly, you never knew who I really was."

"So there's someone in your life now."

"That topic is off limits."

"Why, Rina? Don't you trust yourself?"

In a flash, Rina saw who they used to be together—when it was good between them. "Why on earth would you think that?"

"Because I saw your expression just now when I asked you if you trusted yourself."

"Well, I don't know what you think you saw…"

"I know what I saw."

"It's getting late," said Rina. "Let's quit while we're ahead, Brit—before anything bad happens."

When the maître d' came to tell them their limo was waiting, they stood to leave the restaurant. As usual, everyone turned to look at them, and Rina smiled graciously on the way out. Partitioned from the driver, they had a brief call with Reese from the limo and then rode in silence for the next few minutes.

"Rina, is there ever a time when you think of us?"

"I'm sure I have."

"Are the thoughts ever good ones?"

Rina glanced away and then looked back at Britney. "You and I have been almost everywhere two people can go, except the one place where it all fit together."

"Who is she?"

"No one you know or that anyone you know knows."

"What is it about us? No matter how bratty I've been in the past or how many sarcastic digs you throw at me, we still have chemistry. That's why we were cast opposite one another. We have chemistry— we always have and we always will."

Rina stared into her eyes.

Britney slid close to her. "It's there and you know it."

Britney passed her hand along Rina's thigh.

Rina pushed it away. "I can't believe you. Have you ever had any respect for me or what I want?"

"I can feel the attraction, Rina."

Rina felt her face flush. "Well…"

"Well, what?" Britney smiled and stroked Rina's cheek.

"Well, it's not going to happen. Not this time."

Britney leaned back and studied her. "Were you this loyal to me when we were together?"

With a nostalgic smile, Rina nodded.

"I really did blow it with you. Each time. Okay, have your fling. Knowing you, it can't last forever."

Rina stared at her. "No need to push my buttons, Brit. She isn't a fling, and if I'm lucky enough to have her, I'm hoping it will last forever." *I can't wait to hear Julia's voice tonight.*

Britney smirked. "Nice try. I'm not buying it."

"Why?"

"Because your image, your brand won't allow for it. You would never allow it to get out there. Whoever she is, she'll eventually figure that out and that will be the end of it."

Rina was first out of the limo the instant it stopped in front of the hotel. Britney followed her inside and into the elevator. As soon as the door closed and they were alone, Britney grabbed Rina and planted a kiss on her lips.

Rina pushed her backward. "Stop it!"

The elevator door opened to Britney's floor first. She stepped out, turned back to Rina, and smiled. "That push was a split second too late to actually convince me. Night, Rina."

When the door closed, Rina leaned back against the wall and exhaled hard.

She'll never change! Still *a good kisser, though. Dammit!*

CHAPTER THIRTY-FOUR

Dead on her feet after preparing for the Starlight's next catering job, Julia yawned five times while steering lazily toward home. Somehow, even the sports car seemed to know how tired she was, and it wouldn't drive faster than the speed limit. When her headlights caught a reflection on the dark road near the ranch, she turned on her high beams. Nicki's black Mustang was parked off the road by her gate. She rolled to a stop beside it and got out.

She looked through the partially open passenger window to see Nicki sleeping in the driver's seat. "Nicki? Great. What are you doing sleeping outside my gate? Nicki! Wake up!" Still no response, Julia opened the door, reached across, and blared the horn.

Nicki jolted awake. "Huh?" Bleary eyed, she adjusted her head position and rapidly blinked several times. "Juliaaaa. You're home," she smiled.

"Please tell me you didn't drive drunk!"

Nicki grinned and held up an anonymous bottle wrapped in a brown paper bag. "Nope! Did all my drinking right here, waiting for you. But, but, you get home so late."

"All right, don't drive. I'm going to pull my car inside the gate and then drive your car to the house. Climb into the passenger seat."

Julia pulled her car inside the gate, grabbed her gear, and walked back to Nicki's car. She got in and dumped her stuff on Nicki's lap. "What the hell are you thinking, Nicki?"

"I'm thinking...that's a really nice car, Julia. Where did you get that car?"

Julia backed up the Mustang and jolted it forward. "At a car store."

Nicki laughed. "A car store. That's funny. Am I going to your house?"

"You're already at my house." Julia turned off the engine and grabbed her knapsack off Nicki's lap. She got out and tossed the knapsack onto the porch as she walked around the front end. "Can you get out on your own?" she asked, holding open Nicki's door.

Nicki turned on her side and closed her eyes. "Can't I sleep right here?"

"Sure." Julia closed her door.

"No, wait! I want to come with you."

Julia sighed. "Oh, boy. Okay come on, but you're sleeping on the couch."

"Why?"

"Understood?"

"Fine. Will you make me some coffee?"

"Why? Do you want to be an awake drunk?"

"No. It's what people do. They have coffee. Who am I to fuck with tradition?"

"I've had a long hard day and I'm going to bed early."

"Do I really have to sleep on the couch, Julia?"

"If you want to sleep here, you do." She guided Nicki out of the car and up the steps to the porch. "How did you get this plastered?"

"I didn't eat, and I wanted to talk with you. So I thought I'd wait till you got home." Nicki stopped and turned to her. "But I waited so long—and I was thinking of you, missing you."

"Well, at least you had the sense not to drive." She guided Nicki into the house where the woman fell onto the couch. "Will you eat some scrambled eggs and toast?"

"You're an angel." After a minute, Nicki stood and felt her way along the wall into the kitchen and sat.

Julia lit the stove and grabbed her ingredients. In fewer than five minutes, she had served breakfast. "I'll be back. I need to change out of this and put my gear upstairs."

"Thanks for making this. It's really good."

Julia ran upstairs and changed her clothes. As she was making her way back downstairs, her cell phone rang. She picked up immediately when she saw it was Rina calling. "Hi, honey. I'm still on the move since five this morning." Julia sat on the step. "How did it go today?"

"We have a scene to reshoot tomorrow, in addition to the new scene. Vancouver is a cool place. I think you'd like it here."

"I don't know when I'm going to be able to get away to come up there."

"I'm sorry I couldn't call you the past couple of nights…"

"Yeah, I noticed."

"It was work, eat, and sleep."

"I figured. Same here. Still I missed hearing you say good night." Julia heard Nicki opening kitchen cabinets. "You sound tired, Rina."

"I am. Tomorrow's going to be a challenge but hopefully we're all on the same page now. Neither Britney, Reese, nor I liked a scene we shot today."

"So how's it going with Britney?"

"Fine. Just fine."

Did she just hesitate? Julia tapped her foot against the step. "You sure?"

"Yes, it's fine. How did your last party go?"

"We did great, but it left me exhausted. We're still trying to hire one more person and then things should be easier."

"I have an early call tomorrow for the horse scene and I need to get my beauty rest," said Rina.

"If you get any more beautiful, my eyes may just fall out of my head—once I can open them again."

Rina chuckled. "You're sweet."

"I won't ask you to call with such a busy day tomorrow, but it would be really great if we could talk sometime—have a real conversation. I miss you."

Rina sighed. "I know. All of our conversations are starting to sound like this one."

"You mean like News, Weather, and Sports."

"Yes."

"I love you, you know."

"I love you too, Julia. I'll call as soon as I can. Good night, sweetheart."

"Sweet dreams, babe."

Julia stared at the phone in her hand, shocked out of her moment by Nicki rustling around in the kitchen. "Nicki?" She hopped down the steps and rounded the corner to find Nicki eating a big bowl of chocolate ice cream.

Nicki turned to her. "Oh my god, this is so good. You should have some. There's never been a better bowl of chocolate ice cream anywhere on the planet!"

Julia couldn't help but watch her and laugh. If there was one thing Nicki had that Rina never would, it was a crass simplicity that wasn't without charm. Julia tossed her phone onto the counter, grabbed a spoon, and stuck it into the ice cream container. She stuffed a big bite into her mouth and savored it as it melted down her throat. She looked at Nicki. "You're so fucking right! Best ever."

Nicki laughed. "I told you. I'm actually starting to feel human. I was really out of it when you woke me. I'm finally down to seeing two of you. It was three. Kidding! I see only one of you. The one I want to be with." She gulped some water. "You know, I don't think I really appreciated how talented you are when we were together."

Julia sat on the stool next to her. "Those things were just not what you're into. And that's okay. What wasn't okay was sticking your tongue down that stripper's throat with your hands all over her ass at your party. I was standing right there, Nicki. You humiliated me and hurt my feelings."

"I regret that. I really am so sorry. You didn't deserve to be treated that way."

"Thank you."

Nicki grinned. "Now can I sleep with you?"

Julia slapped her arm lightly. "You have the weirdest sense of humor."

"Don't you believe in second chances, Julia?"

"I'm with someone else."

"Where is she?" Nicki peeked around the corner and sat back down.

"She's not here."

Nicki looked into her eyes. "I am."

"Right. I'm going to walk down to lock the gate and get my car."

Nicki took a deep breath and sighed. "I'll be able to drive in a while, I think."

"Forget it. I've got your keys. When I come back, I'll get you a blanket and pillow. You're on the couch tonight, stud."

Too tired to be exhausted, Julia ambled down the long driveway to her car. Having heard Rina's voice, she finally could breathe again. Still she had that sense—that hesitation she thought she'd felt in Rina when she asked her about Britney. It wasn't from anything she had said—but from what she didn't say. This distance, this communication breakdown, wasn't doing their relationship any good. Starting her car, she realized Nicki was staying over. *Do I tell Rina? Why say anything? It's perfectly innocent—and it's not like I want Nicki here or invited her over. I can't let her drive after drinking. Shit. If I don't tell Rina, will I feel guilty? Now that she's on location our conversations are so short. How do I work, "my ex is drunk and crashing at my place" into that call?*

She closed the windows and turned off the car. When she reentered the house, Nicki was asleep on the couch. Julia gently lifted her head and placed a pillow underneath, then covered her with a blanket. She wondered what would have happened had Nicki never broken up with her when and the way she had. *I would have already left the diner that night, and I'd never have met Rina—and I'd probably still be dating Nicki.*

Julia turned on a night light, turned off the big lights on her way upstairs. She fell facedown on her bed, realizing as she did that she'd left her phone downstairs. *Should plug it in, maybe see if there are any texts from Rina*, she thought muzzily even as she burrowed into the bedding. *Or at least get undressed. Right…*

CHAPTER THIRTY-FIVE

Rina arrived at the stable early the next morning while the tech crew was still setting up. She basked in the set's ambiance, created on what had once been an actual ranch. The brisk air made her think of Julia and how proud she would be that Rina had embraced riding in the way she had. Not to mention how particularly impressed she'd be by how ridiculously early it was and the fact that Rina wasn't even groaning about it.

After her ordeal with Britney's advances, she'd wished she was with Julia, riding up the mountain together at the Y2 after her lover served her coffee in bed. She reflected on their final ride—how the storm had stranded them at the cabin where they had made love in front of the open fireplace. *Cowgirl style!* The thought made her chuckle. *I could use a little cowgirl style right now.*

"So you're my date today, Smokey." Rina stroked the horse's soft nose and patted his neck.

"How do you do, Miss Verralta? I'm Mike, Smokey's trainer. You ready for your scene with Smokey?"

"Nice to meet you, Mike. He's a fine looking horse. Gentle."

"Thanks for noticing. Most actors don't know the difference. He's been in a lot of movies."

Rina smiled. "Good. He can cover for me if I screw up."

"I bet you know how to ride," Mike said with a nod.

Rina had the revelation right there. "Yes, I do."

"You know, you didn't need to come so early."

"I did, actually. I wanted to introduce myself to Smokey and talk to him. Would it be okay if I gave him a light brushing? It relaxes me."

Mike nodded in approval. "Stay off his right hindquarter. He gets a little sensitive to strangers touching him there."

"Are you sure you don't mind me brushing him for a few minutes?"

"He'll love it." The trainer smiled. "I'll leave you to it then. Be back in a few so you can saddle up and I can adjust your stirrups."

"Thanks, Mike."

Rina brushed Smokey, seeking the Zen state she'd always found so easily with Thunder. She wondered what Julia was doing at that moment and then found herself tense about Britney's ambush-kiss. *Why did I hesitate to push her away?*

"Good morning, Rina," said Britney when she entered the barn.

Rina smiled. "Morning. What are you doing here?"

Britney smiled and sauntered over to where Rina stood. "Last night you told me you like to come early before you ride, so I thought I'd come see what this barn magic is all about."

Rina passed the brush lightly along Smokey's back. "This is pretty much it."

Britney laughed. "You've got to be kidding me."

"Sorry to disappoint you."

Britney watched quietly. "You missed a spot back here."

"Smokey is sensitive there and doesn't like strangers touching it."

"About last night, Rina."

"What now?"

"I'm not sorry I kissed you. I don't think you were either."

"You should have respected my wishes—which I made pretty clear in the limo."

"I would have, had I thought that's what you really wanted. You forget that I know you pretty well, too."

Rina remained silent.

"Why can't you admit it, Rina?"

"Leave me alone, Brit. I'm trying to focus. We have a scene to shoot with Smokey, and I don't want a do-over. Especially since we have to reshoot that other scene today."

Britney placed her hand on Rina's hip from behind and whispered in her ear. "Come on, honey, one more chance?"

Rina elbowed her lightly to push her back. "Stop it," she said between clenched teeth.

"You almost sound like you mean it. Almost."

Reese's assistant entered the barn. "Finally!" said the perky intern. "Miss Cavell, I've been looking for you everywhere. They're ready for you in makeup. Miss Verralta, your stylist will be here shortly." She turned to leave and whirled back around. "And Reese said he'll come find you."

Rina accompanied Mike as he led Smokey out of the barn. "You mind if I ride him around the ring?" she asked. "Get to know him a little?"

Mike smiled. "Not at all. He needs to warm up anyway. And I need to see what you can do even though your stunt double will do the runaway scene."

Rina took the reins, mounted Smokey, and Mike adjusted her stirrups.

"That looks right," said Mike. "How's it feel?"

"It's good," Rina replied. She nudged the horse gently. "Come on, boy." After one full lap at a walk, Rina pushed him to go a little faster until they found their rhythm in a trot. She held him at that pace for a few minutes and slowed him back down into a walk. Settling into the lazy sway, she reached forward to pat his neck. "We're going to do fine, Smokey."

Mike leaned on the fence and watched until Rina returned. "You two looked good out there. I like how you ride him. Whatever Mr. Collingworth wants, if it's something you need my help with, say the word. I'll be right here."

"Thanks, Mike." Rina dismounted and handed him the reins. "Just those few laps made all the difference in my day."

Rina walked to the chair that awaited her and sat.

"Not too bad," said the hair stylist. "A little primping and spray and you'll be ready to go. Makeup is on the way for last minute touchups."

"Great," Rina said. In a matter of minutes she would need all her concentration to sell the world on being a horsewoman in the world of horse racing. She closed her eyes and channeled Julia—the best coach she could have ever had. She breathed in her love of the Y2 and the horses and felt Julia's rhythm when they were on Thunder together.

"Good morning, Rina." She looked up at Reese with his Palm Springs tan, wavy hair, and broad white smile.

"Morning, Reese."

"So, I like what you and Britney came up with last night. Where is she, anyway?"

"Makeup needed her. She should be back any time now."

"All right. I'll see you at the corral when you're done."

As Rina waited for the makeup artist to finish powdering and shading her face, she watched Britney pass her.

"There, that's much better," said the makeup woman.

Rina handed the woman the cape that had been draped over her. "Thanks." She walked to the corral and joined Reese and Britney at the fence.

"Okay," said Reese. "Rina, you're going to ride around the ring in that sexy trot you were doing earlier."

"You saw me? Sexy?"

"Yes—Julia has taught you really well. That looked *incredible*. So good in fact, I'm going to let you ride while I keep the camera rolling before we shoot the scene. There might be some things I'll want to use later."

"Whoever Julia is, maybe I should take riding lessons from her, too."

"Brit, I need your focus," Reese said seriously. "I don't want Rina or you getting hurt."

Rina remained stoic. *You get anywhere near Julia and we'll both see a side of me we've never seen before.*

They followed Reese inside the corral. He pointed behind Britney. "Britney, you'll come out from the barn to the fence, right of the gate when Rina is across the corral. Rina, you see her and trot to the fence—and do that little quick stop-and-turn thing you did a little while ago. Britney, you storm through the gate and up to the horse on this side—right here." He stepped onto the mark. "You'll do your dialogue."

"Rina, really escalate so that when Britney pretends to slap the horse it looks real. I want to see that dynamic Verralta-Cavell chemistry."

Reese pointed in another direction. "From that angle, Britney, it will look like you're actually hitting the horse, so make it look really convincing. And Rina, when she pretends to hit the horse, I want you to ride fast all the way to the other side so that I have enough to edit into the stunt. When I call 'cut,' you'll change places with the stunt woman for the runaway horse scene. Any questions?"

"I'm good, Reese," said Rina.

"Me too," Britney added.

When Reese left to take his place behind the camera, Britney couldn't help herself. "So who's that riding teacher, Rina? What else did you ride there?"

Rina's earlobes tingled and burned, but she saved up her anger, ready for her character to unleash it on Britney's character. She mounted Smokey and continued to repeat her mantras to drown out Britney's words. *Breathe. Focus. Breathe. Focus.*

"Rina," Reese called out, "start riding. Keep riding." He waited until Rina had circled the corral several times before he called out: "Okay, that's good."

Rina returned Smokey to her mark, from where they would begin shooting.

The First Assistant Director called out, "Actors ready. Quiet on the set. Roll sound."

"Speed," said the Sound Recordist.

The First Assistant Director nodded. "Roll camera."

"Camera speeds. Rolling," the cinematographer added.

Rina and Britney nodded to each other when the Second Assistant Camera came with the clapperboard that showed the film's name, scene, and the number of the take.

"Scene five, take one," he shouted before he slated the clapperboard and smacked it closed. They waited for the audio and video media to sync.

The cinematographer let everyone know the camera was in position and focused properly. "Set."

"Action!" Reese called out.

Rina rode fast, letting Smokey have a little fun in the process. She increased her speed, felt the breeze lift the hair from her neck. She gave the horse his head and let him out into his natural gait. Britney stormed out from the barn, and Rina raced up to her at the fence, stopping Smokey abruptly and doing the little turn Reese wanted.

Britney's character erupted into the scene in a huff. "If you think for one minute I'm going to let you get away with stealing my company out from under me, you've got another think coming!" She flung open the gate and pounded into the ring.

Rina's character stared her down while steadying the horse.

Smokey snorted at Britney as if on cue.

Rina delivered her lines with command: "You're certifiable, Tess! You know that?" Verralta-Stare-Down Number Eight. "You stole this ranch out from under my family in the dirtiest deal in the horse racing industry. And now you think I'm going to let you get away with it? You'll never get your hands on this ranch again!" Rina lowered her voice and flared her eyes. "Ever. Now Get. Off. My. Land."

"I'll get it back all right, and I'm taking that horse you're on with it!" Britney turned in the direction Reese had directed her to and stepped on her mark. She raised her arm and took an open-handed swing at the horse's rear flank.

Rina shrieked when the horse bucked and then bolted. She squeezed her knees as tightly as she could, hooked her feet behind his front legs, and gripped the saddle with one hand, reins in the other. Smokey nearly threw her off three times. No matter how hard or low she pulled on his reins, once he had taken hold of the bit, he wouldn't respond no matter what she did. Rina's feet slipped out of the stirrups as she lost control, and she crashed onto the dirt, barely a step away from getting stomped on. She rolled away on the ground, and Mike ran into the ring and grabbed Smokey.

"Cut! Cut!" Reese screamed, running toward her. "Get the medic! Now!"

He and Britney raced to the other end of the ring, and Britney fell to her knees at Rina's side.

"Oh my god! Rina, are you all right?"

Rina began to sit up and immediately laid back down on the ground.

Britney leaned over her and held her hand. "Jesus! I'm so sorry. The horse moved. I didn't hit him on purpose! Say something!"

Rina looked up at her and then at Reese. "Get her away from me, Reese." Then she pulled her hand away and screamed it. "Get away from me, Britney!"

"I swear it wasn't me!" Britney pleaded.

The medic raced to the scene. "You need to move, ma'am," he said to Britney as he bent down and opened his EMT bag.

Reese pulled Britney to her feet. "Let the medic do what he needs to do. Come on."

"But…" Britney began. Her hands shook and her breathing became erratic. "Oh, my god, is she okay?" she said looking over her shoulder as Reese led her away.

"Look at me, Brit," said Reese. "Are you okay?" He put his arm around her and guided her to a chair on the set.

"I'm freaking out, Reese. The horse moved at the moment my hand came down. I swear!"

Reese stared at her and ran his fingers through his thick hair. "Stay here." He turned to an assistant. "Bring Miss Cavell some water while I check on Miss Verralta."

CHAPTER THIRTY-SIX

Gigi sat waiting at Clay's kitchen table, drumming her nails in succession, from thumb to pinky and back again.

"I'm here," she called out when she heard Clay come through the door.

"I see that." He set down his suitcase and walked toward her.

"How are you doing?" she asked. "You look exhausted. How's Rina?"

He let out an exasperated sigh. "Man, what a twenty-four hours it's been."

"Were the X-rays normal?"

"She's very lucky that nothing's broken. The doctor said she sustained a mild concussion, but she'll be okay." He tossed a glance at the photo collage on his table. "What's all this?"

"The photos from the private investigator."

Clay leaned on the back of Gigi's chair and stared down at them. He leaned farther over her shoulder. "Is that Julia?" he asked.

"Yep."

"Making out with a guy?"

Gigi looked up at him. "So you see it, too."

"Ugh! I can't handle two nightmares today." Clay took a seat, reached for a photo in the middle of the table and studied it. "I know

Rina doesn't know about these or I'd have had to restrain her on the flight home. She's been trying to reach Julia all day. When were these taken?"

"Two days ago."

Clay slumped back in his chair and exhaled a hard sigh. He rubbed his eyes and then looked over at Gigi. "Worst timing ever."

"I know, right?"

His face twisted. "*Et tu*, Julia?"

"This on the heels of the Britney fiasco! What's going to happen now that Rina isn't on set?"

"They're shooting around her for the rest of the week. The doctor wants her at home to heal. I could strangle Britney Cavell for causing this—Rina could have been permanently injured or killed."

"What exactly happened?"

"Britney was supposed to pretend to hit the horse's rear, but she says that the horse moved at the last second causing her to actually hit him. Her hand just happened to land on a sore spot, causing him to buck and then bolt."

"Is she telling the truth?"

"Who knows at this point? The cameras were rolling so there may be another view where you can see what happened if and when the horse moved. But the scene was shot to make it look like she was hitting the horse. In the meantime, you know Britney as well as I do." He stared at her. "What do you think?"

Gigi rolled her eyes. "That woman is capable of anything." *And I can use that to my advantage.* "What does Rina say?"

"Rina told me that when they went to dinner the night before, Britney came onto her like gangbusters."

"Why am I not surprised?" *Now that I have the photos of Julia, this is almost too easy.* "So did Rina take her up on the offer?"

"No, she physically pushed her away—more than once. How could you ask that knowing how she feels about Julia?"

Gigi held up a random incriminating photo and surpressed a grin. "She's not going to feel that way much longer, is she?"

Clay rested his forehead in his palm. "This is already a big fucking mess."

"Just because Rina denies anything happened with Britney doesn't mean it didn't. Maybe they did have a fling in Vancouver. Do you know for a fact they didn't spend the night together? I mean, without me there it was a perfect opportunity, and it's happened before."

"No, no, no. If that happened, I'd need to start taking medication and take up serious drinking."

Gigi chuckled.

Clay stared at her and then at the photos on his table.

"Clay, you don't think Rina should see these pictures of her lover hooking up with some dude?" *Say yes.*

"God no, Gigi. Not now. I can't believe my eyes." He held up the photo of Julia embracing the man. "I'm shocked. I would never have thought that Julia…"

"Now aren't you glad I hired the investigator?"

"Rina will be devastated." He sighed. "Before I put my pillow over my face and scream, is there any more bad news?"

"Nothing but a stack of photos of Rina's lover all over this guy."

"Put them away. Rina's very fragile right now, not to mention her head hurts and she still feels foggy."

Gigi shook her head. "Has Rina been in touch with Julia since the incident?"

"She said she tried to reach Julia all day but couldn't get through."

Gigi waved one of the photos like a fan. "Maybe Julia was occupied," she said in a snide tone.

"I don't know. I didn't press her for answers about anything. You'd be wise to do the same. She said she'll call you when she wakes up tomorrow."

"How do I face her knowing about Julia?"

Clay borrowed Rina's Blank Expression Number Two and stared at Gigi. "Lie!"

"Don't think I don't know you're flashing me Blank Expression Number Two. What about when she goes back to Vancouver? They've just started filming so there's a long way to go. How is she ever going to work with Britney after this?"

He raised his hands in the air. "Haven't a clue. I don't know what the fuck is going on!"

"What about Susie?"

"What about her?"

"If there was ever a time for her to earn her keep as Rina's publicist, it's now," said Gigi.

"Susie is doing what Susie does. Spinning it. She released a statement to the press saying that Rina had to leave the set because of a riding accident. But she's not mentioning how it happened. Honestly, while all the attention is on this mess, I don't want the press to get even a hint of her relationship with Julia. If that's going south too—and then…ugh! I need sleep."

"With all the speculation about why production was virtually halted, it's only a matter of time before the truth comes out, Clay."

He smirked. "It's all a matter of which version of the truth speaks loudest."

Mine! Gigi nodded thoughtfully. "You really think Britney intended to do Rina harm? I mean, why?"

"Who knows? Britney swore to me she didn't intend to swat the horse's butt. However, Rina said that when they walked out through the barn to do the scene, Britney was trying to persuade Rina to give her another chance. Rina was pissed. She basically told Britney that there wasn't a chance in hell she'd ever subject herself to her again."

Gigi chuckled. "You sound just like her. You don't think that Rina and Britney…you know…hooked up before this?"

"Rina said no. Which means Britney short-circuited. Again."

"Here, this one's my favorite." Gigi tossed over a picture taken with a telephoto lens. Julia was lying on top of the man on a porch lounge. "I told you in the beginning that I didn't trust this girl."

Clay shook his head remorsefully. "This is going to destroy Rina. I've never seen her so devoted to anyone. I really thought they had something special." He sighed. "I guess I was wrong."

"Maybe Julia's lies will take care of this situation for us and we won't have to worry about showing Rina these photos after all."

"One crisis at a time, Gigi."

"As if that's going to make one shit of a difference!"

* * *

Alone in her suite, Rina put on her favorite pair of drawstring pants and a long-sleeve jersey top to warm her. She brewed a cup of hot tea and limped to the sofa. She placed the cup on the table in front of the plush sofa and winced when her left butt cheek met the seat. "Where are you, Julia?" Again there was no answer.

Rina was holding the hot cup with both hands to warm her when her phone rang.

"Julia, I've been trying to reach you for a day!"

"I never received any calls from you. Are you okay? I just heard something happened to you!"

"It was a riding accident."

"But you've been so good on the horses. What happened?"

"I'm foggy and my ass is sore. The doctors sent me home to rest this week. But it wasn't my fault I got thrown—or the horse's for that matter."

"Well, whose fault was it?"

"I don't even want to tell you because I know it will make you crazy."

Julia paused. "It was Britney, wasn't it?" she said in a low voice.

"Yes."

"Answer me honestly, Rina. Have you two…?"

"Don't you dare finish that question! Why would you ask me that?"

"Because it's been a while since you and I have been together, and I'm looking at photos of you two on my computer right now. Britney has her arms around you in the first one, and while you were on the ground she was holding your hand. In fact, she's all over you."

"I don't even remember that."

"Convenient."

"What are you implying?"

"I'm calling because I want to know if you're okay. Since I haven't heard from you, I thought maybe you and she—on location together…"

"You know we went out for dinner two nights ago. That's all."

There was a prolonged and deep silence. "I know. I saw the pictures of you together online, afterward. I hate to say it but you look good together." More silence fell between them. "Were you alone with her afterward?"

"Only on the ride home." *And then in the elevator.* Rina thought of the kiss Britney had given her. "I wish you were here," said Rina.

"I'd come up there if I could."

"It's okay, I need some alone time to think."

"Think about what?"

"Everything."

"Us?"

"I'm sorry, but I can't talk. My mind is foggy and I need to rest now—but I'm glad you finally called."

"You feel so distant right now." Julia waited through a pause that had enough room to land a plane. "And…so you are. Feel better. I love you." Julia barely uttered the sentiment before Rina disconnected.

Rina stood, walked to the terrace doors and stared out, searching in the direction for Catalina Island. "I trust you're there, even in the darkness."

From her bedroom, the soft ambient lighting beckoned. She entered the dimly lit space and glanced at the unkind consensus reflected back to her by the multitude of mirrors. Rina lowered the lights until she could barely see—until the mirrors could no longer judge her.

Her last thought before she fell asleep presented her with an unwelcome choice. *Is it harder to long for something you wish you had or to have something you're afraid of losing?*

CHAPTER THIRTY-SEVEN

After a fitful night filled with unforgiving dreams, Rina stood before the open terrace doors of her living room deck, breathing in the foggy aura of morning-ocean. She answered her phone on the first ring. "Your timing is uncanny, Swan." Her eyes scanned the seagulls flying past.

"I was concerned when I read about some shakeup on the set of your new movie. Are you all right?"

"Right now I'd consider diving naked into a pool of warm liquid Belgian chocolate and eating my way out of it."

The line went silent.

"Swan? Are you there?"

Swan cleared her throat. "Sorry. I was picturing it."

Rina chuckled. "Typical screenwriter."

"Yeah. Sure. I'll go with that. Did you really take a spill off of a horse?"

"Yes, but through no fault of my own. I'll heal on the outside—not so sure about the inside."

"Why?"

"Betrayed by a toxic ex."

"Oh?" She paused. "Oh. I think I just put two and two together. Your meltdown after the Oscars that brought you to rehab? Britney Cavell?"

"Yes."

"Really? From what I've gathered, she can't compare to Julia."

"Except that I spoke with Julia last night and that didn't go so well." She sighed. "I was cold and dismissive, and I haven't even called her yet to apologize."

"Think about our group session with Therapy Brittany where we learned how to dissolve our triggers. Britney obviously triggers you in a way that's calling something else into question."

Rina flashed on Julia and paused. "I'm so in love with Julia."

"Hmm. Are you questioning her loyalty?"

"No."

"Are you questioning your own?"

"N-No."

"Are you sure?"

"I know you're asking because you see a connection, but honestly, everything is still too close for me to see it clearly, I think."

"Then call a timeout."

Rina exhaled forcefully. "Easier said than done, my friend."

"Is it, Rina? Or is that simply the story you're telling yourself?"

"I promise as soon as my head clears, I'll think about that. So tell me, what's going on in your world?"

"I have good news. I got *The Do-Over* fully funded, which means we'll be casting at some point soon."

"Swan, that's wonderful! I'm so happy for you. That film deserves to be produced."

"Thank you."

Rina glanced at the clock. "I may have to call you back—I'm about to have a meeting. But since we're on the subject, is there anything I can do to help you?"

"It might be more like what I can do to help you. While I don't want to pry, I have to ask. Is there even a remote chance you're leaving *The Big Picture?*"

"I'm in a tough position, Swan. But strictly, and I mean strictly between you and me?"

"Of course."

"If I do quit the film, it ain't gonna be pretty."

"Perhaps my timing is good then. I've rewritten the part of Dolly—with you in mind."

"I'm honored to have helped inspire something so creative."

"I've barely come up for air since we last spoke. In fact, the whole story has changed, and I think you'd love it."

"Send the script over."

"Really?"

"Sure. I'll be home the rest of the week. It will be a good diversion."

"It would be my dream to offer you the part—even if you declined. I mean, I know for a fact we can't offer you anything like what you're used to getting paid."

"If the part is right, it's right."

"Promise me that you'll be honest with me when you read it. Like right between the eyes."

"We made that vow in rehab."

"We did, didn't we?"

"You sound good, Amanda."

"You never call me Amanda."

"Well, don't you think it will look odd in the credits? Screenplay by Swan?"

Swan paused. "Actually, I don't—I've taken to the name Swan. Even my friends are calling me that now. It empowers me by reminding me of the beauty you saw in me when I was at my worst."

"I have a suspicion that like Dolly's positive nexus in your story, I'm ready for my own little cosmic do-over. But things here are up in the air right now so I have no idea what's going to happen."

"I don't want to pressure you."

"You're not. I'd really like to see the script. You and that story kept me sane through rehab—it's the least I can do."

"Thank you, Rina. I can't tell you how much this means to me."

"*You* mean a lot to me."

"I'll courier it over today."

"Good. Talk with you soon," Rina said before ending the call. She took a cleansing breath and was staring out to sea when she heard the knock on her door. "Come in, Clay," she said without turning to welcome him.

"You wanted to see me?"

"Do you know what I like best about this view?"

Clay crossed the room and poured a glass of water from the pitcher on the bar. "What's that?"

"Every day I look for Catalina Island. Even on days like today, when it's foggy and not visible, I tell myself to trust that it's still there, even though I can't see it."

Clay joined her. She turned her head, looked into his eyes, and then back out at the sapphire Pacific.

"Why do you do it?" he asked.

"Because it reminds me that there's more to everything than what meets the eye. Including myself. Today is one of those days when I have to dig deep and trust what's there."

"You're acting weird. You okay?" he asked.

"I don't know if I've ever been okay-er."

"Honestly, I expected to find the old you—freaking out and throwing things." He drank the water and placed the glass on a table. "What's on your mind?"

She turned to face him. "I'm quitting the film."

Clay raised his eyebrows. "What? You can't quit the film. You'd be in breach of contract."

"I spoke with the attorneys a little while ago. What Britney did puts her in breach since she hit the horse with me on it. It shows intent to cause me physical harm. According to the contract with both her and with Reese, it's up to me whether or not I continue."

"What if on film it shows it exactly the way Britney said it happened? That the horse moved."

"Then I can get out under the 'Trauma Clause.' If that doesn't work, I'll threaten sexual harassment."

Clay scoffed. "What! She harassed you?"

"I told you she made unwelcome advances. I'll leave it there."

"Were they—unwelcome?"

"What? Why would you ask me that knowing how I feel about Julia?"

"Because it's happened between you and Britney before—a few times."

"I'll tell you what I told her. Not this time."

"You can't have a harassment charge go public."

"Believe me, neither she nor Reese want that out there. Whether the horse moved or not, she never pulled back. I don't believe she wanted to hurt me, but she did."

"You'd get skewered in the press. Britney will say whatever she has to for her to come out looking like the victim—and you, the bad guy. Whether it's about the horse or harassment."

Rina placed her hands on her hips. "How could she possibly spin hitting the horse? It's on film, and the cast and crew can attest to her hitting the horse. Even though I fell off, if Julia hadn't taught me to ride, I'd be dead or paralyzed right now because I'd have fallen off when he bucked. Luckily, I was able to stay on him for a while longer. As for harassment, you're right. That will be harder to prove."

"I'm just grateful you're not permanently damaged." Clay glanced at his phone when it rang and then at Rina.

"Is it Reese?" she asked.

He nodded.

"You can call him back."

"Rina, why not just take these days off to heal and regroup, and go back to finish the film?"

"I don't want to."

"I understand," said Clay. "But you've signed a contract and you're already filming. The legality here will wind up shutting down production at least temporarily. You know that everyone including the studio is going to blame you for it. You'd not only lose financially. Think of your reputation."

"I hate doing this to Reese, but it's early enough in the film that he can recast my role. It'll delay things and cost some money, but they can do it." She paused. "You know who would be great in this role is Emma Thompson. You should tell that to Reese when you speak with him."

"Rina, it really is the role of a lifetime. Are you telling me you'd give up the chance of an Oscar nomination over this? Over Britney?"

"I'm saying…I'm done," she said soft and low. "If I can't give this part my very best, then I should walk away. It's about my integrity as well as my dignity, Clay. And Cavell cannot steal either from me. Britney swore to me at the beginning that she'd be professional, and Reese promised me he could control her. They were both mistaken. I'm the one who's paying the price for it and that's wrong."

Clay sighed. "You pay me to manage you. As your manager, I'm telling you not to do this. Let me fight it. Reese will listen to me. If anything, Britney should be kicked off the project. Let Reese recast her role, not yours."

She breathed in ranch-calm. "It's a nice change."

"What is?"

"My entire career, I've had to do so many wrong things for the right reasons." She turned to him and scraped her hair away from her face. "I've always sacrificed little pieces of my soul in order to get the next big role—to play the long game. No more. For the first time, I can honestly say I'm going to do what's right for me for the right reasons and walk away before any more of my soul becomes numb to all of it."

"I have to say it. You're committing professional suicide if you quit."

"See, Clay, that's the thing. I don't think I am."

"You mean you don't care if you are."

"Do you really have so little faith in me?"

"Rina, listen to me."

She stared into his eyes.

"The hard reality is, roles for women your age are few, and they're rarely powerful leads, let alone with great scripts. You already know this. So what do you think your odds will be if you leave this film midstream with a rep for having killed a Reese Collingworth film?"

She sighed hard. "I haven't a clue. But I'm certain of one thing. It's time for me to stop playing it safe. I'm better than this."

Clay went to the sofa and sat.

"Call Reese and make the arrangements, Clay."

"Don't act on impulse. You only left yesterday. Sleep on it."

"Honey, I've changed. My life is changing."

"I get that, but it doesn't seem to be for the better. Can you say you're completely sure about this—not even a hint of doubt?"

Rina nodded. "I couldn't be clearer on the matter."

"So what then? You're going to do nothing? That'll kill you."

"Actually, there's this little indie film that's just come my way."

"An indie film. What indie film?"

"I worked on it in chocolate rehab." Rina turned back to the open door.

Clay smirked.

"It's okay, Clay, you can laugh. It is rather funny in retrospect but worth every minute of my time for what I learned there. I not only tackled my chocolate issue, but I realized what all that chocolate was masking."

"Such as?"

"My true feelings. Now, after months of not having to stuff down my feelings with chocolate, I actually know what I feel. It's time for me to take a risk. A *real* risk. Call it a later-than-midlife crisis if you like."

"What's the project? And you can call it midlife—as long as you live to be *really* old."

"Swan's film—*The Do-Over*."

"Swan. Who's Swan?"

"The young woman I met in rehab."

"Right. Who's producing it?"

"I don't know anything yet. She's sending over the script today."

"So professional suicide isn't enough? Now you want to commit financial ruin? Do I need to look for a new job?"

"Do you want to look for a new job?"

"No, Rina, I don't. You should know—I got a message from Cavell. She keeps calling to ask how you are, and she let it be known she's looking for a new manager."

Rina chortled. "You'd never be able to scrape that sludge off your shoes. You of all people know how toxic she is. Imagine if you had to clean up this mess from her end."

Clay acquiesced. "I wouldn't betray you that way. We made a deal a long time ago. 'I'm in this through the best and the worst.' You'd have to die to get rid of me."

"All right then, do you want to call Reese or shall I?"

"I will. But first I need to ask. Does this move have anything to do with Julia?"

She turned to him and waited a moment before answering. "It has everything to do with her. Those photos of Britney all over me after the incident made it everywhere. Right now, Julia mistrusts everything we've built in our short time together. I could hear it in her voice. I'm sure she was wrecked by that little stunt, and I'm suffering the fallout from it. I'll be damned before I let Britney ruin the best thing I've ever had."

"The best thing you've ever had?"

"Yes, Clay. The best."

He exhaled hard. "Have a seat, Rina. There's something I need to tell you. Before you quit the film, you need to see what Gigi has on Julia."

"On Julia?" she asked, her expression disbelieving.

Clay nodded.

"W-What is it?"

"Stay calm."

"Calm? Why do I need to be calm?"

"I hate this—that Gigi didn't tell you she had hired an investigator to look into Julia while you were on location."

"Well? What did she find?"

Clay pulled his phone from his pocket and placed the call. "Bring the pictures upstairs. No, Gigi, not in ten minutes. Now."

Rina held out her hand and Gigi placed the envelope containing the photos in it.

"I'm sorry, Rina," said Gigi. "You know I'm just trying to protect you, right?"

"Leave. Both of you."

Clay reached out. "No, I…"

"I'll call you after I've seen whatever is in here."

Rina waited until she was alone. She poured a glass of water and sat on the deck, staring down at the envelope in her lap. Her heart pounded. She steadied herself and reached into the envelope.

The first photo showed Julia with a handsome young man. The familiar background of the Y2 made her shiver inside. She flipped through the photos enough to be sickened by what she saw. Especially the photo of Julia wrapped around the same man, kissing him. Her stomach churned.

Taken with what she assumed had been a telephoto lens, in each consecutive picture the intimacy escalated, until finally the vision of her lover in a passionate embrace with someone else was more than she could bear. *How is this possible? We were so in love. And…she's so…so… gay!* Feeling faint, Rina dropped the photos on the table, and guzzled what remained in her glass.

She picked up her phone, her hands shaking. She stared at Julia's number, angry enough to delete it. A minute later, she placed the call. *I want answers. Now!*

The number rang. And rang. She called again and hung up while it was still ringing.

CHAPTER THIRTY-EIGHT

Two days had passed, and Julia replayed in her mind her last conversation with Rina for the umpteenth time. No matter how many ways she tried to explain it, it still bothered her that despite Rina's cool attitude and the abrupt way she had hung up, she still hadn't heard from her. The pit in her stomach hadn't gone away, her sleep was limited to two-hour stints, and the one time she had called Gigi told her that Rina was unavailable.

What did it mean when Gigi said, "You may want to wait to hear from her instead of calling back"? I've waited long enough!

"Julia!" said Isabel. "We need you. The buffet needs refilling."

"Sorry." Julia filled another tray and brought it out to the party. The food was going fast—always a good sign in her mind.

She saw Nicki approach from her side. "Hey, Julia," she said softly. "I'm really sorry about the other night when I showed up at your door."

Julia looked at her and smiled. "You were actually kind of funny. I'm not used to seeing you drunk."

Nicki rolled her eyes in contrition. "I feel like such an ass. But my motives were pure—I really like you—still, and I don't know how to tell you."

"You just did—in a way that was probably a lot less painful than your day after drinking."

"Yeah, you'd think I'd grow up by now."

"Well, you did make one good point that night."

"What was it?"

"That really was the best bowl of chocolate ice cream ever."

Nicki laughed. "No hard feelings?"

Julia shook her head. "Not as long as you don't make a habit of it."

Nicki gazed around the room. "I may not remember everything I did or said that night, but I do remember admitting that I hadn't appreciated you enough when we were dating. That's what I'd come to tell you. You're so talented. By the way, my cousins are raving about the food." Nicki glanced away for an instant. "I'll understand if you want the sculpture back that you gave me for my birthday."

"No, it was a present, and I made it for you."

"Wow, and I didn't think I could feel worse about myself. At my party, I opened the box and set it aside. What the fuck! Right?"

"You'll get no argument from me there, Nicki. But it turned out okay."

"In what way?"

"I met someone the night you broke up with me."

"What? Who?"

"I'd rather not say yet. The truth is we're going through a rough patch."

Nicki smiled. "So…I still have a chance?"

"I prefer to leave things the way they are."

An hour later, Julia left the party after Jimmy told her he would manage the cleanup.

As exhausted as she was, Julia found herself in the casita sculpting once she arrived home. She stared down at her phone several times, rechecked her missed calls and texts. *Nothing from Rina!* She dismissed the thought of driving to LA, knowing in her gut that something was wrong—something was going on and it was obvious to her that Rina wasn't including her in it.

I can't keep calling her, especially when Gigi told me to wait to hear from her. This is ridiculous!

She spent another virtually sleepless night wondering if the reason for the communication blackout was simply Rina trying to find a way to break up with her. In the days since Rina's fall, more pictures of her and Britney had surfaced online along with articles about the shakeup on the set of *The Big Picture*. *Maybe she'll call today.*

Julia brushed her hair, gathered up her belongings, and drove to the diner, thankful that it was Cass's morning to open.

"Still haven't heard from her?" Cass whispered as she passed Julia in the restaurant.

Julia frowned when she shook her head.

Later that afternoon, Julia answered the phone at the diner. "Starlight."

"Julia?"

Julia felt her lifeblood pump through her heart. She turned away from the customers and cupped her hand over the phone. "Rina?"

"We need to talk!"

"What? Why are you calling me at the diner?"

"Because you won't pick up your damn cell phone. I've *been* calling you for two days!"

"I haven't gotten any calls. I've called you!"

"Oh, that's rich! Any other lies you want to sell me?"

"Gigi told me to wait to hear from you. Why are you yelling at me?"

"I'll be at the Y2 within the hour. Be there!" The line went dead.

Immediately, Julia went to Cass. "I just heard from her. Something is *very* wrong and I'm freaking out. Rina is on her way to the ranch. Can you handle things until closing?"

"Sure, Jules. Go!"

Julia floored the car and sped down the driveway of the ranch. She took a quick shower, freshened her makeup, and then waited on the porch counting the seconds—tapping one foot, then the other—clutching the railing tightly. She'd never heard Rina so angry, nor had she ever been the object of her rage. No matter how hard she tried, she couldn't catch her breath, her heart raced, and she kept her eyes fixed on the entrance to the ranch. It took forever before the Jag turned onto the driveway.

She stepped off the porch and raced up to Rina as she exited the car. When Julia reached for her, Rina sidestepped her and without a word walked into the house.

"Not even a hello?" said Julia. She followed Rina into the kitchen. The actress sat on a bar stool at the island, took an envelope out of her purse, and smacked it down on the counter.

"Rina! Talk to me. What the hell is going on?"

Rina glared at her with Anger Number Six and stared her down. On fire, those electrifying eyes could have burned through a thousand movie screens. She picked up the envelope and dumped its contents onto the island, a rubber band holding the photos intact.

"Not that they need it—but explain these! Now, Julia!"

"Why are you attacking me?"

"Is this why I haven't heard from you?" Rina spat.

"I told you that Gigi said I should wait to hear from you!"

"Then why have you been ignoring my calls?"

"What calls?" Julia glanced down at the top photo and shivered. "This is here, outside the casita! When did you take photos at the Y2?" She picked up the stack, removed the rubber band, and thumbed to the next photo. "Who took these?"

"A private investigator," Rina said coolly. "You couldn't wait for me? Couldn't tell me the truth? Why would you do this?"

Julia lifted her eyes from the photos when Rina's words sunk in. "You—had me—*investigated*? Had someone sneak onto my property and spy on me?" She stared down Rina's scathing expression. "Are you fucking kidding me?"

"I didn't know anything about it, but I'm glad now that Gigi did it!"

"Pfft! Gigi. Why am I not surprised!" Julia slapped the stack of photos on the counter and shook her head. "You let Gigi get away with this?"

"What's wrong? Can't bear to look at the rest of them? I don't blame you. The two of you weren't particularly discreet at the diner. You couldn't keep your hands off each other!"

"I don't need to see the rest of them because I know the truth. You, however, are fucking clueless!"

Rina scoffed. "Obviously! Who's the guy you're all over?"

"You really want to know?"

"You're damn right I do!"

Julia's eyes flared. "I'll be right back. Don't you dare move."

"Excuse me? Dare? How *dare* you speak to me in that tone!"

"You're damn lucky I'm talking to you at all."

Julia returned from the living room scrolling through the photos on her phone. She found one of her and Vitty and held out the phone. "Here. Take it."

Rina accepted the phone, shifting her eyes down to the display. Her slackened jaw signaled the moment when she realized what she was looking at. She closed her eyes and groaned before looking back at Julia in disbelief. "Oh, no. Y-your sister…is a twin? It's your sister?"

Julia nodded. "Yep. That's us. The *two* in the Y2. The Dearling twins." She stood there, her adrenaline surging to the point where she felt like she was vibrating. "So much for trust, huh, Rina!"

Rina scraped back her hair and released a breath that to Julia seemed never ending. "Vitty, huh?"

"'Fraid so." She picked the top photo off the stack and waved it at Rina. "And this is Vitty and her fiancé David."

Seeing the shock still roiling Rina's face, Julia made a determined effort to bring her wrath under control. "What's going on here, Rina? I've never seen you so angry."

"How do you think seeing photos like these would make me feel?" Rina snapped.

Julia felt her face grow hot. "I don't know, Katarina. Ashamed maybe? Upset that your lover's privacy had been invaded? Or maybe you could've drawn *any* other conclusion than the one you jumped to?"

She threw her hands in the air. "The better question is, how do you think *I* feel knowing my lover had me investigated? Huh? You couldn't just ask me? You couldn't trust in my avowed love for you? Trust in every single action I've ever taken with regard to you? I guess not." She flung a spoon from the counter into the sink so hard that it bounced out onto the floor. "You know what? I can't talk to you right now!" Julia stormed out of the kitchen and slammed the screen door.

She put a bridle on Lightning and led him out of the barn. As she mounted him bareback, Rina emerged from the house.

"I'm sorry. Julia, wait! Where are you going?"

Julia looked down at her. "Wherever you're not."

Rina winced. "Oh no, you don't!"

Julia turned Lightning toward the mountain. She heard Rina mumbling and looked over her shoulder to see her stomping toward the barn. "Come on, Lightning."

CHAPTER THIRTY-NINE

"It took you long enough," said Julia when she heard Thunder's hooves come to a stop behind her.

"Well, pardon me, but I'm riding with a concussion after a long emotional day and having saddled a horse for the first time!" Rina answered.

Julia stood from the boulder she was sitting on and spun around. "Concussion? Jesus, Rina, you shouldn't be... slide up in your saddle." Julia held Lightning's reins and climbed onto Thunder, seating herself behind Rina with her arms around the woman.

"Very sneaky way to get your arms around me."

"Enjoy it while you can. I'm still mad. Come on, Thunder." Julia walked the horses back toward the ranch at an unjarring pace. "You had no business getting on this horse—or driving all the way here. Why didn't you get a driver?"

"Because when I saw those pictures again after not being able to reach you, I watched red meet the green-eyed monster. I grabbed my purse and phone and left the house. That's all I have with me."

"You have plenty of stuff here. You know, I've been thinking about it. Did Gigi at least tell you I've called?"

"I got one message. That was the first time I called you from home. No, wait. Bear with me, my thoughts were even foggier after the fall. Okay, okay—I tried reaching you several times after the accident and I couldn't get you then, either."

"If you called me, why didn't you leave me a message?"

"All it does is ring when I call." Rina leaned back into Julia. "I hope you don't mind—I'm not feeling well right now."

Julia rested her hand on the outside of Rina's leg. "We're almost home."

When they arrived, Julia let Rina off at the porch. "I'll be in after I get these guys settled." She rode to the barn and dismounted. She removed Thunder's saddle and laughed at how Rina had put it on. "She's lucky she didn't fall off of you too, Thunder."

Julia returned to find Rina lying on the couch with her eyes closed. She sat beside her and gently stroked back a wave from Rina's cheek. "You look pale, babe."

"I'm not feeling so hot."

"Come on, let's get you into bed. Are you hungry?"

"Yes, but I can't eat yet. The concussion makes me nauseated."

Julia reached around her and sat her upright. "I'll bring you a cup of chamomile tea to calm your stomach. Up we go."

They climbed the steps slowly with Julia's arm tight around Rina's waist—Rina's head on her lover's shoulder.

"I've missed you terribly," Rina said.

"I hated being so far away from you. When do you go back?"

"I'll fill you in as soon as I feel up to it."

They entered the bedroom, and Julia opened Rina's dresser drawer. "Which pajamas do you want?"

"The blue silk."

"Here. You change and I'll be back with some tea."

Rina reached out and touched Julia's arm. "I know you're still angry, but thank you for being so good to me right now."

Julia smiled and kissed her forehead. "Get comfy—I'll be back in a flash."

Holding a cup, Julia stopped in the doorjamb and admired the cozy-looking woman in her bed. "Are you awake?" she asked softly.

"Yes," Rina said, barely above a whisper.

Julia placed the teacup on the night table and dimmed the lights more. She brought a few pillows from the closet and propped herself up against the headboard while Rina took a few sips of tea. "Here. Come lay your head on my chest."

Julia massaged her head.

"That feels so good. If I fall asleep, don't be offended."

"Honey, I'm worried about you. I don't like how you look or how you feel. Do we need to call a doctor?"

"No, I saw mine this morning. It's just going to take some time for the concussion to heal."

"What on earth possessed you to drive all this way?"

Rina sighed hard. "Those photos broke me apart. I don't think you realize…"

"Relax now. Don't think." Julia stroked her hair. "Just rest. Where's your phone?"

"Still in the car. Why?"

"I want to call my phone from it and make sure it's working."

"Oh-kay," Rina's voice trailed off. "The password is 0-7-1-4."

"My birthday?"

"Uh-huh." Rina drifted off.

Once she was sure Rina was asleep, Julia retrieved her phone from the car. She sat in the kitchen with her own phone next to it and called herself. *Why isn't my phone ringing?*

She scrolled through Rina's outgoing calls and saw page after page of calls that the woman had made to her. Julia then opened her own phone and tapped Rina's contact information.

"Sonofabitch! How the hell did that happen?" At the bottom of the list of caller preferences, in black-and-white, the display read: "Caller Blocked."

Julia waited a couple of hours before bringing a tray with food upstairs. She rested it on the dresser, turned on the nightlight, and sat on the bed stroking Rina's hair.

"Umm, where am I?" Rina's gaze landed in Julia's smile. "For a second I didn't know if I was at home or in Vancouver or…"

"I'm right here."

Rina looked up at her and stroked her cheek. "Yes, you are, thankfully."

"You had a good deep sleep. I've been checking on you and you barely moved an inch."

"What smells so good?"

"A delicious soup I made yesterday. Do you feel well enough to have some?"

"I definitely feel better than before. I'm hungry."

"Good. Let's sit you up so I can get some pillows behind you." Julia fixed the pillows the way Rina liked them and placed the tray over her legs. She reached for the dimmer switch.

"Not too bright, please." She swallowed a spoonful of soup. "This is so good. What a treat to be eating your cooking again. I think being with you heals me. I really do."

"I'm glad you're here, no matter how weird this has been. I don't think things between us have ever been as strange as they were today." She sat on the edge of the bed. "While you were sleeping I figured out why you couldn't reach me."

"Why?"

"Somehow your number was blocked on my phone."

"What do you mean 'somehow'?"

"Just that. I have no idea how that would even...oh, wait—a—minute."

Rina stopped eating and looked at her. "What is it?"

"Nicki!"

Rina put down her spoon. "What do you mean 'Nicki'?"

"The night before your accident, I was dead on my feet—got home from work really late and Nicki was in her car, passed out drunk at the gate. I couldn't let her drive, and I wasn't about to drive her all the way home, so I let her crash here."

"You spent the night with your ex?"

"Don't look at me that way. I've had enough Katarina Verralta-wants-to-kill-you looks today to last me a lifetime, thank you. No, I didn't spend the night with her. She crashed on the couch downstairs. I didn't even give her a bedroom."

"Then she was here when I called you?"

"Well...yeah."

"And you didn't tell me?"

"We didn't have much of a talk, Rina. You as much as admitted that during the conversation when you dismissed me after a minute or two. Cut me a break, will you?"

"Look into my eyes, Julia. You're honestly telling me that nothing happened between you."

"Yes." She smiled. "Do you believe me? 'Cause if not, I have some pictures downstairs on the counter I can sell you to bolster your fears—make you really crazy."

"I'm never going to live that down, am I?"

"Not anytime soon, but you will—eventually. I'm going to kill Nicki, I swear."

"But how did she know to block me?"

"I don't know." Julia retraced her motions. "I had left my phone on the kitchen counter right after we talked. I remember that because when I went to bed, I reached for it to plug it in and realized I didn't have it. I was so tired I couldn't go downstairs. I even fell asleep in my clothes."

"Did you at least get my texts after we spoke? When I wrote how much I loved and missed you?"

"No, there were no texts the next morning. Damn, Nicki must have seen them come in, deleted them, and then blocked you."

"Why would she do that?"

Julia smirked. "She was making a play to get me back."

"Were you going to tell me about that?"

"Not really."

"Why?"

"Because you were making a movie and you needed to focus on important things. Not stupid crap like my ex showing up here, too drunk to drive and passed out at my gate."

"You really mean that."

"What the hell do you think I mean?"

"Slow down. It's me—my problem. I've been cheated on and lied to enough times that raw honesty is still an alien concept. So is loyalty. Two of your greatest strengths are my go-to insecurities. I still don't know how to handle the honesty."

"Why? Because it's good?"

Rina nodded. "Yes. And since you're showing me that honesty actually works in a relationship, I'm going out on a limb here. Be kind. Britney came onto me that night after dinner. I turned her down of course, but the next morning before we filmed she took another shot at it—which only pissed me off more. It was right after that that we shot the horse scene where I got hurt."

"My face is tingling right now, Rina. I want to strangle her."

"I've never seen you play the jealous lover before. It's very sexy on you—kind of like the Girl Scouts meet Wonder Woman."

Julia fell back on the bed and let out an exasperated breath. "What is it with these fucked-up women? Do you realize this argument was caused by two other women from our pasts? That and the invasion-of-privacy photos."

Rina groaned. "We need a new game plan."

Julia laid her hand on Rina's leg. "I'm open to suggestions."

"Glad you feel that way. We no longer have to worry about Britney at least—I'm quitting *The Big Picture*."

Julia bolted upright. "You're what?"

"I'm leaving the film. As soon as I'm better, I'm going onto a different project. It's a little indie film written by a friend I made in chocolate rehab. It's called *The Do-Over*."

"So this is a good thing?"

"I think it's going to be a very good thing, and I'll be shooting all of it in LA. But none of it matters if I don't have you."

Julia smiled. "You *so* have me."

"I don't exactly have the strength to throw myself at you," Rina grinned, "but I wouldn't say no if you made a gentle pass at me—like now."

"Now?"

"Why, do you have something better to do?"

"No, Rina, you're my favorite thing to do."

"I'll give it up on one condition."

"Which is?"

"Well, I know you keep emergency lasagna for me in the freezer."

Julia moved close and kissed Rina's neck. "You know that, huh? Maybe it's make-up lasagna."

"You mean like make-up sex?"

"Uh-huh—only—lasagna."

"Can I have some after?"

Julia pulled her closer. "After what?" she whispered in her ear.

"Are you going to make me say it?"

"Yes."

"Fine." Rina tilted her head to let Julia kiss her harder. "After you make me scream your name."

Julia pulled back and looked into her lover's eyes. "Scream? You'd never do that."

"No, not me. Never."

"You must really miss the lasagna."

"Oh, baby. I do."

CHAPTER FORTY

Long beyond the Britney fiasco and far enough from the effects of her injury, Rina submerged herself in her new role as Dolly in Swan's film, *The Do-Over*. Her resolve to quit *The Big Picture* had afforded her all the impetus she needed to embrace the new part. Instead of fighting with the pit in her stomach every morning as she had done during *The Big Picture*, she awoke eager to go to work. She was confident she'd made the right choice every time she showed up on the set. Whether it was Swan's hug or being on a first name basis with everyone, including the caterers, Rina felt less like a movie star and more like a newly working actor determined to earn her stripes.

Through the magnetic words Swan had so brilliantly crafted, Dolly became a valued friend. Nuance, emotion, fantasy—all noble beasts of artistic burden—opened Rina to new feelings of levity and freedom. She found herself confronting her past for the first time, questioning decisions she had made—with the grand exception of her love for Julia. Time to express that love, however, was always at a premium, especially when Julia couldn't accompany her to anything that might cause speculation about their relationship.

For months, their visits were brief and often interrupted or canceled, either due to the film or Julia's business expansion. If they were at the Y2, it meant fitting the relationship between stints of a veritable stew of unending have-tos and sleep. In Malibu, it meant First World Problems, like making the Oscar submission deadline—and sleep. At its best, Malibu included a nice dinner at some fancy restaurant with at least Clay's presence to provide a pretext for Julia's. Luxury meant a walk on the beach or watching an ocean sunset together.

Rina sat in her trailer on the set, going over her script changes for the next scene when Gigi entered. "Do you want to run any lines?" she asked.

"No, I'm ready."

"Julia called."

Rina looked up from her pages. "What did she say?"

"If you need to attend the dinner party alone tomorrow night, she understands. She has a big party coming up this weekend and would feel better if she was available to work it with her new staff."

"Ugh. This can't last forever."

"What?"

"Not being with her."

"You two had a great anniversary weekend."

"That was two months ago!"

"She went wild for the Harley-Davidson you gave her."

"She adores that beast. I was hoping it would keep her occupied on her visits to LA when I'm working."

"The good news is, everyone is confident that the film will be ready before the Oscar submission deadline, and the producers already have the release date."

"Whew! We've all busted our asses for that."

Gigi answered the knock on the door. "Ten minutes, Miss Verralta," the Production Assistant called out.

Not one of Dolly's lighter moments in the film, the eulogy she would deliver in the next scene was her poetic farewell to her lover. Rina stood and rehearsed it one last time.

Like the earliest of autumn leaves.
But it's winter.
Sun warm and alive
And it's winter.
Roses by our pond
The fountain sprays only me *with spring*
This winter.
Yellows and pinks decorate your season.

Then white.
And red.
The final bed
Of winter.

Her assistant stood there, staring at her in awe.

"What is it, Gigi?"

"That was without question your most magnificent delivery. Ever."

Rina smiled. "Really?"

"Really."

"There's something about playing Dolly that defines me completely as an actor."

"It shows. I know the role in *The Big Picture* was supposed to be your role of a lifetime, but honestly, Rina, I've been watching and I wouldn't be surprised if this earned you another nomination." Gigi opened the door to the trailer and waited for Rina to exit. "I'll text Julia and let her know you'll call her tonight."

"Thanks."

* * *

Julia picked up the phone when she came into the house from the casita. "Hi, Vitty, you okay? Isn't it past your bedtime there?"

"Hi, sis. It's late but I've been wanting to speak with you and there's never enough time during the day."

"I know what you mean. I've been working nonstop between the diner, catering, and the retail packaging."

"So things are going well?"

"Really well, except it's been impossible for Rina and me to have any meaningful time together."

"I know you haven't shared the details with me yet, but I can't wait to meet your girlfriend. You sound happy."

"I've never been happier. But you and I need to have a much longer conversation for this."

"Fair enough," Vitty replied.

"So, what's up?"

"There's something I'd like to discuss with you about the ranch."

Julia opened a beer and settled on the sofa. "Okay."

"I know it's only months away, but sometime after we're married—sooner than later—David and I would really like to buy a little house outside the city. You know, get a place where we can raise our kids."

"And?"

"New York is so ridiculously expensive, I wanted to ask you if you would even consider buying me out of the Y2 or at least let me sell off part of the ranch. I know it's a lot to ask."

Sell off the ranch? "Wow. That's a big request. I mean, I'd buy you out in a heartbeat if I had more time to save up."

"I know I should have brought this up long before now—at least on my last visit. Look, it wouldn't have to be right away. David and I aren't going to have kids immediately, but it would sure be nice to pay a mortgage rather than throwing thousands away every month renting in the city."

"Let me think about it. Maybe there's a way to finance part of your mortgage using the ranch as collateral or to put the ranch in my name only and take out a second mortgage…"

"Between the two of us, I think we can come up with something we can both live with, don't you, Jules?"

"Sure. We're smart enough to figure this out."

"I feel bad for asking. You've always been there for me and I know it wasn't easy on you when I left."

"Never feel bad about asking. We're sisters."

"Promise me you won't stress about it, Jules?"

That would be a neat trick. "I won't. Get some sleep and I'll speak with you soon."

"Um…Mom says hi."

The reaction stuck in Julia's throat. She said nothing.

"She's so thankful she'll get to be with us together at the wedding."

"I'm your maid of honor. Your wish is my command."

Vitty chuckled. "Best maid of honor ever."

"Night, sis."

"Night, Juju."

Mother! Sell? Where…how…oh, my head is starting to hurt.

Julia was already in bed when Rina called. She smiled when she picked up. "Hey, Dolly."

"Hello, Cowgirl."

"I prefer horsewoman."

Rina chuckled. "It fits you. How are things there?"

"F-fine."

"Want to try that again?"

"Vitty phoned a little while ago. She wants me to buy her out or to work out a deal to sell off a portion of the Y2. She kind of blindsided me, so I'm lying here thinking about how to do it."

"Why does she want you to do that? She knows what the ranch means to you."

"In all fairness, it's her birthright too, Rina. It's not her fault she wanted a different life. And now she and David are about to get married, and they want a little house of their own—where they can raise kids. She said New York is expensive. I know she wouldn't be asking if there was another way to do it."

"You started by saying, 'In all fairness.' What about fairness to you?"

"It'll work out—one way or another things always work out."

Rina sighed. "Always the grown-up."

"Someone has to be."

"Not always, Julia—and even still, it doesn't always have to be you."

"Tomorrow's another day—I'll sleep on it. How did things go on the set today?"

"Incredibly well. Dolly had to deliver a eulogy for her deceased lover. When I finished the first take, everyone on the set applauded. I can't remember that ever happening before. It brought tears to my eyes—honestly, I was so humbled."

"With everything you've told me about this movie, I can't wait to see it. Just the one day I watched you film was incredible. And I love it when we run lines."

"Listen, I feel terrible that I can't bring you to the gala dinner with me this weekend."

Julia exhaled. "I've gotten used to it."

"What?"

"The whole invisibility game."

"Don't call it that. I love you."

"Enough to actually be with me?"

"We've been over this, Julia. I can't come out."

Julia paused and let it sink in for the fifty-thousandth time. "So when will you be done filming?"

"We'll wrap the middle of next week," Rina said excitedly. "I was thinking I could come down the following weekend."

"I have back-to-back parties. How about the weekend after that?"

"I can't. We have the photo shoot for the press materials. I can't put it off because the photographers need the costume and makeup people there. What about the weekend after that?"

"You'll finally have to see me then in any case. That's when I'm meeting with the gallery owner about my sculpture exhibition. Can I crash at your place?" Julia asked facetiously.

"Julia, it won't always be this way."

"What way?"

"Where life is so busy and crazy."

Julia went silent.

"What are you thinking?" asked Rina.

"I'm thinking about how many days, nights, and weekends we've lost out on being together because you can't be seen with me."

"I don't like it either, but I'll be with you when you're here. We'll go for a nice dinner."

"As long as you stay three feet from me at all times?"

"But I'll be right there to cheer you on when you meet with the gallery people, and again a few weeks after at the exhibition. I'm so happy your work will finally be out there for everyone to appreciate."

"Thanks, Rina. It wouldn't have happened without you."

"Sure it would have. Not knowing the gallery owners, it may have taken a little longer, but I have faith in your talent. You should too."

"Thanks for the pep talk."

"Thank you for always understanding my life. I love you, Julia."

"I love you, Katarina. Good luck tomorrow on the film. Sweet dreams."

"Night."

Julia drifted off to sleep with fairy-tale princesses dancing in her head. Princesses whose ivory towers served as their prisons—just like the one in Malibu. She concluded that if her love was a princess, it too would indeed inhabit an ivory tower.

CHAPTER FORTY-ONE

Months later as Julia reflected again on that phone conversation with Rina, she remembered with clarity how she had felt that night, after Rina had apologized yet again for ousting Julia from her social life, marginalizing her role as lover. Secondhand, second-rate, repressed, closeted. None of it looked good on Julia, not even in the funhouse mirror that was Hollywood.

Now, here she was yet again, ready to take on the role of *her* lifetime. Pretending to not be in love with the love of her life. In public with Rina, she had mastered faking it, to the point where she had learned how to feel nothing at all for her so that no one would see the truth about their favorite star.

But here it finally was—Oscar night. Julia made her way down Sunset to Hollywood. Even though Rina had already won the Golden Globe for her role as Dolly, she knew the woman would be a bundle of nerves.

She parked her motorcycle in the lot of the Hollywood Roosevelt Hotel, just steps away from the Oscar ceremonies, where in a matter of hours, Rina and Dolly would await their fate. She shook her hair loose from her helmet, grabbed it and her backpack, and breezed into the iconic Hollywood Roosevelt Hotel. What caught her eye first were the artistically decorated beams that separated the sections of the recessed Moorish ceiling. The ornate patterns and scrolls that overlaid them offered elegant breathing room in this place of the first-ever Oscars—even for ordinary people like her.

Throughout its dark and shabby period, the Roosevelt had resembled a broken down Hollywood has-been—stories of punk rockers stabbed outside and hookers trolling the streets behind it. But like most Hollywood icons who had made it through rehab, it had regained its real estate among the glamorous with a facelift that had earned it a comeback.

The balustrade framed out the colonnade below, and its current incarnation of tufted leather sofas in the lobby invited and welcomed. Beyond its renovation, the hotel's design still harkened back to the era of glam movie royalty. Julia envisioned the likes of Marilyn Monroe, Clark Gable, and Carole Lombard posing for the cameras, perhaps standing where she now stood. Or maybe Sinatra and Dean Martin, a cigar in one hand, a bourbon in the other. *Except that it's illegal to smoke indoors now—and who the hell drinks bourbon!*

Though the deco candelabra chandelier highlighted the ceiling brightly, it spilled a fallen shimmer onto the centrally placed octagonal fountain below.

A young concierge met Julia as she stepped into the high-arched colonnade that ringed the lobby.

"May I help you?" he asked.

"The penthouse, please," she replied.

He glanced at her backpack and brain bucket. "Your name?" His pen was poised over a clipboard with a list.

"Julia."

"Julia…?"

"Just Julia."

He stared at her soberly and then scanned the list, tapping the clipboard with his pen. "Nice try, but I can't let you go up there."

Julia exhaled hard. She smiled anyway. "Would you please call Ms. Verralta's suite and tell her I'm here?"

He hesitated. "Come with me please."

While following him to the Bell Desk, a litany of flashbacks crashed the present moment. No matter how much Rina said she wanted them to be together, the chasm between them had widened, thanks to too many situations like this one. It was bad enough—the times when Clay had yanked her to his side on Rodeo Drive so that she wouldn't wind up in a photo with Rina. Once they were alone, Rina would always apologize.

"It's ringing," said the concierge.

She's apologized a lot lately. But nothing had changed. She knew there would be a next time—and a time after that. After all, there was a *this* time. And, if there was a way for Gigi to conveniently keep her in the dark about anything or to sabotage her relationship with Rina, the assistant always found it, no matter how many times Rina had "spoken" to her. The routine had gotten stale—tiring. Today, it was simply old. She couldn't remember the last time she had spent a whole day off sculpting in her casita on the ranch.

"Still ringing." The concierge gave her a skeptical once-over. "I have Julia—no last name, here in the lobby, but she's not on my list." His expression immediately turned from concierge to that of a humble bellhop. "Thank you." He placed the handset back on the receiver. "Sorry. But you understand."

She understood all right. Then again, she never understood. If there was ever a time she wasn't in the mood to be seen as a nobody— an intruder no less, this was it. Perhaps Rina's biggest night, and she wasn't even on the list along with the florist and the hairstylist.

Julia rode one of the two old elevators, an express, directly from the ground floor to the penthouse on the twelfth floor.

I see why they named this the Gable Lombard Suite, she thought, taking in its opulence.

The main room of the suite had been converted into a ready-station for the Oscar contender. Rina's team of stylists hovered over her like a coven surrounding a caldron. Gigi sat in the corner doing what she always did—making sure Rina had whatever she wanted whenever she wanted it.

Rina beamed when she saw Julia behind her in the mirror. She swiveled her chair to face her. "Oh good, you're finally here. Mark, this is Julia, whose hair and makeup you'll be doing later."

"I've heard good things, Mark," Julia said. "Nice to meet you."

Mark laced his fingers through Julia's long straight hair. "I'm going to love working with this." He glanced at the brain bucket. "Tell me you're not planning on smashing my creation with helmet-head."

She smiled. "No, at worst, it'll be limo-head."

"We're in no rush," Rina began, "so how about we take a break?"

Mark addressed his two assistants. "Be back in twenty."

Gigi remained seated.

"You too, Gigi."

Gigi nodded at Rina, then glowered at Julia when she left.

Rina waited until they were alone before she kissed Julia. "I couldn't wait to see you. I'm so nervous!" She raised her hands and shook them on limp wrists, as though trying to air dry them—or perhaps expel her demons.

"I would have been here much sooner had someone remembered to put my name on the list."

"Ugh! Not again. I didn't know."

A sad smile graced Julia's lips. "You never do."

Rina touched her cheek. "Look, I know how uncomfortable this week has been."

"This week? This month. Right now. Rina, even you must see how often these things are happening."

"I'll talk to Gigi again."

"It won't change anything." Julia peered out the window. In the distance stood the iconic Hollywood sign—and in the foreground, one for the Dolby Theater next door, from where the almighty Oscars would be broadcast around the world. She tried to act normal. "Will I be able to wish you luck privately—before you leave?"

Rina went to her from behind. She placed her hands on Julia's arms and pressed against her. "I wish you could come with me tonight. But the reason I rented this magnificent suite is to keep you as close as possible and to make it easy for us afterward."

"As close as across the street—rooting for you on TV."

"Remember, if I win, which I really don't think I will—when I touch my earring, I'm telling you how much I love you."

Julia turned to face Rina. "I take it Clay will fill me in on the timing and events for tonight."

"Why do you say it like that?"

"Like what?" Julia retorted.

"Are you angry with me?"

"Maybe. I'm not sure. I'm probably more angry with myself."

"Why? Is it the list thing? Because I promise you I will take care of the list thing. What I know is that I'll see you immediately after the awards—after photo ops. Oh, and if I win there will be interviews. Then you and Clay will pick me up in the limo and we'll go to the Vanity Fair party."

"I see."

Rina gasped. "Oh god, it's Oscar night! I think I just broke a sweat. I've been a little crazy all day."

Julia stepped forward and held her close. "You're trembling."

"I know. I never imagined this little indie film would become a huge hit. That's one of the reasons I did it."

"What were the other reasons?"

Rina pulled back to look into her eyes. "I knew I could just act. Really sink my heart into the role of Dolly. And filming in LA meant we'd be closer."

Julia held back a snicker. "You mean closer to me and my boyfriend? I still can't believe you had me investigated."

"Stop it. I'm so pissed at Gigi for doing that."

"That makes two of us."

"In all fairness, you could have told me your sister was your twin."

"Or you could have trusted me before coming to your own ill-founded conclusions."

"You're right. I'm sorry that happened, but you need to understand how I've been scammed in my life by people who've said they loved me."

"I've done more than that. I've shown you, in every way possible. Still, you assumed the worst. This conversation always starts and ends in the same place. Let's change the subject." She paused. "So, tonight instead of sitting with Britney, you'll be competing against her for Best Actress again."

Rina burned her with a glare. "Why would you bring that up now?"

Julia feigned calm. "It's just that she and everyone else in the room get to be with you during your moment, and I don't. I'll bet Mark's name was on the list downstairs."

"Really, Julia? We're going to do this now? Do you think you can find a better time?"

"Sorry. I'm sorry."

"Thank you. When we get to the after parties, you'll enter with Clay."

Julia fidgeted. "So, I'm Clay's 'date' tonight?"

"No. You're *my* date. It's just that Clay will be escorting you."

"Isn't that the definition of a date?"

Rina placed an emphatic hand on her jutting hip. "All right, Julia. Out with it."

"Mark is doing my hair and makeup. I'm going to stay here in the suite with Clay and watch you on TV, and then I'll get dressed and into the limo with Clay—for the limo queue—but I'm *your* date."

"What are you trying to say?"

Julia scraped back her hair. "Fuck. My timing sucks. I didn't plan this, baby. Honestly, I didn't."

"Plan what?"

"I can't do it anymore—I can't pretend I don't love you down to my very bones without it becoming true. I can't pretend that I don't exist even when you can. I can't go."

"But this is my big night and I want you with me. You have to do this."

Julia shook her head. "No, you have to do it. You chose to do it alone at the Golden Globes—why should now be any different? I would never embarrass you or blow your cover, but standing here I just envisioned a night where a thousand cameras will be taking photos of you—as always. And each time, I'm going to stumble backward into the shadows, pretending I'm with Clay. So, go ahead and do it. You don't need me there. Maybe you don't really need me anywhere."

"No."

"No, what?"

"You can't just bow out. You're my lover!"

"I'm your whatever-I-always-need-to-be, whenever you need me to be it."

"Why are you doing this now?"

Julia shrugged. "I guess that today's the day I saw the big picture. I couldn't love you any more if I tried, Rina, and I don't mind playing by the rules of your life—but not to the point where I don't have one." She sighed, and then decided to say it anyway. "I have no place in your real life. I never have."

Rina's eyes shifted from hazel to gold when she turned toward the light. "What are you saying?" she said in a low voice. "That you won't be there for me tonight?"

Julia bit her lower lip.

Rina stepped over to the vanity and cinched the belt on her dressing robe. "I see. Well, I'm going to get ready now," she said with a hard edge to her tone. "When you leave, you can tell my stylists I'm ready."

The contender sat before the mirror and they locked eyes. The chill that ran down Julia's spine wasn't chased by warmth. The expression in her lover's eyes told her all she needed to know—that the woman had been a better actress than she ever thought. The ice running in Rina's veins stung her through the glare of spellbinding eyes that threw her off balance—every damn time.

"I'll be here before you leave to wish you luck," Julia said as she reached for the doorknob.

"Julia, wait!"

Julia turned and gazed into her eyes from across the room. "I'll be back. You need to get ready now."

CHAPTER FORTY-TWO

Julia exited the hotel, sidestepped the edge of the red carpet, and wandered down Hollywood Boulevard. Already the traffic restrictions were of steroidal proportions on a street where mania held fame's hand and skipped along the Walk of Fame twenty-four hours a day. She strolled down the dirty sidewalk and read some of the names she stepped on—one in particular. *Katarina Verralta.* She kicked a discarded paper cup off of the camera icon and continued on.

It took but a block for the concrete jungle of Hollywood Boulevard to assault her sensibilities. Grubby-looking panhandlers. A throng of foreign tourists mumbling in some language she couldn't have even taken a guess at deciphering. Overwhelming numbers of people jostling hours before the affair to claim their spot behind the railing along the red carpet. Generic American tourists dressed in similar uniforms—sneakers, cheap T-shirts bearing the names of hometowns and schools—and herds of bald middle-aged men who might have all been the same person. She noticed no one in particular in the same way that no one noticed her. Then it struck her that had she been there with Rina, no one would notice her anyway.

Look at me, she berated herself. *Wandering aimlessly, staring at the red carpet—the clandestine lover of one of Hollywood's most beloved actresses.*

Her throat tightened. *I can't live this way anymore! But how do I walk away from the love of my life?*

The twisting in her gut caused her to double over in an alley until it passed. Behind her sunglasses tears filled her eyes even as a surge of gawkers and fans lined up early to get a glimpse of Red Carpet Hollywood.

Leaving Rina wasn't about not being in the spotlight. She couldn't have cared less for the spotlight. Although she loved this woman, the truth she'd ignored was that increasingly she felt like an ornament—a less-than-everything. Maybe in this moment, a less-than-nothing. She wondered if she would ever be enough.

Vitty was right. I live for everyone but myself. Her gut twisted again but not as severely as the first time. *Rina's going to hate me—forever. And worse, I'm never going to love anyone more than I love her. But I just can't be* this person *anymore.*

Validation had eluded her her whole life. After all, wasn't it her job to be happy for everyone else's success? Thinking about it now, she couldn't immediately remember even one person who had been her champion—who had taken the reins when she needed it most. Even Vitty had always treated her as second fiddle to some degree—and not only because she was three minutes older.

Julia stayed away from the hotel until she couldn't any longer. Returning to the penthouse, she found Rina alone in the bedroom lounging in her robe in full makeup and with perfect hair. Her gaze followed Julia when she tentatively crossed the room, sat next to her, and held her hand.

The nominee stared into her eyes with enough star power to make Julia feel lightheaded—again.

Rina sighed. "I don't have a good feeling about tonight."

"All the nominees are heavy hitters. I'll bet every actress in your category is saying the same thing right now."

"I wasn't talking about the Oscar. I was talking about us."

Julia stroked Rina's cheek and looked into the phosphorescent light that ignited relentless passion within her. "I'm so sorry, Rina. I love you with all that I am—but I can't do it anymore. I thought I knew what I was signing up for but…"

"Don't do this, Julia. Don't leave—you can't leave me."

"Can you honestly say that all of this separation between us, looking over our shoulders everywhere we go, shoving me at Clay… that none of it bothers you?"

"Of course it bothers me. But what can I do about it? This is my life, my career that's on the line."

"Come on, Rina, it's 2019! People are *gay* now!"

"It's different when you're famous—especially at my age. I don't want my sexuality out there in the world for everyone to weigh in on it. I have so little privacy as it is."

"And that's where I live. In this ever-diminishing space that you call privacy and I call a prison." Julia stood, took a few steps, and turned. "Do you hear yourself? What can you do about it? It's your life and you can do whatever you want to with it. What I don't understand is why you won't."

"The public is fickle and so are the studios. Are you ready to have cameras shoved in your face and reporters taunting you everywhere you go?"

Julia crossed her arms and stared at her. "Don't you ever just want to be—*with* me? Free to take who we are together out into the world? Do you even know who you are without an entourage that worships your every gesture?"

"I'm in love with you. Can't we just be us for…us?"

"We've done all of it your way. It doesn't work for me."

"I can't believe you're doing this now! We'll talk about it later," said Rina.

Julia's eyes welled up. She went to Rina and gave her a "kiss of last resort." *What am I doing!* She pulled away abruptly and regained her balance. "You know, when we're out at the ranch, I see who you really are. You smile—you're happy. This?" Julia gazed at the luxury surrounding her. "Does denying who you are make you as happy?"

Rina stood, sauntered to the window, and gazed out. "I'm happy when you're part of it," she said in a monotone.

"This will make you happy again once I'm no longer part of the equation."

"Stop it. I don't want to do this with you anymore." Rina went to the bar, poured herself a small shot of vodka, and downed it.

Julia waited until Rina turned to face her before she spoke. "Would you like to know what makes me happy?"

"Sure, why not?" Rina slammed the empty glass down on the bar.

"For me, happiness is bringing you coffee in the morning after we make love. It's you bringing me lemonade out in the barn wearing your thousand-dollar sneakers because you don't know any better." Julia stepped toward her. "It's cuddling with you by the fire on a chilly night watching one of your movies, where you fill me in on all the stories that happened off camera. But most of all—most of all, the *you* that's seared into me is the frightened girl who bolted from the casita on a stormy night to fall into my arms." Julia waited—stood there teetering on the threshold of nothingness in the silence that followed. "Good luck tonight. I mean that." When she stepped toward the door, Rina cut her off.

"Where are you going?"

Julia picked up her motorcycle helmet and backpack. "I'll stop back after you leave to make arrangements with Clay to get my things from the house, if that's okay."

"No! It's not okay. You can't leave me. We have to talk about this."

"We've talked a lot, Rina. But nothing changes. You know it and so do I." Julia scraped back her hair. "I know you've tried, baby, and I'm not making you the bad guy here. Honestly, I'm not blaming you. I don't want anything from you, and I'll always respect your privacy—our privacy. We've simply…run out of road, and there's nowhere left to go."

Her gaze dropped to the floor; she swallowed hard and steeled herself again to meet Rina's stare. "Look, you have a huge night ahead of you and you don't need to be thinking about where I am or how things appear. It's time for you to be the A-lister that you are. As for me, now I won't have to worry pointlessly about every single person who worships you and what I don't know about your history with them. Just go and have a fabulous worry-free evening. You deserve it."

"Without you?" Rina spoke softly. "You're my love. None of it means anything if I can't share it with you. How can I do this without you?"

"I don't know. All I know is that right now it hurts to breathe—and my heart is pounding at the thought of walking out that door!" She turned away.

Rina grabbed her arm, causing the backpack and helmet to fall to the floor. "This is insane. Don't! You're not leaving!"

"Let me go!" Julia pulled away. "I'm riding the bike to Malibu now to pick up a few things. Then I'm headed back to the ranch—where I belong."

"You're not riding a motorcycle through the desert alone at night! Why don't you take the car?"

Julia retrieved her gear from the floor.

Rina sighed hard. "No matter how many pages of the calendar we flip, spring never becomes winter, does it?"

"No. Not even with the best of intentions. It's a cruel twist of fate to be victims of seasons never intended to meet."

Rina reached out for her again and spoke haltingly. "Why—why now?"

"Because you're about to have one of the biggest nights of your life. You need the freedom to take that and run like the wind—like when you race Thunder across the mesa. Without worry or fear, and without me holding you back." Her gaze fell to the floor again and then climbed slowly back to Rina. "You need to let me go."

Rina's stare burned into her. "You're breaking my heart, Julia."

Mine is shattered. "I wouldn't have traded a minute of being with you—you're the love of my life. You always will be."

"If that's true, you'll stay!"

Clay barged through the door, startling both women. "I'm so excited! What a great night this is going to be!" He went to Julia and kissed her cheek. "Certainly, having this gorgeous girl on my arm is going to up my cred."

Julia looked over at Rina. *"Your* date, huh?"

"Uh-oh," said Clay. "What am I interrupting?"

"Sorry, Clay. It looks like I'll be standing you up tonight. On the bright side, you can party like a king since you won't have to watch my every move or lie about who I am."

"Rina?" he said.

There was a catch in her throat that barely allowed her to utter the words. "Julia's...leaving."

"Leaving?" His face twisted. "Don't you feel well?"

Though she answered him, Julia's teary gaze fell upon Rina. "Right now, I think I'd have to die to feel better." She turned to Clay. "I'm heading to Malibu to pack some things in my bike bag. I'll call you to arrange picking up the rest."

"You didn't answer me," said Rina. "Are you taking the car? I don't want you upset and riding a motorcycle all the way through the desert at night."

"You're going home?" asked Clay.

"Best of luck tonight, Rina. You know I'll always be rooting for you. Someday, when things quiet down, give me a call and tell me I was wrong. You know the number."

"Someone better tell me right now what the hell is happening!" said Clay.

CHAPTER FORTY-THREE

Gigi hung up the phone and turned to Rina. "That was Swan. She's downstairs in the limo, but she said you should take your time."

Rina stood before the mirror for a final check, straightening the diamond necklace whose V pointed tastefully toward her cleavage. "I'm so nervous I'm vibrating inside."

"Stop scowling," said Gigi. "You look stunning."

Rina turned to her. "Has she called?"

Gigi shook her head.

"You would tell me if she had, wouldn't you, Gigi?"

"Definitely. Come on, I'll see you to the limo." She held the door for the actress, and they entered the penthouse elevator that awaited them. "Clay and I will see you afterward." She smiled. "I know we'll be on the edge of our seats right along with you in real time—good luck tonight."

"Where *is* Clay?"

"He said he had one last errand."

Rina drifted to thoughts of Julia riding her motorcycle through the desert at night, then to the memory of how Julia had kissed her goodbye—ending it all so abruptly with a kiss that wasn't worthy of either of them.

Gigi gave Rina a final once-over. "Are you all right?"

"Why did you have to forget to put Julia on the list?"

"I thought I had. I'm sorry, okay?" Gigi focused on the lit numbers above the elevator door as it descended.

"Tell the truth," Rina started. "You've had something against her from the start. Why?"

"Because the more time you spent with her, the more she changed you."

"Was that such a bad thing?"

"You can rehash it later. Right now, it's time for you to go and have an Oscar-worthy night with your costars, the director, and Swan."

The elevator landed. "Now, smile."

The elevator door opened.

"And...entrance."

Rina felt every head turn to behold the movie-star-Katarina Verralta as she crossed the lobby. She smiled back at the blur of faces, waved with a gracious "hello" at the cameras.

The concierge greeted her. "This way, Miss Verralta." He ushered her through the door from the Roosevelt and opened the limo door. "Good luck tonight," he smiled.

"Thank you." Rina chuckled when she saw Swan's eager face awaiting her. "Hello, Swan."

"Hi, Rina. I can barely keep it together! How are you doing?"

"I'm a bouillabaisse of emotions from one instant to the next. Worse than the craving for Belgian dark chocolate."

"This is so surreal," said Swan. "I'm nominated, you're nominated. The *film* is nominated!"

"Just to reiterate, we're not mentioning we met in rehab, right?"

"Right," Swan answered. "Besides, I doubt anyone will recognize or want to interview me."

The limo pulled forward and took its place in the line to coast to the next block.

Swan studied her. "Something seems off with you. Are you all right?"

"No, not really. Julia left me—a few hours ago."

"What! Oh, no."

Rina nodded and stared out the window.

"I'm so sorry."

Rina turned to her. "Thanks, Swan, but I don't know how I'm going to do the red carpet interview, let alone fake my way through the ceremony. Will you stand by me tonight?"

Swan smiled. "Sure. Stay present—and remember what Therapy Brittany taught us about staying in the moment. Nothing happens until you get there."

"But we *are* there." Rina's door opened onto the red carpet. She accepted the hand of the young man who offered it and waited for Swan.

"I can feel the buzz in the air, Rina. I'm so nervous—my heart is racing." She took a deep breath and forcefully exhaled. "Gotta get rid of these heebie jeebies."

Rina let her shoulders fall into position—clicked the internal switch that produced the shine her public expected to see. She heard the voice of interviewer Brandon Coyote as he approached, speaking into his microphone. The camera that followed him broadcast the exchange.

"The stars are out tonight," he said. "Here comes Katarina Verralta, looking flawlessly chic." He extended his arm to welcome her.

"Why thank you, Brandon!" Rina smiled Red Carpet Smile Number One and returned his air-kiss to her cheek.

"Congratulations on your tenth nomination, Katarina. A win tonight would be number five on the mantle. Here with you tonight is Swan—the Oscar-nominated screenwriter for your film *The Do-Over*. Congratulations on your first nomination, Swan. So tell us, where did the name Swan come from?"

"Actually, Katarina gave me the nickname and it stuck."

Brandon pointed the microphone at Rina. "Why Swan?"

Rina pulled Genuine Chuckle Number Six out of her ass. "Because she was too pretty to be called Duck."

Swan laughed. "It's true, Brandon. I was feeding ducks when we met..."

"And I have a bad memory for names." Rina put the issue to bed. *Good save, Swan!*

"You look flawless tonight, Katarina—your gown brings back the glamour and magic of classic Hollywood. Who are you wearing?"

I'm wearing what's left of Julia all over me. "This is Dior Couture," she beamed. Rina pivoted to let the camera get its best oblique view of her, allowing the slit over her leg to part.

"So it was custom-made for you."

"Yes."

"The V halter neckline, the fabric—gorgeous. And that shade of green makes your eyes look electric."

Julia was right—this is *my color.*

"Those diamond earrings peeking through your luxurious waves are magnificent, as is that sexy slit on your leg."

"Well, thank you, Brandon." Generic Smile Fourteen—the one with the amused raised eyebrow. "What girl doesn't *love* Dior?"

"Can we get a shot of those shoes?"

When the camera pointed toward her feet, Rina gently lifted the fabric draped over her leg to reveal her heels with the diamond studs on the ankle strap. The cameraman cut back to Rina's face.

"Katarina, what is it you loved about playing this character Dolly in *The Do-Over*?" the interviewer asked.

"Her universality. At some point in life I think everyone has the thought: 'I wonder what would have happened if…' Dolly gets a chance to pick the one defining moment when she wished she had made a different life choice, and she gets to go back and change it. What Swan brilliantly shows is how everything evolves for Dolly from that moment on. In the end, Dolly surprises everyone, including herself."

"I think anyone on a journey of self-discovery can relate to Dolly," said Brandon.

"Thank you," Swan offered graciously.

"This is certainly a unique film," said Brandon, "and it's such a departure from every other role you've had. What made you want to play Dolly?"

"Swan's portrayal on the page inspired me to want to *be* Dolly."

"In a way she already is," Swan interjected. "Meeting Katarina is what inspired the character."

"Katarina, I think a lot of people were surprised to see you sign on to an indie non-big budget film," said Brandon.

Rina nodded thoughtfully. "Once I read the script, I knew I would be kicking myself forever if I turned it down. I mean, Dolly is so strong and she imparts a unique perspective on life that's totally relatable. This film's positive message is that it's never too late to change, no matter what has happened in the past. But to do that Dolly has to take her biggest risk—believing in herself."

"Why do you think people have connected so intensely with this film, Swan?" He pointed the mic at her.

"Many people are feeling uncertainty about life right now. *The Do-Over* is, in a way, every person's journey. We all make mistakes, and I think audiences connect with Dolly's honesty in admitting she took a wrong turn in life. After facing a mountain of obstacles, Dolly turns it around by doing something she never dreamed she was capable of doing. In that sense, she becomes her own hero."

"Can you personally relate to her, Katarina? If you had the chance to go back and change something, would you opt for a do-over?"

Rina's face flushed and she fidgeted. *Steady.* "I would."

"Would you like to share what you'd do over?"

Rina chuckled. "Sorry, you'll have to wait until I'm old and I write the memoir."

Brandon laughed. "Then we'll leave it right there. Thank you, Katarina Verralta, and Swan—screenwriter for *The Do-Over.* Good luck tonight."

"Thank you, Brandon," said Swan and Katarina before they walked away.

"Did I fake it well enough, Swan?" Rina whispered.

"Fake it? That wasn't real?" She shook her head. "Damn, you really *are* a great actress. Devious—but *damn* good."

CHAPTER FORTY-FOUR

With a heavy heart, Julia left Rina's house in Malibu, pointing the motorcycle toward the freeway to head home. She passed the entrance to the interstate and then circled back—three more times—before she abandoned the idea.

A temperate breeze of late winter mixed with early spring bit her cheeks when she accelerated. She turned onto a boulevard and found herself psychically summoned by the gay gods of West Hollywood. Too distracted for the long ride home, she decided to go to the gay video bar on Santa Monica Boulevard where she was sure the Oscars would be playing on every screen.

She had resisted the urge to turn on the TV at the house, afraid that if she saw Rina on the red carpet she would break down completely. Now, however, Julia yearned to see the love of her life—needed to root for her favorite star, Katarina Verralta. Needed to know if she would win.

Julia had second-guessed herself repeatedly about ending the relationship, the gravity of her actions weighing heavily on her. While it was true that she had stood up for herself, she had to think that in doing so she also had taken a stand for Rina and for them as a couple.

Maybe one day she'll see it that way, even if it's too late to do anything about it.

Although her desire to go back to Rina pulled hard like the force when wind collides with water, she was drowning in a tsunami of emotions that pushed her farther away from her only anchor to all that was good.

Julia viewed their relationship as a fractured sculpture. Shards that would forever show cracks, no matter how carefully glued in an attempt to make the art appear whole again.

How long would it take for me to feel imprisoned next time? The time after? She laid rubber and weaved the motorcycle between the cars on Sunset Boulevard the instant the light turned green. She turned off of Sunset onto Larrabee Street and followed it down the hill to Santa Monica Boulevard, where she parked. Julia shook her hair loose from the helmet, letting it spill down over her leather jacket.

"Hey, pretty lady," said a wide-eyed millennial as she passed.

Julia smiled back. She unhooked her saddlebag, latched the helmet to it, and entered Revolver, a video bar. As she had suspected, screens everywhere were broadcasting the Oscars. She ordered a beer, found a seat, and watched the mid-portion of the show, like every other nobody. To her right, two men were discussing the year's films.

"Did you see *The Do-Over?*" said the one closest to her.

"It was fabulous!" his fake-blond friend answered.

"I can't wait to see it. I heard that Katarina Verralta killed it!"

"She did. I think she should win Best Actress."

"Wait—wasn't she supposed to have been in that other film with Britney Cavell?"

The blond laughed. "*The Big Picture?* Yes, but then somehow Emma Thompson wound up playing the part."

"Wow, and all three of them are nominated in the Best Actress category!"

"Rumor has it that Cavell and Verralta had an affair on set. Talk about Hollywood drama."

Julia rolled her eyes.

"Lovers?" said the blond's friend. "Get outta here. Really? No. I've heard stories about Britney Cavell but Verralta's not gay!"

Julia sneered, picked up her gear, and found another bar stool as far away as she could. Mesmerized by the big screen over the bar, she watched film clips of Rina and of Britney Cavell—who had become the first person she'd ever despised without ever having met her. The categories crept by, with occasional cutaway shots to Rina laughing at the host's joke or being a good sport when he picked on her.

Rina has the perfect expression for everything. In her mind she saw the one she had never seen before today. The You're Breaking My Heart, Julia. That one—the one that would haunt her forever. Her gut twisted again. *This is fucking torture!*

It was long dark by the time the show got closer to announcing the Best Actress category. After that there would only be the last trophy—that of Best Picture—after which Rina would enter the limo to find Julia absent.

Gigi must be thrilled that I'm out of the picture.

"Hey, beautiful, can I buy you a beer?" The voice from behind startled her, causing her to teeter on her stool when she whipped around.

"Clay! What are you doing here? You're supposed to be getting ready for the limo and the parties…wait. How did you know I'd be here?"

He took the seat beside her. "I tracked your phone."

"You what!"

"Don't be mad."

"I'm not. I'm impressed. Did Rina send you?"

He looked into her eyes in earnest. "No, she has no idea that I'm here. She's devastated, you know."

"We both are. For the record, even though my timing sucked, I walked away because I *do* love her."

He scrunched his nose. "I don't get it."

"We can't go on like this. You shouldn't have to always be my beard in public. You should see her on the ranch, Clay…"

"Please. Every time I try to picture Rina on your ranch, I cry from laughter."

"She's so genuine there, and she loves who she really is. She doesn't love herself here. Instead, she kills any chance of us having a normal healthy relationship and that's destroying me."

"May I?" Clay didn't wait for Julia to say "yes" before he took a hefty swig of her beer. "Rina's right about one thing. You *are* the grown-up in this relationship. Don't go, Julia. She needs you. Now more than ever."

Julia glanced up at the TV and then settled on Clay's eyes. "She needs this more. It's done—we can't have both love and fame the way that things are. No one, not even Rina, wishes harder that it had turned out differently. But the truth is, I don't exist in her world. At all. I'm invisible. What's most painful about it is that she *is* my world." She killed the last of her beer.

Clay held out his arm to get the bartender's attention, pointed to Julia's beer, and held up two fingers. "Her category is coming up soon."

They watched and waited and then waited some more. Finally, the last of the Oscar-nominated songs was sung and the broadcast went to commercial.

"Why did you stay, Julia?" Clay took a sip of beer.

"Because I need to know if she wins."

"Will that change anything?" he asked.

"For her, it will change everything—she deserves that award. Even sweeter to snatch it away from Cavell. I mean, really, after what that woman did to her? It's so cool that Rina had the guts to leave *The Big Picture* for *The Do-Over*."

"You were the deciding factor."

"What? I was?"

"Rina couldn't bear the thought of Britney's stunts breaking you up. She said she couldn't go back to Vancouver having you wonder about them being together. She refused to be far away from you."

"Really?"

He nodded. "Then she quit the film. And for you? What changes for you if she wins?"

Julia shrugged. "I get to leave knowing I held her best interest at heart."

"You really are something."

"I don't know about that. I'm a regular girl, deeply in love with a woman who's way out of my league. Leagues notwithstanding, I believe when you truly love someone, you have to do right by them, no matter the cost."

He shook his head and thought for a moment. "You're worthy of her—she's worthy of you. Not like Cavell or any of the others. I've known Rina for a very long time. You, young lady, are the love of her life."

"Here it comes," she said as she reached for Clay's hand.

"Jesus, girl, you have a death grip!"

"Sorry. I'm nervous."

"It's her hand you should be holding right now, not mine."

"In public, I'm more used to holding yours."

"Doesn't she look stunning?" Clay said when the camera cut to Rina.

"Positively. The most beautiful woman ever created—inside and out."

Clay leaned close to her ear. "No one would guess that inside she's suffering from a broken heart."

"Oh, come on, Clay. Don't do that to me!"

"And the Oscar for Actress in a Leading Role goes to—" the dramatic pause was excruciating in length "—Katarina Verralta for *The Do-Over!*"

Clay and Julia shrieked at the same instant. They hopped off their stools and hugged each other. Julia buried her face in his shoulder and started to cry.

Clay held her tighter. "Are you okay?"

"No. I have to go." She pulled away. "I'll call you to get my things."

He extended his arm to prevent her from reaching for her gear. "Don't you even want to hear her acceptance speech? Come on, you were with her through all of the rest of it."

Julia exhaled hard. She shot Clay a sidelong glance and plopped back down on the stool. "Sure. What's a little extra heartbreak on the second worst day of my life?"

"What day was worse than this?"

"The day my mother left."

"Your mother left you and your sister?"

"Shh!"

* * *

As Rina walked toward the stage, every other A-lister stood to congratulate her.

"Wow," said Clay. "Reese Collingworth just breached his tribe to congratulate her."

"Ha! Look at that phony Britney Cavell smiling," Julia said with disdain.

Once on stage, Rina returned the kiss on the cheek of the presenter, last year's Best Actor. She accepted the little gold man he handed to her and stared at it. Her halter gown with the V neckline flaunted the sensuous cleavage that made Julia weak, all of it framed by dark chestnut waves that fell to just below her shoulders. Her bright green eyes sparkled in the camera's lens.

"Hold on," said Clay. "That's not Award Ceremony Smile Number Two. Or Number Four for that matter. In fact, I've never seen that smile."

Julia sighed. "She calls it 'I Love You Smile Number Seven.' It's the one she gives only to me."

"Sheesh! You have your own Verralta smile?"

"Well, I did until now, I guess."

Katarina Verralta smiled and surveyed the audience before speaking. "When this indie film came my way, the thing I found most striking was the authenticity of the script—so brilliantly written by Swan. Thank you for Dolly, Swan, and heartfelt appreciation to everyone who worked so hard to make this picture come to life, right down to the caterers who indulged my finicky ways."

The audience chuckled.

"The more I delved into the character of Dolly, the more I realized she had some very important lessons to teach me. So being Dolly didn't exactly end when we wrapped. She's still teaching me to take risks—to follow my heart to my own ultimate do-over. So here goes." Rina stared directly into the camera. "I'm dedicating this Oscar to my partner, my lover, Julia. If you're out there watching, our time has come. Will you marry me?"

The cameras cut away to the faces of Hollywood's shiniest audience. Jaws dropped on their hinges—a few gasps made it past the producers, all the way out—live—around the globe.

Rina eclipsed the reactions, using her microphone. "My deepest gratitude to the Academy and to the other nominees whom I greatly admire and whose performances continually inspire me. I'm praying that this award isn't the only prize I win tonight. Thank you and good night."

The orchestra punched into the end-of-speech refrain and the presenter held out his arm to escort Rina off the stage.

* * *

Julia and Clay stared into each other's eyes, slack-jawed. Julia heard the cacophony rising in the bar—the screeches from a packed house at a gay video bar. Outbursts came from every corner of both rooms and escalated to a din. The reactions played like voiceovers:

"Whoot whoot!"

"Did you hear that!"

"Get it, girl!"

Not only would Hollywood be all over this, but West Hollywood was already making itself heard.

"You heard that right, kids!" the bartender blurted over the PA. "Katarina Verralta just came out!"

"Oh. My. God!" Clay reached for Julia and hugged her. "I can't believe she did it! She came through for you."

Julia hoisted her gear off of the chair and turned to him. "Let's go!"

He ran after her. "Where are we going?"

She grabbed his hand and ran toward her bike. "All that's left is Best Picture!" She unlocked the second helmet and handed it to him. "Put this on!" She hastily secured the saddlebag, climbed onto the bike, and started it. "Hold on tight. Tighter!"

Julia flew through the back streets and up to Fountain Avenue. She broke every law—speeding and running red lights as she zigged and zagged between the cars.

"Julia! You're going to get us killed!"

Julia accelerated and raced toward the theater, bumping them onto the sidewalk to bypass the gridlock. She turned onto La Brea and headed north, passing Sunset Boulevard. The next block would be tricky as it was barricaded at Hollywood Boulevard for the Dolby Theater. If she had any chance of reaching Rina, she would have to come from behind all the madness. She cruised down Hawthorn, the residential street along the back of the Roosevelt Hotel, in an attempt to get as close as she could.

"I'll call the limo driver," said Clay. "We can meet up with him—there's still time to get into the queue."

"No time! You're either in or you're out!"

"I'm in! I'm in!"

Julia navigated around the unattended ROAD CLOSED barrier on Orange Drive and passed the Hollywood High School track.

"You're not going to be able to get this bike anywhere near Hollywood Boulevard!" said Clay.

"Yeah? Watch me!" Julia blew past a cop manning the barrier on Highland Avenue. If she remembered it accurately, she wasn't far from the theater exit. She passed the spot where earlier she had doubled over from stomach pain—before she'd said goodbye to Rina.

The barricade at the next corner was easy to get around. She was so close now. Julia revved the engine and took off toward the orange and white sawhorses that read "STREET CLOSED."

A cop on horseback intercepted them and blasted her whistle. "Stop right there!" the policewoman yelled.

Julia halted, turned off the engine, and engaged the kickstand. She raised her hands in surrender. "Will you bail me out?" she whispered to Clay.

"Get off the bike! Both of you!" the cop said from sixteen-hands high.

Clay's phone rang. "Not now, Gigi, I'll call you back."

"What the hell do you think you're doing?" the cop scolded.

Julia removed her helmet, mustered her most pathetic expression, and read the cop's name off her uniform. "Officer Morrison," she said sheepishly. "Um…d-do you believe in true love?"

CHAPTER FORTY-FIVE

Officer Morrison glared at Julia. "What does true love have to do with you breaking the law?"

Julia put her hands on her hips. "I thought cops were supposed to help people."

Morrison rolled her eyes. "Do I need to give you a breathalyzer?"

"No, ma'am." And then Julia blurted it all out in one ridiculously long sentence. "My lover just proposed to me in front of the whole world from the Oscar stage and what makes it awful is that I broke up with her right before she did it because I love her so much and I have to get to her before she thinks I'm gone and…"

The cop raised her hand as though halting traffic at the Oscars. "The event is over."

"Please, Officer, you have to help me," Julia pleaded. "Can you use your radio to find out from the door if she's still there?"

Morrison unclipped her radio mic from her shoulder and groaned. "Who am I asking for?"

Clay stepped forward and held out his business card. "Here, Officer."

Morrison skeptically took it. "Katarina Verralta?" She stared down at Julia. "*You're* the one? The whole force is talking about this!"

Morrison pressed the button and spoke into the radio. "Brady, this is Morrison. Do you copy?"

A man's voice answered. "I read you, Katy. Over."

"You still at the talent exit? Over."

"Affirmative. Why? Over."

"Has Katarina Verralta left the building?" While Morrison stared into Julia's eyes, she continued to press the Talk button and then let it go when she realized it.

"Hey, Morrison, you know how these little black boxes work, right? Gotta take your finger off the button if you want to hear me."

"Cute, Brady. Katarina Verralta? Is she there or not? Over."

"Affirmative. We just provided an escort to get her into her limo. The press and fans were all over her. We might need to escort her limo to get her out of here! Over."

"Do you have a description of the vehicle? Over."

"Why? Over."

"I have the woman she proposed to here with me. Over."

"It's exactly like the other fifty black Escalade limos I'm staring at right now. Over."

"Copy. Out," said Morrison, staring down at Julia. "Sorry, but you heard the man."

Julia stared down the street, her heart pounding. "Officer Morrison, I need your horse."

"Okay now. Have a good night," said Morrison as she turned the horse away to leave.

"Please, please, please! I'll groom your horse for a month!"

"Are you crazy? I can't just give you my horse! Do you even know how to ride?"

"There's no way in hell I'm going to find her without your horse! I'm an expert rider. Really!"

Clay stood beside her nodding. "She's not joking, officer. She has a ranch in the desert and everything."

"Every second counts," Julia blurted out. "What's your horse's name?"

"Trigger."

"You're joking."

"No, I'm a big Roy Rogers fan."

Julia kissed Trigger's nose and spoke to him calmly. "I'm an excellent rider, Trigger, but I need your help. I can't do this without you." She glanced up at Morrison. "Keep my bike for collateral. Keep Clay for collateral!"

"Hey!" Clay protested.

"The bike is badass—like having thirty Triggers between your legs. Come on, Morrison—what do you say? For true love?"

She grunted. "Okay, okay, but I could get fired for this—and if you take off with my horse that's Felony Grand Theft!" Morrison dismounted. "What the hell is your name, anyway?"

"Julia. Julia Dearling." She swung up and into the saddle in one fluid move. "Come on, boy!" She pulled Trigger around with crowd-control command and began to weave her way between the redundant limos like the cones in a corral.

"Rina?" Julia called out in desperation. She shouted the name at every tinted Escalade window she passed. With the traffic gridlocked, chauffeurs honked at her until she maneuvered Trigger beyond them and eventually onto the sidewalk.

She came upon the last of the police barricades. The row of LAPD sawhorses that closed off the sidewalk were lower than the height she was accustomed to jumping with Lightning. Julia stood in her stirrups to see above the crowds. "Dammit, Rina! Where are you?"

It was useless to think her voice could be heard amid the clarion drone of Rina's fans still calling to her and every other star.

Julia clicked her tongue twice. She turned Trigger around and walked the horse as far away as possible from the barriers, then turned him back around to face them. "Come on, Trigger!" she yelled as she gave the horse a firm tap with her boots. "Ha! Come on, boy!" With a short runway, Trigger sailed over the barricades, and Julia maneuvered him back into the street, weaving to search the limos she hadn't yet seen. From the corner of her eye she saw Officer Morrison crossing Hollywood Boulevard, closing in on her, with Clay following close behind, her saddlebag slung over his shoulder and the helmets swinging from his hands. Julia scanned the limos and called out again from the bottom of her lungs. "Rina!"

The back door to the third-farthest Escalade limo opened. The Oscar winner stepped out onto the boulevard drowning in Dior Couture, wearing diamond-studded heels never intended to touch actual ground. She clutched her Oscar statue—her eyes wide with disbelief. "Julia?"

The cowgirl nudged the horse forward, closed the distance between them, and dismounted so hastily she almost fell. Amid the honking limos, the paparazzi ran to the scene with cameras flashing, shouting a symphony of questions.

"Julia—what are you doing? Where did you get that horse?"

"Did you mean it, Katarina?"

"My speech? Yes, of course I meant it! But what good would it do if you disappear? Is…Is that a police horse?"

Morrison finally arrived.

"This is Officer Morrison, who was kind enough to loan me her horse, Trigger."

Rina stared at the cop in disbelief. "Thank you?"

When Clay caught up, he managed to speak haltingly with labored breath. "Please don't arrest her, Morrison."

"Clay?" said Rina. "What are *you* doing here?"

Officer Morrison waved away the clutter of media pandemonium. "Keep it moving, people! Can we keep it moving along here? Oh. Julia Dearling, you weren't lying."

"No, ma'am, I wasn't. Lying is bad karma." She handed Trigger's reins to the cop. "Rina, if it wasn't for Officer Morrison, I'd be in jail right now."

Rina smiled at the cop. "If you'd be kind enough to contact my office, I'd like to thank you—perhaps with less fanfare."

"Not necessary, Ms. Verralta. You have a pretty persuasive girlfriend here."

"Don't I know it?"

"Fiancée, Morrison," Julia corrected her.

Rina took a step closer to Julia and grinned. "So…that's a yes?"

Julia's eyes opened wide. "Do you think I risked…" she turned to the cop, "Felony what, Morrison?"

"Felony Grand Theft—with serious jail time since Trigger is technically police property."

"Yeah," said Julia, "what she said. Do you think I risked *that* to say no? Hey, Morrison, where's my bike?" Julia took the helmets and saddlebag from Clay.

Morrison turned and pointed across the street. "Happy trails, ladies. Ride safe. Let's get you out of here."

"Meet us at the suite, Clay. Come on, Rina!" She took the Best Actress's hand and led her across the boulevard.

Back on her horse, Morrison tried to separate them from the ant farm of paparazzi that had now surrounded Rina's limo and doggedly pursued them.

"But what about my Oscar?"

Julia took the statuette, laid it gently inside the saddlebag, and hooked it to the bike. "Can you ride in that gown?"

"You do realize this gown is *couture*!"

"And you do realize this is a Harley?" Julia handed her a helmet.

"I'm not smashing my hair with that thing."

"Yes, you are. Good thing your *couture* has a slit in the leg." She helped Rina onto the bike, trying to ignore the onrushing press. Julia climbed into her seat, revved the engine, and rode off into the night, with Rina's arms wrapped tightly around her waist and her head nestled against Julia's back.

CHAPTER FORTY-SIX

What remained of the gaggle of press who lingered at the Roosevelt Hotel blinded the newly engaged couple with camera flashes as they raced through the lobby toward the elevator. Julia held Rina's hand and juggled the helmets and saddlebag with her other hand. Once they were behind the closed elevator door, their eyes barely had a moment to meet before they fell into a kiss that fused them together—that reminded Julia of their very first kiss—the moment she knew she was falling in love. They stepped out into the penthouse.

Rina laughed. "For a cowgirl, you sure know how to make an entrance."

"I learned from the best. And for an A-lister, you sure know how to propose."

"I can't believe you stole a cop's horse out from under her!"

"I hope she doesn't lose her job because of me."

"How did you convince her to give you..."

"Trigger. I asked her if she believed in true love. Next thing I knew I was screaming your name on a horse who jumped those barricades like a pro."

Julia pulled the Oscar statue from her saddlebag and stood it gently on the table. "That sure is pretty—but not as beautiful as

you. Congratulations on your superb performance, Ms. Verralta—
especially that acceptance speech." She smiled uncontrollably.

"And to your performance, Ms. Dearling. Maybe *you* should have
gotten that award. That scene on the boulevard belongs in a movie."

"I'm sure it's uploading to the net as we speak."

Rina stepped forward and stroked back Julia's long hair.

Julia fell deep and deeper still into Rina's almond-shaped gaze, like
Alice falling down the rabbit hole. "What possessed you, Rina? I mean
going from being in the closet to coming out to a billion people?"

"You. Us! That depressing mess we argued about. As soon as you
walked out that door I knew I was going to lose the battle with myself.
You were right. When I was on that stage, as much as I craved this
Oscar, in that moment, I wanted you more. It was right then I realized
that the win meant so little if I couldn't share it with you."

A flood of emotion blurred Julia's vision. Rina wiped away her tears
and smiled I Love You Smile Number Seven. "Now do you believe I
love you, Julia?"

"Say my name again."

"Why?"

"Because I love how it sounds with your accent."

"*Zhooliah*. Now, kiss me like you mean it."

"I *always* mean it."

Clay barreled into the suite huffing and out of breath. He collapsed
onto the sofa.

"Why are you so out of breath?" asked Rina.

"Are you kidding me?" He nodded at Julia. "You try to keep up
with her when she's trying to get to you! The press is camped out in
the lobby near the penthouse elevator, so I had to take the stairs part
way." Clay stood and crossed to them. "Oh my god, Rina! Julia!"

Julia laughed and hugged him. "If it wasn't for Clay, I might never
have stolen that horse because I wouldn't have heard your acceptance
speech."

Rina went to the bar, planted the champagne bottle in the center,
and waited for Clay to pop the cork. She placed three glasses next to
it. "Now this is a story I can't wait to hear." She poured the bubbly and
handed them each a flute.

"Congratulations, you two! I'm definitely going to need this to
deal with the press," said Clay before he drank it all. Rina and Julia
followed suit.

"Oh my, that is good!" Clay said. "I've already heard from your
publicist and from Pinna—" his phone rang again. He pulled it from

his pocket and looked at the display. "And Gigi." He answered the call. "Sorry I had to hang up on you earlier but Julia and I were about to be arrested before she conned an LAPD officer out of her horse." He looked at Rina. "Gigi wants to congratulate you and to know if you're still going to the parties."

Rina raised her eyebrow. "That depends on my future wife." She looked at Julia. "So, are you up for a little celebrating?"

"No," Julia replied, "I'm up for *a lot* of celebrating."

"Tell Gigi we'll meet her at the Vanity Fair party. And Clay, get Mark back up here. Thanks to Julia's helmet, I need some repair work, and so does Julia."

Julia laughed. "So I'm not styling for the after-parties in cowboy boots and jeans?"

Clay nodded at Rina. "Gigi says she already told Mark to come back."

Julia threw her hands in the air. "That helmet was on you for one minute, Rina! I'm so glad I left my outfit here—especially since you're wearing *couture.*"

Rina laughed. "Are you going Hollywood on us?"

"Maybe. But only for tonight," Julia smiled. "I love, love, love you!"

"You'd better. I just risked my entire career to marry you."

"You won't be sorry, Rina," Clay said. "I was with this woman before you pulled that stunt on stage, and all I can say is, it's everyone's dream to be loved the way she loves you. For the first time in my life, I actually understand what it means to be happy that two people have found each other. It's like there's a hole in the universe when you're not together."

Julia kissed his cheek. "I don't know what I would have done without you, Clay. Really! You saved my life tonight."

"Oh sure, that's why you told Officer Morrison to keep me as collateral for her horse?"

"How's that?" asked Rina.

The doorbell to the suite rang and Clay went to answer it. "Hi, Mark, welcome back!"

"Well, look at you!" Mark said to Rina as he crossed the room.

"Why?" she asked, alarmed.

"Because you've never looked more radiant. I heard the news— well, everyone's heard the news—congratulations!"

"But my hair…"

Mark ran his fingers through the long waves and gave her a slightly disheveled look. "Perfect. This is who you really are!" He put his hands on her shoulders and turned her toward the nearest mirror.

"Hmm," said Rina. "I like it. But you'll need to touch up my makeup."

"First things first." Mark turned to Julia. "You, on the other hand, need serious help. Come with me." He led her by the hand to the chair, arranged his makeup palettes, plugged in his straightener, and went to work.

* * *

Rina, Julia, and Clay stopped before entering the most glamorous party of the night.

"You look gorgeous, Julia. Are you ready for this? Your anonymity ends as soon as we walk through that door…"

"Depends, Rina. Are you in it with me?"

"Isn't that the same question you asked me before our first dinner party as a couple?"

"It is," Julia smiled.

"Then I'll give you the same answer now that I gave you then." She beamed the Katarina Verralta Oscar-winning come-on stare. "I'm *deep* in it."

Julia held Rina's hand and with her other hand reached for Clay's hand.

"You don't have to do that anymore," said Clay.

"Yes, I do. You've become my rock during times like this. Besides, I've gotten used to holding your hand in these Hollywood situations."

He smiled and squeezed her hand. "Okay then. You ready, Rina?"

She nodded. "I can't wait for the world to see how in love I am with this woman."

Clay opened the door. As the paparazzi rushed them with every camera in the room clicking away, Clay released Julia's hand, stepped backward out of the spotlight and into *their* shadow.

CHAPTER FORTY-SEVEN

After their jaunt to Hawaii to celebrate Rina's win and weeks at a time spent on the ranch together, Rina had honed her riding skills and learned to assist Julia in the kitchen. She had even modeled for the sculptress in the casita so that Julia could finish yet another bust of her. Not that that was always easy. Julia often got sidetracked, her concentration blown to bits by the mere presence of the woman posing for her. The casita was one of the many places on the ranch that passion was welcome to overtake the moment—to trade it for something much bigger than any single thing either of them could do alone.

The peace Rina felt at the Y2 governed her every move. She breathed in the sweetness of the air and sighed. That peace was being eroded by the wedding that would occur at the ranch that weekend. Julia entered the bedroom while Rina was switching purses.

"I'm nervous about meeting your mother, Julia."

"Why?"

"What if she tries to convince you I'm too old for you?"

"Do you care what a woman who virtually abandoned her twin twelve-year-olds thinks?"

"What I know is, there's more to everything than what meets the eye. You. Me. *Everyone*."

"Fine. It's Vitty and David's rehearsal dinner and that's all I'm going to focus on."

Rina cradled Julia's cheek in her palm and gazed into her eyes. "Part of that means allowing your family to be a family—your mother included."

Julia gave her a peck on the lips. "What if she tries to get me alone?"

"Julia! She's not the big bad wolf. She's your mother, and like it or not she and Vittoria are developing a relationship. I'm just saying, stay open. Few things in life are ever exactly how we paint them—so the trick is to not paint *yourself* into a corner."

Julia placed her hand on her hip. "Okay, can we leave now, Rina?"

"No. For your own happiness, I want to know that you're going to embrace your family."

"Why?"

"David called me last night."

"He did?"

Rina took Julia's hand and looked into her eyes. "He and Vittoria weren't sure how you're going to handle seeing your mother again."

"And?"

"David said that Vitty has tried to talk to you about it, knowing this is hard for you."

"I told Vitty I don't want to talk about Maria."

"David told me something you need to know."

"What is it?"

"Your mother is bringing a plus-one to the dinner."

"What plus-one? I don't know of any plus-one."

"That's why your mother has left you so many messages. She wanted to speak with you about it first. But when you never returned her calls, she asked Vittoria and David, and they said it would be fine."

"It's their wedding, so if they're okay with whoever this guy is, that's all I care about. Ready to go? I don't want to be late."

Rina followed Julia out to the no-longer-scorned sports car. "You know what I love most about your sister's wedding gown?"

"What's that?" Julia closed Rina's door and got behind the wheel.

"It gives me a realistic view of what you'll look like next month when we get married."

Julia kissed her. "Until then, technically we're still courting."

"Courting? What century are you in?"

Julia put the car in gear and held Rina's hand as she drove off the ranch. "Are you ready to be my dinner date at the Wayfarer Inn and Restaurant?"

"To attend the rehearsal dinner for my future sister and brother-in-law. I really like how that sounds! Or, how about this? My fiancée's family."

Julia giggled. "Since you brought it up, I just shivered at the thought of meeting your family before our wedding."

Rina counted them off on her fingers. "My crazy mother, my brother and his wife, their daughters—and two aunts and uncles…oh, then there's my cousin the vintner and…"

Julia threw her a sidelong glance and hit the gas. "You mind if we get through one family at a time? I'm breaking a sweat over here."

* * *

Julia felt all eyes on them when they entered the private banquet room of the restaurant. *Thank god Rina's here—she makes a big enough entrance for the both of us!* She nodded at her mother and saw the empty chair next to her. *Where's her boyfriend?* She smiled anyway, and then they greeted everyone, beginning at the head of the table, the way she and Rina had rehearsed it. Vitty and David stood.

"Congratulations to you both," said Rina. "I'm so excited, but I'm afraid to have alcohol because as it is, every time I see the Dearling twins together, I already think I'm seeing double. You really are dead ringers for one another. Even your voices on the phone."

"We're so glad you could make it, Rina," said Vitty. They hugged.

"I wouldn't have missed it—we're about to become family," she smiled. "Hello, David." He kissed her cheek.

Julia took a step to their right after Vitty and David sat down. "Hello, Mother. This is my fiancée, Katarina Verralta. Rina, meet my mother, Maria Dearling."

Maria stood.

Her mother was slimmer than Julia recalled, and her dark hair was now shorter and fashionably highlighted. And although years had passed since they'd seen each other, Julia thought her mother still looked pretty—her blue eyes sparkling in the way she'd always remembered.

Rina expressed Delight Number Three: Brightly lit smile with a warm handshake. "It's very nice to meet you, Maria. It's clear to me now where Julia and Vittoria got their beauty."

"Thank you, Katarina—although I wouldn't mind being their height." She laughed. "It's wonderful to meet you."

"Please, call me Rina." She leaned closer. "I wouldn't mind being their height either."

As Maria stepped back from her hug with a stiff and stunned Julia, a woman walked to her side. A sharp-looking city type, the olive-complexioned Latina wore a black pantsuit, cream-colored silk shirt, and medium-height heels.

"Julia, Rina, I'd like you to meet my partner Syd," Maria said.

Julia froze. "Your what?" She stared at the curly haired Syd, whose large brown eyes and warm generous smile awaited her.

"My partner, Julia."

"H-Hello, Syd." Julia's lips felt tingly—then numb, and her words formed like she had overdosed on novocaine. She did her best to recover, but her brow knitted, and a thousand-and-ten questions ran through her mind. She glanced at Rina, then Vitty, who nodded at her.

Syd extended her hand. "I'm so happy to finally meet you, Julia. Hello, Rina."

"Lovely to meet you, Syd," Rina added.

Julia led Rina along the table where she introduced her to the other guests, including Isabella, Cass, and David's parents, brother, and sisters. When they took their seats, Julia's gaze darted around the table and she squirmed from the uncomfortable silence. No one had said a word.

Rina squeezed her hand and then broke the ice. "So, David, since we're going to be in-laws, I could use your help."

"With what, Rina?"

"Have you figured out yet how to tell them apart?"

The guests watched the exchange, following the conversation.

"I have," David answered. "It's so simple."

"Well?"

"One is gay. That one's yours. Have I mentioned I admire your taste in women?"

"As I admire yours," Rina replied with stage-like elegance.

Everyone at the table chuckled or laughed.

"Thank you for clearing that up," Rina said with a touch of irony. She glanced at Julia, who could barely take her eyes off her mother and Syd.

David raised his glass and looked out at his guests. "Before we start, Vittoria and I have something we'd like to express—and I was named spokesperson. We want to thank Julia, who has worn herself ragged putting this entire wedding together. From the reception, to the food, and every detail that had her sister spinning out three thousand miles away. You're an amazing sister, Julia, and I can't wait to call you *my* amazing sister."

"Here, here!" said Vitty before she downed the champagne in her glass.

"Thank you, David and Vitty," Julia replied. "I wouldn't have had it any other way."

David's father cleared his throat and stood. "To David and Vittoria and the joining of these two marvelously different families." Again everyone laughed, this time at the unlikely pairing of the nice Jewish boy from suburban New Jersey, marrying the sharp ranch girl from the Southern California desert.

Rina squeezed Julia's hand and whispered in her ear. "I know you're freaking out right now about your mother, but let go and hold my hand."

Julia turned to her and smiled. "I love you," she whispered back.

And then the festive spirit spread throughout the room—glasses filled with champagne, conversations filled with smiles. It left Julia marveling at all the unlikely pairings. Her own—first and foremost. Then there was that little matter of her mother's date being a woman. Another budding match at the far end of the table—the chemistry she observed between David's younger brother and Cass. While deep in conversation, Cass winked at Julia, and Julia returned it with a knowing smile.

The one guest she had difficulty looking at was her mother, who was seated across the table from her and Rina. Julia was still shell-shocked at the sight of Maria, who she caught occasionally staring at her. She studied Syd. *"My partner,"* Maria had said.

Curiosity and confusion had reverberated through Julia since that first revelatory moment, but she had no idea how to react to it. She had always believed that it was her mother's inability to deal with Julia's sexual tendencies that had instigated Maria's move to New York. It was why she had left the girls with Grandmother Lucia in the first place. *Wasn't it? What is she doing with a woman?* Julia filled and emptied her glass several times until she was as numb as the thoughts from her past were.

Only Julia, Rina, Vitty, David, Maria, and Syd would truly understand the enormity of this reunion. The more Julia tried to not think about her mother's abandonment, the more she thought about it. The memory of it made her ache in places she'd long since excised from her life.

By the time dessert and coffee were served, everyone was so engaged in the spirit of the event that Julia was able to slip out unnoticed onto the terrace that faced the mountains. Her connection to these mountains stirred inside of her—the way the sun both rose above and sank below the peaks, the way it was neither day or night, but like all twilight, indistinguishable in the inevitable melding of the two. Not all that different in sensation from her union with Rina. If she could have jumped onto Lightning and ridden like the wind, she would have done it.

Julia turned expecting to see Rina when she heard the footfalls behind her. What she hadn't expected to see was her mother by Rina's side. Rina escorted the woman to where Julia stood.

"Sweetheart," Rina said softly. "I thought this might be a good time for you two to have a moment alone." She smiled, kissed Julia's cheek, and left.

CHAPTER FORTY-EIGHT

Maria stepped forward and leaned on the railing next to Julia, facing her. "I miss this—the rose glow off the mountains when the sun is gold at the end of the day. But what I always miss the most is you. You look beautiful—and so happy. But wow, Katarina Verralta? That was a shock to my system."

"Why? Are you about to tell me she's too famous for me? Too old for me?"

Maria chuckled. "No. Actually I was going to tell how you how perfect I think you are together."

"Why did you come? And, and what—what're you gay now? Because as I remember it, you found it unacceptable that I liked girls. Isn't that why you left?"

"Julia, with all my heart I hope you'll give me a chance to help you understand."

Julia shot her a glance. "Understand what?"

"First of all, to tell you how much I love you, have always loved and missed you."

Julia turned to face her, still leaning against the railing. "You sure have had a strange way of showing it. Did you really expect to come here and all would be forgiven?" She scoffed.

"No, I didn't. But I did expect to finally tell you the truth about why I left and why I left you with my mother."

Julia exhaled. "And here it started out as such a nice evening."

"With the way you feel, which you've made abundantly clear by refusing contact with me for years, I may not get this opportunity again. So there are things you need to know."

"Seems I'm doing fine not knowing."

"Still have that stubborn streak, I see."

"I get it from you."

Maria nodded. "Point taken." She smiled. "I left because I knew I was gay. I knew your life would be hard because, well, let's face it, Desert Bluff is about as big as a noodle."

Julia laughed unexpectedly. "A noodle?"

"Have you forgotten that Lucia raised me too? Back then, that kind of stigma would have made your life very hard. Too hard. It was your grandmother who came up with the solution, not me."

Julia looked at her distrustfully. "Grandmother Lucia told you to leave us?"

"She wanted me to be happy, not ostracized, to not have you and Vittoria suffer the fallout from having a gay mother in a small town. I knew that by the time you grew up things around here would be different for you than they were for me."

"But what about Daddy?"

Maria sighed hard. "We're going to need another four-course dinner—with extra cannoli for dessert and several cappuccinos—for that discussion."

"Did you love him?"

"Yes. But not in the way I should have. In my day, we did what we were supposed to. So even though I knew I liked women, that wasn't even an option here. I did what I was supposed to do—I found a good man and married him because I wanted to have a family. It tore my heart out leaving you and your sister."

"Why didn't you take us with you? You could have taken us with you!"

"Three of us in a two-room apartment for the first three years in New York? You would have hated it. I know you. You were the kid who took off on her horse to places where we couldn't find you. When the mare we had was pregnant, you slept in the barn because you said if she needed you, you wanted to be there."

Julia smiled tenderly at the thought. "I *loved* that horse."

"You've loved every horse. You loved cooking with your grandmother, riding up the mountain before school. I did what I knew was best for you and I tried to keep us together."

"But you hardly ever visited."

"In those early years before I made my own way, I couldn't afford to visit more often. Then, once I could afford it, I couldn't get the time off from work. I came here every chance I could. I was working overtime, sending money to your grandmother for you and Vitty. Then, by the time I could come more often, you were so mad at me that coming here only upset you—set you back. Your grandmother told me how your grades would suffer and your attitude. Even your sleep. She had asked me not to come more than a few times."

"So you left because you were gay?"

"Yes. Why do you say it like that?"

"Damn, I thought you had left because I was gay."

"Forgive me, but I have to do this." Maria wrapped her arms around Julia and pulled her close. She held her so tightly that Julia couldn't get a full breath.

It took Julia a few seconds to respond, but once she hugged her mother back, her eyes filled with tears and buried emotions ambushed her body. She pulled away. "I'm sorry, Mom, but I'm not ready for this." With hurried steps, Julia reentered the restaurant and headed straight into the ladies' room. She wiped her forehead with a cool damp towel and leaned on the sink, feeling lightheaded. She sat on the love seat by the vanity and mirror and looked into her eyes. "How, after all these years, can I still be so overwhelmed by this?"

Julia looked up when the door opened.

"I thought I'd find you here," said Vitty.

"I don't want to talk about it."

"Yes, you do."

"Okay, you're right, I *do* want to talk about it. I just don't know what the fuck to say. Did you know—that Mother is gay? That that's why she left here?"

Vitty nodded. "I did. But I didn't find out until this past year."

"Why didn't you say anything to me?"

Vitty sat beside her and held her hand. "Because you have always shut down every conversation I've tried to initiate. At the mere mention of Maria you went all wonky on me—every time, Jules. Every time."

"I know. Sorry."

"I understand. The one thing you don't do to either Dearling twin is lead her to water and then expect her to drink it!"

Julia laughed. "That's true, isn't it? I need to process this…maybe we could talk after your honeymoon?"

"Deal. Are you all right, little sister?"

"Three minutes! You're only three minutes older."

"Older is older," Vitty grinned. "You have a little mascara under your eyes. Here." Vitty grabbed a tissue on the vanity and tenderly wiped off the makeup.

"I abandoned Rina. Is she okay out there?"

"She's amazing. What a warm and loving woman. Huh."

"What?"

Vitty shook her head. "I'm marrying a Jewish lawyer from Jersey, and my little sister is marrying Katarina Verralta. What universe is this? I've never seen you this happy—well, minus this reunion with Maria. I watch how Rina looks at you, how she treats you. She adores you."

Julia smiled. "Yes, she does. And I'm over the moon about her. It doesn't bother you that I'm with someone so much older?"

Vitty raised her eyebrows. "Bother me? Hardly. From what I've seen, you're not only right for each other—you have that special right kind of right. It's so obvious how in love you both are. Not only that, the two of you are so opposite that you're practically alike."

Julia nodded. "I've never thought of it that way, but that's really true."

"Like I said, you're the right kind of right."

"Come on, Vitty. What do you say we wrap up this dinner and go home so we can all hang out? I have the casita made up for David to stay there tonight."

"What?"

"He can chill with us when we get home, but then I'm kicking him out. Bad luck for him to stay with you before the wedding."

Vitty groaned. "What are you, like, channeling Grandmother Lucia and her superstitions?"

"Hey, she'll always be part of our family tradition."

"Fine, but you're the one who's going to have to tell him."

Julia stared at her. "Oh no, I'm not!" She thought for an instant. "I know, we'll let Rina tell him. He likes her."

"He loves her. Everyone loves her—she's Katarina Verralta, for god's sake! Just get me through my wedding tomorrow and I promise next month I'll do the same for you." Vitty looked down at Julia's hand with the pinky sticking up. "Seriously?"

"Pinky swear." Julia held up her hand.

"What are we, six years old?"

Julia tapped her foot, waiting.

Vitty linked pinkies with her. "Fine! Pinky swear."

CHAPTER FORTY-NINE

A month later, on the morning of her own nuptials, Julia wandered through the Malibu mansion alone, taking in the view of the sapphire diamond-studded Pacific from every room. Workers were bustling across the grounds, setting up for the wedding, carrying large bouquets and placing hundreds of chairs on either side of the wide aisle. Stopping to take in the moment, she awakened to the magic that had become her reality—and it gave her goose bumps.

Although she and Rina had been together long enough to know they wanted to get married, she couldn't help imagine this whole new part of their life—where the shadows she had once painfully occupied were now suffused with light, shining a spotlight on the good they brought forth together into the world.

Rina had come a long way—they both had. Rina was no longer only loved for her talent, but for her philanthropy and her kindness in helping those causes who badly needed her name and commitment. She had told Julia that without her, none of it would have happened—that she would have remained isolated, miserable, without the deepest connection and happiness she had ever known.

Vitty had been right when she said that Julia and Rina were so opposite they were practically alike. But what surprised Julia the most was that never would she have imagined there would come a day when she would view the "closeted" period of their relationship as a good thing. In retrospect, what she finally appreciated was that all the time she and Rina had spent in the shadows had given them what would otherwise have been a lost opportunity.

During that time, they had truly gotten to know each other, to love each other, and away from the public eye, Julia was able to appreciate the side of Rina she loved the most—the girl she had fallen in love with. Not the movie star that the world idolized, but the tender girl inside the woman who had learned to ride a horse, to cook, and who laughed at her silly jokes. And in that time, Julia had learned to make an entrance—and to open herself to a world beyond her imagination.

According to Rina, if it hadn't been for Julia and the Y2, she might never have understood the precious stillness that being far from the spotlight had afforded her. She still maintained that being with Julia is what finally allowed her to see who she really was, even though she had to dig it out from where it was buried under layers, beneath decades of fame.

Julia's thoughts drifted to the night before, to her last conversation with her mother and Vitty—after everyone had gone to bed. After having learned the truth about why Maria had left her and her sister with their grandmother, Julia realized that while the past could never be recaptured, she felt hopeful about their future as a family—a real family. In part, she owed that awareness to her very-soon-to-be wife. *Rina was right—and wise. There really is more to all of us than what meets the eye.*

On her way downstairs through the kitchen, Julia took the fresh flower bouquets and left the main house to deliver them to the guesthouse. Bright and beautiful, they were a harbinger of the peace and joy she would share with those she loved. *Maybe I should sculpt these bouquets. The galleries may want more of my horses, but I'd bet Rina would love to have forever-flowers.*

She meandered along the driveway, remembering her first impression of the estate as the old Fiat, gone now but not forgotten, chugged up to the house. She vowed to someday restore the Fiat that sat idle in her garage on the ranch. Now this would be her home, along with the Y2, or what would be left of the ranch once she sold off the part that would buy Vitty and David a house in New York.

Before knocking on the door to the cottage that David and Vitty shared with Maria and Syd, Julia closed her eyes and inhaled the mélange of scents.

Maria answered the door with a loving smile, her bright blue eyes filled with tears at the sight of her no longer estranged daughter. "Hi, honey." She hugged Julia, and this time Julia embraced her. "Come in. How are you holding up?" She stroked Julia's hair.

Julia exhaled a huge sigh. "I'm nervous as hell, Mom. The ceremony is in a few hours and I keep breaking out in a sweat and reminding myself to breathe." The moment struck her again. *Julia Dearling-Verralta! Oh my god, I'm going to be* hyphenated!

Maria reached for Julia's hand and squeezed it. "Don't worry about a thing—it's all going to be fine. I promise." She looked down at the boulder on her daughter's finger. "If that diamond sparkles any brighter, I'll need sunglasses."

"Rina had our rings cleaned yesterday."

"I can't wait to see your wedding bands. I'll bet they're gorgeous."

Julia chuckled. "When she originally asked me what kind of band I liked, I told her a cigar band would do just fine."

"You didn't!" Maria laughed.

Julia nodded, and inside her, for the first time since the day before Maria had left the Y2 for good, she felt her mother's love—her care. And the trust she had once placed in the woman began to slowly creep back into her heart.

"Vittoria," her mother called out, "your sister is here."

"Hey, Juju, come on in. There are some things Mom and I have put together for you."

"What things?" Julia asked.

Vitty smiled. "Come with us."

Julia followed them into Vitty's bedroom.

"Something old, something new, something borrowed, something blue," Maria said.

Julia lit up when she saw it. "Grandmother Lucia's necklace!"

"Of course," said Vitty. "I wore it at my wedding and now it's your turn. Someday we'll look back at our wedding pictures and argue about who wore it best."

They shared a laugh while Julia removed the Cartier necklace that Rina had given her the first time she'd asked Julia for a commitment. Julia flashed on that moment up in the cabin, the two of them naked in front of the fire. She handed the necklace to Vitty. "Make sure nothing happens to this please."

"That's a maid of honor's job," Vitty said, placing it in the jewelry box that had held their grandmother's necklace.

Maria opened the clasp of the sapphire set in gold that had been handed down from mother to daughter for generations. "This will take care of the something old, borrowed, and blue." Maria placed it around Julia's neck from behind and her hands shook trying to secure it. "I'm so excited, I can't get the clasp locked."

"Here, let me do it," Vitty said.

Once it was on Julia's neck, she went immediately to a mirror to admire it.

"Thank you, Mari—Mom. This means a lot to me."

Maria sighed. "It looks beautiful on you, and I know your grandmother would be so proud that you're wearing it to get married. Vitty? You're up."

Vitty stepped forward and held out a small jewelry box. "Go ahead, look inside. It's your 'something new.'"

Julia sat, opened the box and stared at the locket inside.

Vitty sat next to her. "It's a locket for your bridal bouquet. Open it."

Julia gasped when she did. Tears filled her eyes and she flung her arms around her twin. "She's here with us, isn't she?" Inside the new locket was a picture of Julia as a child, hugging Grandmother Lucia with all her might.

"Of course she's here," said Maria. "Now you have her necklace and a locket for your bouquet."

"Feeling a little better now?" Vitty asked.

"I am. Thank you both. I feel complete now, having my family with me."

Syd had entered the house and watched from the bedroom doorway.

"Oh good, you're back," Maria said. "How was your walk on the beach?"

"Beautiful, honey." She went to Maria and kissed her cheek. "When I came up the stairs from the beach, I saw the set up out back. Julia, it's magnificent. What a backdrop for the ceremony—that endless blue ocean."

"Except for the ocean, all of that is Rina and Gigi and their magic makers. My almost-wife knows how to throw a party in Malibu, that's for sure. Honestly, I'd have been just as happy getting married on horseback out on the ranch."

All three women laughed at her.

"What?" asked Julia. "What's wrong with that?"

"Nothing," Syd answered, "until you see how you're actually going to get married."

Julia's eyes opened wide. "Oh my god, I'm getting married—on a cliff. Oh, somebody make sure I don't fall off that cliff."

"I just got you back," Maria joked. "I'm not losing you to a cliff!"

"You ready to marry the love of your life?" asked Vitty.

"My thoughts are racing, my heart speeds up to where I can't catch my breath...so, yeah, I'm really looking forward to breathing again. That, and not worrying about falling off the cliff would be good, too."

"Where is Rina, anyway?" Maria asked.

"She's superstitious like me, so we spent the night apart, and frankly the house is so damn big, she's tucked away in her suite and I've been relegated to my own. Last night when she called to say good night, she made me promise that we wouldn't see each other until we walk down the aisle."

"I'll get you there, Juju," said Vitty. "Look at the time! Come on, we have to get you back to the house. You need to shower. Rina made me promise to have you ready in time for hair and makeup."

"You spoke to her today?"

"Yes. She said to make sure you eat something. And that it won't be Mark doing your hair—she's sending someone else."

"Who's Mark?" asked Maria.

"He's the stylist who did my hair and makeup on Oscar night."

"The night Rina proposed," Maria said. "With me watching and not knowing the Julia she had proposed to was my daughter!" She grabbed Julia suddenly and held her close. "Oh how I've missed you."

"Quit it, Mom. You're going to make me a blubbering idiot."

Vitty laughed. "You were the lucky one, Mom."

"Why?"

"Go ahead," Julia urged, "tell her."

Vitty continued. "I didn't see the Oscars, nor did I know that the Rina Julia had told me about was Katarina. My coworker's sister works for TMZ and when she saw the viral video of Julia jumping those hurdles on that police horse, she thought it was me. The next morning the press stampeded me outside my office building. I had no idea why until I battled my way inside and my boss showed me the video. That's how I found out."

Julia poked Vitty's arm. "Like you could have jumped those sawhorses."

They shared a laugh and Maria pulled back to look into Julia's eyes. "Right now you remind me of when you were ten and I told you that you could keep Lightning. The expression on your face is exactly the same. Look at my girls, Syd. I couldn't be prouder of you both." She laced her arms around their necks and hugged her daughters.

Vitty squeezed Julia's hand.

"Before you go," Maria smiled, "I want to thank you both for giving me this opportunity—for allowing me back into your lives."

Julia returned the smile. "I'm sure Grandmother would have wanted this for us."

"So, Juju, are you ready?" Vittoria asked.

"Yes." On the way out, she hugged her mother again and then hugged Syd before she and Vitty took off on yet another Dearling Twins adventure.

"See you at the wedding, honey!" Maria called out, waving from behind as the girls climbed the driveway.

* * *

The sisters moved to the side of the driveway when they heard a vehicle behind them.

"What the hell?" said Julia when she saw a horse trailer being towed by a pickup.

Vitty laughed. "We got one over on you but good!"

Julia held up her hand to stop the truck and raced to the trailer's window. "Lightning! Thunder!" She turned to Vitty. "Are you kidding *me*!

"Rina wanted it to be a surprise. She said she couldn't imagine you getting married without having Thunder and Lightning here."

"I can't believe—" Julia placed her hand over her heart. "Could that woman know me any better?"

"Ahem!" said the woman who hopped out from the passenger side of the truck and walked toward them. She scratched her head. "Which one of you is Julia?"

Julia's jaw dropped open. "Officer Morrison?" she said awestruck.

"Hey, Dearling, it's not Officer anymore. That little stunt on Oscar night? Got me into boiling hot water with my captain."

Julia covered her eyes and shook her head. "I'm so sorry. Now I feel terrible!"

"Don't," Morrison smiled. "I'm now the head of security—and horses—here and out at the Y2. It's all been hush-hush until today."

"What? How…I can't believe you're here!"

Morrison chuckled. "Have you ever heard that saying: 'Man makes plans and God laughs'? Well, I think the plan all along was for me to wind up right here. Miss Verralta reached out to thank me a couple of months ago and that's when she offered me the job. So I have you to thank for it."

"She never said a word to me."

Vitty laughed. "That's because you weren't supposed to know about it until today."

"Morrison, if it wasn't for you and Trigger, I wouldn't have gotten to Rina on Oscar night."

Morrison shook her hand. "Congratulations, Julia. I guess we'll be seeing a lot of each other. Well, I'd better get your guys here out for a stretch and some water."

"Thank you, Morrison! You'll never know how much this means to me."

"I already do, Julia—and you can call me Katy. You forget I saw how you rode Trigger. Anyone who can ride like that on a horse they just met is someone who knows and loves horses as much as I do. I'll see you at the ceremony."

"Th-Thanks again," Julia called out as Morrison climbed back into the pickup.

"That was the cop whose horse you stole!" Vitty belly-laughed. "Leave it to you."

Julia laughed. "Trust me. It wasn't funny at the time—when I thought she was going to arrest me."

Half an hour later, Julia was out of the shower when Vitty answered her door.

"Julia? It's me—Marielle!"

"No, I'm Vittoria, Julia's twin."

Julia entered the room and looked at the stylist. "Marielle?"

"Yes! Oh my gosh, you're *the* Julia?"

Julia laughed. "How are you? How did you wind up here?"

"I work with Mark. Since he has to get Miss Verralta ready, he asked me to do your hair and makeup."

"How do you two know each other?" Vitty asked.

"Marielle is a friend of Nicki's. I met Marielle at Nicki's birthday party when we were still dating. How is Nicki?"

"I haven't really spoken to her since that party," Marielle answered.

"But you two were such good friends," Julia said.

"Honestly, when I saw how she had treated you that day, I realized I couldn't be friends with her after what she did."

"But we hardly knew each other."

Marielle scoffed. "She chose a stripper over you and that gorgeous sculpture? Please!"

"Well, that's long in the past, Marielle. It's good to see you. Follow me, I have the vanity cleared and ready for you to work your magic."

"This is great. Congratulations on your wedding. I'm so happy to be here, Julia. You can relax. I'm going to make you look flawless."

"Looks like you're in good hands, Juju. So if you don't mind, I'm going to start getting ready at the guesthouse."

"Perfect. Call me when you're done."

* * *

Vitty left Julia's suite and descended one flight to the kitchen. She went to the refrigerator, took out an apple, and was washing it when Gigi entered.

"You know, Julia, this doesn't change anything," said Gigi in her most snide tone. "I'm still going to be watching you like a hawk for any little slip-ups where Rina's concerned. You still have time to do the right thing and back out."

Vitty turned to her and took a large bite of the apple. She stared at Gigi's smug expression, chewed slowly, and made her wait until she had swallowed the entire bite before responding.

"Here's the deal, *Geege*. It changes everything. You got the wrong Dearling, *honey*. Unlike my twin, I know plenty of women like you—and not one was recognizable when I got done with them. When you took those pictures of me and David, you violated my privacy, not Julia's. If I were you, I'd watch your back. One word from my sister of you undermining her and Rina? Count on me coming back in a flash to make your life a living hell."

Gigi opened her mouth to speak.

Vitty smiled a wicked grin. "I'd weigh very carefully anything you're about to say right now. Anything."

Gigi stared, waited, and then nodded. "Well, aren't you the alpha sister? You might want to tell her before the ceremony that Britney Cavell is here as someone's plus-one."

Vitty felt her cheeks get warm. "No doubt we have you to thank for that. Strike one, Gigi. Two more and I won't even wait for Rina before I take—you—out." She smiled. "Are we clear?"

Gigi raised an eyebrow and nodded.

"Great. See you at the wedding."

CHAPTER FIFTY

As planned, Vitty escorted Julia to the place from where she would exit the house.

"How you holding up?" Vitty asked.

"My legs feel like water, and I'm so nervous I'm shaking. Rina should be here already. Although I'm not surprised she isn't. The woman loves to make an entrance."

Vitty hugged her. "You look magnificent. But…I've been elected to tell you that there's been a change of plans."

"Change? What change? What are you talking about?"

Vitty laughed. "Calm down, you're going to love this. Promise. Come with me." She escorted the bride to a door on the side of the sprawling mansion.

Julia stared out at the sight framed by the open glass wall. "Shut up!" She walked outside. "Rina, are you serious?"

Rina looked down at her from Thunder's back and smiled. "Dead serious."

Julia took a step toward her horses, each draped with a festive lei around his neck. "No wonder this aisle is so wide. You look gorgeous—I can't take my eyes off of you."

Rina sported I Love You Smile Number Seven—the one reserved only for Julia. "Time to get married, Cowgirl. Are you in it with me?"

"*Deep* in it." Julia turned to Vitty and handed her the bouquet. "Hold this."

"Wait!" Clay came from behind with steps for Julia and placed them in front of her. "So you don't mangle that beautiful gown," he said.

"You're so good to me, Clay."

He whispered in her ear. "I don't want you to be shocked, but Britney Cavell is here as someone's plus-one. And yes, Rina just found out. But don't worry—I'll take care of everything. Just focus on this amazing day." He looked at Rina and nodded.

Julia mounted Lightning, took her bouquet from her sister, and reached for the reins.

"Not today, kiddo," Vitty said when she took Lightning's reins.

Clay held Thunder's reins and nodded at the wedding planner. She cued the flute and guitar duo, and Clay and Vitty waited until Rina gave them the go-ahead.

First, Rina took Julia's hand. "You said you wanted to get married on horseback."

"Rina, I can't believe you did this for me."

"I did it for us. For all the special times we've had on the ranch."

Julia winked at her. "And in the barn."

"Don't make me blush—there are cameras. I also have a special surprise. You're now full owner of the Y2."

Julia's eyes opened wide. "What?"

"I bought out Vitty's shares and am giving them to you as a wedding present. It's perfect. She and David get to buy the house, and you get your ranch."

"You mean *our* ranch."

"That too, but best of all—I get you, Julia." She gazed into Julia's eyes and smiled Getting Married Number One for the first time. "I think we're ready, Clay."

Clay and Vitty led the horses slowly down the aisle as the guests they passed stood and applauded.

Julia spoke in a hushed tone. "You really do know how to make an entrance. There are so many famous people here."

"Well, of course. What did you expect?"

"I expected you to be the one making the entrance, not me."

"As you said to me on my first foray into the barn, 'If you need to bolt right now, Lightning here is pretty fast.'"

Julia giggled. "You sure know how to deliver a line."

"When we reach the end of the aisle, there will be steps to dismount."

"Got it," Julia nodded.

"Oh, and I have two more little surprises for you," Rina said as they slowly neared the altar.

Julia stared at her. "I'm not even going to try to guess."

"What's our favorite Steel Eyes song?"

"'If I Ever Had the Chance (I'd Fall in Love with You).' You already know that."

"She, Kenna Waverly, will be performing it for us at the reception."

"Shut up. Are you kidding me?"

"No. You know there's no one in the world I love slow dancing with more than you. Lastly, I've taken the liberty of getting you three weeks off at the diner because we're honeymooning in Paris."

Julia fell down the rabbit hole of Rina's loving gaze. "I've wanted to see Paris ever since your opening scene in *Allies of Night*."

"I know." Rina reached out and squeezed Julia's hand. "With any luck, we'll get a little rain."

Bella Books, Inc.

Women. Books. Even Better Together.

P.O. Box 10543
Tallahassee, FL 32302

Phone: 800-729-4992
www.bellabooks.com

CPSIA information can be obtained
at www.ICGtesting.com
Printed in the USA
LVHW090758310319
612338LV00001BA/26/P